Wow! Joel's book has it all: action, suspense, drama, mystery, romance, and humor. With more twists and turns than a country road, fasten your seat belt, hold on tight, and enjoy!

—Jim Davis, Hebron, KY
President/Senior EHS Compliance Specialist
Environmental Risk Management, Inc.

Bloodline and Betrayal is a captivating and fast-paced adventure filled with betrayal and deceit. Its tapestry of characters is brilliantly interconnected in unforeseen and fascinating ways. The dramatic twists and turns of the plot heighten the excitement and intrigue. I found this book so compelling that I could not put it down. It's the kind of story that lingers with the reader long after the last page is turned.

—Sharon Crovetto, B.S., Ed

Great story, great fun, and a happy ending. I think this story would make a great movie—lots of action, beautiful scenery, car chases, boat chases, pretty girls, heroic guys, nasty villains, both male and female.

—Darrell Smallwood, Business Manger Avon Lakes City Schools,
Avon Lakes Ohio

BLOODLINE
& BETRAYAL

BLOODLINE & BETRAYAL

JOEL HOWARD

TATE PUBLISHING & *Enterprises*

Published by Tate Publishing & Enterprises, LLC
127 E. Trade Center Terrace | Mustang, Oklahoma 73064 USA
1.888.361.9473 | www.tatepublishing.com

Tate Publishing is committed to excellence in the publishing industry. The company reflects the philosophy established by the founders, based on Psalm 68:11,
"The Lord gave the word and great was the company of those who published it."

Book design copyright © 2010 by Tate Publishing, LLC. All rights reserved.
Cover design by Kandi Evans
Interior design by Lindsay B. Behrens

Published in the United States of America

ISBN: 978-1-61663-121-5
1. Fiction / Action & Adventure   2. Fiction / Romance / Suspense
10.03.17

ACKNOWLEDGEMENTS

First and foremost, I thank God for allowing me to do something I deeply love. I thank my wife, Sheila, and my son, Michael, for standing by me and supporting me during all the times they listened while I read this story to them and waited for their input. I also thank my brothers and sisters for their help and support in completing this novel. Last but not least, I want to thank my friends at work for their patience and encouragement throughout the process. Philippians 4:13: "I can do all things through Christ who strengthens me."

CHAPTER 1

Elizabeth Benson had broken her own rule—she had carelessly opened the door to her Queens, New York, apartment after the bell rang, without looking through the peephole to see who was there. Perhaps it was because a man she had loved for most of her life, a man she'd had to love from a distance, a man that no one could ever know about, had just left and she thought he had returned.

It wasn't just the forty-eight years of her life experiences giving her that fatal-mistake feeling in the pit of her stomach, but also the death stare reflecting from the dark, glassy-eyed, scruffy-bearded young man whose mask she had just pulled off as she struggled with him.

"That was a mistake!" he bellowed. He grabbed her, locked his arm around her head, and dragged her to the kitchen. He shoved her head facedown in the sink and turned on the hot water. She screamed until he punched her. He turned her loose, and she fell to the floor. He snatched a knife from the butcher block, grabbed her by the hair, and stuck the knife against her throat. "Make one more sound and it will be your last, old woman!" He lightly slid the blade over her throat, and she could feel it sever the thin top layer of her skin. "Now, I have a few questions for you." All she could do was follow his demands.

He tortured her for information that she reluctantly gave him. When he was satisfied with what she had said, he turned her loose. Blood trickled down her throat from the thin cuts. She jumped up and ran across the room and picked up a vase from a nearby table.

"I've told you what you wanted to hear!" she screamed as she threw the vase at him. "Now get out of here!" As she attempted to evade him, he lunged and struck her on the head with a brass candleholder. She fell in a crumpled heap to the floor. He dropped the candleholder, turned slowly, and walked toward the kitchen. After shutting off the pilot valve and turning on the burners to the gas stove, the perpetrator left the apartment.

After a short time, Elizabeth regained consciousness. Choking from the strong gas odor and bleeding from a large cut above her left eye, she gathered enough strength to crawl to the telephone. Just as she began to dial, the apartment exploded. A ball of fire and black smoke rolled up the side of the building. Glass from the windows showered the street below as the man pulled from the curb and drove away.

FIVE MONTHS LATER

Debra Benson awakened to the ringing of her telephone in her Manhattan, New York apartment. She groaned as she leaned toward her night table, fumbling for the phone. After several rings, she found it. Debra, a twenty-eight-year-old brunette, had lived alone since college. The author of several romance books, Debra was constantly in pursuit of new ideas and had just endured another semi-sleepless night, trying to put the middle and ending to her latest novel. She jerked the receiver from the hook.

"Hello!"

"Hey, Debra." It was her friend Ashley. Debra and Ashley had been friends for about two years after meeting at one of Debra's book signings. They talked afterward and found they had a common interest: politics. Ashley had started a career in politics after college and was an aid and media liaison to New York Senator Jack Braco, who had recently won his party's nomination for president of the United States.

"Hi, Ashley," Debra said.

"So, how did it go last night, Debra?"

"The worst," said Debra with a raspy morning voice. "I just can't seem to concentrate. I should have gone to the rally with you." Even though Ashley was a few years older than Debra, they had become good friends and did many things together. Ashley seemed to find many interesting things for them to do, political rallies, fundraisers, and conventions. Debra glanced at her unfinished manuscript lying on the table by the bed. "What time is it?"

"Uh, it's almost eleven, hon."

"My gosh! That's awful! I needed to get up early so I could try to finish my book." She sat up in bed, frustrated. She rubbed her eyes and pushed some long strands of brown hair away from her face. With a stretch and a yawn she said, "Didn't you have to be at a press conference for Jack Braco this morning?"

"No, actually that is this afternoon. I've been working so hard for this guy. He better win," Ashley said with an exasperated sigh. "Anyway, I called you because I have an idea that I think you'll really like."

"Oh, you have an idea, do you? Like the one where the serial killer falls in love with his victims? Or maybe it's like the one where the alien from Mars woos the girl then takes her home to his planet," Debra said.

"Yeah, well, I admit those weren't the greatest ideas, but I'm not talking about a storyline. My uncle has a cabin in the Adirondack Mountains, and when I told him about your predicament, he was happy to loan me the key." There was a pause in the conversation. Debra switched the phone to the other ear and gave the curtain an irritated jerk to block the sun. "Besides, Debra, you need to get away from those neighbors of yours who party constantly."

"Yeah, they're driving me crazy, but that's not enough reason to go running off to the mountains. I can't leave. I've got to finish my book. My publisher is putting pressure on me to finish it in five weeks."

"That is exactly why you *should* go. It's peaceful and quiet, and you can relax and concentrate. There's no better place to finish your book."

"What about Annabelle, and now there's Oscar?"

"Oscar! Who's Oscar? Do you have a new boyfriend I don't know about?"

"No, I don't have a new boyfriend you don't know about. Oscar is my new bird."

"What? A bird?"

"Yes, a bird. Besides, who has time for a boyfriend?"

"When did you get a bird?"

"I just bought him a few days ago. He's a Brazilian parrot. I saw him in the pet store on my way out of the mall, and he whistled at me as I went by. I just couldn't resist."

"A cat and a bird! Who puts a cat and a bird together?" asked Ashley as she began to laugh.

"Well, as long as you keep them separated, they're fine," Debra said, laughing as well. Annabelle leaped onto the bed, and Debra began to stroke her long fur.

"I'll take care of them," Ashley replied. "Just leave the food and supplies for me, and I'll come every day. I'll keep them apart too."

"That's much easier said than done. Annabelle has already tried to get into Oscar's cage twice. I had to move it higher so she couldn't get to it. Besides, I don't want you to take on my problems. I just don't—"

"It's no problem at all." Ashley interrupted. "You work too hard, and you deserve some peace and quiet."

"It really would be nice to have some quiet time alone to finish my book. I haven't been able to concentrate with these wild neighbors, and since Mom died, it's been really tough."

"I know that was a terrible time for you, Debra. You know I would never do or say anything that would hurt you, and I only want the best for you. Please don't think this is harsh of me, but you have to move on with your life. You need to get away, and I think a trip to the mountains is just the pick-me-up that you need."

"I know … you're right. You're such a good friend, Ashley."

"It's settled, then," Ashley said. "Besides, I wasn't going to take no for an answer. I've already bought a ticket for a commuter flight tomorrow. You leave at one o'clock from JFK airport."

"Well, I guess you've decided for me," Debra said with a sigh. "I suppose it will be a nice, relaxing time for me. Thank you so much, Ashley."

Cheerfully, Ashley replied, "Well, that's what friends are for!"

"I guess I'd better get ready. I have some errands to run and lots to do before I even start packing. I'll see you tomorrow. Thanks again, Ashley!"

"My pleasure. Hey, let's have lunch tomorrow, and I'll drive you to the airport."

"That sounds great," Debra said. She thanked Ashley again, and they hung up. Debra sat momentarily and thought about how much she valued Ashley's friendship. After the tragic loss of her mother, Ashley had been there to comfort her, although she could be a bit overzealous sometimes. "She's right," Debra said, lecturing herself. "I guess it *is* time to get on with my life. I can't live in the past."

She leaned back on her pillow for a few seconds, thinking of all she had to do as she stroked Annabelle's fur.

"Are you going to miss me?" She rubbed noses with Annabelle. "I'm going to miss you, but you better be good and leave Oscar alone." She held Annabelle up in the air as she gently scolded her. "Now, I've got to get going." She put Annabelle down and slid over to the side of the bed. Just as she stood up and walked toward the bathroom, the phone rang again. Thinking it was Ashley calling back, Debra picked up the phone and said, "Okay, what did you forget to tell me? A trip to the Riviera perhaps?" Debra laughed.

The unfamiliar voice at the other end of the line said, "Miss Benson, I'm John Whitmire. I don't think we've ever met, but I was your mother's attorney." Debra was caught completely by surprise. She swallowed hard, and her expression quickly changed to a more serious one.

"Attorney? Why would my mother have ever needed an attorney?"

He avoided the question, saying only, "I really need to meet with you. Would tomorrow be a good time?"

"No … uh … actually, I'm leaving town tomorrow. What's this about anyway?" Debra asked as she tried to recover from the shock. She sat on the bed and listened intently.

"I can't talk about it on the phone." He hesitated. "Can you hold on, Miss Benson? There's someone at the door. My secretary took the day off, so I'll have to let them in." There was a rustling sound as if the man was attempting to get up from his desk. "Okay, never mind, they're coming in now." He hesitated another moment. "Come in; I'll be with you in one moment. Just have a seat. Now, Miss Benson, it's about your mother's will."

Debra was almost speechless from the shock. After a couple of seconds, she was able to regain her composure. "I didn't know my mother had a will. She never mentioned it to me," she quickly replied.

"It's very complicated. Please, can we meet? I think there are some people that—hey, what…what are you doing? Don't—hey, don't, wait—wait!" he yelled. She heard a thud as if the phone receiver had fallen to the floor. There were strange background noises, a loud *bang,* a loud crash, then silence.

"Hello? Hello?" There was no answer. Debra hesitated for a moment, and then she heard someone pick up the phone. "Hello!" No one answered. "Hello…Mr. Whitmire, are you there?" She could hear the person breathing. "Who is this? What do you want?" She heard a popping noise, and then the phone went dead. Puzzled, she stood there wondering. Could this simply have been a prank call, or did her mother really have a will? And who was the person who picked up the phone? What was Mr. Whitmire trying to tell her, and could he really be a lawyer? After a few seconds of pondering, she looked at the caller ID and pushed the redial button. After a couple of rings, a recording came on.

"The number you're trying to reach"—the voice repeated the numbers—"cannot be completed as dialed. Please check the number and dial again."

Debra hung up the phone, and as she tried to understand what the call meant, she decided to get the phone book and look up John Whitmire. After some searching, she found a listing for John Whitmire, Attorney at Law. As she dialed the number, she noticed it was different than the one on her caller ID. After several rings, his voice mail came on. Still not understanding the meaning of the call, she decided against leaving a message and hung up the phone. She stood there, perplexed, cradling her chin with her hand. *Was someone attempting to keep him from talking to me? Should I call the police,* she thought. *If not the police, I probably should do something, but what?* She paced back and forth, trying desperately to think of what she should do.

"If she had a will, what could that mean? She wasn't wealthy. It has to be a prank call, and if it isn't…perhaps he'll call back," she said. "Even if he doesn't, I'll see him when I get home." She decided to go on with her business of the day, but the phone call remained fresh in her mind.

The next day, Debra was finishing packing as she waited for Ashley to take her to the airport when the phone rang.

"Hello?" No one answered. "Hello," Debra said sternly. She could hear someone breathing. "Who is this?" she shouted. "Mr. Whitmire, is that you?" Suddenly, the phone went dead. *Another strange phone call,* she thought. As she hung up the phone, she wondered if it had anything to do with the one from the previous day. She checked the caller ID. "Unknown Caller" was lit up on the screen. She stood there for a brief moment, trying to make sense out of it. After she sat on the bed for a couple of minutes, she decided to focus on packing and to put the phone calls out of her mind.

Ashley came to pick up Debra at 10:30 a.m. Debra put food out for Annabelle and Oscar. After she said her good-byes, they carried the luggage to the car.

As they loaded the luggage in the trunk of Ashley's car, Debra began to get an uneasy feeling, as if they were being watched. Suddenly she heard a noise and looked around. A black car with dark tinted windows was sitting just across the street. As she looked around, someone was rolling up one of the back windows. She noticed that the front fender was dented. Beside the back door, she saw several cigarette butts lying in the street, giving the impression that it had been there for some time. She thought how strange it was for someone to be sitting in their car with the windows up and the car not running. It was late summer, but still warm enough to need the air conditioner. She glanced around at the car again. But then she thought, *The world is full of strange people* and thought nothing more of it. They finished loading the luggage and drove away.

On the way to the restaurant, Debra told Ashley about the strange phone call from John Whitmire from the day before. "What do you think that could mean, Ashley?"

"Probably just a prank call," she said. "I wouldn't worry about it."

"Some people came in his office while he was on the phone with me. When he began to talk about my mother, they stopped him. It sounded as though they were struggling with him. I think they were trying to keep him from telling me something—something about my mother. I believe they forced him off the phone." Debra leaned forward and looked in the side mirror on her side of the car.

"What did he say that would make you think that, Debra?"

"Well, it was more the intensity and tone of his voice. He seemed very anxious and nervous. He said my mother had a will! My mother has never mentioned a will to me before. She only had a small bank account when she died. There wasn't any reason for her to have a will." Debra hesitated for a moment as she pushed her hair back from her face. "After they forced him off the phone, someone in the room picked it up and just held the receiver for a while and didn't say anything. I could hear them breathing. I got another call this morning; they just held the phone and didn't say anything again. I think it was the same person, but the caller ID lit up 'Unknown Caller.' There are some strange things happening, and I don't understand what any of it means. What do you think, Ashley?"

Knowing the type of person Ashley was, Debra regretted asking the question almost immediately. Ashley, being outspoken, aggressive, and always ready to say what was on her mind, emphatically replied, "Come on, Debra. Stop being so melodramatic! It was probably some pervert that read about your mother's death in the paper and thought he could get under your skin, or perhaps some nut that's been watching you and is obsessed with your beauty and thinks he might be able to meet you."

"Ashley! Why would you say something like that?"

Quickly tucking a strand of blond hair behind her ear as she looked over at Debra, Ashley replied, "You know how many weirdos there are on the streets these days." Ashley looked over at Debra again. When she saw Debra's expression she said, "I'm sorry, Debra. I don't mean to be so blunt or to scare you, but I think you've watched too many mystery movies. I think you're making much more out of this than you should." Speaking in a low tone she continued. "I've been worried about you, Debra. That's why I wanted you to go away on this trip." She put her hand on Debra's shoulder. "Since your mother died, you take everything too seriously and you never relax. Don't worry about some stupid phone calls. Just try not to think about them, and have a good time on your trip." While Debra considered Ashley's comments rather strong, she knew that her intentions were that of a concerned, caring friend.

"You're right. Thank you so much, Ashley . . . for being there for me," Debra said as she looked at Ashley and smiled. "I'll figure it out when I get back." Just as quickly as Ashley had shown her humble, caring side, she shrugged it off and with a bubbly smile said, "Great. Now, where are we going for lunch?"

"I don't care—you pick." Debra hesitated for a moment, leaned forward, and looked in the side mirror again. "What about Famous Ray's Pizza? Isn't that your favorite restaurant?" she asked as she remained in the forward position, staring in the side mirror.

"Yeah, that sounds fine. They have the best baked ziti in town," Ashley replied. She looked over at Debra, who was still leaning forward just enough to view the side mirror. "What do you keep looking at, Debra?"

"Ashley, isn't that the same car that was sitting across the street in front of my apartment?"

"What car?"

"That black car that's been following us!"

"How would I know that?" Ashley sarcastically replied.

"When you came to pick me up, I noticed a strange black car sitting across the street. While we were loading the luggage, I had this odd feeling that someone was watching us. I heard a noise, and when I turned around, the back window was just closing. The car wasn't running—just sitting there. There was a pile of cigarette butts lying in the street beside it, as if they had been sitting there for a while. I believe they were watching us, and now they're following us."

"How do you know it's the same car?"

"It *is* the same car. It's black, has dark tinted windows, and there's a ding on the front fender. I can see it from here."

Ashley gave a friendly chuckle. "Okay, Sherlock Holmes, so what if it is the same car." She looked at Debra. "That's a perfect example of what I was talking about. You're so uptight that you can't relax."

Debra sighed. "I know. Maybe you're right, but don't you think it's strange that a car that was sitting in front of my apartment has been following us since we left?" There was a brief pause. Then suddenly Debra gasped and screamed, "Oh my God!"

"What's wrong with you? You almost caused me to wreck!"

"Ashley, what if you're right? What if that was a pervert that made those calls, and he was sitting outside my apartment and is following us right now!"

"Don't be ridiculous. It's broad daylight. He wouldn't try anything now."

Debra took a couple of deep breaths, and while covering her face with her hands, she said, "I'm sorry, Ashley. I suppose you're right.

I–I just can't stop thinking about those phone calls. They're making me crazy." She turned around and looked out the back window. "Well, let's see how far they follow us."

"We'll know when we get to the restaurant, but I don't think they're following us anyway. Didn't we just agree that you were going to stop thinking about that and relax? Now, let's talk about your trip, Debra. Uncle John told me about the cabin. He said it is in a very remote area and there are lots of animals around. It sounds like a wonderful place; I hope this is a fun-filled, relaxing time for you, Debra."

"I hope so too. This was a great idea, and I really need to rest and hopefully finish my book. Thank you so much, Ashley. You're such a good friend." Debra smiled and put her hand on Ashley's arm.

Ashley put her left hand on Debra's, smiled, and said, "You deserve it. I want you to sleep late every day, rest, and have a good time. Try to enjoy yourself. Now, when you land at Saranac Lake, Uncle John said the closest town to the cabin is called Owls Head. It's a small town slightly northwest of Saranac Lake. He said you can hire a driver at the airport to take you there. When you get there, stop at the first gas station you see, and they can tell you where you can hire someone to take you to the cabin."

"Thanks again, Ashley. You're a life saver," Ashley responded with a smile.

They talked more about the trip and all the fun and relaxation that Debra was going to have, but Debra still kept a close eye on the car behind them.

They stopped at the restaurant, and Ashley parked the car. Debra opened the door, and as they stepped out, the black car slowly drove past. They couldn't see inside because of the dark windows. "I told you it was only a coincidence," said Ashley.

"The fact that they're driving on by doesn't mean anything. They're not going to make it that obvious and stop."

"Come on, Debra, they're driving away," Ashley exclaimed.

"Okay, I suppose you're right," Debra said reluctantly as she stood beside Ashley's car, watching the mystery car drive down the street. She breathed a sigh of relief as they walked into the restaurant and waited to be seated. The delicious aroma of homemade Italian food was alluring enough to capture the senses and sway the thoughts of anyone.

They were seated and looking at the menus when Debra noticed a handsome young man who walked into the restaurant, wearing a baseball cap. He sat down at a table across the room. He was alone and began reading a book while he sipped coffee. She looked at him, studied his face, and thought about how his beard made him look much older than she guessed him to be and about how lonesome he seemed to be. She thought of her own life and how nice it would be to have someone she could share it with. She thought of the few romances she'd had that hadn't led to anything. *This is not going to be a sad time,* she thought, and with a smile, she looked at Ashley and said, "This is going to be a nice trip."

After they gave their order and the waitress brought their food, Debra was eating when she noticed that the young man with the baseball cap and beard was looking at her. When she looked back at him, he quickly looked away. To keep from getting any reprisal from Ashley about being paranoid or some other sarcastic remark, Debra didn't say anything to her about it.

They finished their lunch, Ashley drove to the airport and parked the car. Debra walked to the back of the car, and Ashley opened the trunk. Debra looked over and saw the black car with the dark windows two aisles over, driving by slowly.

"There's the black car again, Ashley!" Debra whispered loudly, pointing her finger as the car drove away. Just as Ashley looked up in the direction Debra was pointing, the car turned the corner and disappeared around the building.

"Please don't start that again, Debra."

"It was the same car, Ashley. I'm not making it up!"

"Well, it's just a coincidence," Ashley replied.

"A car at my apartment follows us to the restaurant, and now it's at the airport. That's more than a coincidence, Ashley."

"I guess you're right, but I'm sure it's nothing," Ashley said.

Ashley helped Debra check in her luggage. Her flight was scheduled to depart at one o'clock and fly to Saranac Lake in the Adirondack Mountain Park.

Debra hugged Ashley, told her good-bye, and set off toward the boarding gate.

Debra boarded the plane, and as she walked down the aisle, she noticed a thin-faced, dark-skinned man sitting near the back of the plane. As she walked closer to him, she thought that he seemed to be staring at her. Growing increasingly uneasy, she looked down at the numbers on the seats and pretended not to notice. When she finally reached her seat and placed her carry-on bag in the overhead compartment, she couldn't help but glance back. The man's dark eyes were still intently fixed on her. She turned to push the loose handle from her soft bag farther into the compartment, and another man bumped into her. They exchanged apologies and the man walked to the back of the plane. Debra closed the overhead compartment and prepared to take her seat. She glanced back and saw the man take the seat beside the man who was staring at her. She shook her head as she chuckled, realizing he had been looking at his friend. She took her seat and closed her eyes for a few seconds.

"I must be losing my mind," she muttered. "The phone calls and the black car, all these strange things are making me crazy." Was she crazy? Was that car really following her? Maybe it was her paranoia, just like Ashley said. She sighed, leaned her head against the window, and tried to put it out of her mind. *I'm going to take Ashley's advice,* she thought. *I'm not going to think about it.*

Once the plane was in the air, she watched the clouds out the window. She had never been to the Adirondack Mountains, and the excitement for the adventure that surely awaited her began to outweigh her lingering worries. She leaned back in her seat and settled in for what would be a short flight to the mountains.

CHAPTER 2

When the plane was nearing the Saranac Lake Airport, Debra woke from her nap. She looked out the window and was amazed at how beautiful the Adirondack Mountains really were. The plane landed and Debra hired a driver. She explained to him that she needed to go to a small town called Owls Head. After loading the luggage in the car, they began the short trip. While driving through the park, Debra was awestruck by the beautiful mountains, streams, and lakes.

When they arrived in the little town, she had the driver stop at a gas station while she inquired about getting a ride to the cabin. The station owner directed her to Harry Graddison's General Store on the north end of town. Once they arrived at the Graddison General Store, the driver unloaded the luggage. Debra paid him and went inside with a bag in each hand and one under her arm.

She immediately noticed the aroma of sweet-smelling candy mixed with pickles and sourdough bread. She looked around the room at the odd combination of items displayed on shelves and hanging on hooks. She had read about the alluring odor of a country store and its small-town atmosphere but had never experienced it for herself. As she savored the moment, she noticed an older gentleman sweeping behind the counter.

"Well, hello, young lady," he said with a smile. "I'm Harry Graddison. What can I do for you?"

"Hi, I'm Debra Benson. Someone at the gas station directed me here. He said you might be able to drive me to John Sherman's cabin."

"Okay. I sure can. I have a jeep we use to chauffeur tourists to campsites in the park. Are you traveling alone?"

"Yes, I am."

Debra put the luggage down, and Harry came around the counter to shake her hand. "I have just one question. Why would a pretty young lady like yourself want to go up to a secluded cabin in the mountains alone?"

"I'm a writer, and I just need some time to myself to finish the novel I'm writing," Debra said with a smile.

"Well, it's very remote. There shouldn't be anyone to disturb you up there, except a few campers and hikers and maybe some squirrels or raccoons."

"That sounds great!" Debra said.

I don't think this young lady realizes just how remote that place is, Harry thought. He turned and walked over to the back door that led to the garage and reached up on the wall where several keys were hanging on hooks. He took a set from one of the hooks, opened the door, and tossed them to a short, stocky young man working on a lawnmower.

"Here! Kevin, pull the jeep around front and load up supplies for this nice lady. She's going to stay up in the mountains for a while." Harry looked around with a pleasant smile on his face. "That's my son, Kevin. He's a good, hard-working kid." Harry closed the door and walked over to Debra. "You tell me what you want to take with you, and as soon as we load the jeep, he can take you to the cabin."

"Great," Debra said, with a smile. "It would be nice if we could get there before dark."

"If you leave right away, you'll make it just before dark."

"I'm not sure I know what to tell you to pack for me," Debra said as she lightly bit one corner of her lip. "I've never stayed in a cabin in the mountains before."

Harry chuckled as he went behind the counter and picked up a pad of paper from underneath the shelf.

"I'll make a list for you." He looked at her and smiled. "So, what do you write about, Miss Benson?" Harry asked as he walked back over to her.

"Please, call me Debra."

"Okay, Debra, what do you write about?"

"I write romance novels," she replied.

"My wife reads those, but I never had any use for them myself," he said with a blank expression. Debra smiled. She could tell by his actions and tone that he wasn't putting her down; he was just being himself.

"How do you know John Sherman?"

"I don't really know him. I've never met him. I'm friends with his niece, Ashley Bolton. She arranged for me to use Mr. Sherman's cabin."

"I haven't seen John around lately," Harry said. He began to write on the pad of paper. "But he's kind of a loner, anyway."

He placed a cardboard box on the counter and put several items in it. "So, how long are you going to be staying at the cabin, Debra?"

"My publishers are expecting my book to be finished in five weeks. Do you have the supplies I need to stay four or five weeks?"

"I have all the supplies you need right here, but I suppose John's niece didn't tell you that there isn't any electric power in those remote mountains?"

"No, she didn't," Debra exclaimed as she stared at the storeowner blankly. He chuckled at Debra's sudden apprehension.

"There's a portable generator in the shed behind the cabin, and we have the diesel fuel you'll need to operate it," he said with a smile.

"That's great," Debra replied. "I don't think this city girl is ready for total darkness in the mountains." She and Harry both began to laugh.

"I'll make a list of what you are going to need and then you can add anything you like," Harry commented.

"That's wonderful; I'm really looking forward to this trip."

Debra helped Harry pack the items. "If you could send Kevin to pick me up in about four weeks, that would be great. I'll pay you for your trouble."

"It's no trouble at all, Debra. It's my pleasure. As soon as we get the jeep loaded, you can be on your way."

"How far is the cabin from here?"

"With road conditions, I would say at least a ninety-minute drive," Harry said as he stood scratching his chin. He hesitated for an instant and said, "John's cabin is located just north of the Blue Line."

"What's the Blue Line?" Debra asked.

"That's what they call the Adirondack Mountain Park boundary. His cabin is several miles past the boundary, but then the park circles around behind the cabin. The roads in the park are well maintained, but some of the roads outside the park are rough, due to heavy rain and lack of maintenance. That's why we're taking you there in the four-wheel-drive jeep."

Kevin drove the jeep around to the front of the store and introduced himself to Debra. They loaded the supplies she had purchased, including diesel fuel for the generator. Harry explained how to start the generator and how the cistern water supply worked. Then he stood and looked at Debra for a moment with a concerned expression.

"I really have some reservations about you being in those mountains alone for four weeks, Debra. I don't think you realize how rough and remote it is up there. Are you sure you want to do this?" She hesitated for an instant. Then she gave a big wide smile.

"Yes, I really want to do this. I'll be fine, but I appreciate your concern."

"Okay, but if you need anything, John has a satellite phone in the cabin. You call right away. If you should get hurt or sick or anything, it will take a long time to get there, so please be careful," Harry said, still showing concern.

"Thank you so much. I'll be fine," Debra said, reassuringly. She leaned forward and hugged Harry and thanked him again. She appreciated Harry's quick display and genuine concern. Since she never had a father, this was a new experience for her.

After the last of the supplies were loaded, she and Kevin climbed into the jeep for the bumpy trip up the mountain to the cabin.

During the trip, Debra talked about life in the big city. Kevin was envious of her, and he explained how he planned to someday live in the city where the pace was much faster. "I don't like living in such a small town. There's just not enough excitement," Kevin said with a frown. "Nothing ever happens here. It's just a boring little town."

"After living in the city for all these years, I think I can use a little boring time," Debra said.

"I met John Sherman a couple of times. He's been in the store. He's friends with that senator. What's his name…oh, nuts…you know, the one that's running for president."

"Are you talking about Senator Jack Braco?" Debra asked.

"Yeah, that's him. He's been in the store with John Sherman."

"Really? Senator Braco has been in your store with Mr. Sherman?"

"Yes, he has."

"Are you sure it was Senator Braco?"

"I am positive it was him because my dad got his autograph!" Kevin swerved around a small deer as it crossed the road in front of them.

I wonder why Ashley didn't mention that Jack and her uncle are friends and that they have been here together, Debra thought.

After driving for more than an hour, they finally reached the cabin. They traveled over rough roads and through remote areas, a distance that could have been traveled in a lot less time had it not been for the potholes, ruts, and trenches washed out by the rain in the partly gravel and dirt roads.

It was nearly dark when they reached the cabin, but as they approached, she could see that it had a nice porch on three sides, with a rocking chair on either side of the front door. Debra unlocked the front door. Kevin helped her unload the supplies, and they put them in the cabin.

"I'll take the diesel fuel to the shed," Kevin said. After he came back, he asked, "Are you sure you're going to be okay?"

"I'll be fine. Thanks for your help."

Kevin told her good-bye and drove away. She suddenly was faced with the reality of being alone. She hadn't brought a cell phone because she didn't expect there would be a signal in the mountains. However, she remembered Harry telling her about John's satellite phone in the spare bedroom.

She stood still for a moment, looking around. A slight grip of fear crept over her at the thought of being alone in such a remote place. But she was used to being on her own and completely independent. She had faith in God and in her own ability. She had always been able to adapt and rise to the occasion when necessary. As a small child, her mother taught her to pray for God's guidance, to be optimistic, and to see the best in everything. *When things are tough, make the best out of what life sends your way.*

After taking a tour of the cabin, she saw how well it was laid out. The cabin was rustic, with the natural wood showing inside. It had two bedrooms, a hallway separating them that led to the back door and a large living room with a fireplace at one end. The kitchen and bathroom were off to one side of the living room.

She walked to the shed in the backyard and found the generator. She filled the generator with a can of fuel, and after a few pulls of the rope, it started. The shed was far enough from the house that the roar of the generator could hardly be heard at the cabin. As she ran the warm water into the tub, she wondered how clean the water really *was*. After all, it was rainwater from a cistern. Harry had explained to her how it worked, and he told her there was a water-purifying filter system on the water lines.

She was thankful to have power and some comforts of home in such a remote place. After getting into the tub, she soaked for a while. The warm water felt so good. It had been such a long day, and she was extremely tired. As she lay there relaxing, she dozed off for a short time. Suddenly, she was awakened by a noise. She climbed out of the tub, wrapped herself with a towel, and went to the window. It was still just light enough that she could see the outline of the yard. She looked closely at the edge of the woods and saw the bushes shaking at the end of the backyard.

"Probably just an animal," she thought out loud. After getting dressed, she found a flashlight in one of the drawers in the bedroom. She went to the shed, turned off the generator, and got ready for bed. When she turned the flashlight off, the cabin was engulfed in total darkness—darkness unlike anything the lifelong city girl had ever experienced. As she lay in bed, she wasn't afraid, but she wondered what might be in store for her in the next several weeks. She thought about the strange phone call from the day before and wondered if her mother really had a will and why her mother wouldn't have told her about it. *I'm really too tired to think about it anymore tonight*, she thought. After lying there for a short time, she said a prayer and drifted off to sleep.

She awakened the next morning to the glow of the sun coming in the cabin, and she could hear the birds singing. Knowing what a beautiful day it was, she quickly got dressed-and ate a bowl of cereal before venturing outside.

When she walked outside, she looked all around the cabin and saw just how beautiful it was with rabbits and deer playing in the backyard. The cabin was on a slight hill, and the front yard sloped down to a beautiful lake with crystal clear water. There were morning glory flowers and sweet-smelling honeysuckle vines on one corner. Several ducks were swimming on the lake, and the birds were singing in the trees. Having been limited to city life and unfamiliar with the natural beauty of the country, Debra thought, *This is the most beautiful place I've ever seen.*

It was a nice, warm, sunny day, so she decided to go for a walk. As she walked down by the lake, she noticed that the water was smooth as glass. She put her hand in the water, and it was plenty warm. She looked all around and didn't see anyone, so she decided she would go for a swim, knowing how secluded this area was.

With a mischievous smile, like a child sneaking a piece of cake before dinner, she undressed down to her underwear and stepped slowly into the water. She swam a few strokes and after a few minutes, dunked her head under the water. As she came up and wiped the water from her eyes, she heard a rustling on the shore behind her. She turned around expecting to see an animal, but instead a young man about her age was walking along the bank. He had brownish-blond hair and was very handsome and rugged looking. He was wearing jeans and a white tee shirt. He looked straight ahead as he walked. At first she thought, *If I don't move, maybe he won't see me.* But he spotted her clothes by a small bush. She took a deep breath and slowly dunked her head under the water, hoping he would walk away before she had to come to the surface. She stayed under as long as she could, but finally she had to have a breath. When she came to the surface and wiped the water from her eyes, she saw him staring straight at her.

"Who are you and what do you want?" exclaimed Debra as she swam farther away from the shore. Realizing she had nowhere to go, she turned around and tried to cover herself with her arms.

"I'm sorry, miss. I don't mean to scare you. I'm camping back in the woods and decided to go for a walk, but I never expected to find anyone here."

"Would you throw me my shirt, please?" Debra demanded, but her shaky voice belied her false courage.

"Well now, miss, looks like you're in a rather precarious position," the man said, smiling. "What if I'm a pervert of some kind and I took your clothes and left with them?" He began to laugh as he picked up her shirt.

"I'm glad you see the humor in this. Now toss me the shirt, please!" Debra demanded again. The young man tossed the shirt to her.

"Now, turn around!" she said sternly. He turned his back to her.

"I'm just funning with you, miss. I'm as harmless as a puppy."

She hurriedly put the shirt on as she got out of the water, but she couldn't help but smile at his last remark, even with her teeth chattering from the air hitting her wet body. She put on the rest of her clothes while she quizzed him.

"What are you doing wandering around here, anyway?" asked Debra, trying to sound aggravated. "This is private property; this is not part of the park."

"Well, I could ask you the same question. I don't see John Sherman around, and you could be someone who just wandered in here too."

"Well, I–I got the key to the cabin from his niece, Ashley Bolton," she said with an unsure tone. "You can turn around now," Debra said, after she finished getting dressed.

"My name is David Kimble." He put his hand out to shake hers. She looked at him and then turned and started to walk up the hill toward the cabin.

"I won't hurt you, miss. If you're going to be here for a while, maybe I could show you around. I'm camped a short distance away, just inside the park." She stopped, turned around, and looked at him for a few seconds. He had a pleasant smile and a kind and gentle look about him. He seemed to be someone she could trust, and after the slight hesitation, she walked back to where he was standing and put out her hand.

"Hi … I'm Debra Benson," she said. Then she looked closer at him and said, "There's something familiar about you. Have we met before?"

"No, I don't think so. I'm sure I would remember," he said.

"Oh, well, my mistake." She leaned over to one side and squeezed water from the ends of her long hair. "I'm a writer, and I came here for some peace and quite. I hope to finish a novel I've started."

"A writer. What kind of writer?"

"You wouldn't be interested," replied Debra.

"Maybe I would. Try me."

"How do you know Mr. Sherman?" Debra asked, changing the subject.

"I met John Sherman once before while camping up here, but I haven't seen him in a while. I normally camp about a quarter of a mile east of here."

"I've never met him," she said while watching a flock of wild ducks land on the far end of the lake. "So, David, what do you do?"

"I am a forest service agent, and I love the outdoors."

"I'm beginning to as well. I grew up in the city, but I could get used to this place. I have never seen any place so beautiful, peaceful, and quiet," she said as she glanced around and motioned with her hand.

"There's only one place that might be more beautiful. Maybe I will be able to show you sometime."

"A place more beautiful than this? I would love to see it," Debra said, squeezing water out of her shirttail. "I guess I better get out of these wet clothes. I'll see you later," she said and turned to walk toward the cabin.

"Yes, you will," David commented. She turned sharply and looked at him. "I—I mean if it's okay with you. I'm just east of here, if you need anything."

She smiled at him as she turned and walked back up the hill toward the cabin. As she walked, she wondered why he looked familiar to her, but she shrugged it off. She was excited about David being close by. She felt safer now, and he seemed to be nice. She felt so at ease around him, almost as if she had known him for a long time. She had never had a first impression like that about anyone before.

She went back to the cabin, changed her clothes, and settled in for a day of writing, but she could not concentrate. She couldn't stop thinking about David. She thought about how handsome, tall, and muscular he looked, and she wondered if he could possibly be as nice as he seemed. She focused on her writing the rest of the day, but every time she thought of her meeting with David, she could not help but smile.

Over the next week, David came back to the cabin every day and offered to do things for her, such as putting fuel in the generator and starting it each morning. She began to feel more and more comfortable with him and they quickly developed a mutual bond of trust and attraction.

One morning, after a light rain, Debra decided to go for a walk. As she breathed in the fresh, crisp, rain-washed air, she reflected on her life and how she felt about David. Even though she had only known him for one week, she felt as if she had known him for years. She had never thought about destiny before, but this felt right. *I don't want to rush into anything, I need to find out more about him,* she thought.

Later that evening, Debra was preparing food for dinner when someone knocked on the door. She went to answer it and found David standing there, holding a bouquet of wildflowers. Debra smiled and invited him in. Trying to hide the excitement she felt because he was there, she took the flowers from him and put her nose in them.

"They smell wonderful," she said delightedly. "Thank you so much!"

"You're welcome," David said with a smile. "Am I interrupting anything?"

"No, I was about to have some dinner. Would you like to join me?"

"What are you having?"

"Chicken and noodles—my mother's recipe."

"That sounds great. Much better than Beanee Weenees®."

"Well, the chicken came from a can, but it's good."

"It still sounds better than Beanee Weenees®," he said with a chuckle.

They walked to the kitchen, with Debra leading the way. She had an excitement deep within her, a woman's intuition that this visit from David was going to be special.

"Could you please get some plates while I find a vase for the flowers?" David put plates and bowls on the table. Debra found a vase in the cabinet and filled it with water. She put the flowers on the table, spooned two bowls of noodles, and got soft drinks from the refrigerator. They sat down at the table across from one another, but the flowers were blocking their view. David took the vase of flowers and moved them to one side.

"I'd rather see your face," he said with a grin. Debra smiled but quickly jumped up to get some napkins.

"I didn't bring a cooler," David commented. "I didn't want to drag one way back here in the woods, but it sure is nice to have something cold to drink."

"I've been meaning to ask you, how did you get here, anyway? I haven't seen you driving a vehicle"

"I had a friend bring me up here to stay a few days. I like to come and camp alone occasionally. It gives me time to think."

"So much for alone—you've been working for me every day," she said.

"Yes, but it's nice to share time with someone," he said as he looked at her and smiled.

Each time he smiled at her she could feel the excitement growing inside. She smiled back and then quickly changed the subject.

"I really appreciate you putting fuel in the generator for me. As you know, I don't run the generator all the time. I didn't bring enough fuel to last as long as I plan to stay."

"You haven't told me yet how long you plan to stay."

"Probably four or five weeks; my novel is due then."

"Good, I'll get to see you for a while … uh … that is, if you don't mind?" He looked at her with his deep blue eyes and her heart leaped with excitement.

"No … uh … I–I don't mind." They both smiled.

After they finished their dinner, David built a fire in the fireplace to combat the night chill. He took a couple of cushions from the couch and put them on the floor in front of the fireplace and asked Debra to sit next to him. They sat on the cushions and leaned back against the couch. Debra could feel the chemistry between them. It was a feeling unlike any she had experienced before. She felt excited and warm sitting next to him, and she knew it wasn't just from the fire. "David, tell me about yourself."

"There's not much to tell. I grew up in Kingston, New York, in the foothills of the Catskill Mountains, and I went to work for the forestry service right out of college. I'm an only child. What about you, Debra?"

"Well, after college I tried my hand at writing. I've always loved to write, and it seemed to come natural for me. I've been lucky enough to have a few books published. I'm an only child also. My grandparents died before I was born, so my mother raised me alone. I don't know much about my father, only what my mother told me. She used to say, 'He's influenced by other people, and that's why he can't be around.' When my mother talked about him, I could tell she really loved him, but there was a slight sense of fear. I can't really explain it. She would stare off into space, and tears would come to her eyes. For that reason, I didn't ask about him very much. My mother died just over five months ago in a fire. The fire department said the gas stove caused an explosion and that it was an accident. For some reason, I don't believe that, but I just can't imagine why anyone would want to harm my mother. She was the most kind and gentle person on earth."

"I'm sorry," David said as he gave her a sympathetic glance. "I'm sure you miss her. She sounds like a wonderful person."

"Thanks. Yes, I miss her terribly."

"Tell me about your novels."

"Romance novels."

"Okay, romance novels."

"I don't know why my books have been a success. My own life, as far as romance goes, sure hasn't been anything to write about."

"A pretty young lady like you, I would think you could have your choice of men," David said.

"No, that's not the case. Besides, I have such a busy schedule," she said, looking down at the floor.

"You mean you don't have a boyfriend who's going to come breaking through the door any minute to rescue you from a strange man?"

"No, I don't, but you don't seem too strange to me." She looked at him and smiled. "I think I could take you anyway," she said with a giggle as she put up her fists.

"Oh, yeah?" He took hold of her fists, and they began to wrestle. He rolled over onto the floor on his back and pulled her on top of him. She squealed but was able to break loose from him and roll over beside him on her back. David leaned up on his left elbow. He was captivated by her beauty. With the glow on her face from the reflection of the fire, she looked like an angel. As their faces came close together and their eyes met, their expressions changed to more serious ones. David looked deep into her big, brown eyes, and he could not resist the passion of the moment. He leaned forward and kissed her softly. Debra kissed him, but after a few seconds she drew her face away from his and moved to one side.

"Uh … it's getting late; you better go," she said.

He gently pulled her toward him and looked into her eyes. She could not hide the passion that was building, and he could not resist his own mounting passion. He kissed her again, and even though her heart was pounding and excitement was echoing throughout her body, she still was able to resist and pull away from him.

She stood up, dusted off her clothes, walked across the room, and stood with her back to him for a few seconds. Then she said, "Please, David. It's getting late; please go."

David stood up from the floor, walked over to her, and stood looking at her.

"Okay, Debra, I'm sorry," he said. He slowly turned, walked to the door, and stopped. He turned around and looked at Debra, still standing with her back toward him. He walked over and put his hand on her shoulder. She closed her eyes. The warmth of his hand and the excitement of his touch were almost irresistible, but she didn't move.

"I'm sorry, Debra. I don't want to offend you," he said and then turned and left the cabin.

After a short time, she turned and rushed toward the door, but David had already walked off the porch and was gone. Debra stood there motionless for what seemed like an hour, not knowing what to do.

It was just a kiss, but I'm so stupid. I ran him off, probably for good. He may never come back again, she thought.

As much as she tried to convince herself that it was only a kiss, she still could not dismiss the way she felt inside.

She cleaned up the dishes, put them away, and got ready for bed. As she lay there thinking about the night and the kiss from David, she thought of how long it had been since she had cared about anyone romantically. No one had ever stirred her emotions with a kiss the way David had. As she thought about him, she smiled and got a warm feeling all over. He was unlike anyone she had ever known. She wondered if he would ever come back. But down deep she knew he had felt the same way, and she finally drifted off to sleep thinking about him.

The next morning she got up, fixed some breakfast, and began to work on her novel, but she wasn't able to concentrate very well. After working for a few hours without accomplishing much, she stopped and prepared lunch. It was almost noon, and she had just cleaned off the table and put her dishes away when she heard a knock. When she opened the door, David was standing there looking at her through the screen. She tried not to show the excitement she felt just to see him. He took a step closer to the screen door, opened it, and stood looking at her.

"I'm sorry about last night. I didn't mean to scare you. I know we've only known each other for a short time." He looked at the floor. "I guess I come on too strong sometimes, but I don't want to move too fast for you. I really like you a lot, Debra."

"It's okay, David. I just haven't been close to anyone for a long time. I feel so stupid about the way I acted."

"No, don't feel stupid. It's okay." He took her by the hand. "Please come with me. I want to show you something."

Debra walked out onto the porch. She smiled at him. "Where are we going, David?" Debra asked.

"I have a surprise for you."

He held her hand as they walked back through the woods, about a quarter of a mile from the cabin. There was a path that led to the end of a large row of trees. He told her to close her eyes, and she did as he asked. She staggered and stumbled as she tried to walk. She kept giggling like a young schoolgirl on a first date. David was holding one hand and she had her eyes covered with the other as he led her toward the end of the trees.

"No peeking," he kept telling her.

When they reached the edge of the trees he told her to open her eyes. They were standing at the edge of a large meadow with a sea of beautiful wildflowers. There were purples, reds, yellows, blues, and whites.

"Remember I told you the other day about a place that was even more beautiful than where we were? Well, this is it," David said with a smile.

"Oh my!" Debra exclaimed and put her hands over her mouth. She took a few steps forward, looked from side to side, and spun around in a circle, extending her arms out as she turned. She could not believe all the beautiful flowers.

"Here are some flowers that are exclusive to this area," David said. "They're called Basil Mountain-mint and Torrey Mountain-mint." They were white with dark specks.

"They are so beautiful! This is great; this is so wonderful!" exclaimed Debra.

They sat down in the middle of the flowers and talked for hours. Suddenly they realized how time had slipped away. It was late in the evening when they began to walk back toward the cabin. As they neared the cabin, David took Debra by the hands and pulled her gently toward him. He looked into her eyes, and then he kissed her. This time she didn't resist. She put her arms around his neck, and they kissed passionately for a few seconds.

After they kissed and said their good-byes, David left. She was so excited as she walked along toward the cabin. *Surely fate brought me here and allowed me to meet such a wonderful man,* she thought.

The following week, they spent almost every minute together. The more time she spent with him, the more she enjoyed his company, and she knew David felt the same. This was the happiest she had ever been. She realized she was falling hopelessly and helplessly in love with him.

CHAPTER 3

One day, David came to the cabin carrying a fly rod and told Debra that he would catch some fish for their lunch. She kissed him and watched him walk toward the lake. Then she went in the kitchen to prepare some canned vegetables to eat with the fish. She was singing a song in low tones and thinking about David and how happy they were together.

Suddenly, there was a knock at the back door. Debra walked down the hall to the door, thinking it must be campers needing something. She opened the door, and there stood a young man. He had dark hair and eyes and wasn't dressed like a camper. He looked lost and out of place.

"Can I help you?"

"My name is Ben Butler. I'm from the FBI. We have been investigating a bank robbery, and we have followed a male suspect to these mountains. Miss Benson, we believe the man you have been seeing is this man." Debra stood petrified and instantly went numb. She could do nothing but stare at the man. Finally she managed to force words from her mouth.

"Wha–what? Do you mean ... David?" Debra asked as she looked at him in total astonishment.

"Yes, the man fishing at the lake right now."

"I don't believe you! How do you know who I am anyway?" Debra asked.

"I know all about you, Miss Benson. It's my job to know."

"How do you know my name? I want to see some ID," she demanded. The man produced a badge with FBI across the front.

"It's my job. We know all about you, and we've been watching David Kimble for some time now. He pulled a bank job a few weeks ago down in Schenectady, New York. He's been hiding out in these mountains for several weeks."

"I just don't believe it!"

"You better believe it, miss. He's dangerous."

"There must be some mistake."

"No mistake. It's him for sure."

"What gives you the right to spy on me?" She glared at him. I want you to get out of here right now!"

"Forcing me to leave doesn't change the situation. I told you we know all about Mr. Kimble. You had better watch out. If you continue seeing him, you could get hurt."

"Well, what I do is none of your business, and I want you to leave—now!" She tried to slam the door, but Butler put his hand up and took hold of the door.

"Calm down now, Miss Benson. We need your help, and if you're not involved, you should be glad to help us."

"What do you mean, if I'm not involved? I can assure you I'm not involved in anything!" She turned away briefly. But then she quickly turned around with a snarl and shouted, "Why should I believe someone who just shows up out of the blue waving a badge? Maybe you're lying. We *are* in the middle of nowhere, and there's no one here to corroborate your story."

"I'm telling you straight. We need your cooperation in order to apprehend this criminal, miss."

"If what you're saying is true, then why don't you arrest him right now?"

"We think he hid the money around here somewhere, and if we try to arrest him now, we won't be able to recover it. So we're going to need your help."

"I don't care. I can't do that. It sounds much too dangerous to me, if he really *is* a criminal. Besides, you said yourself that he's dangerous, so I'm not willing to take the chance."

"Yes, but we would be close by and—"

"I don't care," Debra interrupted. "I'm not going to do it!" She tried again to push the door shut.

"Wait! Hear me out," Ben said, holding onto the door. "If you are going to continue to see him, then we would like for you to keep an eye on him for us. We're hoping he leads us to the money."

"Who's the 'we' you keep referring to? If there are people with you, then you don't need me," she said.

"You think about it, and I'll come back. In the meantime, just string him along. I'll be in touch, miss." Butler then left without further explanation.

Could this be true, she wondered? She stood there in total shock. Her knees got weak, and she had to sit down. She was so upset she couldn't think straight. *How can the man I have fallen in love with be a criminal,* she thought. She choked back tears. At that moment she heard David whistling as he came up the path to the front porch, so she wiped her eyes. She wondered if she should mention it to him, but she decided against it and pretended everything was normal.

After David cleaned the fish he had caught, Debra prepared them for lunch. She spoke very little. She was afraid he would suspect something, so she pretended to not feel well. She put the food on the table, but her appetite was gone.

What if that man was telling the truth? After all, what do I really *know about David,* she thought. *Only what he has told me.*

She tried not to show her nervousness, but she was shaking. She could not hide her feelings. David came over and tried to put his arm around her, but she walked away from him. He walked over to the table and sat down.

"Debra, what's wrong?"

"Nothing. I don't feel well."

David saw how upset she was, so he didn't press her anymore. He decided to wait a while.

After eating lunch, they were sitting at the table when David asked Debra again.

"Come on, Debra, tell me what's wrong. You hardly touched your food, you won't talk; something is wrong." David walked around the table and stood next to her. "I caught this great-tasting fish, and you barely touched it."

"Are you sure you have told me everything about yourself, David?" she asked, looking up at him.

"Yes, I have. Why do you ask?"

She suddenly decided to take a chance to see what he knew.

"A man came to the back door." She hesitated for an instant, and just as quickly she changed her mind. "Oh, never mind. I have a headache. I want to be left alone."

"A man came to the door! What did he say, Debra?"

"Nothing … nothing, just a camper needing directions. I told you I don't feel very well. Can you please leave?"

"Tell me what he said. Maybe I can explain whatever it is that you don't understand about me."

"Just leave! Please!" She put her hands on her forehead, leaned forward, and rested her elbows on the table. She sat there looking down at her plate. David picked up the dishes from the table and started to put them in the sink. Debra jumped up and took them from his hand.

"I'll put them away," she said. David just looked at her. Then he walked to the door, picked up his fly rod, and walked off the porch.

Debra sat down for a long time without moving. Finally she decided to go for a walk by the lake. Tears streamed down her face as she thought about how much she cared for David. Heartbroken, she tried to determine what to do next. *Maybe I should just call Harry to come and get me. I'll call him tomorrow,* she thought.

That night Debra couldn't sleep. She hoped and prayed that what the FBI agent had told her wasn't true. She finally cried herself to sleep.

The next day Debra tried working on her book but with very little success. She kept delaying the call to Harry. It was late morning when David came to the cabin and knocked at the front door. When Debra came to the door, she said, "I don't want you here. Please leave. I need time to think."

"What's wrong?"

"You haven't been truthful with me, David. Just leave and don't come back!"

"Who did you talk to, Debra?" She just stared at him. "Whatever they told you is not true."

"Just never mind!" She slammed the front door. She couldn't control her emotions any longer; she began to cry again. *How could this have happened,* she thought. *Just when I meet someone who seems to be wonderful, he turns out to be a criminal.* She went in the bedroom, fell onto the bed, and sobbed uncontrollably.

After some time passed, she heard a knock at the back door. She wiped her face and eyes and went to the door. As she jerked the door open, she yelled, "I told you to leave me alo—!" But before she could finish, she saw Ben Butler standing there.

"Miss Benson, I thought you were going to keep Mr. Kimble occupied for me."

"I never agreed to that. I told him to leave me alone. I don't know you, and I don't owe you anything. I want you to leave me alone too. I want no part of this!" She turned and slammed the door. She went to the kitchen and stood over the sink and cried for a short time. After she had calmed down and gotten her emotions under control, she washed her face. She decided some warm tea might make her feel better. After drinking most of the cup, her head began to spin. That was the last thing she remembered.

When Debra awoke, she was disoriented and the room was spinning. It took a few seconds for her to remember where she was. She tried to move her arms but could not. She looked down and saw that she was tied to one of the kitchen chairs. Not knowing what had happened or how long she had been unconscious, she closed her eyes to stop the room from spinning. *What is going on?* she thought. *Who could have done this and why? Could David have done this? Maybe he suspects that I know about the bank robbery. I have to get free before he comes back.* She began to panic as she struggled against the ropes. She knew she could not walk in her present state, so she decided to wait until her head had cleared before attempting to free herself.

After she had regained complete consciousness, throbbing pain streaked through her head. She struggled to free herself from the ropes. She stood up, and the wooden chair she was confined to came up with her. The room began to spin again. She sat back down quickly. *I've been drugged,* she thought. *It must have been in the tea.* She waited a short time and stood up again. She fell backward onto the legs of the wooden chair with all her strength. The chair made a loud cracking noise, but it didn't break. She landed flat on the floor, almost like a turtle landing on its back. She struggled and struggled and finally was able to roll to her side and get back up. She fell backward several times, putting all of her weight on the chair. Finally the chair legs broke and the ropes loosened enough so that she could free her hands. As she was loosening the last rope, she heard someone knock at the front door. She finished loosening the rope. She ran from the kitchen to the hall. Suddenly she heard David shout as he opened the front door, "Debra, I'm coming in! I want to talk to you."

She ran out the back door before David saw her. She raced across the backyard and toward the woods. But then she stopped, remembering the satellite phone. But she knew David would catch her before she could get to it, so she kept running. Still dizzy, she held one hand on her head as she ran. She stopped and held on to some small trees to keep her balance. She wondered what this was all about and why David had drugged her and tied her to a chair. Once she caught her breath, she began running toward the woods again. When she was still several yards from the trees, she looked back and saw David coming out the back door of the cabin.

"Debra, wait!" he shouted.

"Leave me alone!" she yelled. She hesitated for a moment as she looked in his direction, but then she turned and kept running. Still groggy and unsteady on her feet, she ran as fast as she could, trying desperately to make it to the woods where she could hide.

"Wait! Debra, I just want to talk."

"Why are you doing this, and what do you want?" she yelled while running.

"What are you talking about?" David shouted. Trying to catch up to her. But Debra had a good lead, and he knew she would make it to the woods before he could catch up to her. He kept pleading for her to stop so he could talk to her.

"Why did you drug me?"

"I didn't do anything!"

"Stay away from me!" she shouted.

David kept insisting for her to wait. She ignored him, ran back into the woods several yards, and hid behind a big rock. David ran into the woods and looked all around as he called her name. He turned to his left and went up the hill, looking for her and calling her name. When she couldn't see him anymore, she slipped quietly down the hill toward the road. She was shaking so badly with fear that she could hardly walk. Suddenly she smelled a strong odor, a smell that a lifelong city girl had never smelled before, but her instincts told her it was something that had been dead for a long time.

As she approached a large clump of bushes, she noticed the smell getting stronger. Walking by the bushes, she glanced over and saw what looked like a partial human hand sticking out. She took one hand and moved some of the brush back, revealing an older-looking man lying there. He had been dead for several days. The body showed evidence of animal and insect infestation. Debra was horrified at what she saw and jumped backward, screaming. She tripped and fell, focusing on the clump of bushes, and crawled backward on the ground. Finally, after she was able to control the terror and nausea that gripped her, she scrambled to her feet and started to run, but David came up behind her and grabbed her. She struggled to get loose from him.

"Oh my God! That's John Sherman!" he yelled suddenly. "Debra, listen to me! I'm not the enemy here!" She jerked loose from him and turned and faced him.

"You killed him!" Debra screamed. David grabbed her and pulled her to him. "Let me go, you murderer!" She beat her fists against his chest and tried to free herself from his grip.

"It wasn't me, Debra. I swear. It must have been Ben Butler!" David said, holding on to her arms.

"Butler? He said you were a bank robber!" she yelled as she kept struggling with him.

"Debra, I'm here to help you."

"Get your hands off me! You drugged me and tied me to a kitchen chair!" She turned and tried to pull away from him.

"Debra, listen to me!" he said. He spun her around and looked into her eyes. "I'm the same person that you knew two days ago, before Ben told you all those lies about me. Now, if you were tied to a chair, Ben must have done it. For what reason, I don't know, but you've got to believe me. I'm here to help you."

"I don't believe you, David. Ben Butler showed me an FBI badge!" Debra said. She jerked loose from him, turned, and tried to run away.

"He's not from the FBI, Debra. He's lying!"

"How do you know him, David, if he's not telling the truth?" She tried to move farther away from him. "I can't explain it right now. You need to trust me," David said.

"Leave me alone!" she shouted, trying to run.

"I didn't want to do this, but you give me no choice," David said. He grabbed her by the shoulder, pulled a gun out of his waistband, and put it next to Debra's face with the barrel pointed forward. She stopped struggling. "Now listen to me; I'm here to help you."

"How? By sticking a gun in my face!"

"If I was going to hurt you, don't you think I would have before now? I've had plenty of chances. Now listen to me. We have to get away from the cabin while I explain what is going on. At least the part that I know."

David took Debra by the arm and forced her to walk deeper into the woods. He began to tell her his side of the story.

"Debra, I want you to listen to me, please. Your life depends on it. I'm an undercover FBI agent." She stopped and stared at him.

"If you're from the FBI, where's your badge?"

"I'm undercover. I don't have a badge with me." They began walking again.

"Let me see if I understand this," Debra said. "Ben Butler has an FBI badge and you don't, but you are the FBI agent and he's not. He's lying, and you're telling the truth. How do you think that looks and sounds from my perspective, David?"

"I know, Debra. I came here to watch Ben Butler. I believe he's working with someone, but I don't know who it is yet. The two of them are blackmailing Senator Jack Braco."

"I'm supposed to believe you?" Debra sarcastically replied. David stopped walking and took hold of her arm.

"Yes, you've got to trust me. Your life may depend on it."

"If this is true, why didn't you tell me before now?"

"There are lots of reasons, but you need to trust me," David said.

"Okay, let's say you're telling the truth. Why are they blackmailing him, and what does that have to do with me?"

"I don't know yet, but if Ben has talked to you, then he is planning something. You asked me how I knew Butler. I work out of the FBI office in New York City, and during my investigation, I heard him talking to someone about you on the phone. He used your name." She turned her back to him and took a couple of steps forward. She spun around and said, "Ben said you've hidden money that you stole from a bank, David."

"That's not true, Debra. I don't know what he's talking about. He's just making up stories to turn you against me," David said, shaking his head in disgust.

"Why would he make up a story about you, David?"

"I don't know, but he's up to something."

"How do I know who's telling the truth, David?"

"You've gotten to know me over the past couple of weeks, Debra, and I haven't told you any lies about myself. Ben just shows up out of the blue one day, and you believe everything he tells you."

"You just forgot to tell me about working for the FBI, right?" Debra said.

"I couldn't tell you—not yet anyway."

He pulled her down beside him as he sat on the ground. "I'm going to put this gun away if you promise me you won't run."

"Okay, I won't run. Where would I go anyway? Let me ask you something, David. Are you going to shoot me if I don't do what you say?" Debra asked as she looked at him with a solemn expression on her face.

"Of course not. You know I could never hurt you, Debra." She turned away from him, looked at the ground, and said nothing.

After a short time, they stood up and David took her by the arm. They continued to walk deeper into the woods. Debra's concern of her situation became greater with each step they took. She still didn't know if she could trust the man she had fallen in love with.

It was getting late in the evening when they stopped to take a break.

"We'll have to spend the night here. We can't take a chance on going back to the cabin. I don't know what Ben has planned. If he tied you up, he's up to something. You've got to believe me, Debra. I'm on your side." Debra turned away and ignored him.

During the long walk, Debra had had time to think about the situation. She decided to quiz David. "David, if you didn't put something in my tea, then that means Ben did. Why would he do that?"

"I don't know, Debra. But he has something planned, and I believe it involves you," David replied.

"But I don't even know him."

"I know that, but he's the bad guy, not me, Debra."

Debra hesitated briefly, and her mind reflected back to John Sherman's dead body. "That poor man that someone killed and left laying in the bushes—what kind of person does it take to do such a thing to another human being?" Debra said, beginning to cry.

"I'm sorry, Debra." David moved closer and tried to put his arm around her.

"Don't touch me!" she screamed as she jerked away from him. "For all I know, you killed him. Maybe he found out about you robbing that bank. Maybe he knew where you hid the money."

"I told you, Debra. Those are all lies. There is no money. Why won't you believe me?"

"I just don't trust anybody, David." She moved away from him and piled up some leaves and laid down on them. Dressed in jeans and a flannel shirt only, she wrapped her arms around herself, trying to stay warm from the night chill.

"I know you're cold, but we can't have a fire." He took off his jacket and offered it to her.

"You keep it. I don't want anything from you," she said as she turned her back to him.

After a couple of hours, David took a pack of crackers from his coat pocket and gave them to Debra. She refused them at first, but she was so hungry that she finally gave in. After eating, David piled up leaves to make a bed to rest for the night, but Debra wouldn't let him get close to her.

Debra spent the night tossing and turning. Occasionally David would hear her start to cry, but she rejected any comfort or affection he tried to show her.

The next morning when Debra awoke, David's jacket was laying over her. She slowly sat up and saw that David was still asleep. It was barely daylight, and she knew he would be awake soon. She saw her chance to escape. She slowly rolled over. The leaves crunched under her when she moved. Her heart began to race with fear that he would awaken. She stood up and quietly hurried down the hill in the direction she thought might lead to the road. After she walked through rough terrain for about an hour, she finally came to the gravel road that ran past the cabin. She stood momentarily, trying to decide what to do. She decided to walk in the direction that led back to town.

What am I going to do now? What if all that Ben said is true? I have the worst luck with men, she thought. "I'm going to walk back to town and just leave everything behind me. I'm going to forget that I ever met David Kimble," she mumbled. Tears came to her eyes. "This was supposed to be a quiet, relaxing time so I could finish my book," she said, choking back tears. She wiped the tears from her eyes and walked on toward town, not knowing what to make of all that had happened.

After walking down the gravel road for another thirty minutes or so, she heard a car coming north from Owls Head. She was so excited that she ran as fast as she could to meet the car. She ran around a small curve in the road, and just as she turned the corner, she could see a small SUV coming up the road toward her, splashing water from the chug holes. As the vehicle came closer, she could hardly believe her eyes. Her friend Ashley was driving. She drove up beside Debra and rolled her window down. "Debra, where are you going?" Ashley asked.

"Oh my God! Ashley, I'm so glad to see you, but what are you doing here?"

"I hadn't heard from you, so I decided to come and see how you are doing."

"Ashley, you've got to help me!" Debra shouted as she ran around to the passenger side of the SUV. "There are some men chasing me. I don't know what they want, but we've got to get back to town and get some help!" She jumped in the seat and hugged Ashley.

"The road's too narrow to turn here. We'll have to drive until the road is wide enough to turn around," Ashley said. She hesitated for a moment and looked at Debra. "What's this about, Debra?"

"I don't know! I believe these men are going to kill me if they catch up with me."

"Who are they, and why do they want to kill you?" Ashley asked as she sped away.

"Their names are David Kimble and Ben Butler. I don't know what they want, Ashley, but we have to get to town and contact the sheriff."

Ashley hurriedly looked for a place to turn around. As they rounded a bend in the road, Debra saw David walking toward them.

"There's one of them! Don't stop! Go—go faster! He has a gun!" she shouted. As they came closer, Ashley began to slow down. "What are you doing? Don't stop!" Debra shouted as she looked at David. As the SUV came to a stop, Debra looked at Ashley. Ashley was holding a gun in her hand, and she was pointing it at Debra. "Ashley, why do you have a gun in your hand? And why are you pointing it at me?" Debra said. Ashley didn't respond. The SUV came to a stop beside David and Ashley rolled the window down.

"You were supposed to watch her. Why was she walking down the road?" Before David could respond, Ashley pointed the gun at him. "Take your gun out and throw it on the ground."

"Ashley, what are you doing?" Debra yelled.

David stared at Ashley with no expression and complied with her demands. Debra tried to open the door and get out, but Ashley pointed the gun at her.

"Don't you move. You're not going anywhere!" she shouted and gave Debra a hateful glare. Debra sat motionless, in total disbelief of what was happening. Ashley motioned for David to step back. She opened the door and jumped out of the SUV, picked up David's gun, and quickly stepped back keeping the guns pointed at each of them. "David, I want you to get in the driver's seat." Ashley opened the back door. "I want you to get in slowly." As David climbed into the driver's seat, Ashley jumped into the backseat. "Now drive back to the cabin," she demanded, pointing a gun at each of them. Debra was in total shock as she stared at Ashley.

"What are you doing, Ashley?"

"You'll know soon enough, Debra. Now just keep your mouth shut."

"So David was right about Ben," Debra said, looking back at Ashley.

David had his right hand on the seat beside him, and he motioned it back and forth, trying to signal for Debra to be quiet. Debra looked down and saw him signaling her.

"What did David say about Ben, Debra?"

"Oh, nothing; Ben told me some ridiculous story about David, that's all," Debra said. She turned and faced forward in the seat, hoping Ashley hadn't caught on to her comment. Debra was beginning to realize that David could possibly be telling the truth. When she saw him signaling for her to be quiet, she knew he didn't want Ashley to know who he really was.

Ashley then turned her attention toward David. "Ben told me about the two of you and how you were carrying on, so I don't trust you, David. I think you just might try to help her escape."

"What do you mean 'escape'? Escape from what? What are you doing, Ashley?" Debra asked. "Why won't you tell me what this is about?"

"I told you to keep your mouth shut!" Ashley jammed one of the guns against Debra's head. "I want both of you to keep quiet until we get back to the cabin and I can find out just what kind of mess Ben has made."

"So, Ashley, you're Ben's partner? I was wondering when we were going to meet," David commented.

"I know all about you, David, but you don't need to know anything about me. Just keep your eyes on the road and your mouth shut!"

Debra sat, petrified, as she tried to figure out why Ashley was doing this. She was beginning to understand why David didn't want to go back to the cabin. She wished she had listened to him and trusted him. She worried that they were both in danger now. David quietly contemplated his next move as he drove over the bumpy road to the cabin.

CHAPTER 4

As they approached the cabin, Ben was walking from the woods toward the porch. David parked and shut the engine off. Suddenly he jumped out of the car and ran into the cabin. He went to the spare bedroom and pulled the satellite phone out from under the bed.

Ashley jumped out, jerked the door open, grabbed Debra by the arm, and pulled her out of the seat. Debra screamed as Ashley shoved her to the ground.

"Get David, Ben!" Ashley shouted. Ben ran up the steps to the porch and charged inside, but David jumped out the back window of the cabin and raced toward the woods. Ben climbed out the window and gave chase. He stopped and fired a shot at David just as he entered the woods.

"Are you crazy? Don't shoot him!" Debra screamed.

David disappeared into the woods. Ben could not tell whether the shot had hit its target. He ran toward the woods, trying to catch up to him.

Ashley grabbed Debra's arm and jerked her up from the ground. She forced her up the steps to the porch.

"Let me go!" Debra screamed. Ashley shoved her toward the front door. Debra spun around. "Stop shoving me, Ashley, and tell me what you want!"

"I told you to keep your mouth shut!" Ashley shouted. She pointed both guns at Debra. "Get in the house now!" Debra turned, opened the door, and walked into the cabin. Ashley pushed Debra down into one of the chairs, just as Ben came back from the woods... without David.

"Where is he?" Ashley demanded.

"He got away! I found the satellite phone; I must have hit it when I shot at him. It was in pieces."

Thank God. At least he got away, Debra thought.

"How much does David know, Ben? What exactly have you told him?"

"I haven't told him anything, Ashley!" Ben shouted.

"We can't have him running around out there. Who knows what he'll do. You better fix this, Ben. I've waited too long for this, and I'm not going to let anyone screw this up. Do you understand?"

As Debra listened to Ashley and Ben talk, she thought, *What is Ashley talking about, and why is she doing this? I should have listened to David. He was telling the truth.*

After they finished their discussion, Ashley took hold of Debra's arm and pulled her up from the chair. "Take her out behind the cabin. If they are as chummy as you said, when we threaten to kill her, he'll give up."

"Ashley, how can you talk about killing me? You act like it's nothing. We're supposed to be friends!" Debra said.

"Just keep quiet, and do as you're told," Ashley said.

Debra tried to pull away, but Ashley put her gun to Debra's head. "I said you do as you're told if you want to live."

They forced Debra into the backyard. "David, if you don't come out we're going to shoot her!" Ben shouted. There was no response. "I'll kill her right now if you don't come out."

He grabbed Debra by the arm and put his gun to her head. Terrified, she closed her eyes tightly, leaned her head away from the gun barrel, and began to tremble.

After a brief moment of silence, David shouted, "Okay, I'm coming out. Don't hurt her!"

David slowly emerged from the woods and walked toward them. "I told you," Ben said as he looked over at Ashley and smiled. Ashley turned and looked at Debra with an astonished expression and then a sarcastic smile.

"Well, Debra, you two must have really gotten cozy."

When David came up to them, he looked at Debra. Ben grabbed him by the arms, tied his hands behind him, and forced them both into the house. "Who did you call on the satellite phone, David?"

"I didn't get a chance to call anyone. When you shot at me, the bullet struck the phone and it was destroyed."

"If you called someone, and they show up here, I'll kill her right in front of you, and then I'll let you have it next!" Ben shouted.

"What kind of mess have you made, Ben?" Ashley said. "I thought David was helping us, and then I find him and Debra both wandering down the road on their way back to town. If I hadn't come along when I did, she would have gotten away and this deal would have been over."

"When I got here, instead of David watching her, those two were hanging on to each other all day every day!" Ben said.

Suddenly David began to struggle with Ben. Ben forced him toward the back bedroom. David kicked Ben, and Ben began punching David in the face.

"Stop! You're hurting him!" Debra shouted. Ashley pointed her finger at Debra.

"Don't you move!" Ashley turned and took a few steps toward the bedroom door. When Ashley turned away and walked toward Ben and David, Debra knew this was her only chance to escape.

Debra screamed David's name as she knocked Ashley down and ran out the back door. She ran as fast as she could toward the woods. She could hear Ben running behind her. She was so scared that she ran without paying attention to where she was running or in what direction. She ran through heavy brush that scratched her face. It was so thick that she couldn't run fast, so she didn't get very far. Ben came running up behind her and grabbed her. She screamed as he pushed her to the ground. He put his knee in her back and stuck his gun to her head.

"Be quiet, or I'll shoot you right here!" he shouted.

"Are you going to kill me, like you killed that old man?"

"So you found John Sherman. That was a loose end we had to tie up."

"What do you want from me?"

"You'll know soon enough. Just keep your trap shut. Get up and get going—now!"

"I'm not going anywhere!" Debra shouted.

"I told you, I will hurt you bad. Now get up and start walking toward the cabin!" He grabbed her by the hair. She kicked her foot backward and hit him in the groin. He swung his arm down and hit her in the back of the head with his gun. She lay there dazed, holding her head. He twisted her arm.

"You're hurting me!" she screamed as he pulled her up on her feet and shoved her in the direction of the cabin.

"If you don't do what I tell you, it's going to hurt a lot worse!" he said.

"I knew you weren't from the FBI," Debra said as she walked in front of him.

"Oh, you figured that out, did you?"

"You were lying about David too, weren't you?" She looked back at him.

"David isn't as innocent as you think he is, Debra." He shoved her forward, trying to force her to walk faster. "He's in on this little scheme up to his neck."

"If that's true, then why do you have him tied up?"

"He tried to sneak you out of here, so Ashley doesn't trust him, and neither do I."

"She's really got you wrapped around her finger, doesn't she?" Debra said, glancing back toward him with a condescending look.

Ben drew back his fist and swung at her. She jumped forward and ducked her head, so he missed with his swing.

"I told you to be quiet!" he shouted.

Debra stayed just far enough ahead of him to keep him from punching her.

"Why won't you tell me what you're doing and what this is about?" Debra pleaded, holding on to the bump that had now formed on her head.

"Does wittle Debwa's head huwt?" he asked mockingly in an Elmer Fudd tone of voice.

"Yes, it does, you jerk!" Instead of punching her, he grabbed her by the hair, jerked her head backward, and then shoved her forward.

"Oh!" Debra screamed. She spun around and slapped him across the face. His face flushed with rage, and he swung his left hand backward and hit her across the cheek. She fell backward on the ground, holding her jaw. Ben stood over her and said, "You can make things much easier on yourself if you cooperate and do as you're told." He grabbed her by the arm, jerked her off the ground, and shoved her forward.

"Stop shoving me and tell me what you want from me."

"We have a surprise for you back at the cabin," Ben said. He began to laugh. "A really big surprise; you're going to like this surprise." He was still laughing as they walked out of the woods and into the backyard.

When they reached the cabin, Ashley was in the bedroom where David was tied up. Ben shoved Debra inside, tied her hands behind her, and forced her to sit in one of the chairs in the living room.

"I demand to know how bad you've hurt David."

"You'll have to ask Ashley." Ben laughed again.

Ben went just inside the bedroom door. Debra thought about jumping up and running out the front door, but with Ben still in view, she knew she wouldn't have time to get away this time either. When Ben came back into the room, Debra leaned forward again and demanded to know what was happening.

Then she heard a noise from the bedroom. "David, are you okay?" she shouted. There was no answer. Ben pushed her back in the chair.

"We were not going to reveal any of this to you just yet, but things have changed. I suppose now is as good a time as any to explain what's going on," Ben said. He pulled a picture from his pocket and shoved it in front of her. It was a picture of Debra tied up and unconscious in the kitchen chair.

"You're the one who drugged me."

"I put a little something in your tea after I spoke with you that first time, Debra. Remember after you forced David to leave you went for a walk down at the lake that day? You shouldn't be so trusting; you should keep your doors locked. All I had to do was wait around until you drank the tea."

"Why did you take a picture of me tied to the chair?"

"Ashley and I sent a picture just like this one … to your father." Debra looked at him in astonishment. "That's right, Debra, your father. Your father is Senator Jack Braco."

"What … come on … is this some kind of sick joke?"

"Does this look like a joke, Debra," Ben said, shaking his gun back and forth.

"I don't believe you! How would you know that? Did someone tell you this?"

"I told you we had a surprise for you," Ben said with a big grin. "Maybe Ashley can explain it better." He turned and motioned toward the spare bedroom door. Ashley walked out with her gun in her hand.

"Ashley, why are you doing this?"

"Were you surprised when you saw me drive up on the road today, Debra?"

"I asked you, why are you doing this, Ashley?"

"You need to learn to be patient, Debra. They say patience is a virtue. Do you believe that, Debra?" Ashley said with the same irritating smile.

"Would you just cut the crap, Ashley, and tell me what you want from me?"

"I'm calling the shots here. You better settle down and relax."

"I'm your friend. What's this about?"

"It's about the money, Debra!" Ashley emphatically replied. "I got tired of working my tail off waiting on Jack Braco and catering to him like a servant. I helped make him who he is today, and he has never once acknowledged that fact. I heard from a reliable source that when he wins the presidency I'm not even going to be a part of his administration." She turned and began to pace in front of Debra. "I have decided to collect some money for services rendered. I think I deserve it."

"I demand you cut me loose right now!" Debra shouted.

"I told you, I'll decide what happens here, and you're in no position to demand anything. Now sit there and listen to what I have to say." Debra slouched back in her chair.

"I want to know how you came to the conclusion that Jack Braco is my father."

"I told you to keep your mouth shut and listen." Ashley continued pacing.

"Didn't you think it strange that your mother never told you who your father was, Debra? You had to suspect that he wasn't just a run-of-the-mill, average Joe. I suspected there was some connection between you and Jack Braco because he was so inquisitive about you. One day Ben and I followed Jack to your mother's apartment. He tried to hide the fact that he was going there. He even tried to change his looks to keep from being recognized, but I knew what he was up to. I knew Jack had some secrets he didn't want anyone to know about. I knew there was money to be made if I could find out what those secrets were. When I saw Jack at your mother's apartment, it all seemed to come together. I remember he would ask me about you from time to time because he knew we were friends."

"Some friend," Debra sadly expressed.

"Hush! Let me finish. I decided I would capitalize on one of those secrets, but I needed proof. He gave me the slip several times before when I tried to follow him, but not that time. We had him, so we waited until after he left, and Ben went in to get proof of what I already knew. After seeing Jack there, I knew that you were his daughter, but we wanted to make sure. After some persuasion, your mother finally admitted it, but then things got out of hand—I'm sorry about that part, Debra..." Debra could scarcely believe her ears. The blood rushed to all of her extremities, and she suddenly became almost numb. Seconds later, the initial shock subsided.

"*You* killed my mother!" she screamed. "All this time you pretended to be my friend! What kind of monster are you?" Debra tried to get up, but Ben shoved her back into the chair. Ashley walked over and stood directly in front of Debra.

"I'm sorry, Debra. It wasn't supposed to be that way...it just happened."

Debra tried to jerk away from Ben.

"I knew my mother was murdered!" She looked at Ashley as she gritted her teeth and said, "I could never understand why anyone would hurt her. The person responsible, my best friend, was with me at her funeral, crying beside me and pretending to be upset!" The more Debra shouted, the angrier she became. "Ashley, how many times did you try to console me when I was suffering over the death of my mother? That was all fake! How could you do that, Ashley? What kind of an excuse for a human being could do such a cold-hearted and vicious thing?"

Ben had his hands on Debra's shoulders. He was standing behind her chair, holding her down. Debra kicked her foot toward Ashley and Ashley moved aside.

"I told you it wasn't planned—it just happened. During the struggle she pulled Ben's mask off; she was going to call the police. She could have identified him. He had to keep her quiet."

Debra was angry, hurt, and began to tremble. Her emotions were at their brink. Her eyes were wide and her face flushed red.

"Don't you even speak to me, you conniving, lying...scumbag!" Debra screamed. She looked at Ben and yelled, "Get your filthy, murdering paws off of me, you animal!"

Ben shoved Debra over sideways in the chair.

"Shut up if you want to know what this is about!" Ashley yelled.

"I don't care what it's about, Ashley. I know everything I need to know. The person who claimed to be my friend, someone I have known and trusted for the past two years, has betrayed me!" Debra hesitated for a moment. She looked directly into Ashley's eyes with a look that practically went through her. "You're responsible for killing my mother. Doesn't it bother you that people suffer—and for what, money? I hope the money is worth it. How can you live with yourself, Ashley?"

Ashley turned away from Debra, walked across the room, and stood quietly, staring out the window.

After Ben saw that Debra had calmed down somewhat, he walked over and sat down across from her.

A short time later, Ashley walked back to where Debra was sitting, and with a cold, hard look on her face, she shrugged off everything Debra had said. She methodically began to finish her story.

"Ben and I knew Jack didn't want the public to know about his relationship with your mother, so we began to blackmail Jack about five months ago. He only paid us twice, and then he suddenly stopped. I wasn't ready to make this scandal public just yet. I knew there was more money to be made." She turned and began to pace back and forth again in front of Debra as she spoke, switching the gun from one hand to the other. "We decided to make Jack think that you had been kidnapped. That's why we had to get you up here. So you see, Debra, it's not blackmail any longer. Now it's a ransom demand for your life!"

"What makes you think Jack Braco is going to pay ransom for me?"

"Oh, he'll pay."

"So was that Ben who followed us to the airport in the black car? Is that why you kept telling me everything would be okay?"

"No, I don't know anything about that, other than you being paranoid over nothing." Ashley looked at Debra with a slight grin. "Anyway, I knew Jack would pay a hefty ransom to keep anything from happening to his precious daughter."

"If this is all true, how do you know Jack Braco doesn't want to see me disappear? I mean, look at what he has to lose," Debra said.

"Yes, that's right; he has two things to lose: you and the presidency. Besides, I saw that 'father' look on his face every time we spoke about you, Debra; he'll pay," Ashley said.

"What about John Sherman? I'm guessing he wasn't really your uncle, and I suppose that's why you didn't mention that he was a friend of Jack Braco's." Ashley stopped, turned, and gave Debra a puzzled look. "The general store owner's son, Kevin, told me that John Sherman and Jack Braco knew each other and were good friends. I suspected something wasn't right, but I wouldn't let myself believe it. I suppose Mr. Sherman was just someone else that you used and then disposed of when you were finished with him?"

"I wasn't going to give you any information you didn't need," Ashley said and kept walking back and forth across the room. "No, John Sherman was not my uncle, and yes, he was a friend of Jack's, or I should say a crooked colleague. He was willing to extort money from Jack—but anyway, that's how I got to know him. He gave us the key to the cabin, but he overheard Ben and me talking about the kidnapping plan and wanted in on it. We agreed to let him in, but he got too greedy. He wanted half the money or he was going to turn us in, so I had Ben take care of him." Debra looked past Ashley at Ben.

"Don't you see how she's using you, Ben? She *really* has you wrapped around her finger."

"Shut up!" Ashley shouted.

"I bet Ashley hasn't killed anyone, has she, Ben?" Debra looked at Ashley. "That's what she has you for, isn't it, Ashley?" Ashley stopped pacing and stood in front of Debra. She bent over and drew her hand back to slap Debra. Debra quickly leaned forward and spit in Ashley's face.

"You murderer! I hope you get what you deserve!" Debra screamed.

Ashley shoved the barrel of her gun under Debra's chin, pushing her head backward in the chair.

"Go ahead, pull the trigger," Debra said. "You won't have me to use anymore!"

"No, Ashley, don't!" Ben yelled, jumping up and running toward them. "Don't do it, Ashley!" Ben yelled again.

"Go ahead, Ashley," Debra screamed again as tears began to well up in her eyes. "There'll be no ransom paid for a dead body!" While hovering over Debra, Ashley quickly drew the gun back and hit Debra across the cheek. The impact knocked her head sideways, cutting a gash on her left cheekbone as she fell over onto the chair arm.

Ashley stood up, wiping Debra's spit from her face. Blood began to trickle down Debra's cheek as she turned and looked at Ashley with a detesting stare. Ashley moved around behind Debra and grabbed a handful of her hair and pulled her head backward over the back of the chair. She put her face down close to Debra's, and with clenched teeth she growled, "Don't do that again, you sniveling, spoiled little brat!"

Debra struggled against the ropes that held her hands tied behind her. She tried to get loose from Ashley's grip on her hair. Her eyes were clenched shut and a pain-stricken look was on her face. "Something you better keep in mind, Debra: I didn't specify to 'Daddy' what condition you would be in when he gets here. You best watch your mouth!" Ashley jerked Debra's head back even farther and then turned her hair loose and walked across the room.

Trembling and shaking with fear and anger, Debra screamed, "I don't care what you do to me! I'm going to tell you exactly how I feel about you, you backstabbing liar!"

Ashley spun around in mid-stride and yelled, "I don't want to hear another word, or I will finish the job right now!" With fury in her eyes and shaking from anger, she put both hands on the gun and pointed it at Debra. Ben ran over to Ashley and pleaded with her to calm down. Ashley lowered the gun, jerked loose from Ben, and went to the kitchen to wash her face.

All of Debra's emotions were spinning inside her like a tornado. She felt as though she could cry at anytime, but she refused to give in to any emotion that could be perceived as weakness. Her rage was beginning to control her, and sudden hatred began to form for her once good friend.

Ben turned and looked at Debra, and with a low, calm, and serious voice he said, "The only way you're going to survive this is to not antagonize her." Then he walked back and sat down.

Debra knew they were not going to kill her. She knew they would lose their money if she wasn't alive, so she decided to make them earn it. She stared at Ben for a few seconds, and the rage within her surfaced to the top.

"Don't speak to me, you filthy, murdering pig! You can just keep your advice to yourself. The two of you are like parasites sucking the life out of humanity. Why don't you do the world a favor and shove that gun in your mouth and blow your brains out!" Debra snarled.

"Just keep pushing it, and I'll turn Ashley loose on you," Ben said, glaring at her.

"You're not going to do anything to me. You're both full of hot air. I'm your meal ticket!" she shouted. "Now, I want to know where David is, right now!"

"Just keep your mouth shut. You'll be told when I get good and ready," Ben sternly replied, waving his gun at Debra.

"You mean when *Ashley* gets good and ready. She has you trained just like a little puppy. I bet you have to ask her when to use the bathroom, don't you, Ben?" Debra said with a smile. "Men like you make me sick. You're a spineless wimp that has to have someone do the thinking for you. Ashley's a controller, but it wasn't much of a stretch for her with you. I bet if she clears her throat you jump like a little kid who's afraid of his abusive father."

"Shut your mouth, or I'll shut it for you."

"Was it fun mistreating my mother, Ben? Did it make you feel good to beat on an old woman, someone helpless and not as strong as you? I believe in karma, Ben. What goes around comes around. So it's coming back your way, Ben. You and Ashley both ... wait and see. It's coming your way."

With his anger brewing, Ben jumped up, ran across the room toward Debra, and drew his hand back to slap her. Debra tried to avoid him by leaning over to the right side of the chair. He stopped in mid-swing, grabbed her by the hair, and gave it a quick jerk.

"I told you to keep quiet!" he yelled. After regaining control of his anger, he sat back down.

After a short time, the tension level decreased and everyone cooled off slightly. Ashley came back in the living room, sat down, crossed her legs, and began swinging her foot back and forth. Debra sat in the chair, still reeling from all that had happened. With mixed feelings of hate and revenge, she stared at Ashley so intently that she scarcely blinked her eyes.

"I don't think Jack wants the media to find out that he has a bastard daughter," Ashley said. She scornfully swung her head from side to side while staring straight at Debra with squinted eyes and the same irritating smile as before. "Especially since Jack's gotten the nomination to run for president. I also believe he just might come to rescue his only daughter and be willing to pay lots of money to keep this scandal quiet. I put that picture in the overnight mail to your daddy, Debra. He has until midnight tomorrow to get here with four million dollars, and if he doesn't, or if he goes to the police, then I *will* finish it!"

With all the different levels and mixtures of emotions, Debra began to experience a new one. She sat with a blank stare, unable to move from the shock of all that had taken place. She kept her eyes fixed on Ashley. It was hard to believe she was living this terrible nightmare. Her best friend was responsible for murdering her mother. It was as though the world had suddenly stood still. *This isn't real—it can't be. When am I going to wake up from this nightmare?* she thought. As she stared at Ashley, she knew she was helpless against two people with guns. She wondered when the nightmare would end, but deep down she had a strong feeling it was not going to be soon.

After trying to cope with all that had happened, Debra was beginning to get even more aggravated with both of them. They kept avoiding the questions about David.

"What about David? How badly is he hurt?"

"Don't you want to know about his involvement in this, Debra?" Ben asked.

"I don't believe anything you say. You're a murderer!" Debra shouted.

"He was in on this with us from the start. I met David through an acquaintance. He wanted money. When we found out that he knows his way around these mountains, we decided to include him," Ben said. "He was only getting a small share of the money, but we needed him to keep an eye on you. With his knowledge of these mountains, we thought he might come in handy, but he was getting too close to you. I had to do something to separate you two. That's when I decided to use the fake badge and make up the story about him being a bank robber. I knew if you got too chummy with him, he wouldn't go along with what we had planned. We were hoping to draw this out a little longer. We hadn't planned for Ashley to be here until tomorrow, but you wouldn't cooperate. So I called Ashley; we had to speed things up a little." Ben looked over at Ashley. "Ashley didn't trust me to handle this alone. When she heard about how close the two of you were getting, she came a day early."

"Is David still in the bedroom?" Debra asked.

Ben began to smile. Debra got a sick feeling in the pit of her stomach. Her first thought was that Ashley had killed David while Ben was chasing her through the woods.

"What have you done with him?" she demanded again.

"He's not dead … not yet, anyway. If something should go wrong with our plan, we may need him to help us escape from these mountains," Ben said and then stood up and went into the bedroom. Debra breathed a sigh of relief. Ben came back in the living room, dragging David by the arm. He was gagged, bound, beaten, and bloody, but he was conscious. Debra's mouth dropped open with shock when she saw the condition he was in. Ben took the gag out of his mouth.

"David, are you okay?"

"I'm okay, Debra."

"You didn't have to treat him like that. You two are nothing but uncivilized animals."

"Why are you defending him? He was helping us with this kidnapping caper," Ben said.

"I wouldn't put him in the same class with you two animals!" Debra yelled.

"You can save your insults for later, Debra," Ashley said.

Ashley stood up and put her hands on her hips. Debra began to smile slightly. She thought how childish Ashley looked standing there, demanding attention like some little girl being ignored at a birthday party.

"Now that we're all reacquainted," Ashley said, "this is how things are going to go down. If your daddy pays the ransom, he can take you home with him. In the meantime, we're all going to have to get along until midnight tomorrow. I think I'll fix something to eat. Ben, you watch these two. You two had best not try to escape, or you'll *both* get a beating next time," she said with a loud cackle as she walked toward the kitchen. Ben walked over to the kitchen door but didn't go in. He stood by the door so he could keep an eye on David and Debra.

Debra looked at David and asked, "David, are you part of this?"

David leaned closer to Debra and whispered, "No, I'm not part of this. I told you yesterday, I'm an undercover agent from the FBI. I know I should've told you earlier." Debra stared at David for a brief moment. "I'm sorry, but I couldn't tell you until I knew I could trust you. Yesterday I still wasn't sure how much you knew about all of this." David hesitated. "I work in the extortion and blackmail division of the FBI, where Bill Rogers is the director. Bill told me that Senator Braco had come to him and said he was being blackmailed. He wanted us to keep the investigation quiet because of the circumstances involved. He said it would ruin his career. Bill wouldn't tell me why they were blackmailing him, but he said it would come out during my investigation. If I were caught, it would be best if I didn't know. He only said it was a mistake from the senator's past. He said it was better if we kept it quiet. I trust Bill, so I didn't push it. Bill asked me to go undercover to investigate the blackmail. To keep anyone else from finding out, no one else would know that I was undercover. So I agreed to do it." David hesitated for a second when Ben looked toward them. When he looked back toward Ashley, David continued. "During my investigation, I discovered that Ben was behind the blackmail. I knew he had someone working with him, but I didn't know who. I reported to Bill what I had found out, but I didn't know whether or not you were in on the blackmail with Ben." Debra looked at David with an even more puzzled look on her face.

"You thought I was in on the blackmail? I didn't even know who my father was until tonight!"

"Keep your voice down!" he whispered as he slid himself across the floor, closer to where Debra was sitting. "I know that, Debra, but I had to be sure. My plan was to watch you and get information. I was in the restaurant the day you left to come here. I was sitting at a table alone, reading a book." David paused for a moment because of the look he was getting from Debra.

"I saw you there. That's why you looked so familiar to me when I first met you that day at the lake. Why did you have on the fake beard, and why were you watching me?"

"I had to get close to you to get information on them and find out if you were part of this blackmail plot. I didn't want you to recognize me when I got here to the cabin."

"How did you know I was going to be here?" Debra asked.

"I put a bug on Ben's telephone. I heard part of a conversation between him and a woman, but I didn't know who it was. Ashley never used her name. I knew they were watching you, but I didn't know why. The day you left, I was able to arrange a meeting with Ben through a street informant that I know. I met John Sherman through Ben that day also. Ben wasn't going to be at the cabin for several days, so I made a deal with him. He wanted me to watch you." Debra's stare became more intense.

"Even after their conversation, you still felt that you had to get information from me and you had to watch me?"

"Yes. I wasn't sure what was going on. I thought this was still part of the blackmail plan. Ben only slightly mentioned that there was lots of money to be made. Ashley hadn't said anything about any ransom when she talked with Ben on the phone, and I certainly didn't know they were going to kill John Sherman. I left immediately after you. I came here to stay close to you and get as much information as possible."

Debra's face flushed red. She looked down at the floor, trying to keep from showing her humiliation and embarrassment. Then the embarrassment and humiliation quickly turned to aggravation and anger. She looked up and glared at him, and with complete disgust in her voice said, "So you only wanted information from me. You were even going to be paid to watch me. That's just great." Debra shook her head from side to side. "So, tell me, David, was what happened between us just part of the plan too? Did it mean nothing to you?

I hope you weren't disappointed. I hope you got plenty of information." She looked back down at the floor.

"No, Debra, that wasn't part of the plan. It was something wonderful that just happened."

She raised her head and looked straight at David. "Why didn't you tell me all this last night?"

"I still didn't know who Ben's partner was."

"You had to know it wasn't me."

"Yes, you're right, but I suppose I was reluctant to tell you because I didn't know how you would react and I had no idea that the woman I heard on the phone was your friend. When I saw Ashley that day at the restaurant, I had no way of knowing she was involved."

"You were just using me like Ashley's been doing." She looked up at the ceiling, shaking her head, and said, "What an idiot I am. I must be the stupidest human being alive not to realize when I'm being used by everyone around me." She looked down and just stared across the room.

"No, it's … uh … not that way at all, Debra." David dropped his head, looked at the floor, and then looked up at her and said, "When I realized what a wonderful person you are, I knew you could never do anything to hurt anyone. I've gotten to know you and how sweet and kind you are. I have never met anyone like you. The more I saw you, the more I wanted to see you. It wasn't just my job anymore. I wanted to tell you several times, but I didn't know how you would react. I wanted to tell you last night, but I was afraid I would lose you. I would never do anything to hurt you. I never planned to fall in love with you, Debra." David hesitated for a moment. "But I did. Please … please, forgive me. I love you. I'm glad I took this job because I was able to meet you, Debra."

Debra looked into David's eyes. She realized that he had to watch her as part of his job and that he never planned to hurt her in any way. The man she had gotten to know over the past couple of weeks could never intentionally hurt anyone. She knew by the look on his face that what he was saying was coming from the heart. She also knew she felt the same way. Even with all the emotions and the mixed-up feelings and thoughts going through her head, she still loved him. It was a kind of love she had never felt for anyone before, love that can't be pushed down or held back; pure, heartfelt love.

"I love you too, David," Debra said, partially smiling, her face still hurting from the cut from Ashley's gun. "David, how are we going to get out of this mess?"

"I don't know. Maybe if I tell them who I am I could reason with them."

"No, I think they're just crazy enough to kill you now instead of later."

"Maybe we'll get a chance to reason with them at some point," David said and leaned back against the side of Debra's chair.

They both hoped this would be over soon, but there was a mutual sense of understanding between them that this just might be the beginning of their problems.

CHAPTER 5

After preparing some food, Ashley came back from the kitchen, with Ben following her.

As they walked close to David and Debra, Ashley commented, "Hey, love birds, Ben said you two were whispering. What are we whispering about? Planning an escape?"

"No, actually we were talking about being used by people."

"Oh, come on, Debra. Let it go. You are so gullible; it was easy to use you."

"I guess so, if you're the type of person that easily uses people."

"Whatever," Ashley said with a sigh. "Okay, we're going to the kitchen to eat a bite. I hope we're not going to have any problems from the two of you between now and tomorrow night."

"Untie our hands so we can eat. We won't try to get away," said Debra, as they entered the kitchen. Ashley agreed, but then she gave them a warning.

"I'm going to be watching you really close, and I won't hesitate to use this gun if I have to," she said while pulling the hammer back on the pistol and pointing it at Debra. She grabbed a lock of Debra's hair and pulled her head back slightly. Ashley put the gun barrel to Debra's ear; then she gave a devious grin and released the hammer. She walked over to the table and sat down and put the gun beside her plate.

Debra was scared but was able to conceal her fear, and she boldly asked Ashley if she could clean the cuts on David's face before they ate. After some discussion and more threats of violence, Ashley finally agreed. Debra and David went to the bathroom, with Ashley and Ben following. Debra dampened a washcloth with warm water and washed the cuts on David's face and the cut on her face from Ashley's gun. She also cleaned her scratches from the chase through the woods. The cuts on David weren't as bad as they looked after she cleaned the dried blood away.

When Debra was finished, they went to the kitchen to eat. Debra kept her eyes on Ashley while trying to eat some tough noodles that Ashley had cooked. The more she stared at Ashley, the more irritated she became. She was beginning to experience another level of the emotional rollercoaster that had been running since this nightmare began. The rage within her began to surface again, and she saw one more chance to hurl another insult at her former friend.

"I understand now why you were never married, Ashley."

"Why is that?" Ashley asked while she glared at Debra.

"Because no one could eat this slop," Debra said, shoving her plate forward.

"You can eat it, or you can starve!" Ashley snarled. She stared at Debra for a moment. "Okay, smart mouth, between now and tomorrow night, you can fix all the meals. We'll see how Miss Susie Homemaker does at cooking."

There were hateful stares and very little conversation while they finished their meal.

After they had finished, Ashley said, "Now, Debra, since you know so much about the kitchen, you and lover boy can clean up these dishes."

Debra didn't look in Ashley's direction as she and David cleaned up the kitchen and washed the dishes. It was late in the evening when they all walked back to the living room. In spite of Debra and David's objections, Ashley had Ben tied their hands.

Debra could do nothing but sit and stare at Ashley, wondering what had happened to her that would cause her to harbor all of this hate and deceitfulness. *What kind of a person can be so kind and sweet to your face and be planning to hurt you at the same time behind your back,* she thought. For the two plus years she had known her, Ashley had never shown the personality that was now evident. Debra began to think that maybe she had always had this hate dwelling inside her. Perhaps her sudden disdain toward Jack Braco triggered these pent-up feelings that had surfaced. She knew that the best thing she could do was pray that Ashley would come to her senses and this nightmare would end soon.

After it had been dark for a short time, Ashley stood up and said, "We're going to bed now."

"Untie our hands, Ashley. I promise we won't try to escape," Debra said. After some strong arguing, Ashley finally agreed.

They each took turns using the bathroom, and then Ashley announced, "We are all going to sleep in the same bedroom so I can watch you two."

They chose the bedroom where Debra had been sleeping. Ben took the mattress from the other bedroom and put it on the floor at the foot of Debra's bed. He went to the shed and got a hammer and some nails and nailed the bedroom windows shut. He began to tie their hands to one of the bedposts.

"Don't tie our hands. We won't be able to sleep. Our hands will go numb," David said.

"I don't care," Ben replied.

David looked at Ashley. "Ashley, you agreed earlier to leave our hands untied. We won't try to escape. Where would we go anyway?"

"I don't believe you," Ben said.

"It's okay, Ben," Ashley said. "I'm not a heavy sleeper. If they move, I'll know it. I'll have my gun in the bed with me, and I'll use it." She looked at Debra with squinted eyes and an evil grin. Debra just looked at her with no expression on her face. *What an evil person. How could I have been so mistaken to ever believe this person was my friend,* she wondered.

Debra and David lay down on the mattress, Ashley slept in the bed, and Ben slept in the chair, blocking the doorway. When all was quiet, Debra whispered, "We have no way to escape."

"I know; we can't get past Ben in the doorway, and the windows are nailed shut. We're going to have to wait until tomorrow and see if we get a chance to escape," David replied.

"Didn't you plan to have any of your FBI friends watching?" Debra asked.

"No, remember, only Bill Rogers and me knew about my being undercover. I don't have any identification, other than my driver's license. I spoke with Bill briefly on the satellite phone when Ben was chasing me. I told him that Ashley was the woman working with Ben on the blackmail. Ben's bullet knocked the phone out of my hand, and I wasn't able to tell him anything else. I didn't have my gun, so I had to give up when they threatened to harm you," he whispered.

"Those two are real tough as long as they're holding a gun," Debra said.

"Debra, if we can't get away, I want you to go with your father when he pays the ransom."

"No, I'm not going anywhere without you."

"Don't worry about me. I'll be okay."

"I'm not going without you. I love you, David." David kissed her as they moved closer to each other.

"Debra, there are campers scattered in these mountains, so if we can get away tomorrow, we might be able to get some help."

"David, promise me you won't do anything to provoke those two. All they would need is an excuse to shoot you."

"I promise. I won't do anything to cause a problem, but the first chance we can escape, we have to take it," replied David. "Debra, don't get into any more arguments with Ashley. She's just crazy enough to shoot you."

"No, I think she's just trying to act tough. She won't hurt me— I'm her meal ticket. She knows she won't get one penny if I'm dead, and for that reason, I may just make her earn her money."

"What do you mean, Debra?"

"Well, I'm not going to take her mouth."

"Debra, I want you to promise me you won't try to provoke her."

Debra hesitated for a brief moment and then whispered, "She's responsible for my mother's death."

"I know, Debra, but now is not the time for revenge. We have to focus on getting away. You'll get your chance—just bide your time."

"Okay."

"Please promise me," David whispered with distress in his voice. "She's a nut, and money or no, I think she would shoot you in a New York minute, especially since you can identify her. Now promise me you won't antagonize her."

"I promise ... I'll try," Debra whispered. She laid her head on his chest, and they held on to each other the rest of the night.

The next day, Ashley followed through with her threat. She forced Debra to make breakfast for them. Ashley agreed to leave their hands untied, but she watched every move they made.

Later that afternoon, they were resting in the living room when they heard a vehicle driving up to the cabin. Ashley jumped up and looked out the front window and saw a green jeep driving up the road to the cabin.

"Someone's coming," Ashley said. They could hear the jeep come to a stop at the far end of the cabin. The door opened and then slammed closed. Instantly Debra saw Ashley's arrogant, I'm-in-charge confidence dissipate with her ghostly pale complexion, and for the first time, she had the look of fear on her face. Ashley hesitated for an instant, and then she grabbed Debra by the arm and pulled her up from the chair. She poked the gun at Debra's ribs and forced her to the door.

A male voice called, "Hello, in the cabin."

"Hello," Debra answered through the screen door. Ashley pressed the gun against her back.

"Walk out on the porch and talk to him and get rid of him. Just remember, I'm going to have a gun pointed at your boyfriend's head, so be careful what you say." Ben forced David over behind the door with Ashley. She put the gun to David's head.

David's brain was racing, trying hard to think of something. But any plan of making a noise or struggling with them was quickly hampered by the thought of Debra being hurt or killed by these two maniacs. He knew that now was not the time. He could only stand helpless to their commands and follow orders.

Debra walked out on the porch before the man had time to walk up the steps. She looked toward the end of the porch and saw a man in a green and tan uniform with matching broad-brim hat standing in the yard. He had a pistol on his side and a badge on the left front side of his shirt. He was standing at the right side of the porch.

"Hi, I'm Don Smith, the conservation officer for this area. Are you Debra Benson?"

"Yes, I am."

"When I was in town at Harry's store a few days ago, he told me you were up here at Sherman's cabin. He said you were alone, and he wanted me to check on you. Since I was going to be up this way today, I thought I would stop by." He took off his hat and wiped his brow with a handkerchief.

"It's nice to meet you, Don. That was very thoughtful of you and Harry, but I'm fine."

"I have a few minutes to spare if you need me to come in and help you with something, or if there's anything at all you need me to do." He put one foot on the bottom step.

Ashley whispered out the door, "Get rid of him." Debra walked forward, to the end of the porch.

"Thanks anyway," she said with a smile, "but I'm really busy right now. I appreciate you coming by, but I'll be fine."

"Okay, miss, it was nice to meet you. Sorry to bother you."

"That's okay. Thanks for stopping by," Debra said with a smile and a wave. With that, Don stepped back into his jeep, gave Debra a wave good-bye, and drove away. Debra stood on the porch and watched him drive back down the road from the cabin.

After he was gone, Ashley shouted, "Get back in here!" Debra came back inside. Ashley met her at the door and followed her to the middle of the room. "Why did he want to come in? You didn't give him some kind of sign, did you?" Debra glared at her.

"You don't think I'm going to risk David's life, do you?"

Ashley began to smile. "Oh yes, I forgot how precious David's life is to you." Ashley turned and slowly walked toward David. "Well, well, well. Little Debra is in love. Isn't that sweet?" Ashley said in a most condescending tone and with a smirk on her face. She put her gun in her waistband and began to smile as she rubbed her hands across David's face and head. He quickly tried to pull away from her. Ashley kept her eyes fixed on Debra as she moved closer to David. She pressed her body to his, wrapping one leg around him while rubbing her hands all over him. Her evil grin and her antagonizing stare were more than Debra could stand. Her blood practically boiled, and she could not control her anger. She lunged toward Ashley and grabbed her by the hair. They fell to the floor, fighting and scratching each other. Debra was on top of Ashley, both hands full of Ashley's hair. She was screaming, pulling her hair, and slamming Ashley's head against the floor. Ben began laughing hysterically as he walked over and made a halfhearted attempt to separate them.

This was the chance David had been waiting for. He ran over and knocked Ben to the floor. Then he grabbed Debra by the arm, jerked her up, and they ran out the front door. Ben and Ashley scrambled to their feet and quickly followed.

Debra and David ran as fast as they could, desperately trying to make it to the woods. They were almost to the tree line when a gunshot rang out from behind them. The bullet hit the ground only feet from David. Dirt showered him, and they stopped in fear.

"Hold it right there! That was a warning shot. The next won't be in the ground!" Ben yelled.

Ashley grabbed Ben by the arm. "Are you crazy? Someone may have heard the shot!"

Ben glared at her and jerked his arm from her grasp. He looked back at David and Debra, his gun still trained on them. He motioned for them to walk back to where he and Ashley were standing.

"Stop harassing her! If they had gotten away, it would have been because of you!"

"I know what I'm doing," Ashley replied sharply.

"Then start acting like it," Ben said. He grabbed David by the arm and shoved him toward the cabin.

"Get back to the cabin," Ashley commanded through gritted teeth as she grabbed Debra by the arm and shoved her forward.

Ashley's eyes were wide, and she was furious. She shoved her gun against Debra's back as they walked.

"You try that again, and it will be your last time!" Ashley shouted.

"What are you going to do, shoot the only chance you have of getting your money? I don't think so!" Debra said.

"Just keep pushing it, Debra, and you'll find out!" Ashley said, still shoving Debra toward the cabin.

When they reached the cabin, Ashley tied their hands and forced them to sit in chairs in the living room. She sat down across from Debra, and they stared at each other intently.

While sitting there staring at each other, Debra decided she would try to find out exactly why Ashley had begun to hate her.

"Ashley, maybe you can tell me exactly why you hate me so? I mean, what did I do to cause you to hate me the way you do?"

Ashley raised her eyebrows and gave Debra a surprised look.

"Okay, you really want to know? I'll tell you. I have never met anyone as lucky as you. Everything just falls into place for you. Let me ask you, Debra, has anything ever *not* worked out for you? An example: you write a book, and it sells. Your father, even though you're a bastard child, is a rich senator and possible soon-to-be president of the United States. And if that's not enough, I trick you into coming up here to this secluded place, and somehow you manage to find the love of your life." She shook her head and said, "That doesn't happen to normal people, Debra. Just you!"

Debra looked at Ashley and began to smile. "You're right, Ashley. I had never thought of it that way. Thanks for reminding me. I feel much better now."

Ashley, quivering with fury and hatred, jumped up and stormed toward the bedroom. She gave an irritated glance toward Ben. "Ben, if either one of them moves, shoot them!"

Debra looked across the room at David, and they both smiled. "I'll wipe that smile off your faces tonight when this is over," Ben said, pointing his gun at them. He walked over to the bedroom door and tried to console Ashley by reminding her of the money they would be getting. "Four million dollars, Ashley. Think of what we can do with four million dollars," Ben said.

"I'll be glad when this is over and I won't have to see her face anymore!" Ashley shouted.

"You called me, Ashley, and said, 'Oh, Debra, I only want the best for you. Oh, Debra, you need to go on this trip, so you can relax.' You pretended to be my friend, and all the time it was only about money! You are a selfish, manipulative liar!" Debra yelled, from her chair in the living room. Ashley came back to the bedroom door and pushed Ben out of the way. Ben grabbed her by the arm. "No, Ashley. Leave her alone." With a look of hatred on her face and the sound of contempt in her voice, she yelled.

"One more word out of you and Daddy will be picking up a corpse tonight."

"Sit there and be quiet, or I'm going to get a gag and put it in your mouth," Ben said, pointing his finger at Debra. Debra stared at Ben with no expression on her face. Ashley went back to the bedroom and sulked while Ben kept watch over David and Debra.

The day came to a close with Debra making sandwiches for them, but the tension was high.

While they were sitting at the kitchen table, Debra said, "Ashley, aren't you going to be a little cautious? I haven't seen you look out the window one time. What if my father sends the FBI to rescue me?"

"He's not stupid enough to try anything like that. He won't jeopardize his little girl's life."

"Are you sure about that? Or maybe my father doesn't care that I have been kidnapped. After all, he did stop paying the blackmail, didn't he?"

"Yes, but he's not the kind of man that would do anything to cause harm to anyone. He's a spineless wimp. Besides, he knows that we are willing to go to the media with information about his illegitimate daughter. He'll be here. He's ahead in all the election polls, so he's not going to do anything that would endanger this election. Now, just shut up and be patient," she said with a smirk on her face. "Daddy's going to come to the rescue."

After dinner, Ashley agreed to let them go to the bathroom and clean up one at a time while she and Ben took turns watching the bathroom door.

It had been dark for about an hour, and Ben and David were sitting in the living room. Ashley and Debra came back from the bathroom, and as they walked into the living room, Debra stopped beside David's chair, which was located near the back of the room, by the hallway. She began to talk to him. Ashley had kept walking, but she stopped and turned and looked back at Debra.

"Get over here!" Ashley said in a most hateful tone.

"I'll come when I am good and ready," Debra replied as she knelt down beside David's chair and put a hand on his shoulder.

Ashley had walked over near the front door. She stood there glaring at Debra and motioned toward her with her gun. "I said get over here and sit down," she demanded.

"Debra, you had better do as she says. She's crazy," David commented.

"That's right, Debra—I'm crazy! Now, I'm only going to say this one more time. Get over here and sit down right now!" Ashley demanded, stomping her foot on the floor.

Debra stood up and looked at Ashley. As she began to smile she said, "Do you realize how pathetic you look standing there stomping your foot like a spoiled five-year-old?" Debra began to get angry. "What are you going to do? Shoot me? I don't think so. I've had enough of your orders!" Debra shouted with her fists clenched. "Now you go ahead and use that gun, or come over here and make me do as you say," Debra said, waving a clenched fist toward Ashley. Ben jumped up and took hold of Ashley's arm just as she started across the room.

"Can't you two get along just a little while longer, until we get this thing finished? I'm sick of your bickering, both of you. Now, Ashley, let her sit beside him for a little while. What's it going to hurt? And you, Debra, keep your mouth shut and don't antagonize Ashley anymore."

Debra knelt down beside David, breathing hard and shaking. She was so furious she could hardly contain herself. "Calm down, Debra; you'll get your chance to get even when this is all over, so just be patient," David whispered.

"I would like to wring her neck!" Debra said with her teeth clenched and her voice quivering. Ashley jerked away from Ben and looked at him with detest.

"Go tie her hands, Ben—unless you think it might make her uncomfortable," Ashley sarcastically replied. Ben walked across the room and left Ashley standing there. He took a piece of rope lying on a small table and walked toward Debra.

All of a sudden, one of the windows by the front door exploded with a loud crash and a large piece of firewood sailed through the window into the cabin. Glass showered the room. Bright lights and gunfire came through the broken window at the same time. At that point the cabin door swung open and gunfire came through the open doorway. Ashley jumped to one side of the room.

Ben leaped to the floor behind the couch and yelled, "Get down, Ashley!" But she was already on the floor, firing her gun.

"Ben, I'm hit! Help me!" Ashley screamed.

Ben sprang up from behind the couch, shooting wildly at the open door and the window. He jumped over the couch toward Ashley screaming, "Ashley! Ashley!" as he landed on the floor in front of the couch.

When the shooting started, Debra grabbed David by the arm, jerked him out of the chair, and they dove onto the floor of the hallway that led to the back door.

"Keep your head down, Debra!" David yelled. They struggled to their feet as bullets exploded all around them, blowing splinters of wood from the corners of the hallway. David slammed into the screen door, shoving it open at the back of the cabin, knocking a man holding a handgun down onto the ground. When the man fell, he hit his head and was dazed for a brief moment. When David saw the gun, he ran over to the man as he began to get up and kicked the gun out of his hand. The gun sailed a few feet and fell into the grass of the dimly lit backyard.

"Run, Debra!" David shouted. Debra ran toward the woods, with David close behind her.

As they raced across the backyard, they could still hear gunfire from inside the cabin. The man David had knocked down rolled over and began looking for his gun, crawling on his hands and knees in the grass.

When they reached the woods, they hid behind a large pine tree. Breathing hard, David asked, "Are you okay, Debra?"

"Yeah, I think so; just scared!"

"See if you can untie my hands." Debra was shaking so badly she could hardly get the ropes loose.

"Why did you kick the gun away from that man, David?"

"They sent a man to the back door. I wasn't sure if he was here to help us or hurt us. I believe that was a professional hit."

"Who do you think is doing all the shooting, David?"

"I don't know. It can't be your father's men. I don't believe they would have just started shooting. And why would they send a man to the back door unless he was there to block our retreat?"

"It was almost like they were trying to shoot us, too," Debra said.

"I know; it seemed that way."

"If it's my father's men, why would they be trying to shoot us? That just doesn't make sense."

"They don't know me, or why I'm here, so maybe that's why they were shooting in our direction. We'll know in a few minutes," David said. He suspected something wasn't right, but he didn't want to alarm Debra.

"David, I'm afraid," Debra said, beginning to cry.

"It'll be okay, Debra." He put his arms around her. "Let's sit down here and wait and see what happens next. Maybe this is finally over," he said, desperately trying to reassure her.

The mixture of excitement and anxiety was almost overwhelming as they waited with great anticipation to see who would come out of the cabin.

CHAPTER 6

When the gunfire in the cabin stopped, the back door of the cabin flew open. Debra and David were hoping to see Senator Braco, or at least his men identifying themselves. But two men came out the back door and joined the other man. The man David knocked to the ground had found his gun and stood there as the other two began reloading their guns. The man standing in the middle became very agitated and began yelling at the man David had knocked down.

"I'm sorry, Carmine. It happened so fast I didn't have time to react," the man said.

"Don't use my name, you moron; they can hear us," Carmine said. He grabbed the man by his collar. David and Debra didn't know what to make of their conversation as they watched the man try to explain why they were able to get past him.

It was a moonlit night, and they could barely make out the faces of the men. After putting a new magazine in his gun, the man standing in the middle lit a cigarette. When Debra saw the man's face by the flash of his lighter, she recognized him as the thin-faced man from the plane, and the man beside him was the man who had bumped into her.

"David, the man who just lit the cigarette, the one the other man called Carmine, looks a lot like a man I saw on the plane on my flight up here, and the man standing beside him was on the plane too."

"Are you sure, Debra?"

"Yes! I believe it's them—they must have been following me."

Carmine said, "I know you two can hear me. We're early. It's only a little after nine o'clock, but I would like to get this over with long before midnight. So, Debra, if you and David give up now, you can save everybody a lot of trouble." David and Debra looked at each other with a puzzled look.

"How does he know who I am?" David said, staring at Debra.

"I know you're disappointed, Debra—you were expecting Daddy. Well, Daddy's not coming." He began to laugh. "The senator sent us to take care of this little problem for him. So you and David just come on out. I promise I'll make it quick and you won't have to suffer."

Debra could scarcely believe her ears. She grabbed David's shoulder, trembling and scared. With her voice cracking and trying to choke back tears, she whispered, "Oh my God. David, he's saying that my father wants me dead! They *were* shooting at us."

"That's why they sent a man to the back door, Debra—they were trying to kill all of us."

"When I told Ashley yesterday that my father could possibly want me to disappear, I didn't really believe it myself. Do you think Jack Braco is that kind of person, David?"

"I've never met your father. I don't know much about him. I just don't know if they're telling the truth."

"The senator is not going to pay any more blackmail or ransom money to keep this scandal quiet," the man said. "We are here to end it once and for all. Those two amateurs in there won't give him any more trouble. I can't believe they were only asking four million dollars for the ransom. I'm getting almost that much to do this job." The man put his cigarette in his mouth, pulled the slide back on his semiautomatic pistol, and chambered a round in the barrel. "This is one skeleton from his closet the senator wants buried. He's not willing to let the public find out about a bastard child from his past," he said, his cigarette jiggling from his lips as he spoke.

Debra sat motionless as she listened to the man speak of the hatred that her father had for her. She was horrified at what she was hearing. David noticed how nonchalant they were as they talked about killing Debra. He didn't know whether Debra would be able to grasp what they were capable of doing in order to collect their money. He knew their situation had suddenly become even more dangerous than before. These men were not the amatures they had been dealing with. They are professional, ruthless killers that would stop at nothing to see their mission accomplished.

"They killed Ashley and Ben. What are we going to do, David?" Debra trembled with fear as she held on to him.

"We don't have any weapons to defend ourselves. Ashley took the only gun I had with me. The only thing we can do is run. The only chance we have is to make it to a phone so I can call the FBI."

"It must be miles to the nearest phone, David."

"Hopefully we'll be able to find some campers on our way to town. Maybe they'll give us a ride."

David took Debra's hand, and they sneaked down through the woods. The moon was shining brightly, and they could see just well enough to walk in the shadows of the trees.

When they were far enough away, without making noise, they began to run through the woods as quietly as possible. They circled around so they could follow the road as best they could. They determined they were not being followed and stopped running. When they stopped, Debra was struggling to breathe.

"I can't ... I ... can't ... go on. I have to rest," Debra said. She bent over and put her hands on her knees. David stopped running and slowly walked back and stood beside her. He put his hands on his hips, half bent over, and began to pace back and forth.

"We can rest here a few minutes," David said, pausing to breathe. "I don't believe they're following us."

Carmine called to them again from the backyard. When there was still no response, he walked farther out into the yard, turned, and faced the other two men and said, "There's no point in trying to chase them through the woods tonight. Go in the cabin and get the guns that those two were using, in case they come back here after we leave. We'll go back down to that little town. I'm sure that's where they're going."

When the three men had arrived at the cabin earlier, they had parked back in the woods, far enough to keep from being heard. After getting the guns from Ben and Ashley, they walked back to where they had parked their SUV and drove toward town.

While they were resting, Debra and David heard the SUV start up and saw their lights as they drove down the road just below the cabin. "They'll be waiting for us back in town, Debra. We'll stay here tonight, and we'll leave first thing in the morning, as soon as it gets light."

They sat down between the aboveground roots of a big tree and leaned back against the tree for a while, holding on to each other.

After all that had happened, Debra's thoughts were spinning around in her head. She wondered how they would ever get out of this mess alive. She kept thinking, *This must be a dream. When will I wake up?* But, she didn't have to pinch herself to know she wasn't dreaming. As she tried to relax, she began to listen to the sounds of nature's nocturnal creatures around them, from the hoot of an owl to the scurry of a fox through the leaves. She thought about how the world was still going on even though this terrible thing had taken place. *Time didn't stop, the moon is still shining, and the sun will come up in the morning,* she thought. *Thinking outside reality, you imagine everyone should know about what just happened, but within reality, you quickly realize that it's not possible. It's only you, faced with the crazy twists and turns that an evil world has thrown your way, and you're forced to deal with it.* She lay pondering all these new and strange thoughts as she tried to keep in perspective this horrible nightmare.

David didn't say anything to Debra about how difficult it was going to be to try to get out of this. He knew they had to get to a phone and call for help. He would have to draw on all of his past experiences and his extensive training in law enforcement if they were to survive.

With thoughts of this bizarre situation dancing around in their heads, some time passed before either one of them spoke. Finally, with her mind back to reality and with a trembling voice, Debra said, "David, I'm so scared. If they catch up with us, there won't be any negotiation. They're going to kill us!"

"We'll figure something out in the morning. It'll be okay," David replied in a reassuring tone, trying not to show any sign of anxiety or doubt.

"Maybe we could go back to the cabin to see if they left Ashley's and Ben's guns. Then maybe we would have some way to defend ourselves."

"I thought about that, but I'm sure they took the guns from Ashley and Ben. Besides, one of them might have stayed behind to see if we *do* come back."

"Do you think Jack Braco is really paying those men that much money to kill me?" Debra said, her voice breaking as she choked back tears.

"I don't know, Debra. Maybe part of their strategy is psychological. If they can get in your head, then they can break down your will and determination and you won't fight back as hard. I wouldn't believe anything they said," David said, pulling her closer to him. "I think they're doing it for fun, as well as the money. I've dealt with people like that before. They're just mean and evil to the core. They enjoy hurting people. Don't worry, Debra. We'll figure a way out of this. I'm not going to let them hurt you. Now try to get some sleep. We have a long walk ahead of us tomorrow. He held her close to him and tried to be upbeat and reassuring, but he knew just how grave their situation really was.

The few times Debra was able to fall asleep, she had nightmares and would wake up screaming. David spent the night trying to console her.

After a night of very little sleep, they were both awake when it was light enough to see. They decided to start the long trek to the small town after making the best of a quick nature break. They stayed off the road as they made their way toward town.

About three hours into their trip, they came upon a deserted campsite. They looked for food, but all they found were three candy bars in one of the tents. After eating the candy, they walked on toward Owls Head. Suddenly they saw a man walking close to the top of a ridge.

"Hey, mister, we need your help!" David yelled. The man looked at them and started to run.

"Please help us!" Debra shouted. The man stopped, turned, and looked at them. He stood there for an instant and then walked toward them. As he approached them, they could see that his hair and beard were ragged and long. After introducing themselves, David explained the predicament they were in. The man told them his name was Steve Tanner, he was homeless, and that he lived in these woods in a cave. He told them to follow him and he would give them some food.

They followed him to the bottom of a hill, where they saw a wall of rock that formed a cliff, with one rock protruding out slightly near the bottom, creating an overhang. It wasn't really a cave, but a small, open space with very little depth. He invited them to rest and asked them to spend the night.

After David and Debra sat down, David asked, "How long have you lived in these woods, Steve?"

"For the past four years. I'm a veteran. I was in Vietnam. When I was released from the service, I couldn't go home. I just wandered around for years, until I came to Owls Head. I like these mountains. I just don't like to be around people," Steve said. He handed each of them a piece of meat.

"What is this?" Debra asked.

"Fried squirrel," the man replied. Debra looked at him with a blank stare. David laughed at the expression on her face.

"It's okay. I just cooked it this morning. I use a trap to catch them. They're good to eat." David took the piece of meat and began to eat. Debra looked at David, and then she too ate the fried squirrel. She was surprised at how good it tasted. *Maybe it's because I'm so hungry,* she thought.

As they sat there, David kept looking at Debra and smiling as he watched her eat the squirrel. She noticed him watching her eat. She turned and shoved her face toward him, a piece of squirrel hanging out of her mouth. She had her eyes squinted, her nose drawn up, and a big grin on her face. He started laughing. She took her hand and swung at him, but he dodged it and then grabbed her and pulled her close to him as they both continued to laugh.

They sat eating and enjoying nature as their predicament remained in the back of their minds. When they were finished eating, David looked at Steve and said, "It must get awfully cold in the winter. How do you survive?"

"I don't stay here in the winter. Harry Graddison, who owns the general store in town, lets me stay in a small shed behind his store. He even puts an electric heater in there to keep me warm. He's a really nice man." He hesitated for a moment. "The park rangers have told me that I'm not supposed to be here, but they've never tried to force me to leave. There are still some nice people left in this world," Steve said.

Debra's eyes filled with tears as she listened to Steve talk about his situation. *It doesn't matter what kind of problems you have, there's always someone else who has problems equal or worse,* she thought.

Steve picked up a cloth bag and pulled a nice leather belt out of it.

"I make these belts, and Harry sells them in his store. I trade them for food and clothes. I can make about five or six of these in a month. They're all handmade," Steve said as he handed the belt to David. "I catch a ride into town with the park rangers and deliver the belts to Harry." David looked at the small strands of leather woven together. The workmanship was excellent. David complimented Steve as he handed the belt to Debra.

"How often do you see the park rangers?" David asked.

"About once every two weeks," Steve replied.

"Maybe we'll get lucky and see one today," commented Debra.

They were on the northwestern edge of the park, and David knew there was a slim chance of seeing a park ranger in a park with millions of acres. He also knew they needed to leave because Steve wasn't going to be able to help them. Each time David talked about leaving, Steve kept insisting that they stay.

"I suppose it would keep the people that are chasing us guessing if we delay our presence in town," David said.

They agreed to spend the night and slept on an extra blanket that Steve gave them.

The next morning, they dined on eggs, squirrel, and coffee. Afterward they thanked Steve and started their trek toward Owls Head. They walked almost all day, taking periodic breaks. It was late afternoon as they were nearing the little town. Just before they reached the perimeter of town, David said, "We're traveling south, so we will be coming into town on the north end. Isn't that where Harry's store is?"

"Yes, it is."

"If we can get to his store without being seen, then I can use the phone and get some help."

They continued to walk the short distance to the end of the trees that bordered Owls Head. As they neared the edge of town, they could see Harry's store about three hundred feet from the woods. There was a short parking lot and then the street, with Harry's store on the other side. The road that came through town made a left turn at the north end of Harry's store.

They looked around and didn't see anyone, so they ran across the parking lot to the street. They quickly crossed the street toward the store. As they neared the front of the store, they saw a man climb out of an SUV, just down the street on the opposite side. The man started walking in their direction and they recognized him as one of the shooters from the cabin. He began to walk fast as he crossed the street toward them. He had one hand under his coat. They threw the door open and ran into the store, where Harry was stocking shelves. He looked up as the door flew open.

When he saw Debra and David, he said, "What are you—?"

Debra interrupted him before he could finish. "Harry, the man coming in the store behind us is trying to kill us!" she yelled as she ran through the store. "We need to borrow your car!"

"What?" Harry stood there for a second with a puzzled look on his face.

David jumped to the left of the door and stood there. At that moment, the man chasing them threw the door open and rushed in with his gun drawn. David jumped from behind the door and grabbed his gun hand. When David jumped on the man, his momentum shoved him forward. As they struggled for the gun, David punched him in the face, and they fell to the floor. The gun fell out of his hand and slid across the floor. He jerked loose from David, jumped up, and ran toward the gun. Harry ran behind the counter, and David scrambled to his feet and ran toward the back of the store.

Debra was hiding behind a shelf when David grabbed her hand and ran toward the back door leading to the garage.

As they ran, David yelled, "Call the FBI and tell them David—!" A loud bang interrupted David, and a bullet zinged past his head, landing in the middle of garden tools hanging on the wall near the back of the store. The impact of the bullet knocked several of the tools to the floor with a loud crash. Debra screamed as she and David dove behind a support post for the roof. Before the man could get off a second shot, he was interrupted.

"Hold it right there, mister!" Harry yelled. He pulled a double-barreled shotgun from beneath the counter. The man turned toward Harry, and his eyes grew wide as he looked down the barrel of the shotgun. He raised his gun slightly. Harry pulled the trigger on one of the barrels of his shotgun. Just before he fired, the man jumped behind a shelf. Canned merchandise exploded all around him from the shotgun blast.

While Harry and the man exchanged gunfire, David and Debra jumped up and ran out the back door. David grabbed the two sets of car keys hanging from the hooks by the door as he ran.

The man jumped up and fired a couple of shots at Harry as he ran toward the front door. One of the bullets hit a large glass jar of candy on the counter. The jar exploded, and the colored balls of hard candy scattered all over the floor. Harry stood up from behind the counter, took a step forward, and aimed at the man as he retreated. Just as he fired his shotgun, he slipped on the balls of hard candy. His aim was off, and he missed the man by a wide margin. The blast blew several cans of paint from a shelf. A shower of paint spread across the front of the store as the paint cans exploded. The man jerked the door open and ran out of the store.

In the meantime, David chose an old Chevrolet suburban from the two vehicles in the garage. He tried one set of keys and it wouldn't fit, so he tried the other set. The ignition fired, and the engine roared in the old truck. After opening the garage door, Debra ran around the front of the truck and jumped into the passenger seat.

The SUV came to a quick stop in front of Harry's store just as the man Harry had been shooting at ran out the front door. He jumped in the SUV with Carmine and the other man from the cabin. As he climbed in, David and Debra's stolen suburban came around the building. The big truck slid sideways, burning the tires as they turned onto the street and headed south. The men in the SUV took off quickly behind them. Harry came running out the front door, reloading his shotgun, but the SUV had driven away. Harry ran back inside to call the sheriff.

As David and Debra reached the outskirts of town, they were slightly ahead of the SUV, but the SUV caught up as they made a quick turn onto State Route 30 and drove south. The SUV rammed the back of the suburban several times but couldn't move it much. The man on the passenger side leaned out the window and began shooting at them. The back window to the Suburban exploded and Debra screamed as glass flew all around.

David yelled, "Get down!" He swerved from side to side, but Carmine was still able to maneuver the SUV up beside the suburban as David steered toward them, trying to force them off the road. They continued to pepper the sides and the back of the truck with bullets. David continued to steer the truck from side to side. He used his right hand to push Debra down on the floor. The SUV pulled alongside the suburban again and slammed into the left rear side. Trying to avoid them, David stepped on the gas pedal and was able to pull ahead of the SUV.

He saw a road to the left and quickly turned off of State Route 30 onto the side road. The road was gravel, and the suburban slid from side to side when David made the quick turn. Just as David regained control, the SUV turned behind them and came up beside the suburban again. David jerked the wheel to the left and slammed into the side of the SUV. The big truck forced the smaller SUV off the road, through a fence, and out into a field. David sped off as the men jumped out and fired at the suburban.

Carmine began pounding his fist on the front fender of the SUV after the suburban was out of sight. "Come on; lets get this thing out of here before the cops get here!" he shouted.

After seeing the SUV go off the road, David looked down at Debra and said, "You can come up now, Debra. They ran off the road." David reached over and put his hand on her shoulder. "Are you okay?" Her whole body quaked with fear. She crawled up into the seat. With trembling hands, she wiped the tears from her eyes.

"Yes, I'm okay." She looked at him. "David, they're going to kill us." She began to cry. She leaned her head back on the seat and covered her face with her hands. David reached over and took hold of her arm.

"It'll be okay, Debra. I won't let them hurt you," he said, trying to reassure her. "We've got to find a telephone so I can call the FBI office."

Debra straightened up in the seat and wiped her eyes. "Maybe Harry called them," she said.

"I hope so, but I don't know if he heard me. If he called the local police, they're not going to know anything about the case," David said.

They drove another twenty miles and then all of a sudden, the truck began to miss and sputter, the engine shut off, and the truck rolled to a stop. David looked at the gas gauge and saw that it was on empty.

"We're out of gas. It was full when we left. I guess one of the bullets must have punctured the gas tank." They climbed out, and David walked behind the truck. "We have to hide this truck so they can't find it." They were able to push the truck off the road, down a small embankment, and into some heavy brush.

It was nearly dark when they began walking. They stayed off the road and walked through the woods and the brush as much as possible.

"Where are we, David?"

"The Adirondack Mountain Park. Six million acres," David said.

"How are we going to get out of here?"

"I guess we'll have to walk out."

"Not tonight; I'm so tired I don't think I can go another step," she said.

"We can camp here tonight if we find a level spot. I'll make a bed out of leaves," David said.

After walking a short distance, they found a place that seemed to be level and a nice spot for a bed of leaves. At that moment they heard the roar of a small engine.

"That sounds like a motorcycle," David commented. "Maybe we can flag them down and they can help us."

The sound was coming from the gravel road, so they ran in that direction. They followed the sound for a few minutes as the roar of the engine became less and less audible. Then suddenly they could not hear the motor any longer. They kept walking in the direction where they had last heard the sound. David stopped. "Wait," he said. They stood still for a few seconds, straining to hear the engine, but instead they heard the faint sound of music in the distance. They looked at each other, and then David said, "It's probably campers."

"Maybe they can help us, and maybe we could get some food. I'm starving," Debra said. "The fried squirrel from this morning is long gone."

While walking down the road in the darkness, they followed the sound of the music. David spotted a narrow, barely visible dirt road that turned off the gravel road.

"The music is coming from this direction. I think this road leads to a campsite. Let's follow it," David said. They kept walking toward the sound. After several minutes of walking, the music grew louder and they saw the glow from the campfire. As they walked around a small turn in the road, three young men came into view. They were sitting around a campfire, listening to a radio. As they came closer, Debra recognized one of them.

"It's Kevin, Harry's son," she said as she ran ahead of David. "Kevin, it's me, Debra!" she yelled, still a few yards away. Kevin saw her coming toward him and jumped to his feet. "You remember me? You drove me to John Sherman's cabin a couple of weeks ago," Debra said as she held out her hand.

"Hey! What are you doing way down here?" He shook Debra's hand.

"Listen, Kevin, there're some men chasing us, and they're trying to kill us. We need your help."

"What? What's going on?"

"It's a long story," Debra said. "We need to get to a telephone so David can call the FBI." Debra quickly explained their situation and assured them that the killers wouldn't be able to find them.

After David walked up and introduced himself, one of the young men spoke up and said, "Hey, dudes. I'm Darrell, and I've got a truck. It doesn't run very fast, but it does run."

"Do you guys mind if we camp here with you? We're just too tired to try to go anywhere tonight," David said.

"No, we don't mind at all," said Kevin.

After making introductions all around, Kevin said, "Robert and I rode here on our dirt bikes. We've been fishing in Meacham Lake most of the day. We just came back from there a few minutes ago." He turned and motioned toward Darrell. "In the morning, Darrell can drive you back to town in his truck."

"Hey, dude, I don't mind at all."

"We can't go back to Owls Head. They'll be looking for us there. We'll have to find another town nearby or someplace where we can use a phone. We'll figure that out in the morning. Right now we're just too tired and hungry to think about it."

"I hope you like hotdogs roasted over the fire. We have marshmallows too," Kevin said.

"With Hershey bars and graham crackers to make s'mores, I hope!" Debra said.

"Absolutely!" Kevin replied. "You can't go camping without making s'mores."

After they ate some hotdogs and roasted some marshmallows, Debra took the Hershey bars and made s'mores.

"I haven't done this since I was in the Brownies when I was a little girl," Debra said with a wide smile. The fun they had around the campfire took their mind off their situation for a little while.

Kevin loaned them a blanket to put down on the ground. After lying down for the night, even though she was exhausted, Debra wasn't able to sleep. Part of the problem was sleeping on the ground, but mostly it was because of everything that had happened in the three previous days. She thought about how they had gotten into this mess; about her best friend and how she had betrayed her; how she only pretended to be her friend, had used her just for money, was responsible for her mother's death, and now was dead. Something she had always wanted was a father, and now that she knew who he was, she found out he was trying to have her killed. The more she thought about all these things, the more upset she became. She began to tremble, and she could not hold back the tears.

David could sense her restlessness. When she began to shake and he heard her sobbing, he knew what she was thinking. He put his arms around her and pulled her close to him.

"Debra, I'm sorry about all that's happened to you in the last few days. I know your world has been turned upside down, but we'll get through this … I promise."

With her head on David's chest and holding on to him as tightly as she could, she said, "Ashley said everything always goes my way." She hesitated for a moment, choking back tears. "But it's not like that at all. There's nothing good about this!"

"I know, Debra, but I'm not going to let anything happen to you. We'll see this through to the end, whatever it takes." Debra looked up at David and smiled with her tearstained face.

She knew there was a reason they had met, and she knew she would not have made it through this without David's help. She had always been independent and able to handle any situation, but this was all new. For the first time, she would have to depend on someone else if she was going to survive this terrible ordeal. With renewed confidence, she began to relax. She felt better knowing she had someone like David with her, someone who loved her and wanted to take care of her. They both felt more determined than ever to get through this alive. The physical events of the day finally began to take their toll, and they drifted off to sleep.

CHAPTER 7

The next morning Debra and David told Kevin about the shootout at the cabin and his dad's store. They asked Kevin if he could send the police to the cabin to recover Ashley and Ben's bodies, and he said that he would.

"My dad was in the military during the Vietnam War. He served two tours and was one of the last men to ship out of Vietnam after the war ended. He's pretty tough. I wouldn't want to mess with him. If those guys made it out of there alive, they better feel real lucky."

"We had to borrow the old Chevy suburban in the garage. I grabbed two sets of keys as we ran out the back door. I threw the extra set on a workbench next to the door after we were able to get the suburban started. Tell your dad that I'm an agent from the FBI and that I'll see that he gets paid for his truck when this thing is over. It's all shot up and out of gas. We abandoned it and pushed it off the road a few miles from here. We had to leave the store in a hurry, so we didn't have time to explain anything to him. Tell him thanks and that we're sorry about the truck."

"Don't worry about that old truck. It had a lot of miles on it, but I'll tell him what you said."

"If he hasn't called the FBI yet, tell him to call and ask for Bill Rogers. Tell him that David Kimble is trying to reach him. I will be coming into New York City, and I have Debra Benson with me. Tell him some dangerous people are trying to kill us. Can you remember all that?"

"I think so. I'll tell him as soon as I get there," Kevin replied. "I guess we better pack now."

He and Robert packed up their camping equipment and put it in Darrell's truck.

They waved good-bye and rode off down the dirt road.

Darrell packed his camping gear in the truck. It was a small, lightweight truck that could seat three, but not very comfortably.

"Hey, dudes, this little truck is only a four cylinder. It won't go fast, but it's better than walking. Get in and tell me where you want to go."

"Where is the closest town from here, besides Owls Head?" David asked.

"From here, if you want a big town, dude, I would say Saranac Lake."

"That's where I flew into," Debra said.

"But that is southeast of here," Darrell commented. "Hey, dudes, we're near the ski resort, but they're closed for the season, and no one is there until this winter, except for one old security guard who is only there a couple days a week."

Trying not to laugh and trying to ignore some of Darrell's strange, offbeat comments, David said, "Let's go to Saranac Lake. Maybe we can get a flight out of there."

"Hey, dudes, there's a scenic train that runs from Saranac Lake to Utica. It's much slower than a normal train, so people can enjoy the beautiful scenery."

David and Debra looked at each other and then at Darrell. With a smile they both said at the same time, "Darrell, we're not on vacation!"

"Hey, dudes, it was just a thought." Like sardines in a can, they squeezed in the small truck with Darrell driving, Debra in the middle, and David next to the passenger door.

After a short distance, they came upon the area where they had pushed the old suburban into the bushes. They could see the top of it sticking out of the brush. They drove the twenty miles or so down the gravel road that led back to State Route 30.

Darrell approached the intersection of the gravel road and State Route 30 and came to a stop. He signaled and made the turn south toward Saranac Lake. After driving south for a few miles, they met Carmine and the other two men in the banged-up SUV driving north on 30. Carmine was on the passenger side. He looked over and saw Debra and David in the little truck and motioned with his hand. The driver of the SUV suddenly slammed on the brake and tried to bring the vehicle to a quick stop. David and Debra stared in disbelief at the untimely encounter. The driver attempted to turn the SUV around in the road.

David yelled, "The men in that truck are the ones that are chasing us! Go fast, Darrell, Go, go, go—faster!"

The truck quickly picked up speed. Darrell held the pedal down, driving as fast as the little truck would run. He hoped to get a quick jump on the villains.

With the lack of power of the little truck, David knew the SUV would catch up to them shortly. They hadn't gone far when they saw another road on the right.

"Turn here, Darrell," David said. Darrell quickly made a right turn.

"Hey, dudes, this road goes by the ski resort I was telling you about earlier," Darrell replied.

"It doesn't matter; we have to hide from them," David said.

"But, dudes, like I was telling you, there's no one there this time of year."

"As long as we can give them the slip, it won't matter, Darrell," David said.

After turning the SUV around, Carmine and his henchmen tried desperately to catch the little truck, but Darrell had turned onto the side road before the SUV was able to catch up to them.

As Darrell drove along, they noticed that the road began to get steeper and steeper. As they neared the top of the long hill, they came upon another road on the left. They saw a large sign with the name of the ski resort.

"That road leads to the ski resort," Darrell said.

"We need to stay on this road to see where it comes out," David said.

After turning down the other side of the mountain, they drove several miles. Just ahead, they saw a big yellow sign: "Caution! Reduce Speed Ahead." Darrell looked back and could see the SUV behind them.

Suddenly, Carmine saw the little truck. The SUV came up quickly behind the small and less powerful truck.

"Hey, dudes, they're right on my tail! What do we do?"

"Just do as I tell you. When they get beside us, I want you to slam on your brake as hard as you can. There's a deep curve ahead, and with this steep grade they won't be able to stop very easily," David said.

The SUV came barreling up beside them.

"Now, Darrell!" David shouted. Darrell slammed both feet onto the brake pedal. The little truck came to a quick stop, and the SUV went sailing past the little truck and into the deep curve.

"Turn around, Darrell! Hurry; hurry!" David shouted. Darrell quickly turned the truck and headed back the way they came.

The SUV came into the curve, and the driver slid the truck around and the front end went into the ditch.

Carmine jumped out and yelled, "You idiot! Let me drive." He jumped into the driver's seat, switched the truck into four-wheel drive, and backed out of the ditch. He turned the truck around, and they took off quickly, trying to catch the little truck again.

Darrell drove back to the top of the hill and made a right turn onto the ski resort access road. They drove around behind two narrow buildings that were connected in the middle by a small breezeway. Darrell parked the truck behind one of the buildings. "I'm going to see if any of the phones are working," David said, opening the passenger door.

"Hey, dude, I told you they're closed for the season except for that old security guard who is very seldom around," Darrell said. David ignored Darrell, stepped out of the truck and hurried to the closest door. It was locked, but David used his elbow to break the window. He reached through and unlocked the door. He went inside and looked around and finally found a phone. He picked it up and checked for a dial tone. There was none.

"You were right, Darrell. There's no one here and the phones don't work, but I had to try." David said after returning to the truck.

They sat there in the truck for about ten minutes, plotting their strategy, while Carmine and the two other men looked for them. Suddenly they heard someone yelling. David looked to the right and saw the security guard exiting a small building near the back of the property. The guard came running toward them. At that moment, the SUV came around the end of building where they were hiding.

"Go, Darrell! Go the other way!" Darrell backed up and took off as the SUV came up behind them.

"Call the police!" David shouted at the security guard as they drove past him. The security guard ran after the two vehicles, yelling for them to stop.

Darrell made a quick left turn and drove into the breezeway. The space connecting the buildings was very narrow, and the small truck just squeezed into the opening, pushing a small patio table and chairs along in front of it as they drove through. The passage was so narrow that both sides of the truck were scraping the walls, and the mirrors were torn off each side. The table and chairs caught onto the concrete, and the truck rolled over them. One of the chairs hung underneath the truck and was dragged for an instant before it came loose.

Carmine slid up to the narrow passageway. He knew the SUV would not fit between the buildings, so he put it into reverse and began cursing. He turned around and drove back toward the end of the building.

The forte of an evil minded man is to enjoy inflicting pain. Such was the case with Carmine. As he drove up to the security guard, he began to smile. He steered his vehicle directly at him. The security guard jumped sideways, fell to the ground, and rolled over, narrowly escaping the wheels of the SUV.

By the time he scrambled to his feet, Carmine had turned the corner at the end of the building and he could not get the license plate number. Carmine was still smiling as he drove around the building.

Darrell's quick thinking had allowed them to stay ahead of the killers, even though his vehicle was much slower. After driving through the narrow space between the buildings, Darrell drove back to the road in front of the ski resort. He turned right and headed back toward Route 30.

"Great job, Darrell!" David shouted.

"My mirrors are gone," Darrell said.

"We'll buy you new ones, Darrell," Debra said, putting her hand on his shoulder.

They drove as fast as the truck would run, trying to make it back to State Route 30. Darrell turned right onto 30 and headed south toward Saranac Lake. After they had driven a few miles, the SUV caught up to them again.

"Hey, dudes, here they come again!" Darrell shouted.

Carmine came up to the little truck quickly. The SUV bumped the truck from behind and pushed it around to the right. Darrell held the gas pedal down, straightened the truck, and pulled away from the SUV.

"Darrell, you have to go faster."

"Hey, dude, I've got the pedal to the floor now. This thing won't go any faster!" The SUV bumped the little truck in the back, and Darrell almost lost control. The truck swayed back and forth on the road.

"Hold it steady, Darrell!" David yelled.

"Hey, dude, I'm doing my best. I'm not a racecar driver!"

Carmine stomped the gas pedal to the floor and bumped the little truck again. It turned almost completely sideways.

"Darrell, you're losing it!"

"Hey, dude, I can't help it. They're pushing me all over the road!"

Carmine steered the SUV up to the left corner of the truck bed. He didn't give them time to slam on the brake this time.

"Watch this!" Carmine shouted as an evil grin crept across his face. He swerved into the side of the truck bed. The little truck turned sideways and began sliding. Darrell struggled to regain control of the truck, but he couldn't hold it. Debra screamed as the truck turned on its side and rolled over twice and then slid several feet on its right side before coming to a stop.

The SUV spun around sideways, and the front end dropped off the side of the road into a ditch on a small hill. Before Carmine and his thugs could get out, the SUV slid down into the ditch. The front bumper hit the bank at the bottom.

When the little truck stopped, it was lying on its passenger side. The tailgate of the truck was near the right side of the road as it slid to a stop. The windshield was broken out, and the top was crushed down part of the way from the rollover. The two vehicles were about two hundred feet apart when they each stopped moving.

Debra was forced to put her hands down on the glass-covered road as she crawled out through the broken windshield, crying. She was bleeding from a cut on her forehead. David had a cut on his right hand and one above his right eye. His face was covered with blood. Darrell was hanging by his seatbelt behind the steering wheel. Smoke began to billow from underneath the hood.

Debra staggered to her feet and looked around the truck at the SUV. She screamed at David, "Come on—get out! They're coming!"

There was no one else around, and she knew that if the killers were able to reach them before they could get away, they would shoot all three of them.

Carmine and the other two men began to climb out of the SUV and make their way up the bank from the ditch to the road. David struggled to help Darrell out of his seatbelt. The smoke under the hood had now turned into flames. The flames were coming out through the grill and around all the seams of the hood and front fenders.

"Come on!" Debra screamed.

Debra was consumed with fear, but she was able to keep her head. She knew what she had to do. Suddenly she was running on pure adrenalin and had the strength and physical ability of someone twice her size. She kicked out what was left of the broken windshield and grabbed David by the hand. With all her strength, she pulled him through the opening of the broken windshield. Darrell came out behind him, and they crawled away from the burning truck.

Carmine and his men were running toward the truck by now. Debra grabbed David by the hand, and they jumped to their feet. "Come on, Darrell," shouted Debra.

"I'm not leaving my truck," Darrell said. He sat down in the road.

David wiped the blood from his face as they turned and ran down the bank next to the road as fast as they could. They ran into the bushes and disappeared.

The three men came around the front of Darrell's truck with their guns drawn. Darrell was sitting in the road about fifty feet from the truck, holding his bleeding head and looking at his truck. The men ran up to Darrell and Carmine stuck the gun in his face.

Darrell looked up at them and said, "Hey, dudes, look what you did to my truck!"

"Where did they go?" Carmine shouted. Darrell just sat there holding his head and looking at them blankly.

Debra and David kept running as fast as they could through the brush and trees. All of a sudden there was a loud boom. They stopped, looked back, and saw a large plume of black smoke and fire billowing above the trees.

"Poor, Darrell. There goes his truck," Debra said, pausing briefly to breathe.

"We can't do anything about that now," David said and grabbed Debra's hand and started running again.

The blast from the truck sent all three men diving to the black-top. Pieces of burning debris landed close by them. They held up their hands to shield their faces from the heat while they climbed back to their feet.

Carmine looked at Darrell and said, "Thanks for your help, punk!"

The three men turned and ran down the bank, into the brush in the direction they thought David and Debra had gone. Darrell sat holding his head and watching his truck burn, with the same blank stare.

David and Debra ran for several minutes along a small creek that was now dry but at some point had been a small, flowing stream. Big rocks were sticking up above the banks. They could hear the men running through the brush behind them. Debra stopped abruptly, half bent over and breathing hard.

"We're not…going to be able to…outrun them…are we, David?"

"No, we're not," David said, wiping blood from the cut on his head with his sleeve. He paced back and forth, trying to catch his breath. "We may not be able to outrun them, but let's see if we can't outfox them," he said, grinning. "Let's see if we can hide in among some of these big rocks." He pointed in the direction of the dry creek bed.

They climbed down into the ditch and began looking for an opening or some type of large crevice to hide in. While searching frantically for a place to hide, they heard one of the men tell the others to split up and go in different directions to search for them.

David and Debra came around a large rock that protruded out into the dry creek bed. Several large rocks were above it, creating an overhang. The bank on the opposite side was very steep. They stepped back into the large opening just as they heard one of the men walking down the ditch.

"David, I can hear someone coming," Debra whispered fearfully.

"We have to defend ourselves by whatever means," David whispered. He ran over and picked up a large tree limb lying on the ground. It was about twice the size of a baseball bat. David stood at the edge of the protruding rock, drew back the big stick, and waited to see if the man came their way.

While standing there listening to the brush and the leaves crunch underfoot as the man came closer and closer, Debra began to tremble with fear. Her heart was pounding so hard it felt as though it would jump out of her chest. The sound of each crunch of the dry leaves as the killer came closer and closer seemed to define what was left of her short life. As she stood contemplating their deaths, it felt as though time had suddenly stood still. *Is this how it ends?* she thought. She put her hand on David's shoulder, every emotion and nerve of her body at its peak.

David turned and whispered, "It's going to be okay." He smiled and motioned for her to step back into the shadows of the rock. His smile and expression of confidence gave her a boost of hope, almost like a shot of adrenaline.

It seemed like forever before the man stepped around the rock. Just as he came into view, David swung with the big tree limb as if he were going for a home run at Yankee Stadium. The blow struck the man across his midsection. The man doubled over, gasping for air, and dropped his gun into the leaves and brush.

Just as he swung the big stick and hit the man, David yelled, "Run, Debra!"

Debra started running down the ravine, David close behind her. After catching his breath, the man began fumbling around for his gun.

"Carmine, Carmine! They're over here!" the man yelled, pausing momentarily as he struggled to breathe. "They're running down this ditch!"

Nearing the end of a row of several trees that lined the banks of the ravine, David and Debra could hear what sounded like a train. The ravine was getting wider and deeper as they came to the end of the tree line.

David grabbed Debra's hand, and they stopped momentarily and listened.

"Come on, Debra!" David yelled. He practically pulled her off the ground when he started running again. "Maybe we can catch that train!" They ran even faster toward the sound. A small railroad bridge crossed the ravine just ahead of them. As the bridge came into view, a train was just beginning to cross the bridge. "I think that's the scenic train Darrell was talking about," shouted David. David was in the lead, and Debra could barely stay up with him as he pulled her along by the hand.

They came out in a clearing around the bridge and ran up the left side of the ravine. The train was headed south, and most of the cars had already gone by as they came up the side of the bank. It was traveling slightly faster than they were running. They ran with all the energy they had left to catch up to the train. As they ran along beside the tracks, David noticed that some of the train cars had a top on them but the sides of the cars were open. He could see people sitting in seats. He knew immediately that this was the scenic train Darrell was talking about. He reached out and grabbed on to the handrail of the steps of one of the open cars as it went by. He jumped onto the step of the train car. It was next to the last car on the train. As soon as he was on the step of the car, he immediately turned, leaned over with his arm outstretched, and yelled to Debra, "Come on, Debra! Grab my hand!"

She stretched her arm out as far as she could, and David grabbed her by the hand. With all the strength he could muster, he pulled her 120-pound frame up onto the step of the train car.

Just then the three men came running out in the clearing and up the side of the bank by the bridge that crossed the ravine and saw Debra jumping onto the train as it disappeared out of sight.

"They're getting away!" one of the men yelled.

"We'll see if we can't do something about that," Carmine said.

Carmine and the two other men turned and started running back toward their vehicle. "We have to get out of here before the cops show up," Carmine said as they ran back to the SUV.

The three men ran back to where Darrell was sitting, watching his truck burn. Two cars had stopped near the accident, but the people were still in their vehicles because of the burning truck. Carmine and his men put their guns away, and Carmine ran over to Darrell. He motioned toward his gun under his coat.

"Where is that train going?" Darrell didn't say anything. He just sat there still holding his head. "Are you some kind of a retard?" Carmine shouted as he grabbed hold of Darrell's shoulder.

"Hey, dude, it stops in Utica," Darrell said, looking at the three men fearlessly.

"You better keep your mouth shut, kid, or I'll be back and I'll shut it for you! Now you tell these people and the police that we were not involved in this accident. We stopped to help. Do you understand?" Darrell just looked at them with the same blank stare. The three men ran and jumped in their SUV and drove off, leaving Darrell sitting there.

David and Debra looked back and saw Carmine and the other two men come out of the woods. They watched the three men stand and stare at the train as it moved out of sight.

With a sigh of relief, they caught their breath for a few seconds. They turned around, and all the people on the train car were looking backward, staring at them. They were holding on to each other, out of breath from running. Their clothes were torn; their faces were dirty, sweaty, and bleeding. A man came over, helped them to a seat, and gave them a handkerchief and a bottle of water. They thanked the man, sat down, and took turns drinking the water. Debra took the handkerchief and dampened it with the water. They took turns using the handkerchief to clean each other's face. A woman sitting nearby asked them if they were okay and gave them some bandages to put on their cuts. Debra tried to give the woman an explanation, but the stunned expressions on the faces from all the people who heard her story forced her to keep it short. David wrapped the handkerchief around the cut on his hand. They sat and relaxed for a while before either one of them spoke to each other.

Finally Debra said, "Poor Darrell. I feel really bad about his truck."

"I do too. Maybe we can make it up to him when this is all over."

"Is this ever going to be over, David?"

"Sure it is." He looked at Debra and gave her a smile from his bandaged, cut, and bloodstained face. "I mean, look, we've been able to stay away from those men up to now, haven't we? Besides, Darrell said we should catch the scenic train." He looked around with a slight chuckle. "Look's like we caught the scenic train."

"Yeah," Debra said. She looked at David and began to smile. "I guess that means we are on vacation, right, David?" They looked at each other and burst out laughing.

David asked some of the passengers where the train was going. They told him that it was going to Utica.

"Debra, we need to find a telephone as soon as we get to the train station. I'll call Bill Rogers and get some help," David said. "If I can't get him, I'll call the FBI office in New York City."

"David, shouldn't the FBI be looking for you? I mean, they haven't heard from you since that call you made when Ben shot the satellite phone out of your hand."

"Yes, but I didn't have time to tell Bill anything about our situation. Because I was undercover, they will wait for me to contact them. If they know about what happened at Harry's store, they could possibly be trying to find me." He hesitated for an instant. "Oh well, let's just enjoy the ride. Maybe this ordeal is almost over," David said. He looked at Debra and smiled.

They tried to relax and enjoy some of the beauty of the scenic train ride, but the anticipation of the nightmare ending still lingered in the back of their minds.

CHAPTER 8

The train pulled into the station at Utica; Debra and David exited the train. All of a sudden, police officers came out from everywhere, with their guns drawn. When the passengers saw the police with their guns drawn, they began running in all directions, screaming.

"Debra Benson and David Kimble, put your hands up!" one of the police officers yelled into a megaphone. "Everyone else get down on the ground!" Stunned, Debra and David stood there for a second. "David Kimble and Debra Benson, put your hands in the air—right now!" repeated the cop. When they raised their hands in the air, everyone around them moved away quickly. Several people lay down on the floor of the station. The police moved toward them, stepping over the other passengers. One of the cops had a picture printout of David and Debra.

"I am an FBI agent," David said.

"Yeah, and I'm Tinker Bell!" one of the cops replied.

"I'm an FBI agent! I'm undercover," David said again.

"If that's true, let me see you're badge. You better do it real slow!"

"I don't have a badge. I'm undercover! That's what being under-cover means!" David yelled, frustrated.

"Don't get smart with me, punk!" the cop said.

"I have a driver's license and that's all!" David said.

The officers surrounded them and pulled their arms down behind them. "We received a call from the FBI, and they said you were on this train. They said to pick you up and hold you until they get here."

"Did they explain what's going on?" David paused momentarily and then asked another question. "Didn't they tell you that I am an FBI agent and that I am undercover?" David asked.

"No," one of the cops replied. "There wasn't any explanation."

"I guess Harry or Darrell called the FBI. I suppose they talked to someone other than Bill," David said as he turned and looked at Debra. "It's okay, Debra. We'll be safe now." The police began to put handcuffs on them.

"Why would you put handcuffs on us? We're not criminals," David exclaimed.

"We'll find out when we get to the station," one of the cops said, latching the cuffs around their wrists. David and Debra looked at each other, but they didn't complain. They were relieved at the thought that this ordeal could be over. One of the officers loaded them into the backseat of a police car.

Once at the station, a large, chunky man with a bad case of acne scars on his face came up to them. In a deep, coarse voice he said, "I'm Sheriff Dale White. My job is to keep you safe until the FBI gets here. I am going to put both of you in a cell."

"I'm an FBI agent, undercover. I don't think it's necessary to lock us up."

"Well, I do. Until I find out what this is all about, you two are going in a cell. For all I know, you could be killers. The FBI didn't explain anything. They just said to hold you, so I'm going to do that—the way I see fit."

"We haven't done anything wrong," Debra said. "People are trying to kill us!"

"Well, miss, if people are trying to kill you, then where could you be anymore safe than in a jail cell?" Debra just rolled her eyes. "We do things by the book here, miss, like it or not. Now, some of my men will be here all night, so if the FBI doesn't come today, you'll have all night to rest up for your trip with them tomorrow." One of the deputies locked them in two separate cells next to each other.

"Call the FBI," David said. "Ask for Bill Rogers. He'll verify that what I am telling you is the truth."

Sheriff White quickly walked back to their cell and said, "I have talked to the FBI. Besides, it's the weekend. You can't get in touch with very many government agencies on the weekend. Anyway, they just said to hold you until they get here. So that's just what we're going to do." The sheriff turned and walked back to his office.

"David, do you think it's the FBI that's coming to get us?" Debra asked.

"I'm sure it is. Darrell must have called them. They said the FBI told them we were on that train."

"David, how did the FBI know we were on that train? What if those men that are chasing us called and pretended to be from the FBI?"

"Darrell must have told them," David replied. "He knew that the train ran through there. Besides, I don't think these cops are stupid enough to just take someone's word over the phone that they are who they say they are. I'm sure it was the FBI. There's nothing to worry about."

Trying to reassure her, he put his hand through the bars and stroked Debra's face. David tried not to show his suspicion that something was wrong. The more he thought about it, the more he could not understand the situation. *If they had talked to Bill Rogers, why hadn't he explained the situation to the police? Why wouldn't the sheriff call the FBI? He should know the FBI could be contacted anytime, even on the weekend.* He kept these thoughts to himself and tried to disregard any notion of underhandedness by the police or the FBI. As he suppressed his true feelings, he tried to be upbeat and make the best of what he hoped would be a short stay.

One of the deputies brought them soap, bandages, and towels. After they cleaned up and dressed their cuts, the deputies gave them some food.

They spent the rest of the night in the jail cells, with no sign of the FBI. The next morning, the FBI still hadn't shown up. One of the deputies brought their breakfast.

"Get the sheriff in here right now," David demanded. The deputy walked to the door and called for the sheriff. He came into the room.

"What do you want?" he growled.

"How long are you going to hold us here?"

"Until the FBI comes to pick you up, so you best relax, sonny."

"I demand that you let us make a phone call."

"The FBI will be here soon, and then it won't be necessary to make a phone call, now will it?"

"I work for the FBI, and I know my rights. We have not been charged with anything. I demand you let us make that call right now."

"You can demand anything you want, but we do things my way here. Now pipe down," Sheriff White said as he pulled his baton and smacked the bars. "Now get over there, sit down, and eat your food." He turned, put his baton away, and left the room whistling.

David couldn't keep what he was thinking to himself any longer.

"Something is wrong, Debra," he said, looking at her with a concerned expression. "They should have been here by now. Jack Braco has a lot of money. Maybe these cops have been bought off. Or at least that sheriff may've been."

"What can we do?"

"We can't do anything right now. If they won't let me make that call, we'll just have to wait and see what happens."

When they were finished eating, a young deputy came to pick up the dishes. He kept looking behind him at the open door as he picked up Debra's plate. When he came close to the bars of David's cell, he bent down.

"You're in danger," he whispered. David moved over closer to the bars.

"What do you mean?"

"I heard Sheriff White talking on the phone. He is going to take you out of here. You better be careful!"

"You have to help us," David said. The deputy stood up and moved away from the bars. David could see the fear in his face.

"I can't help you. I overheard Sheriff White say something about two hundred thousand dollars when he was speaking with them on the phone. People can get killed for that kind of money. I'm not willing to take that chance," he whispered. He took David's plate and quickly rushed out of the room. David walked over to Debra and looked at her through the bars. She could see the concern on his face.

"Debra, the first chance we get, we have to try to get away. I think the sheriff may be planning to turn us over to the people who are trying to kill us."

"Why would he do such a thing?"

"For the money—that's the only reason. I don't think it was the FBI that called. I think you were right. I think it was Jack Braco's men. That's why the sheriff keeps refusing to let us make a phone call."

"We can't let them take us. Do you have a plan, David?" Debra asked, her voice breaking with tension and fear.

"No, not really. We'll have to take advantage of any situation that gives us a chance to escape. So be ready to run at anytime." David looked at Debra and saw how upset she was. Her face had lost its color and her hands were trembling. He reached through the bars and took her hand.

"I'm so scared, David!"

"We're not going down without a fight, Debra. If the sheriff has made a deal with those killers and if he has any human compassion, then maybe I can talk him out of it. But if not, when the time comes, we'll have to resort to other measures. But I'm not going to let them hurt you."

They could do nothing but wait. The anticipation was almost unbearable. David kept walking the floor, racking his brain to come up with a plan. They were trapped, like animals in a cage waiting to be offered up as a sacrifice.

Sometime later, the sheriff came in and said, "I'm going to take you to meet the FBI."

"Why doesn't the FBI come here?" David paused for a moment, waiting for Sheriff White to respond. Sheriff White just looked at him. "I think we should wait for the FBI right here," David replied.

"Well now, some time ago you couldn't wait to get out of here. Now you want to stay. I know it's not the hospitality that is making you want to stay. No, I think you're coming with me."

"I think we both know you're not going to take us to meet the FBI." David looked at the deputies. "If you men let him do this, you're accessories to murder," he said.

"You shut your mouth and put your hands through this slot so these men can cuff you." Sheriff White stepped back and motioned for the deputies to put handcuffs on them. David took a couple steps backward in his cell. "Turn around and put your hands behind your back and put them through this slot so these men can cuff you!" Sheriff White said in a loud, stern voice. David looked at Sheriff White and the three deputies. "If you make us come in that cell, son, my deputies are going to be swinging these batons." The deputies took out their batons. David saw the fear on Debra's face as she stood with her bottom lip quivering. He told Debra to put her hands behind her and do as they said.

After putting the cuffs on them, they took them to a police car and put them in the backseat. After climbing in the driver's seat, the sheriff told his deputies to stay there. He explained that he was going to take them to meet the FBI.

"He's going to turn us over to the people who are trying to kill us," David shouted at the deputies. "You have to help us!"

Sheriff White took his baton and smacked the wire screen behind his seat and yelled, "Sit back and shut up!"

David could see the deputy who had told him about the conspiracy standing behind the other deputies. Sheriff White slammed his door and drove away.

"You're going to take us to those men who are trying to kill us, aren't you?" David shouted.

"Well, that all depends on how much money is involved," he said with a greedy smile.

"You can't do that. You're a police officer, and you've sworn to uphold the law!" David yelled.

"You said that you do everything by the book when we came here," Debra said.

"This job doesn't pay me enough to uphold the law or go by the book. I work long hours, and I still can't get ahead." He cleared his throat. "I've been honest all my life, and where has it gotten me? I live from paycheck to paycheck; a little extra money sure would be nice."

"A little blood money, you mean," David said. "You just don't know who you're dealing with. They have already killed two people that we know of."

"The person I spoke to said you two had killed two people in a cabin up in the mountains."

"They're only trying to give you some justification for what you're doing," David said.

"Just sit back and relax. We have a long way to drive," Sheriff White said. He took a piece of paper with directions he had written down and looked them over. David tried to reason with him several times, but nothing he said had any impact on Sheriff White.

After they had driven sixty or seventy miles southeast, he turned left onto another road.

"Listen to me. You can't trust these people; they're coldblooded killers. They're going to kill us and you too," David said.

"Maybe you're right, but I'm not as stupid as you think. I'll be ready for them. We only have a few more miles to go. When we get there, you two just keep your mouths shut and let me do the talking." With that, he turned the stereo on and began listening to music. He used the music to help him ignore David's pleas for help.

David whispered to Debra, "I can't reason with him. When we get out of this car, I'm going to distract them, and I want you to run away as fast as you can. You can get away if they're busy with me."

"No, David, I'm not going without you."

David looked into her eyes and said sternly, "Listen to me, Debra. They're going to kill us both. I'm trying to help you, so please do as I ask."

"No," Debra said.

David's tone of voice changed. "Look at the mess you've gotten me in, Debra." Hoping to make her think he didn't care so maybe she would try to get away, he said, "I don't want you around me anymore. Why don't you just leave me alone."

"Can you look me in the eyes and tell me that you don't love me, David?" David looked at her and said, "No, I can't do that. You know I love you. I just want you to be safe."

"I think we stand a better chance together," Debra whispered with tear-filled eyes.

"I suppose you're right. We've managed to stay alive so far. Just pray that we are able to survive this time too," David said with a smile. At that moment, the sheriff turned onto a short gravel driveway leading to a large grass field that was surrounded by trees on three sides. After pulling into the field, he turned right, made a half circle, and stopped. The driveway to the field was to the left of the car. There was a black car with dark tinted windows sitting at the far end of the field. He turned the stereo off and looked back toward David.

"Just in case you're right about these people, young man, I'm going to wait right here and see what happens."

Debra recognized the car as the one that had followed her and Ashley to the restaurant and to the airport. "David, that's the car that followed me to the airport," whispered Debra.

"Are you sure?"

"Yes, I believe it is," replied Debra.

A man opened the door, stepped out of the car, and motioned toward the sheriff.

"Pull on down here, and let's have a look at the merchandise," the man shouted. The sheriff stepped out of the car and stood on the ground by the open doorway, looking across the top of his car.

"Here's how this is going to go down, sonny. You walk up to me and bring the money!" he yelled. The man leaned inside the black car, talking to someone in the passenger seat. Someone handed him a briefcase. He closed the door and began walking toward them.

"Take these handcuffs off," David said.

"Shut up!" Sheriff White yelled.

The man was getting closer with each step. Debra began to cry. "David, what are we going to do?"

"I don't know, Debra. I just want you to be safe."

"Promise me—no matter what happens—that you'll always love me. I can't make it through this without you."

"I promise," David said. "Now promise me you'll run away when you get the chance, whether I'm with you or not."

"Okay, I promise."

With their hands still cuffed behind them, Debra looked into David's eyes and smiled. With the expectation of certain death just minutes away, she leaned toward him and pressed her salty, tearstained lips to his, and they shared a long, possibly last, kiss.

"I love you, David," she said and drew back from him.

"I love you too, Debra."

As the man came closer, his coat moved enough to reveal a pistol in a shoulder holster on his left side. Sheriff White put his right hand down to his side, unsnapped the strap on his holster, and rested his hand on his gun. The man stopped about thirty feet from the car. "Pull the microphone and cord off your radio and throw them out on the ground."

"What's wrong, sonny—you scared?" Sheriff White said with a half grin.

"No, just cautious. If this is a trap, I don't want you calling for help," the man said.

"Well, if you give me the money, I won't need to call anyone, will I?" Sheriff White said as he leaned across the top of his car door while still resting his right hand on his holstered gun.

"If you want the money, pull the microphone and cord out and throw them on the ground." He looked at the man for a moment, and then he bent down, reached in, and pulled the microphone and cord from the radio and threw them on the ground. The man came to the front of the car and stopped again.

"Move out from behind the car door," the man said.

"No, I'll be fine right here."

"Move from behind the door!" the man said again in a loud, stern tone of voice.

"I said no!" Sheriff White yelled. Suddenly the man dropped the briefcase and drew his gun. Before he could get a shot off, Sheriff White drew his gun and shot the man. He fell just to the left side of the car. When Sheriff White made a move to get back in the car, a gunshot rang out from the nearby brush, and the impact of the bullet spun Sheriff White around. He staggered and fell on his back in the doorway of the car. Blood was oozing from his chest as he tried to move.

"Oh my God, David. We have to help him!" Debra screamed, even though she knew they were helpless and trapped in the backseat of the car.

"Give me the keys to the handcuffs," David said.

Sheriff White reached up and took hold of the steering wheel and drug himself up into the car just as another shot rang out and blew the glass out of the open car door. He started the engine, jerked the car down into gear, and took off out of the field. The car door was partially open. Several more shots came from the surrounding brush. Debra screamed as bullets tore through the front fenders and doors of the car. David shoved Debra down in the floor and lay on top of her. The back windshield was hit in one corner, but it only cracked.

"Here—take these cuff keys," Sheriff White yelled and passed them through the wire screen behind his seat. David took the keys and began fumbling to unlock their handcuffs while staying as low as possible in the back of the car. The car was hit on all sides with bullets as they left the field.

They drove a few miles back down the same road they had used to get there. David looked behind them, but he could not see anyone following them. "You...were right. I–I...really messed...up,"

Sheriff White mumbled, and at that moment, he slumped over the steering wheel. The car coasted off the road, down a small bank, and into some brush. His foot was stuck on the gas pedal, and the car picked up speed. They traveled a great distance into the brush before his foot came loose, and the car lodged against a large bush. The car stopped, still in gear, with the engine idling.

"Sheriff White!" David shouted, but there was no response.

"How do we get out of here, David? These back doors only open from the outside."

"The glass is cracked on this side," David said. He flipped around sideways in the seat and began kicking the glass. David knew that even though they had traveled a great distance from the road, they were still in danger of being caught.

"Hurry, David. They'll be coming any minute."

He was able to kick the glass out, reach through, and open the back door from the outside. David jumped out, ran around, opened the driver's door, and pulled Sheriff White out. Debra helped drag him to the back door. She opened the back door and climbed into the backseat, and David put the sheriff across Debra's lap.

Even though he was going to turn them over to the killers, she had compassion for him. As she looked at him, she began to cry. His breathing was shallow and he was bleeding badly.

"We have … to get him … to a hospital," she said, between sobs.

David jumped in the driver's seat. He looked down and saw Sheriff White's gun lying on the floor of the car.

"At least now we have a gun to defend ourselves with," David said and put the sheriff's gun on the seat beside him. David tried to back the car out of the brush. The tires began to spin, but the car started moving slowly backward.

"Hurry, David!" Debra yelled. The brush was so thick David had to back the car out on the same path they came in. He was able to get back to the road, but just as the back of the car came up the bank to the road, the front suspension hung onto a small tree stump. The rear tires began to spin. David pulled the gearshift from reverse to drive, but the car only moved a few inches.

"We're stuck!" David shouted.

David kept jerking the gearshift from reverse to drive, but the rear tires kept spinning, and the car only moved a few inches each time he rocked it from reverse to drive. He could not get the car loose from the stump.

Suddenly, the black car slammed into the back of the police car, sending it careening forward off the edge of the road. Debra screamed as she and the sheriff were thrown backward and then forward against the back of the front seat.

When the car stopped, David grabbed the gun and slid across the front seat of the car. He jerked the passenger door open, moved to the back door, and opened it. He grabbed Debra by the arm and pulled her out of the car and slammed the back door.

"Get down, Debra, and as soon as you get a chance, run," he shouted. He stood up and leaned over the trunk of Sheriff White's car and began firing into the windshield of the black car. The men in the black car were just starting to exit when David began firing. The three men scrambled back into the car. The driver jerked the gearshift into reverse and quickly backed away. He slid the car sideways, with the back half of the car off the road about forty feet from the police car. David kept shooting.

The police car was down under the small bank just off the road, and the front passenger door was open. Debra knelt down behind David, next to the open front door of the car. Carmine and two other men bailed out of the car, on the opposite side from David. They began shooting across the hood and the trunk of the black car, using it as a shield.

Suddenly David fell back on the ground beside the car, holding his left shoulder. Debra screamed as David fell to the ground. She knew he had been hit. With mixed emotions of anger and fear, the adrenaline rush gave her the strength of three men. She grabbed him by the arm and dragged him through the open door, up into the front seat. The car was still running as she jerked the shifter into reverse. The passenger door was still open as the car moved backward. The impact of the black car had dislodged the sheriff's car from the tree stump. She held the gas pedal to the floor. As the car moved backward, the tires slung dirt and gravel from the side of the road. When the tires caught the blacktop and began to spin, smoke rolled from underneath the back fenders as the powerful engine roared.

The three men kept shooting as the police car came backward toward them, picking up speed as it came. The back windshield exploded and glass sprayed into the car. Debra screamed and ducked her head as she continued to hold the gas pedal to the floor. She slammed the back end of the police car into the side of the black car. She held the pedal down and pushed the car sideways off the road and into the ditch. The three men were running backward while shooting as they tried to get away from the moving car. One of the men tripped and fell, and the car slid on top of him.

Debra jerked the gearshift down into drive and sped away in the same direction they had been traveling when they ran off the road. Carmine and the other man quickly pulled the third man out from under the black car. The man only had a few cuts and bruises. Carmine ran into the road, cursing, as he watched them drive out of sight.

As Debra drove away, the wind pushed the open passenger door closed. While driving, Debra said, "David, how badly are you hurt?" She looked over at him. David was lying on the front seat, holding his left upper arm. Blood had soaked his shirt around the wound. "Oh my God, are you okay?" she said, horrified.

"I'm okay, Debra. I don't think it's very bad." David sat up in the seat. He ripped the sleeve off his shirt and tied it around his wound. The bullet had taken a chunk out of his upper arm.

"Are you going to be okay?"

"I'm okay," he quickly replied. "Pull over and let me drive, and you try to help Sheriff White." She stopped and quickly jumped out and climbed in the backseat. David moved over underneath the steering wheel and drove away.

"Are they following us?" David asked.

"No," Debra said. "I pushed their car in the ditch when I backed into them. I don't believe they're going to be able to get out very easily."

"We can't take that chance. We have to hurry," David said. Debra lifted Sheriff White's head and put it in her lap.

"I don't know if he's alive, David!"

"We have to get him to a hospital and find a place to hide," David said.

Sheriff White regained consciousness for a couple of seconds and moaned.

"I–I'm sorry," he mumbled. He moved his left arm and one leg. He exhaled a long breath, and his body went limp. Debra began to cry as she checked his pulse. She moved out from under him.

"Is he still alive, Debra?" David asked. She didn't answer him.

"Is he still alive?" David yelled.

"Don't yell at me!" she cried. "I've ... never had someone die in my lap!"

"I'm sorry, Debra."

"What are we going to do now?" Debra said as she wept.

"We have to get off this road. Help me look for a side road or some place we can hide for a while."

"Do you still have his gun?" asked Debra, still crying.

"No, I dropped it when I got hit, but we have the shotgun," David said. He took hold of the shotgun that was attached to the dash. The gun was locked in its holder. "Debra, look at Sheriff White's gun belt. See if there are some keys hanging on it. Check his pockets too."

Debra wiped her eyes and checked his gun belt and his pockets. "I can't find any keys."

"We have no way of getting this gun unlocked," David said.

At that moment David saw a narrow dirt road on the right. He quickly stopped, backed up, and turned in. The road was so narrow it was hardly visible from the road. The brush and trees rubbed the sides of the car as they drove down the narrow path.

"This must be an ATV trail. It's too narrow for a car. If they are following us, I hope they don't see our tracks where we turned off the road. We'll hide back here until dark." They drove through the heavy brush and trees until they could no longer see the highway. David stopped the car. "After dark we can get back on the road and try to find a phone booth at a gas station."

When they stepped out and walked around the car, they saw just how riddled it was with bullet holes. The trunk lid was pushed in, and the back bumper was pushed down from the impact with the black car. After using a seasoned piece of wood to pry up the dented trunk lid, they struggled together to put the sheriff's large body in it.

David walked toward the front of the car and saw steam coming from under the hood. "Looks like the radiator is leaking. I suppose a bullet or a tree limb punctured it," David commented.

"How do we fix it, David?"

"If we can find a stream and something to put water in, we can fill it up after it cools down." After searching under the seats and in the trunk, they found a coffee thermos. They walked through the woods a short distance and found a small, shallow stream. David filled the thermos, and they walked back to the car. They waited for an hour to let the steam subside and the radiator cool down. David took a small stick and shoved it in the hole in the radiator.

"This will have to do until we can get to a gas station."

After several trips he was able to fill the radiator. They walked around the car, and Debra said, "This is like some crazy dream that you hope you are going to wake up from anytime, but then you pinch yourself and you know it's real."

"We'll get through this. Just pray, and it will all work out," David said.

After getting back in the car, David turned the computer on. "If I can determine where we are, then maybe we can find a town close by where we can get some help."

After trying for a short time, David could not get the computer to work. Then a voice came over the radio. It was one of Sheriff White's deputies. "Sheriff White! Sheriff White! Come in," he called again and again.

"We have no way to respond. They're going to be looking for him," David said.

"Maybe they will help us, David."

"Yes, but if they find him dead in the trunk of this car, they may not be too sympathetic with us. Regardless of what we say, they may think we killed him. I just wouldn't want to try to explain that to his deputies while they have a gun trained on me."

"You're right. The police are going to think we killed him! Now the police and the bad guys are after us?"

"Maybe not. If I can get a call in to Bill Rogers, I can explain it to him and he can get in touch with the police. Don't worry. It'll be okay. As soon as we get to a phone, we can explain it all. We had better rest for a while now."

Debra stretched out in the backseat and David in the front, but they didn't sleep very well. They were thinking about the predicament they were in and how they were going to get out of it. Debra kept thinking about the sheriff's body in the trunk and how terrible it was that she was partly to blame for his death. *How can money be so important to someone—important enough to be willing to take a human life? How can this world be so evil; how can there be people that bad?* she thought.

"David, are you asleep?"

"No."

"I can't sleep either. I keep thinking about Sheriff White's family. They don't even know he's dead. It's all because of me. In a way, it's my fault he's dead."

"No, Debra. It's just bad people that are to blame—the world is full of them. Debra, as a law officer, I've seen people who just don't care who they hurt as long as it means money in their pockets. So don't blame yourself."

"David, remember I told you that black car they were driving was the same car I saw following us the day Ashley drove me to the airport. These people were watching me then. They must have been at that lawyer's office. I wasn't sure then, but now I think they murdered him to keep him from telling me about my mother's will. They called me the day I left and just held the phone. Even before I came to the mountains, I believe they were planning to kill me, David. Why is this happening?" Debra began to cry. David opened the front door, jumped out, and climbed in the backseat with Debra. "It's bad enough that my best friend murdered my mother, but now these killers hired by my father are trying to kill me. David, I'm just a little, insignificant person. I've never done anything to anyone in my life. How can all these people be out to kill me?" Debra trembled as she cried from a broken heart. David put his arms around her.

"You're not insignificant. I love you, and I'm going to stand by you. It'll work out, Debra. I promise. I'll keep them away from you." David held her close and stroked her head as he tried to console her.

"I thank God that we met. I just could not get through this without you, David," Debra said, clinging to him.

After they talked for a while longer, David was able to convince Debra that everything would be okay. Debra finally began to relax. She faded off to sleep with David holding her.

CHAPTER 9

David and Debra were exhausted and didn't wake up until about an hour before daylight. David started the car and began the difficult task of turning around. As he maneuvered the car back and forth on the narrow road, he bumped into several trees. After turning the car, they drove back to the highway. Due to the extensive damage to the car, only the left headlight was working.

David turned right and drove southeast, hoping to find a gas station with a payphone. His wound was beginning to hurt very badly; he could scarcely move his arm.

"I'm going to have to get some peroxide to clean this wound before it gets infected. It's starting to hurt a little." Debra knew that if he was complaining about the pain, it must be much worse than she thought.

"If we find a grocery store or gas station, we can buy some first-aid supplies, and I'll bandage it for you," Debra said. She leaned over and put the back of her hand on David's face. David reached up and held her hand.

"I'll try to contact Bill Rogers first," he said and smiled at her.

"Is he going to be at the office this early in the morning?"

"No, but I have his home phone number."

After driving for a few miles, they saw a gas station on the right. By parking at the end of the building, he hoped to keep anyone from seeing the banged-up, bullet-riddled police car. He went inside and asked the attendant if there was a telephone he could use. The man told him it was in the back, in the hallway near the restrooms. David thanked the man and turned to walk toward the back of the store. The attendant looked at him and said, "You don't look like a cop."

David stopped and turned and said, "What?"

"Well, you drove up in a cop car, but you don't look like a cop," the man said.

"I'm not exactly a cop, but I don't have time to explain it right now." He hesitated for an instant. "What is the closest town to here?"

"Burtonsville is thirty-three miles that way," he said and pointed east. David noticed the man looking at his left arm, with the blood-soaked shirtsleeve tied around it.

"What road are we on?" The young man gave David a puzzled look.

"You're on 163. If you follow it to 168 and then turn left and follow the signs, it will take you to Burtonsville."

"Thanks," David said and walked back toward the telephone. David knew that he had not satisfied the young man's curiosity. He could feel the man staring at him as he walked away.

He picked up the phone, dialed the operator, and asked to place a collect call to Bill Rogers' home number. After the phone rang several times, Bill answered. The operator explained the collect call, and when she was finished, he told her he would accept the charges.

In a groggy voice, Bill said, "Hello."

"Bill, it's me, David."

"David, where have you been? What's going on? I haven't heard from you since that short call the other day!"

"I can't explain it all right now, but you have to come and get us as soon as possible."

"Is the girl with you?"

"Yes, but, Bill, Senator Braco is trying to kill us. He was being blackmailed because Debra Benson is his illegitimate daughter. He has men chasing us, and they're trying to kill her. We need you to pick us up as soon as possible."

"Okay, where are you?"

"We are thirty-three miles from a little town called Burtonsville. We're on 163, but we will be turning east onto 168. I'll call you when we get to town."

"Where are you calling from now? Can't you just wait there?"

"We're at a little gas station, but the attendant is asking questions. We can't stay here," David said.

"So the girl will be there with you too, right?"

"Yes, she'll be with me."

"Call me when you get into town, and I'll be there as soon as I can."

"Bill, the people who are trying to kill us killed a sheriff from Utica. We're driving his car now. We put his body in the trunk. Bill, explain to the police that we are not responsible for his death. I don't want to get shot by some cop out for revenge."

"I'll take care of it, David. Don't worry." David hung up the phone and walked back through the store. He picked up bandages, gauze, peroxide, and radiator stop leak. He also picked up a gallon of water and some drinks and snacks. He paid the attendant and went back to the car and handed Debra the snacks and medical supplies. He pulled the hood latch, loosened the radiator cap with his shirttail, and filled it with the stop leak and the gallon of water. He climbed back in the driver's seat.

"That should hold for a while," he said as he looked over at Debra. She was sitting in the front seat with her head in her hands.

"It's going to be all right, Debra. I talked to Bill Rogers. He's going to help us. This will be over soon."

"Thank God!" Debra said with a sigh of relief.

David turned around in the seat so she could clean and dress the wound on his left arm. She used the peroxide to clean his wound, put the bandage on, and wrapped his arm with gauze. When she was finished, she held his face in her hands and kissed him.

"What's that for?" he asked with a smile.

"A get-well kiss. I'm happy because this nightmare is almost over." David started the car, and they drove out of the parking lot. The attendant was watching as they drove away.

As they shared some of the snacks, Debra asked, "How did you pay for this?"

"I used cash. We can't use a credit card, and Ben took almost all of the money I had with me. I only had a few dollars. I don't have any left now."

"I don't have any either. All the money I had with me is in the cabin. It doesn't matter. We won't need it now," she said with a smile.

When they were finished eating and drinking, Debra asked, "Did you tell Bill that those men killed Sheriff White?"

"Yes, I did," David said. He hesitated for a few seconds. "It's kind of strange, though."

"How do you mean?" she asked, glancing at his slightly green-tinted face, reflected by the dimly lit dash lights.

"Well, Bill didn't seem surprised, or even question me, when I told him that Senator Braco was trying to kill us. He didn't seem surprised by anything that I told him. Come to think of it, he was very interested in whether or not you were with me."

"Is that why you didn't want to wait for the FBI at the gas station?"

"No, I knew we couldn't wait around—the attendant was asking too many questions. I didn't want him to call the police." He hesitated and then he looked over at Debra. "We can't trust anyone right now, not even the police. We can wait for Bill to come and get us in Burtonsville." David reached up and scratched his head and said, "Maybe I'm making more out of this than I should. We'll just have to wait and see what happens when I call him again after we get into town."

They drove the short distance to Route 168. The sun was beginning to come up after they made the turn east toward Burtonsville. They had driven about ten miles when a voice suddenly came over the police radio.

"All units be advised, we just received a tip that the missing police car from Utica is going east on route 168 near Burtonsville." David and Debra looked at each other. "The two suspects—one male, one female—are to be approached with extreme caution. Suspects are believed to be armed and extremely dangerous. They're believed to be responsible for the kidnapping and possible death of Sheriff Dale White. All units respond."

"Oh my God," Debra gasped. "They know where we are, and they think we're criminals. We have the police after us too! What are we going to do now, David?"

"We have to get to a safe place to hide and wait for Bill to come and get us."

"How could the police have found out where we are?"

"I don't know. Maybe the kid at the gas station called them."

At that moment they met a state police car with its lights flashing and driving at a high rate of speed. Just after the two cars passed each other, the police car slid around in the road and came after them. Debra turned around and looked through where the back window once was.

"David, that policeman turned around. He's coming after us. You should just pull over and see if we can convince them to help us." Before David could respond, the officer came over the police radio and reported seeing Sheriff White's car. He came up to the back of their car very quickly. He called for backup, turned his siren on, and then yelled over the PA, "Pull over now!"

"David, you better do as he says. Maybe they can help us."

"Bill told me he would set it straight with them, but I'm not sure I want to try to explain why Sheriff White's dead body is in the trunk of this car. It may not sit too well with the cops if they think we killed one of their own," David said.

"Pull over!" the officer yelled again.

"We have to stop, David. We can explain it to them!" Debra said. Suddenly, two more police cars came up behind them.

A voice came over the radio and said, "Officer Johnson, I got a tip that there's a dead sheriff in the trunk of that car. They're cop killers! Let's show them how we handle cop killers. Run that dirtbag off the road!" David stepped on the gas and sped up.

"They're trying to kill us. How could they know about the sheriff's body in the trunk?" David said. "Why didn't Bill tell them who killed Sheriff White? He's helping the senator. Why would he do this to me?"

Officer Johnson was driving the car directly behind them. He drove up to the left side of their car and slammed into it. David steered his car to the left and forced the police car off the road and into the ditch. The police car spun around and rolled over and stopped on its right side. One of the cops stopped to help Johnson out of the police car, as it lay halfway in the road.

A shot rang out, and the side mirror exploded on the driver's door of Sheriff White's car.

"Get down, Debra!" David yelled. Debra rolled down onto the floor.

She looked up at David and said, "Why are they shooting at us? Are they crazy?" Another shot blew out the left rear tire. David tried desperately to hold the car straight, but it slid around sideways, went off the road, and over a steep embankment.

"Hold on Debra!" David shouted.

The front of the car buried into the ground when the car reached the bottom of the hill. As soon as the car stopped, David jumped out and ran around to the passenger door and pulled Debra out. He could hear the cars above him sliding to a stop on the highway. After pulling Debra out of the car, he took hold of the shotgun and jerked it, trying to free it from the holder on the dash. It was still locked and wouldn't budge.

"Go on, Debra—get out of here! I'll be right behind you!"

"Come on, David!" Debra screamed as she turned and ran. At that moment, two police officers came down the hill. One of them fired his gun, and the bullet went just over David's head.

"Hold it right there—put your hands in the air now! I'm Captain Fred Martz of the New York State Police. If you make another move, I'll be forced to shoot you!" he shouted. David put his hands in the air. The cop kept his gun pointed at David as he walked down the hill. He was a large man, and he struggled to walk. His double chin swayed from side to side as he waddled down the hill.

"Run, Debra!" David yelled. Debra stopped for a brief moment and looked back. She saw the police surrounding David. She turned and started running again.

"Freeze, or I'll shoot!" one of the cops shouted. Debra kept running. The cop fired a shot, this time toward Debra, as they were surrounding David.

"Stop shooting at her! What's wrong with you people? Are you insane?"

"You shut your mouth, boy," Officer Johnson said and punched David in the kidney and shoved him against the car. David spun around and punched the Officer Johnson in the jaw. He fell backward on the ground. Captain Martz hit David across the back of the neck with his baton and knocked him to the ground. Officer Johnson jumped up and started to kick David, but Captain Martz pointed his finger at him and yelled, "Johnson, you get the girl!"

Johnson turned and began running after Debra. Captain Martz and the other cop grabbed David by the arm, jerked him up from the ground, and threw him up against the car.

"I'm an FBI agent, undercover," David said as he rubbed the back of his neck where Captain Martz had hit him.

"Is that a fact? Well now, Mr. Undercover FBI Man, why don't we look in the trunk and see what we find."

"Look, Captain, there're some really dangerous people trying to kill us, and they killed Sheriff White. We just barely escaped with our lives. I have a bullet wound on my upper arm to prove it," David said.

"Look, all I know, young man, is that we received an anonymous phone call that said the two of you killed Sheriff White, his body was in the trunk, and you two were driving his car on route 168. Sheriff White has been missing for some time now and was last seen with the two of you, and I can tell from the uniform I see between the seams of that banged-up trunk lid that all we need to do is call the coroner."

"Bill Rogers." David hesitated for a moment. "He's to blame; they must have gotten to him."

"Yeah, well, you can explain it all to the judge, Mr. FBI Man!" They all laughed. "You can make your phone call when we get you to the police station in Burtonsville. In the meantime, you better just keep quiet and try to impress me," Captain Martz said. He turned and started to walk away.

"You have to listen to me!" David shouted as he tried to jerk loose from them.

"I told you to keep your mouth shut. You had best save your explanation for the judge. The court doesn't take kindly to cop killers," Captain Martz said.

"I told you, we didn't kill anyone," David said.

"And I told you to keep your mouth shut," Captain Martz said. He turned sharply and gave a hateful look to David. David could see that his pleas were falling on deaf ears. He decided to bide his time and try to argue later.

They read David his rights, forced his hands behind him, and put on the handcuffs. After taking him up the hill, they stood beside one of the police cars. Captain Martz was leaning on the police car, breathing hard from the walk up the hill.

"Maybe you should cut back on your breakfast doughnuts," David commented. Captain Martz jerked his nightstick out and smacked the trunk of his car.

"I told you to keep quiet, boy, or you're going to force me to use this on your head," he said. He then paused to catch his breath.

Debra ran as fast as she could through the heavy brush and trees. She heard a gunshot and looked back. The bullet went over her head. She could hear it tearing through the trees. *These people are crazy,* she thought. *They're going to kill us.* Limbs scratching her face, she ran even faster. She was so scared she didn't know what to do. She began to cry.

She couldn't help but wonder what would happen to David. *I won't be able to help him escape if I'm captured too,* she thought. *I have to get away.*

Although excitement and danger had command of her instinct and self-survival, her senses were still working perfectly. She was acutely aware of her surroundings. She caught the scent of the damp-ened-earth smell that people enjoyed on nature adventures through the woods. She caught herself wishing she was miles away. *Maybe I should give up,* she thought. Just as quickly, she became angry and refused to give in to any thoughts of giving up or getting caught. She wiped the tears from her eyes and kept running with renewed confidence.

She could hear one of the policemen running behind her. She stopped and hid behind a tree to catch her breath.

"I'm Officer Johnson of the New York State Police. Come on, miss, don't make it any harder on yourself than it already is. Just give up now!" he shouted. She could hear him coming closer. Just as she started to run again, the cop came running up behind her and caught her by the arm. She struggled with him as she spun around and was able to break loose from him. He grabbed her by her long, brown hair as she tried to run away. He pulled her head backward and then pushed her to the ground. She screamed as she fell forward.

"Don't make me get my gun out," he said as he fell on top of her, forcing her face into the dirt and leaves. He was able to pull her arms behind her back. He reached back and took his handcuffs out of their holder. Debra struggled loose from his one-handed grip on her arms and rolled over on her back.

"Let go of me!" she shouted as she fought with him. The hand-cuffs slipped out of his hands and fell in the leaves beside them. He grabbed her arms, forced them down against the ground and put his knees on them. His weight was enough to push them down into the soft leaves and dirt.

"Now, aren't you a pretty little thing," he said with a smirk. I should get something for all that running you made me do, and now you caused me to lose my handcuffs," Officer Johnson said.

"Let me up!" Debra shouted. She could not move her arms, regardless of how much she struggled. Johnson leaned forward and put his hands on her face. She jerked her head away from him. He slowly moved his hands down to her breasts. Debra screamed and struggled with all of her might, but she could not get free.

As they were trying to put David in the police car, he heard Debra screaming. He braced one foot on the rocker panel of the car, below the back door. He lowered his shoulder and shoved his upper body forward with all his strength and knocked two of the policeman down. He ran back down the hill in Debra's direction, screaming her name, with his hands cuffed behind him. The cops caught up with him and shoved him to the ground.

"If you bastards harm her, I will hunt you down and kill every one of you scumbags!" David screamed with all his might.

They held David on the ground as he continued his threats. "Settle down, son," Captain Martz said as he walked down the hill. They pulled David up from the ground. "Hacker, go down there and see what's going on."

Debra struggled to get loose from Johnson. The more she struggled the more he poked, prodded, and laughed at her resistance. She spit in his face. He instantly became angry and drew back his fist. When he shifted his weight, his left knee came off of her right arm. She jerked her arm free, grabbed a piece of dead tree limb lying on the ground next to them, and hit Johnson across the side of the head. With a groan he rolled off her, into a ball, holding his head and moaning. He reached for his gun. Debra jumped up and hit him across the back of his head. He dropped his gun and howled in pain. She dropped the stick and started running through the woods again.

Officer Hacker came to where Johnson was lying on the ground moaning. "What happened?" he asked.

"That stupid woman hit me with a stick! Go after her," he demanded, pointing in the direction she had run.

Debra ran until she was exhausted. She stopped for a few seconds behind a big tree. After a short time, she heard Officer Hacker running in her direction, so she started running again as fast as she could. She ran up to the edge of a rock cliff. It was straight down. There was a fast-flowing river at the bottom with a big pool of water. She looked to her left and then to her right, but the rock cliff ran as far as she could see in both directions. She knew she could not climb down. She had nowhere to run; she was trapped.

"I'll have to jump. God, help me," she said.

She knew she had no other alternative. Thinking of David and her determination to help him escape, she began to tune out all of her fears and emotions. Suddenly, the instinct to survive took control. She quickly turned around and ran back several feet. She stood looking in the direction that the cop was coming from. She prayed he would not appear, but she could hear his footsteps coming closer and closer. As the cop came into view, she turned and ran as fast as she could. When she came to the edge of the cliff, she closed her eyes and jumped, feet first, with all of her might. She could feel the wind whistling past her as she fell. A death scream that sounded as though it came from the very pit of her soul echoed through the mountains as she fell.

Just as she jumped, Officer Hacker came running up behind her and saw her jump. He ran over to the edge of the cliff and stood there with his mouth open in total shock. He watched as she hit the water. He stood still for a few seconds, in disbelief of what he had just witnessed. He waited a short time, and she never came up.

Hacker went back to Johnson who was still on the ground, still holding his bleeding head and complaining. Officer Hacker helped him back to where they were holding David. He had to practically hold Johnson up in order for him to walk.

Captain Martz saw them coming, and he looked at Johnson and said, "I have two questions: What happened to you, and where's the girl?" he demanded.

"She hit me with a club," Johnson said.

"She did a swan dive off that sixty-foot cliff back there. I saw her hit the water, and there's no way she could have survived—no way," Hacker said.

From inside the car, David heard what they said. He screamed at them, "You bastards! I told you, if she's dead, I'll kill all of you!" He turned around sideways in the back of the car and started kicking the door.

Captain Martz smacked the side window with his hand and said, "Pipe down in there. We don't know she's dead, yet. Now, Hacker, what makes you think she's dead?"

"I saw her hit the water, and she never came up. Besides, we used to jump from that cliff when I was a kid, but we had a spot that we jumped from that was about ten or fifteen feet from the water. No one was ever brave enough, or crazy enough, to jump from the top. It's at least fifty or sixty feet to the water. She's dead, all right. No one could survive that," Hacker said.

"Well, I guess we'll have to call the Water Rescue Squad to see if they can recover her body," Captain Martz said. He climbed into the passenger side of the patrol car, and Hacker got in on the driver's side.

Captain Martz shouted out the window, "Johnson, call Donnie and tell him to bring his tow truck and tow your car to the shop."

"Why me? I'm injured—I need a doctor," Johnson replied.

"You'll be okay. Now, do as you're told. Besides, you wrecked the car—you take care of it. When the coroner gets through with that body in the trunk, have Donnie pull that police car from Utica out too. Tell him to take it over to Earl's Salvage Yard, and you go with him and put a barrier up around it. I don't want anyone messing with it. We may need it for evidence," Captain Martz said. Johnson stumbled away complaining.

Captain Martz picked up the radio microphone. "Hey, Joyce, call Jim Procter and tell him to go about twelve miles west out on 168. A couple of my men will meet him there. We have a dead body in the trunk of a car sitting over the bank. He needs to inspect the body. Tell him it's that missing sheriff from Utica. Tell him to hurry before the body decays even more than it already has. Thanks, darlin.'"

David's wound had started to bleed again from his struggle with the cops.

"I need this wound tended to, if it's not too much trouble!" David said.

"We may be small-town cops, but we're not stupid enough to take you to the hospital, where you can try to escape. I'll have a nurse come over to the jail when we get there, so just calm down," Captain Martz said.

"I hope you fine police officers are proud of yourselves. You just killed the daughter of Senator Jack Braco, the next president of the United States."

"Yeah, and I own the Brooklyn Bridge," Captain Martz said, chuckling.

"I'm telling the truth!" David said.

"It doesn't matter who she is, Mr. FBI Man. She should have stopped when she was told to stop. Now you just keep quiet and worry about your own skin. When we get to town, we have a nice jail cell waiting for you." He and Officer Hacker started laughing as they drove off toward Burtonsville with David in handcuffs.

CHAPTER 10

Tom and Kate Browner had lived on the little river that flows by Burtonsville for the last forty years. This particular day, Tom had decided to take the evening off from his daily hobbies of working in his garden or playing with his pet goats. He picked up his fly-fishing rod and headed toward the river for his favorite pastime, fly-fishing for trout.

When Tom walked down to the riverbank, he noticed that the river was high and moving faster than normal because of the storm that had gone through two nights before. He knew he would have to find a pool of water that wasn't moving so fast in order to catch any fish. He was looking for just the right pothole of water. He walked around a big rock and saw something lying in the water. As he came closer, he realized it was a young woman. He dropped his fishing equipment, ran over to her, and checked her pulse. She had a weak heartbeat, and she was breathing shallowly. He pulled her out of the water, carried her near the tree line, and laid her down in some soft leaves.

He hurried back to the house and told his wife about the young woman. He hooked up the wagon to his old tractor, and he and Kate went back to where the young woman was lying.

When Kate saw her and brushed the hair back from her face, she said, "Oh my, her clothes are all torn, and she has cuts and bruises on her face. What could have happened to this pretty, young woman?"

"Wonder how she ended up in the river," Tom commented.

Kate moved her around and took hold of her arm. "Tom, help me load her in the wagon."

They loaded her in the wagon and took her back to their house. Tom carried her inside to a bedroom and put her on the bed.

"Now, Tom, you go out and feed the goats, and I'll take care of her," Kate said.

"Shouldn't we call the life squad and the police?"

"No, I don't think she has any life-threatening injuries, maybe some slight hypothermia. There's no telling what kind of trouble she's in."

"That's exactly why we *should* call them," Tom said.

"No, Tom, I think it's our duty as parents to help her. Besides, she reminds me of Peggy. Wouldn't you want someone to help your daughter if she was in trouble?"

"Of course I would, but we know nothing about her. She could be a dangerous criminal."

"She doesn't look very dangerous to me." Kate gave a motherly smile. "Now go on, Tom, and feed the goats."

Tom hesitated for an instant. "I suppose it's the right thing to do," he said.

"Okay, you go on now, and I'll get her cleaned up." Tom left the room reluctantly.

Kate used soap, a cotton washcloth, and a pan of warm water to clean the cuts and bruises on Debra's face. Debra faded in and out of consciousness. As Kate cut Debra's torn and tattered clothes and gently removed them; she noticed Debra had a really bad bruise on her left leg. She washed off the dirt, put a nightgown on her, and covered her with a blanket.

That night, Kate slept in a recliner next to Debra's bed. The next morning, at the break of dawn, Debra woke up screaming.

Kate walked over, sat on the side of the bed, and put her hand on Debra's arm. "There, there now, dear, it's okay," she said.

"Where am I?" Debra asked as she sat up in bed and began to gingerly rub her eyes.

"You're near a town called Burtonsville. I'm Kate Browner. My husband, Tom, pulled you out of the river."

"I remember," Debra said, her eyes wide. "There are some people trying to kill me!"

"What's your name, honey, and who's David?" Kate asked. She put her hand on Debra's shoulder and pushed her hair back from her face.

"I'm Debra Benson, but how do you know about David?"

"You talked in your sleep last night, dear. You kept asking David to help you. What kind of trouble are you in, Debra?"

"It's a long story, but I can't stay here. I have to go help David!" Debra exclaimed. She slid over to the side of the bed and put her feet on the floor. She screamed in pain and grabbed her left leg. Holding her leg and trying to balance herself by holding on to the bed, she said, "Where are my clothes?" Then she began crying hysterically. She put her hands over her face, fell to her knees on the floor, and put her face on the bed.

Kate came around the bed, knelt down beside her, and put her arm around her.

"I have to find David. They're going to kill him. He may already be dead. What am I going to do?" Tom rushed in the room when he heard all the commotion.

"It'll be okay, honey. We'll help you, but you're in no condition to go anywhere. You can stay here with us until you feel better. Then we'll help you find David, right, Tom?" Kate said reassuringly.

"Sure we will," Tom said in a raspy morning voice as he scratched his head and yawned.

"I'll get you some of our daughter's clothes, dear. I had to cut your clothes off of you. They were all dirty and torn. Don't be upset; everything is going to work out. You wait and see," Kate said, stroking the back of Debra's head.

"I'll go start breakfast. That'll make you feel better," Tom said, yawning again as he turned and left the room.

Kate helped Debra back on the bed and left the room to get her some clothes. She brought the clothes to Debra, and put them on the bed.

"Our daughter, Peggy, left these here a few months back. You look about the same size." Debra wiped her eyes and took the clothes.

"Thank you."

"Perhaps you would like a hot bath before we eat breakfast? Then we'll see if we can't help you work out your problems," Kate said with a smile.

"You're so kind." Debra smiled. "A bath would be nice."

Kate helped her to the bathroom. Debra climbed in the tub and let the warm water run over her bruised and scratched body. It felt so good that she didn't want to get out. While soaking, she began to relax and let her mind wander. She caught herself wishing that she and David were miles away, relaxing on a beach in the warm sunshine.

Kate told Tom about Debra's injured leg while helping him with breakfast. When breakfast was ready, Kate went in and helped Debra get dressed. Tom brought an old crutch in and gave it to her. "Maybe this will help with your injured leg."

"I really appreciate what you wonderful people are doing for me," Debra said with a smile. She put the crutch under her arm and walked into the kitchen.

After breakfast, Kate asked Debra to tell them what kind of trouble she and David were in.

Debra explained everything, from her mom's death to Ashley's betrayal. She told them about being chased by the police and three killers that may have been hired by her father. She went on to tell them about David being an undercover FBI agent and how she ended up having to jump off the cliff to escape the police. They listened in astonishment at all she had been through.

"Young lady, I know the rock cliff you're talking about. It's about a mile back upriver. If you can survive a jump from that cliff, you're one lucky lady. The good Lord was watching over you," Tom said, shaking his head in amazement.

"You're right, Tom. I believe God was watching over me," Debra said. She took a sip from her coffee cup. "Well, that's my dilemma, but I don't expect you nice people to get involved in this. It's much too dangerous."

Just then they heard cars coming down the drive. Tom jumped up and looked out the window. "It's the police!"

"Oh no! What am I going to do?" Debra said. Using the crutch Tom had given her, she stood up from the table.

"I'll go out and keep them occupied. Kate, you take her to the big closet in the back bedroom."

Kate and Debra made their way through the house as quickly as they could. Tom went out the kitchen door and saw several police cars coming to a stop at the front of the house. He walked around the end of the house to where they had parked.

"Good morning, officers? What's going on?" Tom asked as he walked up to one of the cops.

"I'm Captain Fred Martz, and we're looking for a fugitive—a young woman; her name is Debra Benson. She's wanted in connection with the death of a sheriff from Utica. Have you seen anyone around?"

"No, I sure haven't, Captain."

"We caught the other suspect, a young man. They were traveling together. I spoke to some of your neighbors, and they all said you know this river better than anyone. If a young woman jumped off that big cliff a mile back up the river, where would she end up? We had the water rescue team search the pool of water at the bottom yesterday evening. They searched most of the river down to here so far today, and she's nowhere to be seen," Captain Martz said.

"Well, I assume you know you're looking for a body because no one could survive a jump from that cliff."

"We suspect that she may be dead, but the FBI wants her body found."

"There's lots of rapids and fast-moving water on that river, with the storm we had three nights ago. A body could be several miles down stream by now," Tom said.

"You don't mind if we look around, do you? Just in case she's still alive and may be hiding somewhere nearby."

"No, no … help yourself," Tom said. "Oh, by the way, what's going to happen to the young man that you captured?"

"We're going to turn him over to the FBI. They're coming to pick him up soon. It's their investigation. They pulled rank on us local boys. You know how that is—we do all the work, and they take the credit. Why do you ask?"

"Oh, no reason. Just curious," Tom said and gave a slight laugh. He turned and went back inside the house.

The police began to check the barn and all the surroundings, as well as the riverbanks and the brush.

Tom went to the back bedroom, where Kate and Debra were. He walked over to the closet door and opened it.

"Debra, they *are* looking for you. There's a Captain Fred Martz and four other state policemen out there combing the brush, but the good news is that your friend David is going to be turned over to the FBI," Tom said.

"I ... I don't think that's good news," Debra said. Tom gave her a puzzled look. "Bill Rogers is the only person at the agency who knows David is undercover, and he's the only one who knows that David and I are innocent. But I think he just may be the reason the police were chasing us. He was supposed to tell the police who really killed that sheriff, but he made them think that we did it. I don't know for sure, but I believe he wanted the police to kill us. I have to get David away from them somehow."

Suddenly, one of the cops walked up to the bedroom window. Tom pushed Debra back in the closet and closed the door. Kate walked over, stood in front of the window, looked out, and waved at the cop. The cop turned and walked away. Tom opened the closet door.

"I can't put the two of you at risk," Debra said. "I have to get away from here." Kate walked over and stood beside Tom. She looked at Debra standing there in the closet with the crutch under one arm.

"You can't even walk, Debra. You need to stay here for a few days," Kate said.

"They won't hurt David until they find you," Tom said. "That's why they're so interested in finding you or your dead body. If they know you're still alive, they may try to use David as bait to get to you." Tom walked to the window and looked out. "So I agree with Kate. You need to stay here until you're better. We can keep you hidden until the police leave."

"I guess you're right. I can't get around very well."

"It's settled, then," Kate said.

Suddenly there was a knock at the front door. They closed Debra up in the closet, and Tom went to the door. Captain Martz was standing there holding a piece of cloth. "My men found this about twenty yards from the riverbank. We think it could be from the shirt that woman was wearing." He cleared his throat. "I think we're going to have to search the house."

"Do you have a search warrant?"

"Yeah, I keep it in my shoe!" he said. He shoved Tom out of the way and stepped inside the door.

"Hey! You can't come in here without a warrant!"

"It's called reasonable suspicion, old man. Now get out of the way before I have to arrest you for interfering with police business." Kate came over and took hold of Tom's hand. She stood beside him, trembling with fear.

"You're scaring my wife!" Tom yelled.

"We'll be out of here in a couple of minutes... if she's not in here."

He motioned for two of his men to come in the house. Debra had the door to the closet cracked, and she could hear the conversation. Captain Martz sent one of the men toward the back bedroom and one to the front bedroom. Debra heard the cop coming to the back bedroom. As quietly as possible, she eased the closet door closed.

The cop came in the room and looked under the bed and in the bathroom. He opened the door to the big walk-in closet. Debra had hidden as far back behind the clothes as she could. When the cop walked into the closet, she could see him through the hanging clothes. She recognized him as Officer Johnson, the man who had put his hands all over her the day before. Rather than fear, rage began to build quickly. She tightened her grip on the crutch in her hand as she clenched her teeth. Johnson began moving clothes out of the way on the opposite side of the closet. Debra slowly moved the crutch out through the clothes and aligned it so that it was between his legs.

With all of her might she jerked the crutch upward and practically crushed his testicles. He let out a blood-curdling howl as he bent over and grabbed his crotch. Debra hobbled out from behind the clothes, grabbed his gun, and yanked it from his side holster. She forced him toward the door of the closet as he held on to his groin, grimacing in pain.

Captain Martz heard the commotion and came running toward the back bedroom. He met Debra, with a handful of Johnson's hair in one hand and his gun in the other. She had the barrel of the gun pointed at the back of Johnson's head.

She came from the bedroom with a sudden jolt of uncontrollable anger. All the frustration and stress from the mistreatment and near-death situations that had been building up inside came to the surface. She was like a person outside of her own body, and her anger reached its limit. Debra had always been a calm and well-reserved person, always in control of her emotions. She had always been able to control her temper and not let it get the best of her, but this time she gave in. This situation had pushed her to the breaking point. A stranger inside her, someone she didn't know existed, had begun to emerge, a person with a totally different character. Fear and anger had created this stranger that took control for a short time.

When Debra caught sight of Captain Martz, she began screaming at him from the very pit of her soul. "Get out of this house, you fat tub of lard, or I'm going to blow his head off," Debra screamed as she hobbled along behind Johnson, shoving him forward while still holding a handful of his hair.

Captain Martz began stepping backward as he pointed his gun in her direction. "Tell the rest of your men to lay their weapons down right now!" she shouted.

"Drop that gun and let Officer Johnson go," Captain Martz said as he backed into the living room. Ignoring him, Debra looked over at the cop that had come from the other bedroom. He had his gun trained on her.

"Drop that gun! Do it now!" Debra yelled. When the young cop saw the look on her face, he knew she wasn't in any mood for negotiation. He glanced over at Captain Martz and then quickly dropped his gun.

"Now, I want you to go outside and tell the rest of those cops that if they call for help over their radios, your captain here is going to get a bullet right between the eyes. Now get out of here!" she yelled. The young cop ran out the door.

"You better drop that gun, miss," Captain Martz demanded again. Debra gave him an intense stare.

"I'm only going to say this one more time, Captain … Martz, is it? I want you to get your fat gut out of this house and leave these people alone. They had nothing to do with my being here. I was holding them hostage." She looked at Tom and Kate, who were standing there numb with fright.

Kate, despite her fear, spoke up with a trembling voice and said, "Now, honey, you know that's not true." Debra looked at Captain Martz and motioned toward the door.

While aiming his gun at her, Captain Martz started moving backward toward the door that led to the front porch. Debra kept her slender frame well hidden behind Johnson as they moved closer and closer to the door, forcing Captain Martz out of Tom and Kate's house.

"You best drop that gun, young lady, and let him go, if you know what's good for you," Captain Martz said.

"If I know what's good for me?" Debra's fury elevated to an even higher point. "Oh, I know that turning myself over to you or this pathetic excuse for a human being that I have here is definitely not good for me … especially after what he did," Debra said, jerking Johnson's head back and forth. Johnson began to whimper and whine.

"Now, Miss Benson, Johnson was only doing his job. I'm sure it was because you resisted arrest and nothing more," Captain Martz said.

"Resisted arrest? He put his filthy hands all over me." She raised the knee of her injured leg and kneed Johnson in the behind. He let out a yell. "Stop crying like a baby!" she shouted. "It's not much fun to be humiliated is it?" She hesitated. "I didn't get a chance to resist arrest, isn't that right, Johnson?" He didn't respond. She jerked his hair, pulled his head backward, and shouted in his ear even louder, "Isn't that right, Johnson?"

"Yes!" he bellowed in pain.

"Now, we're going out that door to the porch, Captain."

"Come now, Debra," Kate said. "This is only going to make things worse."

"I don't care," she said. "I'm sick of being treated like a criminal by these people, and I'm sick of running from them. I have had it. I'm going to give to them what they've been giving to me. It's time people stood up to bullies like this." She jerked Johnson's hair and shoved him forward. He howled in pain. "Now, Captain, I want you to put your gun on the floor," Debra said in a low, demanding tone.

"I'm not doing anything of the sort."

"You'll do it, or I'll shoot this pervert right here." She shoved the gun even harder against Johnson's head.

"Captain, please! Do as she says!" Johnson yelled. "She's crazy! She'll kill me if you don't!"

"That's right—I'm crazy!" Debra screamed. "Just crazy enough to use this gun on all of you if I have to!"

"Just calm down now," Captain Martz said, standing near the front door. Debra raised the gun and fired. Johnson jerked his head sideways and grabbed his right ear as he let out a scream. The bullet hit the doorjamb just beside Captain Martz's head. Plaster dust and splinters of wood blew out from the wall and doorjamb. He ducked his head and put his left hand up to shield the debris. He looked over his left shoulder as plaster dust drifted past his head. He was scared out of his wits, but trying not to show it. He had been in situations before, but none like this one.

"I've had firearms training and a self-defense course, so I know how to use this gun. Now I'm tired of getting kicked around. I'm a desperate woman," Debra said. "The next one is going to be between your eyes, if you don't drop that gun right now!" she yelled. He looked into her eyes and saw complete determination. That, combined with her belligerent and aggressive demeanor, was enough confirmation of her resolve. He knew negotiation was out of the question.

Trying not to show any signs of weakness or loss of control of the situation, reluctantly he said, "Well, I don't want to see anyone get hurt, so I'm going to put my gun down. Now you just calm down." He dropped the gun and backed out onto the porch. Debra shoved Johnson through the doorway and onto the porch. She looked around and saw three police cars and three cops standing there. Two of them were pointing their guns at her and yelling for her to drop her gun. Debra said, "Captain, tell your men to drop those guns now, or I will splatter Johnson's brains all over this porch!"

"Okay, men, drop those guns!" Captain Martz said, retreating down the steps and off the porch. The cops dropped their guns.

Tom and Kate had followed them out on the porch. "Tom, what do you have to drive? Debra asked.

"I have an old truck parked in the barn."

"I'm going to have to borrow it."

"I'll go get it," Tom said, hurrying off the porch and running toward the barn.

Getting angrier and feeling more and more humiliated by the minute, Captain Martz said, "You're not going to get very far, young lady."

"Shut up! Now, I want all of you to move over there." She pointed to the left side of the yard. There was no response as they stood there with blank expressions on their faces. They were trying to deal with the embarrassment of knowing this woman had complete control of the situation. "I said move!" She motioned with her gun. They took a few steps in the direction she had pointed. Suddenly, Johnson tried to spin around and twist away from her. She held on to his hair, drew the gun back, and hit him on the side of the head. He went down to his knees, screaming in pain. Captain Martz and his men rushed forward and bent down to reach for their guns. Debra raised Johnson's gun and fired into the ground beside them.

"Hold it right there!" she yelled. They stopped and jumped backward slowly moving away from their guns.

Tom brought the truck from the barn. "I heard a gunshot. I thought you may have shot one of them," he said.

"No, but not because they don't deserve it," she said, giving Captain Martz a detestable look. "Tom, I want you to collect all their guns, take them down to the river, and toss them in—and don't forget the two on the floor in the house."

She waited until he had gathered up all the guns and taken them to the river. "I hate to keep causing you all this work, Tom, but could you collect their hand radios and their car keys and put them in the bed of the truck." After a brief pause, she said, "Oh … don't forget the microphones from their car radios too," as she looked at Captain Martz and smiled. Tom did as Debra asked.

Captain Martz was fuming. He raised his hand and pointed his finger at Debra. "I'll find you wherever you go! Nobody makes a fool of me and gets away with it!"

Debra ignored him. At the moment, Captain Martz's following her was the least of her worries; getting out of there alive was her number-one priority. "Now, Tom, I want you to unplug all the telephones in your house and put them in your truck."

"I'll help," Kate said.

Tom and Kate came back with two phones and put them in the truck. Reminded of his own daughter, Tom held out some money for Debra.

"Maybe this will help," he said. Debra smiled, took the money, and stuffed it into the front pocket of her jeans.

Debra had calmed down somewhat, but she still kept her gun trained on Johnson. "Thanks, so much, both of you. I'll see that you get this back. You've been so kind," Debra said with a smile. Kate came over and looked at Debra and hugged her.

"Take care of yourself, dear," she said with a sweet, motherly smile. Debra had a flashback of her own mother and how much Kate reminded her of her. Debra held on to Kate as her eyes welled up with tears. She turned Johnson's hair loose and pushed him forward forcing him to walk around the truck. She opened the passenger door.

"How far is it to the highway, Tom?" Debra asked.

"It's about four miles," he replied.

Debra was still simmering with resentment for Captain Martz, and she saw another chance to get in one more jab before parting company.

"Well, Captain, I can honestly say it has not been a pleasure," Debra said in her most condescending tone. "But here's your chance to work off some of those doughnuts you've been eating all these years at the taxpayers' expense. Just as soon as I leave, you can run those four miles to the highway; maybe someone will pick you up. That is, if there's anyone left in this area that doesn't hate you or that you haven't kicked around." Captain Martz just looked at her and gritted his teeth. "I'm going to take Mr. Pervert Johnson with me for a short distance, just for insurance," she said.

"If you take him, you can add kidnapping to all the other charges," Captain Martz said.

Debra looked at him and replied, "It doesn't matter anyway. My life is such a mess now that one more mistake is not going to make any difference." She forced Johnson into the passenger side of the truck and told him to move over under the steering wheel. "Tom, I'll try to leave your truck someplace where you can find it."

Johnson started the truck, and they drove away. Debra sat motionless for a short time. Her hands began to tremble, but she made sure that Johnson didn't see her. As the adrenalin began to subside, she started to gain control of her emotions once more and the well-reserved young woman began to emerge.

"How far is it to Burtonsville from here, Johnson?" Debra asked.

"It's about ten or twelve miles. Are you going to kill me?" he asked with a whimper.

"Do you think I should?" she asked as they came to a stop at the highway.

"No, ma'am. I'll cooperate. I'll take you wherever you want to go." Trying not to laugh, Debra looked away.

"Turn right, toward Burtonsville," Debra directed. Johnson complied.

They drove a few miles. "Do you have a wife or a girlfriend, Johnson?"

"Yes, ma'am. I have a girlfriend."

"You don't treat her like you did me in those woods, do you?" Before he could answer, she said, "Are you one of those spineless wimps that likes to beat on people that are not as strong as you?"

"No, ma'am. I'm really sorry about that."

Debra saw a gas station ahead on the right. "Pull over at this station, behind the building." He did as she commanded. "I'm going to put you in that restroom around the side of the building, and you better keep your mouth shut for at least thirty minutes, until I get away. I might stay around and see if you wait the full thirty minutes, so you better be quiet." Debra kept trying not to laugh.

"You think I'm stupid or something?" Johnson asked. "As soon as you leave, I'm going to yell my head off."

"You do that, and I might just be waiting outside the door to shoot you!" Johnson looked at her with no expression. Debra told him to get out of the truck, put the gun in her pants pocket, and pulled her shirt down over it. She opened the door to the women's restroom, and they went inside. Ordering him to remove his shirt and sit down on the toilet, she cuffed him to the handrail on the wall, stuffed paper towels in his mouth, and tied his shirt around his face. He was whimpering, whining, and cursing.

"Now, you remember what I said about not making any noise for thirty minutes." He mumbled a few words that were too distorted to understand. She walked out the door and closed it behind her. She found a piece of paper in a garbage dumpster behind the building, took an ink pen from the glove box of Tom's truck, wrote "Out of Order" and hung it on the doorknob. She listened, but she couldn't hear a sound from the restroom. "I guess Johnson is stupid enough to think that I might wait around to see if he makes any noise." She began to chuckle.

Debra climbed in the truck and drove away. *What am I going to do now,* she thought. She drove toward Burtonsville, still wondering what to do, when she saw a little motel on the right side of the road. Debra pulled Tom's truck behind the building and parked so it couldn't be seen from the road. After renting the last room on the opposite end from the motel office, she went in and sat down on the bed. Trying desperately to figure out how to get David out of jail, she walked over to the window. Looking out the window, she noticed an old, dilapidated gas station that was closed and abandoned across the road from the motel. There was a telephone booth standing out near the road. "I'm going to find out, Bill, if you are a good guy or a bad one," she said out loud.

She went to the front desk and asked the manager to check the air conditioner in her room. When he left the office, Debra lagged behind. She switched room keys for the room two doors up from hers. She then followed the manager back to her room. After he checked the air conditioner and found nothing wrong, he said a few words in a foreign language while waving his hands and left the room. Debra just shrugged her shoulders and smiled. After he left, Debra looked out the door and watched him walk back into the office. She quickly slipped into the room two doors up and locked the door behind her. She lay on the bed and began to devise a plan.

CHAPTER 11

The same day Debra jumped off the cliff to escape them; Captain Martz and his men arrested David and took him to the Burtonsville jail. He kept telling them to call the FBI and they would be able to explain everything, but Captain Martz just laughed.

"I told you, son. You can make your own phone call when we get to the jail."

They parked in front of the jail and took David inside and put him in a cell. They sent for a nurse to clean and dress his wound. After the nurse left and they were finished with their paperwork, David said, "I want to make my phone call now." One of the cops took him out of the cell and handed him a phone. Just as he began to dial, Captain Martz came in the room, grabbed the phone out of his hand, and slammed it down.

"I just got off the phone with the FBI, and they said for us to hold you until they get here. They said there's a felony warrant out for you, for the murder of two people. Their bodies were found in a cabin in the Adirondack Mountains. So there will be no phone call for you today."

"Who did you talk to? Let me guess, Bill Rogers, right? I bet he called you—am I right again?"

"It doesn't matter. You're staying in one of those cells until they get here." He took David by the arm and forced him across the hall. He shoved him into one of the jail cells and slammed the door.

"Didn't you recognize his voice? I bet it sounded a lot like your anonymous phone caller, didn't it?" Captain Martz looked at him for a few seconds. "You know I'm right, don't you? It was the same person who told you exactly where we were. And the same person who told you about Sheriff White being dead in the trunk of that car, wasn't it?" David said. Captain Martz just stood there looking at him. "You know I'm telling the truth. But you're not going to do anything about it, are you?" David shouted, slamming his hand against the bars of his cell.

"Just shut up and sit down! I have to go back to the river; the FBI wants us to find that girl's body." As he turned and walked away, he shouted, "Hey, Joyce, call the Burtonsville Water Rescue and tell them to meet me out on 168 about ten or twelve miles west of here. Thanks, darlin'!"

"Captain Martz, don't you see? Bill wants to make sure she's dead! She can cause problems for Senator Braco!" David yelled at the top of his lungs. Captain Martz just kept walking away.

David sat down on the cot in his cell. He clenched his fists and gritted his teeth. *This thing is getting bigger and more complicated every day,* he thought. *How can I explain it all to anyone without any proof? Bill is the only one who knows the truth, and he's using his FBI status to control these cops.* He thought about what he would say to Bill. "I have to try to convince him to tell them the truth," he said.

As he sat pondering what to do next, he thought about Debra. *What if she died when she jumped off that cliff? How can this be happening? I met the most wonderful woman in the world, and now she may be dead. It's entirely my fault,* he thought. *I should have done more to protect her.* He slammed his fist down on the bed then lay down and tried to think of a plan to get out of this mess.

Captain Martz came back to the jail a short time after dark. David heard him come in. He jumped up and began to yell for Captain Martz to come in and talk to him. Captain Martz walked in the room near David's cell. "Did you find her?"

"No, my guess is when we go on down the river tomorrow, we'll find her body."

"Or maybe she got away," David said with a smile.

"Either way, we'll get her. Don't you worry; if she's alive, she'll be in here with you tomorrow," he said as he turned and walked away.

"You are going to take her alive, aren't you, Captain?" David asked.

Captain Martz stopped and turned around and looked at him. "That all depends on her, now doesn't it. If she gives herself up, there won't be any problems—but she won't get any special consideration because she's a woman," Captain Martz said. He turned and walked away.

David lay back down on the bed. He was so relieved that they hadn't found her dead. *There's still a chance she's alive,* he thought.

As he lay there thinking about the time he had spent with her the last few weeks, he began to smile. *They've been the happiest days of my life,* he thought. He thought about how much he loved her and what it would mean if she *was* dead—how empty his life would be without her. Even though he had only known her for a short time, he knew his life would never be the same. Before he closed his eyes, he said a prayer, and he was able to sleep with the hope that she was still alive.

The next morning, before he went with the water rescue team, Captain Martz went to talk to David. "The FBI said they would be here today to talk to you. They want us to bring back that woman's body, and then they are going to take over the investigation," he said with an aggravated look. "We do all the work, and they take all the credit."

"You have to help us, Captain. They're going to kill us."

"There's nothing I can do. I have to go and meet the water rescue team," he said. Then he left the room. David stood staring in disbelief of his lackadaisical attitude.

Several hours later, he heard someone walking into the room. He stood up and walked over to the cell front. He saw his friend, Bill Rogers, and one of the cops walking up to his cell. "Well, if it isn't my boss and friend here to rescue me."

"David, this officer is going to escort you to the interrogation room where we can talk," Bill said.

"Interesting choice of words, Bill. Who's going to be interrogating whom?"

"We'll talk when we get in there." The cop told David to put his hands through the opening in the door so that he could put the handcuffs on. He then opened the cell door and took David to the interrogation room, with Bill following.

They sat down at a table across from each other. After the cop left the room, David quickly said, "Okay, Bill, I know you're the reason those cops were waiting for us at the train station in Utica, and I know you're working with those killers Jack Braco hired. Now, do you want to explain why you're doing this and what's going on?"

"I can't right now, David, but you have to tell me where Debra is."

"Are you kidding me? You bastard, you almost got us killed. Why didn't you tell the police who killed that sheriff?"

"I can't explain it right now, but you're going to have to trust me. Now where is Debra?"

"Trust you? That's a laugh. I don't know where she is, and I wouldn't tell you if I knew."

Bill reached across the table and slapped David across the face. David jumped up; his hands cuffed behind his back, and shoved his chair against the wall with his foot.

"Why don't you take these cuffs off and try that again?" They were glaring across the table at each other. "You had it all planned out from the start, didn't you, Bill? That's why you didn't want anyone else to know that I was undercover. It wasn't just to protect Senator Braco's reputation, was it?" He paused for a second and glared at Bill. "You wanted to keep everyone else from knowing where I was and what I was doing! You planned to get rid of me too! Didn't you?" David yelled.

"David, I knew you could find out who was blackmailing Senator Braco. Neither of you was supposed to survive the shootout at the cabin, but I knew if you did survive, you would bring Debra back with you. You don't understand the implications if the public were to find out about Debra being Jack Braco's daughter. You just don't realize what certain people are prepared to do to make sure they don't find out."

"Bill, I'm not going to stand by and let you and Jack Braco kill her!" David paused for a second and said, "What happened to you, Bill?" Bill turned and walked toward the door. "Is money that important to you that you're willing to sacrifice human life for it?" Bill took hold of the doorknob, pausing for a second, his back toward David.

"That police captain seems to think she's dead." He turned around and looked at David. "That would solve everyone's problems—everyone's but yours, David." He paused for a moment longer, and then he began to smile. "I'm going to see that you go to prison for murdering that sheriff!" He jerked the door open and walked out. David kicked one of the chairs toward the door as Bill left the room. One of the cops came in and took David back to his cell.

David lay on the cot, thinking about the situation. The longer he thought about it, the angrier he became. He could not believe that his friend had betrayed him and used him like this for money.

Later that day, David was resting on his cot when he heard loud noises and commotion. Captain Martz came in huffing and puffing. He paced back and forth in front of David's cell.

"I'm going to get that little smart-alecky girlfriend of yours if it's the last thing I do on this earth!"

David jumped up and took hold of the bars, and a big smile came across his face. He knew Debra was alive.

"What happened?" David asked with great anticipation.

"She held me and my men at gun point, kidnapped Officer Johnson, and got away. She left us at a farmhouse, and one of my men had to ride that farmer's tractor to go call for help. She even took the telephones from the house with her." David just stood and laughed as Captain Martz was ranting, raving, and describing the aftermath of his meeting with Debra.

"Do you think that's funny?" Captain Martz stepped forward and grabbed the bars of David's cell and shoved his face up close to David's.

Without moving or backing away, David emphatically replied, "Yes, actually I do!"

Just then one of the cops came in and said, "They found Johnson in the women's restroom at a gas station out on 168, west of here. He was bound and gagged." David laughed even louder. Captain Martz turned and stormed out of the room, complaining and swearing as he went.

David was so excited he could hardly contain himself. "She's alive!" he shouted. "She's alive!" He lay down on his cot and thanked God for sparing Debra's life.

After some time went by, Bill Rogers came back to David's cell. As he walked up he could see the exhilaration on David's face.

"Well, Bill, looks like the fly is in the ointment again," David said with a great big smile.

"You knew she was alive, didn't you?"

"I kind of suspected it. She *is* resilient—that's what I love about her. Besides, she told me she was on the diving team back in high school," David said. He moved forward, glaring straight at Bill with squinted eyes and a condescending smile.

"I'm asking you again, David, where is she?"

"And I'm telling you again, Bill, I don't know, and I wouldn't tell you if I did!" David said through clenched teeth.

"You're going to regret this, David! I promise you, you're both going to regret this!" Bill shouted. David just gave him another big grin. Bill slammed his hands against the bars, turned, and stomped away.

Debra walked out of the motel room and went to the phone booth across the road at the abandoned gas station. She asked the operator to connect her with the police station in Burtonsville. When a police officer answered, she asked if there was an FBI agent there by the name of Bill Rogers. They told her to hold on. Bill came to the phone. "Hello, this is Bill Rogers. Can I help you?"

"Bill, this is Debra Benson."

Bill caught his breath, hesitated, and said, "Can you give me the number to where you are?" He moved the receiver to his left ear and then asked the person behind the counter for a piece of paper. He took a pen out of his shirt pocket and said, "I'll call you back." She gave him the number of the payphone. After they hung up, Bill went outside, took out his cell phone, and dialed the number. Debra answered.

"Debra, I was just talking to David and Captain Martz, and it looks like we have this little mix-up all worked out. Now—"

Bill," Debra interrupted, "I have a proposal for you to pass on to the police. I'll turn myself over to them if they let David go. He has nothing to do with any of this."

"Okay, let me see what I can do. Where are you?"

"I'm at an abandoned gas station a few miles west of Burtonsville on 168. I'll be waiting in the station. Tell the police to let you bring David with you, or there's no deal." Debra hesitated for a second and then said, "I need a phone number where I can get in touch with you."

"Okay, I'll give you my cell phone number, but the reception is not very good in this area." He gave her the number. "Now, if there's nothing else, I'll be there as soon as I can."

"No, that's all," Debra said. They hung up, and Debra went back to her room. Bill made a couple of other phone calls, and then he went to his car and left the police station.

Debra was sitting in the motel after calling Bill. She suspected she could not trust him, but she had to be sure. She planned to wait in the room to see who showed up at the abandoned gas station. After about an hour and a half she heard tires squealing. She went to the window and moved the curtain just wide enough to see out. She looked across the road, and getting out of a car were the three men who had been chasing her and David.

Bill's predictable, she thought. She watched as the three men went in the building with their guns drawn. Her blood boiled with anger. *They're going to kill David if I don't do something.* She watched as they came out of the building. One of them stood and looked across the road toward the little motel. He called the other men. They got in their car, drove over to the motel, and went in the office.

When Debra saw them coming across the road, she moved back from the window. After spending a few moments in the motel office, they came to the room the manager had given them. Debra was standing by the door of her room listening as the men walked past and went to the room she was supposed to be in. She became nervous and trembled with fear as she heard them kick the door open. After kicking the furniture around for a short time, she could here them swearing as they came back out of the room. They had done exactly what she had suspected they might. She listened as they went back to their car and drove back across the road to the gas station. She peeked through the crack in the curtain and watched as one of them got out of the car and went to the phone booth. After making a call, he went back to the car and they drove off toward Burtonsville. Debra went over to the bed and sat down, still shaking. She began to cry, and then after a few minutes she pounded her fists on the bed.

Bill was on his way back to the police station. It had been about two hours since he had spoken to Debra when his cell phone rang.

"Hello."

"Bill, this is Debra."

"Debra, I was just going to call the num—"

"Cut the horse crap, Bill!" Debra interrupted. "I know you set us up. I know you're working for my father, and I know you're part of the group that's trying to kill me. So now that we both know where we stand, I have—!"

"Wait, Debra I sent some—"

Debra interrupted him again, saying, "Shut up! You sent those men to kill me. They were the same men who killed Ashley and Ben at the cabin. They are the same men who killed that sheriff, and they have been trying to kill David and me. So I don't want to here any more of your lies! Now, where is David?"

"I'm working on getting him out of jail."

"I said for you to stop lying. You work for the FBI. You can get anyone out of jail," she said. Bill's tone of voice changed.

"Well, just so you know where I stand, Debra, I'll kill him if you don't do exactly as I say!" There was a long pause.

Then Debra said, "I'll call you back, and the next time, you better have David with you!" Debra slammed the phone down in the phone booth and hobbled back across the road to her room.

"Wait, Debra! Don't hang up!" Bill began cursing as he slammed his cell phone closed and threw it on the passenger seat.

He drove back to the police station and asked to see David's personal items. He took David's belt and watch and looked them over. Then he gave them back to the police officer behind the counter and went in to see David.

"I had an interesting phone call a couple of hours ago and then again just a few minutes ago. Seems our Miss Benson wants you released. So I made a phone call to a friend, and they sent some people to take care of her."

"The same people who came to the cabin to kill Debra and me. I wondered how they knew my name, but I didn't put it together. I thought I could trust my good friend," David said as he glared menacingly at Bill. "I just wouldn't let myself believe that you would be involved with those types of people. How stupid was I?"

"David … David, just chill out. This thing is much bigger than you or me. You're way too sensitive anyway."

"Let me out of this cell without any handcuffs, and I'll show you some bare-knuckle sensitivity," David said.

"Just settle down. This will be over soon," Bill growled. David stood staring at Bill, motionless as he tried to understand this strange behavior from a once-decent person.

"Debra is much smarter than I gave her credit. She wasn't where she said she would be. I suppose she wanted to test me. I had the number she gave me traced. The second phone call came from the same phone booth. I'm going to look for her myself, and I'm going to take you with me so you can see what happens to her when I find her."

David grabbed the bars to his cell and yelled, "You better not harm her, or I'll kill you!" Bill ignored him and went in and filled out extradition papers. Afterward, they gave David his personal items. Bill had the cops put handcuffs on David and put him in the backseat of his car.

"Where are you going?" Captain Martz asked.

Bill leaned out the window with a slight grin. "I'm going to take him back to Utica for prosecution."

"He's lying. He's going to kill me, and the girl too!" David yelled out the window of the car. David sat looking through the window at captain Martz as Bill drove away. Bill looked at David through the rearview mirror.

"You need you to keep your mouth shut!"

"Where are we going?"

"Debra was supposed to be at an abandoned gas station just west of here. I believe she's close by. I'm going to use you to lure her out, so I can end this once and for all."

"How much money is Senator Braco paying you to betray a friend and kill human beings, Bill? It must be a lot," David said.

"You just don't understand, David. There's more to it than just money." David leaned back in the car seat.

"There're only two things that will make a man do crazy things, things out of the ordinary," David said. "One is money, and the other is a woman. We know there's money involved; I guess there must be a woman too."

"Just sit back there and keep your mouth shut," he said.

Bill drove west on Route 68 until he saw the abandoned gas station. He looked over to the left at the motel as he drove slowly by. Then he turned around and came back.

When Debra heard a car slow down, she got up from the bed and looked through the crack in the curtain. She saw a car drive by slowly, and then it sped up and kept going. A short time later, she watched as the car came back and turned into the parking lot of the motel. She moved back away from the curtain.

Bill pulled up next to the motel office and parked the car. "Carmine checked this motel, and she wasn't here. I think I'll check for myself. She has to be here," Bill said. "She's made two phone calls from that phone booth, and she wasn't at that old gas station when Carmine came to look for her. She's probably staying here." He got out of the car, came around to the back door, and loosened one side of David's handcuffs. He stepped back and put his hand on his gun under his coat and said, "Put the cuffs around the pull handle of the car door, David." David just looked at him and didn't move. "Don't make me shoot you right here."

"I'll have to put my hands in front of me," David said.

"Just do it," Bill said. David did as Bill commanded. "Now get back in the car and keep your trap shut. I'm going to see if the person at the desk has seen her," he said with a smirk. He took a picture of Debra out of his pocket as he closed the car door.

"Don't move," he said. He walked toward the office.

After the car stopped at the motel office, Debra moved over to the door. She cracked the door open and watched as a man opened the back door on the right side of the car and David stepped out. She was so happy to see him that she almost jerked the door open, but she forced herself to wait. She saw him force David to handcuff himself to the car door. Then he made David get in the backseat of the car and close the door. After the man went in the office, Debra eased out of her room and closed the door. She slowly and quietly turned to her left, trying to be as inconspicuous as possible. David was looking left, watching Bill through the front windows of the office. He didn't see Debra sneaking out the door of her room.

Debra went around behind the building and climbed into Tom's truck. She sat there momentarily, thinking about what she should do. She knew Bill was going to hurt David if she didn't do something, and she began to get angry. The longer she sat, the angrier she became.

Bill showed the manager the picture of Debra. The manager explained how Debra had been there but that when the other men had looked for her, they hadn't found her. After a few more questions, Bill turned and walked out of the office.

Debra became furious at the thought of Bill hurting David. She started the truck, jerked the gearshift into drive and took off. She drove around the building extremely fast. Bill had walked out of the office and was standing by his car. He had just taken hold of the door handle when he heard the truck coming around the building. He opened the door as he looked around in the direction of the sound.

When Debra saw Bill standing by the car with the door half open, she stepped on the gas and drove straight toward him. When he saw the truck and the speed at which it was moving, he knew he only had seconds to react before the truck would be on top of him. He jerked the door open and jumped in the car. Just as the door closed, the big truck slammed into the side of his car. It smashed through the door, breaking the driver's door glass and the rear door glass as well. Debra put the truck into reverse and backed up about fifteen feet. Bill pulled himself up out of the seat by holding onto the steering wheel. He was covered with glass.

Debra jerked the truck into gear and came forward again. David moved over as far to the right side of the car as he could. Bill was stunned from the first impact and could not respond quickly enough before the second one. The truck pushed the door on top of Bill, and he screamed as the door pinned him. Debra saw the top of the car disappear as the truck crushed the side of the car and moved on top of it. She jerked the truck into reverse and backed up. She jumped out with the gun she had taken from Officer Johnson in her hand. She hobbled over to the driver's side door and shoved the gun inside the smashed car, pointing it directly at Bill. Bill was lying under the door, semi-conscious and bleeding from cuts on his face.

"Debra!" David yelled. Debra hurried around the back of the car to the other side and opened the back door. David stood up with his hands still cuffed to the door. She grabbed David and hugged him.

"David, I was so afraid I would never see you again," she said, choking back tears.

"Debra, I thought you were dead," David exclaimed, "but we don't have time now. We have to get out of here! Get the keys to the handcuffs, and get his gun." Debra jerked open the front passenger door and checked Bill's coat pocket. He was moving around and groaning. She found the keys, put her hand under his coat, and pulled his gun from the holster. She took the cuffs off David's hands, and they hugged briefly.

"I missed you so much, David. I was so scared!" Debra exclaimed, hugging him.

"Let's go, Debra."

She handed him Bill's gun and then hobbled around the back of Bill's car to the driver's side of the truck. The manager of the motel came running out just as Debra climbed into the driver's seat.

Debra took off out of the parking lot, spinning the tires and throwing gravel. The manager chased after the truck, waving his arms, shaking his fists, and yelling at them in a foreign language.

"Go east toward Burtonsville. There's a road that turns off before you get into town," David said. Debra turned the truck toward Burtonsville. "My gosh! Debra, that was the most incredible thing I have ever seen! What happened to that girl I first met?"

"What girl?" she said with a smile.

"You know? The mild-mannered girl who's been asking me, 'What are we going to do, David' in every situation we have been in since this mess started."

"Oh … that girl. That girl is gone. I've had enough mistreatment from these people!" Debra exclaimed. "Besides, they were about to hurt the man I love," she said. She looked over at him and put the back of her hand on his face.

David took hold of her hand and began to caress and kiss it.

"I heard what you did to that police captain and his men," David said with a chuckle.

"They made me mad. They were mistreating that nice elderly couple that helped me, so they deserved it."

"Well, remind me to never make you mad."

"Speaking of that nice couple, this truck belongs to them," Debra said.

"I guess we'll have to pay for another one when this is over. It looks like it is damaged awfully bad, and there's steam coming out from under the hood," David commented.

"It won't go very fast. It seems to be losing power."

"We won't be able to get very far," David said.

David looked at Debra with excitement in his voice and said, "Tell me how you were able to survive that jump from that rock cliff. Is that how you hurt your leg?"

"Yes, I thought I was going die," she said. "When I hit the water, I just held my breath and hoped I would stay under until the cops had walked away. Remember I told you I used to be on the diving team in high school? I would spend hours practicing holding my breath underwater. Over time, I began to get really good at it, but I never dreamed it would become useful in a life-and-death situation." She looked at him and smiled. "I must have passed out. I don't remember anything after that until I woke up in Tom and Kate Browner's house. I bruised my left leg really bad. They helped me and let me spend the night. Kate gave me some of her daughter's clothes. Then that fat cop came and started pushing those nice people around."

"I'm glad they were there to help you, Debra."

At that moment they came to a road that turned off 168. "Turn left here," David said. Debra made a quick left turn. They were still heading east.

"This may be a truck route around town; let's see where it takes us," David said.

They talked at length about Bill betraying David and what they could do to keep him from catching up to them. They drove east in the old, battered truck, wondering what Bill Rogers and his thugs had planed for them next. Knowing they couldn't trust the cops or the FBI, they decided to try to make it to the FBI office in New York City.

CHAPTER 12

The manager of the motel came over to Bill and helped him out from under the car door. Bill stood up and staggered slightly.

"I call police!" the manger shouted in his heavy accent.

"No, no—here is something for your trouble," Bill said. He took out his billfold and gave the man some money. "Don't call the police." He pulled out his badge and showed it to the man. The man took the money and went back in the office. Bill hobbled around to the back of his car. He opened the trunk, took out a briefcase that held another pistol, and put it in his shoulder holster. He took out his cell phone and checked the screen. It read "no service." He limped into the motel office and asked to use the phone. The man told him he could if he would rent a room. Bill knew he had several things to do before the motel manager involved the police, so in order to keep the manager happy, he agreed. He dialed the phone, waited a few seconds, and someone answered.

"It's me," Bill said. "No, they got away, but I have a little surprise for them." He paused. "What? No, it's okay…don't worry. I'll take care of it. Tell them to meet me at that little motel across from that abandoned gas station. They'll know what you're talking about … don't worry … I will." He hung up the phone. He asked the manager for the room key and then asked, "Do you have any bandages and alcohol?"

"I charge for bandages and alcohol," the manger said.

"Okay," I don't care!" he said and handed the man his credit card. The manager gave him the alcohol and bandages.

After renting the room, he went to his car and took a small briefcase and a bottle of scotch out of the trunk and took them to the room. He set the bottle on the night table and laid the small briefcase down on the bed then went to the bathroom. He used the alcohol to clean the cuts on his head and face and then put bandages on them. He took a glass from the bathroom and poured himself a drink of scotch.

An hour or so later, he heard a car pull up. He went to the door and motioned for the men to come in. Carmine and the other two men came in the room.

"What happened to you?" Carmine asked.

"Just shut up and listen." He opened the briefcase and took out a small, thin box that looked like a laptop computer. He opened the screen, flipped a switch, and a little red light came on, and a computer screen lit up.

"This is a tracking device; we use it in kidnapping cases at the bureau. We hide a transmitter in with the money. The closer you get to them, the faster the red light will blink. A dot will appear on the screen when you get within ten miles of them. It also shows the direction they're traveling. I planted a bug on David; he should lead you right to the girl. No screw-ups this time. You're being paid good money to fix this mess—now go do it!" He turned the machine off, closed the lid, and put it back in the briefcase. He handed it to Carmine.

"The motel manager said they headed east toward Burtonsville, but there's a road that turns off 168 before Burtonsville. He said the truckers use it to bypass town. Go that way; they shouldn't be hard to find. The manager said that truck they're driving is damaged badly, so they can't get very far. Here's my phone number in this room. Call me as soon as you capture them. Now go earn your money," Bill said, giving Carmine a stern look.

They left the motel room, got in their car, and opened the brief-case. Carmine activated the tracking device, and the red light began to blink. They drove away in the direction David and Debra had gone.

Bill went in the office. "Now you can call the police."

When Tom's truck overheated and had very little power, Debra pulled over to the side of the road. "We had better try to hide this truck," David said.

With the engine barely running, they drove off the road and into the brush and trees as far as they could. Then they left the truck and began to walk. "I told Tom I would leave his truck where he could find it. I guess he won't be able to find it here," Debra said.

"When this is over, I'll see that he gets a new one," David said.

As they were walking along, Debra suddenly stopped and took hold of David's arm. "I left the gun I took from Officer Johnson in Tom's truck." She threw up her hands. "Oh well, I'm not used to car-rying a gun with me. Do you have Bill's gun?" Debra asked as they began walking again.

"Yes, I do, but hopefully we won't have to use it since they don't know where we are," David said and took Debra's hand.

"That's right. They won't be able to catch up with us now," Debra commented.

With Debra's injured leg, they had to walk slowly. After they had walked a couple of miles, they came upon a truck stop. As they came into the parking lot, they noticed several big semi trucks parked all around. It was almost dark, and they were both very tired.

"I'm starving," Debra said. "There is a restaurant and a grocery store here. Let's go inside and get some food. Tom gave me some money."

"We don't have time to go to the restaurant. We have to be careful—the police will be looking for us. We'll have to buy some snack food at the grocery store; something we can take with us that won't spoil. We may be traveling for a few days. If we get a chance, we can ask one of these truckers for a ride," David said.

"I don't care. I'll take food of any kind right now," Debra replied.

They went inside, and after using the restroom, they picked out several kinds of snack food.

The cashier totaled the items, Debra handed her the money. The lady turned to put the money in the register just as a news program flashed photos of Debra and David on the TV screen behind her. The lady stared briefly at the photos and then turned and looked intently at Debra as she handed her the change. Debra took the change and picked up the bag of food items. David grabbed Debra by the hand, and they hurried out the door.

It was dark outside, and the parking lot was dimly lit. They ran across the parking lot and hid behind a truck. David saw another truck with the engine idling at the end of the parking lot. The truck had a car hauler with several cars on it. He told Debra to wait behind the truck until he came back. He went to the truck with the car hauler and climbed up in the cab. After a couple of minutes, he came back with a handful of car keys.

He took Debra by the hand, and they cautiously hurried to the car hauler. Crouching down, they looked all around to make sure no one was watching. They climbed up on the trailer and went to the driver's side of one of the cars. David chose the car on the bottom section at the front of the car hauler, nearest to the truck cab. It was the highest one off the ground on the bottom section of the car hauler. He knew no one could see inside without climbing up onto the trailer. David tried the keys until one of them opened the door. They climbed inside in the backseat and lay down. David locked the door and put the rest of the car keys in the front seat.

"I think it's dark enough that no one saw us. We'll be safe for a while," David said.

After being still and quiet for a few minutes, they heard the driver get in the truck, and then they began to move. The trucker was driving away.

"Thank goodness," David said. "I know that lady recognized us and called the police. We can relax, at least for now." They knew they had narrowly escaped.

After eating some of their snacks, they held each other close in the cramped backseat of the car.

"Debra, I think we're going to have to do what we discussed before. We need to get to the FBI headquarters in New York City and turn ourselves in. There are some people there that I can trust. I'll call them as soon as we get close enough for them to pick us up. We're headed southeast, but we're still a long way from New York City, and it would be nice if this truck would be going there," David said.

She laid her head on David's shoulder and held his hand. "David, when we were separated I was so scared. I thought they were going to kill you," she said, her voice cracking. "I don't know what I would do without you." He put his hand on her face and looked into her eyes.

"When I heard that you had jumped off that cliff, it was like my world had ended. I didn't want to live if you were dead. I was so relieved when that police captain came in and said you were alive," David said with a smile.

"We have to fight these people with everything in us. We can't give up, no matter what," Debra said, burying her head in the nape of his neck.

"I will do whatever it takes to keep them from getting to you, Debra. I love you, and as long as there's breath in my body, I won't let them hurt you," David said, pulling her tightly against him.

"We should be home free now, shouldn't we? They don't know where we are."

"Yes, we should be. I can't see how they could find us now. Don't worry anymore; we'll be okay." They tried to relax and enjoy sharing the time together.

The trucker drove until late in the night before he pulled into another truck stop to rest. David and Debra woke up just before daybreak, and one at a time, they went to the restroom and quickly returned to their hideout.

About an hour after daylight, the trucker climbed out of his truck and walked around the trailer with a bar in his hand, smacking the tires, checking them for air pressure. David and Debra stayed down in the seat as low as they could to keep from being seen. The trucker climbed back in the cab, turned his stereo up, and drove away.

Carmine and the other two men slept in the car for a couple of hours. It was daylight as they drove along, watching the red light blink faster. Then the little dot began to light up on the screen.

"We'll catch up with them soon. I don't want the two of you to botch this up," Carmine said. They took out their guns and checked the magazines to make sure they had bullets.

After driving a few more miles, they came up behind the car hauler. The light was blinking really fast, and the dot on the screen was not moving.

"They must be in one of those cars on that trailer," Carmine said. He dropped out from behind the trailer into the left lane and drove up beside the car hauler.

The trucker had been driving for about an hour and a half. David and Debra had just finished eating what was left of their food from the night before when they heard a car come up beside the car hauler. David noticed the car did not drive around the truck; it stayed beside them. David raised his head to look out the side window, expecting to see kids hanging out the window of a car, gawking at the cars on the trailer. Instead, he saw Carmine and the two other men who had been chasing them. He ducked his head down.

"Debra, they've found us!"

"What?" Debra asked, horrified. "How is that possible?"

Suddenly the side window exploded and glass covered them. Debra screamed while trying to shield her eyes.

"Keep your head down!" David shouted, trying to shield her face from the flying glass. The truck driver was listening to his music and didn't see or hear all that was going on outside his truck.

"How did they find us?" Debra screamed again as more bullets hit the car.

"Stay down on the floor, Debra!" David yelled as he climbed over the front seat. He squeezed onto the floor of the front passenger seat, opened the door, and climbed out of the car.

"David, please be careful!"

David climbed up on the top rack of the trailer. He made his way back to the last car, staying on the right side of the trailer. When

Carmine and his men saw David, they slowed down enough to get behind the truck.

The man on the passenger side fired a couple of shots. Trying to keep from being hit, David worked his way over in front of the last car on the top of the trailer. The man on the passenger side leaned out the window and kept shooting as they drove directly behind the trailer.

David pulled out the gun he had gotten from Bill and leaned to his left around the front of the car and fired a couple of shots at their car. Carmine swerved back and forth. David put the gun back in his belt, and then he loosened the metal handle on the straps that were holding the car onto the trailer. The trailer was sloped where the last car was strapped. When David loosened the straps, gravity took over and the car began to move slightly, pulling against the straps. David pushed with all his might, and the car slowly moved backward.

Carmine drove up beside the trailer, and David fired more shots at them, forcing Carmine to drop back behind the truck. When enough of the car was hanging off the trailer, it became unbalanced and then flipped off the back of the car hauler.

Carmine saw the car start to fall and tried to slow down. When the car flipped and hit the road, it slid around sideways and began rolling over. Carmine swerved to miss the car but could not get out of the way. He slammed into the car as it rolled over, and both cars went off the road. Carmine lost control of his car as it tangled with the other car, and began to roll over, ejecting the man on the passenger side. As the man was thrown out the window, the car rolled on top of him.

David began making his way back to the front of the trailer. At that moment, the driver of the truck saw the two cars rolling over, and he slammed on his brakes. David slipped and fell down through the top section of the trailer. He landed on the hood of one of the cars below. By the time the driver brought the big rig to a stop, David had climbed down from the car hood. He made his way to Debra and helped her out of the car. The truck driver jumped out of the truck and ran toward the accident. He looked up and saw David and Debra on the trailer.

He stopped and yelled, "What the heck is going on here?" He stood staring in amazement at them as they climbed down from the trailer.

"Those men are trying to kill us!" David yelled. "You have to help us!"

"But my load! You destroyed one of my ca—" The sound of a gunshot rang out and interrupted him. The bullet zinged past them and hit the trailer, with a loud bang of lead-to-metal. Debra screamed, and they all ducked their heads. David pulled his gun and fired two shots in Carmine's direction. Then his gun was empty. David grabbed Debra's hand, and they ran toward the cab of the truck. David jerked the door open, they climbed onto the running board, and David shoved Debra up in the truck. The truck driver just looked at them.

"What are you doing?" he shouted, not waiting for an answer. He turned and looked in the direction the shot came from. He saw Carmine staggering toward him. He had blood on his face and was pointing his gun in the truck driver's direction. Carmine fired another shot that hit the road just to the left of the driver. A small gash exploded in the blacktop. The bullet made a ricochet zing and tore through the brush off to the side of the road in front of the truck.

"I'm going to kill you two!" he screamed, staggering toward the driver.

"Come on!" David yelled, motioning to the driver as he hung out of the open door of the truck. The driver turned around and began running toward the truck. Carmine tried to wipe some blood from his eyes so he could see where he was shooting.

Debra and David had moved back into the sleeper section of the truck cab. The driver jumped in the seat and threw the truck in gear. He took off as quickly as the big rig would move. Carmine raised his gun and tried to fire another shot, but his gun was empty. He knew the police would be there soon, so he hid the gun in the back of his wrecked car. Two other cars drove up and stopped next to Carmine's car, which was lying on its top, resting against the car David had shoved off the trailer.

The second man was crawling out of the broken back window of Carmine's car. Carmine was waving his arms, yelling, and swearing as he hobbled back toward the tangled wreckage.

The truck driver turned around in the seat, his eyes wide. "What's going on? What was that all about?" the truck driver said as he grabbed the CB microphone.

"Don't call anyone," David said. The driver ignored him and kept dialing the knob on the radio, trying to bring up the emergency channel. After tuning to channel nine, he began to make an emergency call. David grabbed his hand and said, "Please, don't do that." The driver hesitated for a brief moment, looked back at David and then at Debra. He felt compassion for them and hung up the microphone on the CB radio.

"Okay, I know there's a sad story here, right? I've always been a sucker for a sad story, so let's hear it."

"It's a long story," David said, "but you can't call the police. Those men that are trying to kill us also set us up with the police. The police think we killed a sheriff."

"Are you two the ones they're talking about on the news?" the driver asked.

"Yes, that's us." David said. The trucker began to smile.

"It's okay, young man. I haven't exactly always been on the right side of the law myself," he said with a loud chuckle.

"I'm an undercover FBI agent," David said.

"Uh ... forget what I just said," the driver said as his expression changed to a more somber one. David began to laugh.

"I'm David Kimble, and this is Debra Benson."

"How do you do?" he said. He shook David's hand. Holding the steering wheel, he stuck his head around David and glanced back at Debra. "Howdy, ma'am. I'm Delbert Jackson from down in the great state of Georgia."

"Pleased to meet you, Delbert. Thanks for helping us," Debra said with a smile.

"It's always my pleasure to help a beautiful young lady in distress." He reached back and took hold of her hand and pulled her forward, directing her to the passenger seat. "Now you just sit down right there and tell old Delbert all about it, and we'll see if we can't help. Since you have a sidekick here with you, I guess we'll see if we can help him too," Delbert said with a big, wide smile.

Debra smiled. It was a great pleasure to meet someone so understanding, especially after David had destroyed part of his load, she thought. "We're sorry about the car that came off the trailer."

"That's okay, that's why I have insurance," he said, smiling.

Delbert looked to be about fifty years old. He wasn't tall, but he was a big, muscular man. He had a bubbly personality and an ear-to-ear smile. The first impression of him was that he was always positive and upbeat and was someone who could have a good time even under difficult circumstances.

Debra proceeded to tell their story. Delbert was surprised to hear all they had been through. When she finished, Delbert said, "You folks are in a real fix, all right. I'm not going all the way to New York City, but I'm going as far as Newburgh. I have to layover there for a few days, but you're welcome to ride with me that far if you like."

"That sounds great, doesn't it, David?" Debra turned and looked at David. He was sitting on the sleeper bed, with a puzzled look on his face.

"Our problems are far from being over."

"What do you mean? Those guys are not going to be following you for quite a spell. Their car is completely out of commission," Delbert said with a chuckle.

"I know, but first of all, how did they know where we were? I've been trying to figure it out. There's no way they could have known, unless…" David hesitated, and then he began pulling off his shoes and checking the soles and inside them.

"What are you doing?" Debra asked.

"I'm checking for a tracking transmitter."

"What? A tracking transmitter?"

"Yes, a tracking transmitter. That's the only way they could possibly have known where we were. Bill probably put one in some of my personal things back at the Burtonsville jail. The FBI has access to these little transmitters that can be put on your clothing or the arch of shoes. They're sticky on one side and very easy to conceal."

He put his shoes back on. He took off his watch and checked it thoroughly, and then he took off his belt and checked it. "Here it is! It was on one of the brads that attached the buckle to the belt. This is how they knew where we were. I knew it," David said, holding up a small, round disc about the size of a button, only much thinner. "This was stuck to the back of my belt buckle. We use this at the bureau in kidnapping cases; we hide it in with the money for tracking. We have a small electronic tracking device that will pick up the signal from these little transmitters several miles away. They can even pinpoint what direction you're traveling."

"David, they're probably still tracking us now," Debra said with concern.

"We have to get rid of this as soon as possible, but we can't just leave it somewhere; it has to keep moving. Otherwise they'll find it too soon," David said.

"Couldn't we just destroy it?" Debra commented.

"No, they know the direction we're going," David said, scratching his head. "If we can make them think we are still running, but in a different direction, that would be great."

"Maybe I can help you there," Delbert said. "There's a truck stop down the road about another thirty or forty miles. I'll see if I can't find someone going in the other direction. Maybe we can send those guys on a scenic tour."

"That sounds great, Delbert," David said.

David lay down on the sleeper bed and Debra sat back in the passenger seat, and they both breathed a sigh of relief.

"I want the two of you to sit back and relax. Let me tell y'all some stories about my childhood," Delbert said. "Some people seem to think I should write a book about how I grew up. So now you're going to hear a few stories that won't sound real, but they're true."

"That sounds great," Debra said with a smile. She knew he was trying to get their minds off their predicament. *What a nice man,* she thought.

"I hope you don't get bored," he said with a laugh.

As they listened to his stories Debra and David began to relax and it took their minds off their problems for a short time. They enjoyed his stories the rest of the ride to the truck stop.

CHAPTER 13

After the motel manager called the cops and Bill explained to them what had taken place at the motel the police put an APB out for them.

They towed Bill's wrecked car back to town, and he rented another one. He returned back to the motel, where he spent a sleepless night waiting for word from Carmine about the two fugitives.

The next morning, he was lying on the bed resting when the phone rang. Carmine was on the line, and he was very agitated. He began yelling and talking so fast Bill could hardly understand what he was saying.

"Slow down and tell me what happened."

"They got away! One of my men is dead!" Carmine said.

"How could you let them get away?" Bill said.

"Some trucker helped them after your FBI buddy pushed a car off the back of a car hauler and caused me to wreck! They're still with that trucker."

"Where are you now, and what about the tracking device? Is it still working?"

"We're at a gas station, and yes, it's still working, but I don't have a car. I might be able to get one from the station manager." He hesitated for a moment and said something to someone close by. "Bill, the cops are all over the place. They're asking questions about the accident. What am I going to tell them?"

"You don't tell them anything. You pretend it was just an accident. You were driving along, and the car came off on your car, and the driver of the truck didn't even know that the car had fallen off the trailer. You're on a truck route, so there couldn't have been very much traffic. Do you think anyone saw anything?"

"Some people drove up after they were gone, but, no, I don't think so."

"Good, now—"

"Wait!" Carmine interrupted. "The cops saw shell casings in the road. How do I explain that?"

"Use a little wit. You do have some wit, don't you? Just don't let them see your gun. Now, I want you to find a car and go after them. I'm getting tired of your incompetence! Finish the job!" Bill slammed the phone down. He pounded the bed with his fist and then hesitated for a moment. He picked up the phone and dialed a number. After several rings, someone answered.

"Your man Carmine and those idiots he has helping him botched it up again. I should have gone after them myself...I'm aware that they were able to get away from me too." He reached over, picked up his glass of scotch, and took a drink. "I think David is too smart to not figure out about the tracking transmitter. Most likely he's found it by now, but I told Carmine to continue to follow them ... okay, I'll keep you informed." Bill hung up the phone and stared off into space for a few seconds. He picked up the bottle of scotch and poured another shot. As he sat down on the bed, he thought about his ex-wife and wondered how he had gotten into this mess. Then he thought how he had compromised his scruples and morals by taking money to kill people. Bill had never been a drinker, but as he pondered these thoughts, sipping the scotch seemed to make the lump in his throat go down much easier. He tried to think of what to do next. He picked up the phone again and dialed some numbers.

"Hello, Carla. Put me through to John Parks." After a couple of minutes, John picked up the phone.

"Hello?"

"John, Bill Rogers here. Have you heard from David Kimble?"

"No, can you believe what they're saying about him? They're saying he killed a sheriff. Was he working a case, Bill?"

"Yes, I heard about it. And no, he wasn't working a case. He's mixed up with a bad woman. I guess he just flipped out. Listen, John, I know you and David are good friends. If you hear from him, I would appreciate it if you would give me a call. I'm trying to help him, John, but he's so mixed up—this woman has messed up his mind. He'll probably tell you some ridiculous story about me, but don't believe it. I'm only trying to help him."

"Sure, Bill. I'll call you as soon as I hear from him."

"Here's the number where I can be reached." He gave John his cell phone number. "If this number doesn't work the first time, just keep trying. The signal is very sporadic in this area."

"Where are you, Bill?"

"That's not important. Just call me when you hear from him, but don't tell him you're going to call me. He won't understand, John. He's under that woman's spell. Contact me immediately after he calls."

"Sure, Bill. I'll let you know."

"Thanks, John." Bill hung up the phone. He laced his fingers behind his head, leaned back against the head of the bed, and as a big smile came across his face, he said, "I got you now, David."

Delbert pulled his truck in the parking lot at the truck stop. "You two stay here," he said, turning to face them. "Now give me that little device." David handed him the transmitter. He looked at David and smiled. "We'll see what we can do with this." Delbert climbed down from the truck.

After about fifteen minutes, he came back. "Problem solved. I gave it to my friend Carlo Mason. He's from Tennessee; he and his cousin are taking a load up to Maine."

"What are they hauling?" David asked.

"Well, let's put it this way: it's kind of a smelly load. They'll be in for a big surprise when they stop Carlo. I told him to hide that little device in his trailer." Delbert leaned back, lowered his air ride seat, rubbed his hands together, and said, "Okay, does anyone need to use the restroom? You better go now because we have a long haul ahead of us." Debra and David climbed down from the truck one at a time and went to the restroom. They borrowed a cap from Delbert and took turns wearing it inside the building, hoping no one would recognize them. When they came back to the truck, they lay down in the sleeper to rest as Delbert drove south.

After retrieving his gun and keeping it hidden from the police, Carmine rented a car from the gas station manager. He had answered all the questions from the police. He told them he was driving along and the car came off the trailer and was able to convince them that this was nothing more than an accident. Carmine sat down in the driver's seat of the rented car. The man with him put the tracking device in the seat between them, and they drove south. The tracking device was working well. They drove for about forty-five minutes. Suddenly the light on the tracking device began to flash faster.

The man with Carmine said, "We must be getting close—the light is flashing faster."

"We're catching up with them already?" Carmine commented in a puzzled tone.

"Yes, we are." The man paused for an instant and then said, "Hey, something's not right. The dot on the screen is moving north, toward us!"

"Let me see that!" Carmine grabbed the device and turned it around so that he had a good view of the screen. "They must be trying to sneak back past us. Maybe they're trying to hide back at that little town," he said. "They think that coming back this way we might miss them, but this little device is going to lead us right to them." He began to laugh. "How stupid can you be? We have them now, and they don't even know it," he said, laughing even louder.

They drove another five miles and then met Carlo in his truck. The light flashed faster as the truck went by, and the little dot began to travel away from them.

"They must be in that truck!" the man yelled to Carmine after it had driven past them. Carmine spun his car around in the road and took off after the big rig. They caught up with the truck and drove up beside Carlo. The man with Carmine began motioning for Carlo to pull over. Carlo looked out the window and saw the man waving his hand. He turned toward Cledus.

"Hey, Cledus, there's a couple of fellers over here in a car, and one of them is wavin' his arm. I thank they want us to pull over. You reckon it's them fellers Delbert told us about?"

"I reckon it is; we may as well git it over with," Cledus said.

Carlo pulled over in a wide place on the side of the road and set the air brakes on his trailer. Carmine and his sidekick could hear the pigs squealing and smell the stink as they got out of the car.

"There's some nasty animals in there," the man traveling with Carmine said.

"This is going to be easier than I thought," Carmine commented. "You check in the trailer, and I'll handle this stupid truck driver."

"Why do I have to look in the trailer?"

"Because they may be hiding in there, and I told you to—that's why! Now just shut up and get in there!"

"I'm not getting in there with those nasty pigs!"

"You'll do as you're told if you want to get paid," Carmine said.

The man stomped over and opened up the trailer door. He pulled his gun and climbed in with the pigs, cursing and complaining. He took a few steps and slipped and fell down in the middle of the pigs. The pigs began squealing as the man shoved them to the side. Scrambling to his feet, he stood up swearing and complaining even louder.

Carmine walked up to the driver's door, his gun in his hand. He reached up and took hold of the door handle and jerked it open. He moved the gun over to his left hand and took hold of the handrail on the cab of the truck with his right hand. He looked up at Carlo as he pointed his gun at him. He didn't see Cledus climb down out of the passenger seat and walk around the front of the truck.

Carmine waved his gun back and forth at Carlo. "Where are they?" he yelled.

Carlo just looked at Carmine for a few seconds with no expression on his face. Then he asked, "Do y'all know my cousin Cledus?" Carmine looked at Carlo with a dumbfounded expression.

"Now, how would I know your cousin Cledus, you dumb, stupid, redneck?" The door shielded Carmine's view of Cledus as he rounded the front of the truck, carrying a baseball bat.

At that moment, Cledus jerked the door open a little wider and Carmine stepped back and turned loose of the handrail on the truck. Cledus swung the baseball bat down on Carmine's left arm, and it cracked loudly. He dropped his gun and screamed as he fell facedown on the blacktop.

He staggered to his feet, screaming, "You broke my arm, you son-of-a bi—" That's all he could say before he caught sight of Cledus. Cledus stood six-foot-four and weighed about 350 pounds. He looked like a mountain as he hovered over Carmine. Carmine started backing up in disbelief, his eyes almost twice their normal size.

"*Now* ya'll know my cousin Cledus!" Carlo said as he and Cledus burst out laughing. Cledus bent down and picked up Carmine's gun. The smile left his face and his expression changed to a more serious one.

"Y'all better git your asses outta here before I really hafta git rough!" Cledus growled. At this point, Carmine was running backward, holding his left arm with his other hand. He began yelling for the other man to get out of the trailer. The man came out the back of the trailer, cursing.

"Now I have pig crap all over me!" he shouted. He looked up and saw Carmine running toward the car, holding his left arm. When he saw Cledus standing there, holding Carmine's gun in one hand and a baseball bat in the other, he turned and started running too. They jumped in their car, Carmine moaning and complaining about his broken arm, and they took off spinning their tires and headed north.

"I thought you were going to take care of that stupid truck driver," the man said to Carmine.

"Shut up! Just shut up, and help me find a hospital," Carmine said.

Cledus stood there holding his bat and Carmine's gun as they drove past the truck and disappeared out of sight. "Boy, them there fellers shore left in a hurry, didn't they, Carlo?"

"Yeah, they shore did, Cledus." They both continued laughing.

"What do ya reckon a feller ortta do with this here gun, Carlo?"

"Aw, just unload it and pitch it in with them hogs back there; we shore don't want nobody's youngins to git a holt of it."

Cledus unloaded Carmine's gun, went to the back of the trailer, and tossed it in with the pigs. He latched the doors to the trailer, climbed back in the truck, and they drove away.

Carlo called Delbert on the CB radio. "Hey, Delbert, we met up with them two fellers you told us about."

"What happened?" Delbert asked.

"Well, let's put it this a way. That one feller ain't gonna use his left arm fer a while after Cledus got done with his ball bat. They took off like scalded dogs with their tails between their legs and headed back north," said Carlo.

"Thanks, Carlo. I'll talk to you later." Delbert hung up the CB microphone.

"Well, Carlo and his cousin took care of those men who were chasing you guys." They all began laughing at Carlo's story.

Carmine drove back to Burtonsville to the nearest hospital. He told them he fell and broke his arm. The doctor looked skeptical, but he set the bone in his left arm, put it in a cast, and gave him some pills for the pain.

It was dark when Carmine's sidekick drove him to the motel where Bill was staying. They went to Bill's room and knocked on the door. Bill answered the door with his gun in his hand. When he opened the door and saw Carmine with his arm in a sling, he said, "Let me guess," as he shoved his gun in his shoulder holster. "They got away, right?"

"They found your tracking device, Bill," Carmine said in a condescending tone as the two men walked in the room. "They put it in a truck trailer that was hauling hogs, and those redneck truck drivers broke my arm with a baseball bat."

"That's just great!" Bill shouted as he turned and kicked a small table across the room. "I want you guys to go south toward New York

City and just hang out somewhere. You do have a cell phone, don't you?"

"Yes, I do," Carmine said, "but, like yours, it doesn't work all the time in these mountains."

"Give me the number, and I'll call you when I catch up with them."

"What makes you think you can catch up with them?"

"I have a couple more aces in the hole," he said with a devious smile. "You two can stay here tonight, but I'm going to leave now so I can be close to them when my aces come in." He grabbed his overnight bag, loaded it in his car and drove away.

Speeding quickly down Interstate 90, Delbert took the loop that merged with Interstate 87, and they drove to Kingston. Delbert pulled into a truck stop for the night. Debra and David wore Delbert's extra cap to try to disguise themselves. They went in and bought some clothes with the money Debra had gotten from Tom Browner. They showered and freshened up at the truck stop and spent the night in the top bunk of Delbert's sleeper. It was a little cramped, but they didn't mind.

The next morning, they shared a quick breakfast of coffee and doughnuts Delbert had bought at the truck stop. "I asked around, and the other truckers said the cops are looking all over for you two. You're going to have to stay in the truck to keep from being seen," Delbert said. David and Debra agreed.

After finishing breakfast, they headed south on Interstate 87. After they had driven for about two hours, Delbert said, "I'm going to stop at the next exit. There's a little store and restaurant combo there. I'd like to go in and visit the owners for a few minutes. They're a nice old, oriental couple. I stop and see them whenever I'm up this way. Besides, they have the best Chinese buffet you ever ate."

"That sounds great to me," Debra said. "I haven't had Chinese food for quite some time, but it's a little early for lunch."

"Well, we'll call it brunch then if that makes you feel better," Delbert said with a laugh as he took the exit. He geared the truck down, made a right turn off the exit, and drove a short distance to the store. They pulled in the parking lot. The sign over the door read, "Wong's Wok."

"Do you think we should chance going in here, Delbert?" David asked.

"I don't know. This isn't a normal stop for trucks, and I've never seen any cops around. You may be okay."

They decided to take a chance. They climbed down from the truck and went inside. After exchanging greetings with the old couple, Delbert introduced them to David and Debra. Mr. Wong gave the three of them a table in the corner, with two of the chairs facing the front of the building.

After about thirty minutes of just chatting and eating, Mr. Wong came over, and in his strong accent, he told Delbert a policeman was outside looking at his rig.

"You two stay here, and I'll go talk to him. Don't do anything; I'll be right back," Delbert said as he stood up to walk outside.

David took hold of his arm and said, "We can't let you get in trouble because of us."

"No, Delbert, don't go," Debra said. "Maybe we should just give ourselves up, David. If he's not a jerk like the some of the other cops we've dealt with, maybe he will help us."

"Would you two relax? I've dealt with these people before. I'll take care of it. Now, finish your meal." He hesitated for a moment and then said, "If you see him coming this way, go hide in the restroom." He turned around and quickly walked out the door.

The cop standing behind his truck was wearing a New York State Highway Patrol uniform.

"Is this your truck, sir?" the cop asked as Delbert walked up to him.

"Yes, it is. What can I do for you, officer?"

"Could I see your license, registration, and logbook please?"

"Yes sir, officer," Delbert said. "What's this about?"

"We had a report of a truck fitting this description that lost one of its vehicles from the trailer, and that vehicle caused a fatal crash. I can see you have a car missing from the rear of your trailer."

Delbert glanced at the trailer and said, "Yes, I do, but a fatal crash? I didn't know the car had come off the trailer until I was miles down the road, and I certainly didn't know about any fatal crash. I reported it to my dispatcher when I discovered it missing."

"There's also a report that two murder suspects may have been hitching a ride in one of the cars that you're hauling." Pausing, he looked intently at Delbert. "If I find any evidence that you are helping cop killers, you won't be driving a truck anymore. You'll go to jail."

"What? What are you talking about?" Delbert asked.

"A young man and woman killed a sheriff."

"I saw that on the news. That's terrible," Delbert said with a concerned look on his face. "That has nothing to do with me."

They walked toward the front of the truck. The cop looked over at the car directly behind the truck cab. He saw the bullet holes and the taped-up glass in the car. "What happened there?" asked the cop as he paused.

"Some kids vandalized the car," replied Delbert. He climbed up in the truck.

After getting his registration and logbook, he climbed down, took his CDL license from his billfold, and handed it to the cop. After looking them over, he handed them back to Delbert.

"I suppose you won't mind if I take a look in your truck and in the cars you're hauling?" the cop asked, a condescending grin on his face.

"Go right ahead. I don't mind."

Delbert placed his logbook and registration back in the truck as the cop looked inside the cab. Delbert walked back and stood beside the trailer while the cop looked inside the cars. He checked the car with the taped-up windows. When he went around to other side of the car and looked in the backseat, he saw all the food wrappers and papers Debra and David had discarded when they had hidden in the car. He stepped back on the trailer and drew his gun and pointed it at Delbert.

"Put your hands up and get down on your knees—now!"

"Hey, man, are you crazy?" Delbert yelled as he put his hands in the air.

"I said get down on your knees!" Delbert knelt down on his knees.

"What is wrong with you?"

"Where are they?" the cop yelled, holding his gun on Delbert as he climbed down from the trailer.

"I don't know what you're talking about."

"You're going to tell me where they are."

Debra and David were watching from their table. David jumped up from the table and started for the door. Debra grabbed him by the arm.

"David, you can't go out there. He may shoot you!"

Mr. Wong was watching from the window. Suddenly he threw the door open, ran out, and began waving his arms and yelling at the cop. "You no hurt Mr. Delbert! You no hurt Mr. Delbert!" The cop spun around and pointed his gun at Mr. Wong.

"Hold it right there! Don't you move!" the cop yelled. "Get down on the ground! Now!" Mr. Wong just stood there, asking the cop not to hurt Mr. Delbert. The cop ran over and shoved Mr. Wong to the ground.

"Don't hurt him!" Delbert yelled as he jumped up from the ground and ran toward the cop. As he came close to him, the cop spun around, pointing his gun at Delbert. Delbert grabbed his gun hand, and they began to struggle. Delbert fell backward to the ground, with the cop on top of him.

David could stand it no longer. He ran out the door, ran over to the corner of the trailer, and pulled his gun. He knew his gun was empty, but he had to take a chance.

"Drop that gun, and turn Delbert loose!" The two men stopped struggling when they heard David's shout. The cop looked up and saw David pointing a gun at them. He had a deer-in-the-headlights expression on his face. Delbert grabbed the gun out of the cop's hand. "Now stand up, and put your hands up!" David yelled. The cop did as David said. As Delbert stood up, he slapped the young cop across the back of the head and his hat fell to the parking lot.

"What's wrong with you? Were you going to shoot me?" He ran over to Mr. Wong and began helping him to his feet. "Or maybe you were going to shoot this old man!" Delbert yelled as he waved the cops gun around.

"Bring me the gun, Delbert," David said. The cop looked at Delbert.

"You help him, and I'll see you go to jail."

"Oh yeah? I should give the gun back to you, right? You moron! You need to stop watching those cop shows on TV and come back to reality—treat people with respect." As he preached to the young cop, he walked over to David and handed him the cop's gun. A couple of people were watching from across the parking lot. David walked over to the cop, his gun down to his side, and whispered.

"Put your hands down. Tell these people that this was just a mis-understanding. I'm an FBI agent."

"Everyone, go on about your business. This is just a misunder- standing," the cop said. The people began walking away. "There's no misunderstanding here, you're a criminal—you killed a police officer," mumbled the young cop. Debra heard what he said as she walked up and stood beside David.

"You don't know what you're talking about. We didn't do any- thing to anyone. There're some people trying to kill us, and they're the ones who killed that sheriff," Debra said.

"Can you prove that?" David and Debra looked at each other for a moment. "I didn't think so," he said with a half chuckle and a smile.

Delbert walked over and stood close to the cop. "You want me to slap that smile off his face, David?" Delbert said as he gave the cop a menacing stare.

"No, Delbert. I don't want you to get into any more trouble." He paused. "Debra, get the extra magazine from his belt." Debra walked over and took the extra magazine from the cop. David kept the cop's gun pointed at him while he handed Debra his empty gun. He told her to put the magazine in the gun. She ejected the empty one and slid the loaded one into the handle. The cop looked at David.

"Your gun was empty?"

"Yes, it was, but the extra clip from your Glock will fit this one just fine," David said with a smile. The cop's temper instantly flared, and he gave David a hateful stare.

David looked at Mr. Wong. "Mr. Wong, could we borrow your car?"

"Yes, is around behind building."

"Thanks, Mr. Wong. I'll get it back to you as soon as I can. Del- bert, can you go with Mr. Wong and bring the car here?"

Delbert went with Mr. Wong, and they brought the car around to where they were standing. It was a 1963 Chevrolet Super Sport Impala with a V-8 engine and a four-speed, manual transmission.

"Car belongs to nephew. He likes big, American sports car. Get terrible gas mileage. You keep long as you like," Mr. Wong said. David looked at Debra.

"Can you drive a standard-shift, Debra?"

"No, sorry—I never learned how." David kept his eye on the cop as he walked over to Mr. Wong and shook his hand.

"Thank you very much, Mr. Wong," David said. He walked back over to the cop. "I want you to give me your handcuff keys." He handed David the keys. "Now I want you to put your hands behind your back, put the cuffs on, and get in the front seat."

"Think about what you're doing," the cop said with a stern voice. "This is kidnapping a police officer!"

"No, it's not kidnapping," David said with a smile as he bent down and picked up the cop's hat and stuffed it on his head. "Mr. Wong wants you to ride in his car—that's all." David's expression changed to a more serious one. "Now shut up and get in!" he growled.

He glanced at Debra. "Debra, you watch him from the backseat, and I'll drive."

David opened the door, and the cop sat down in the front passenger seat. David thanked Delbert for all his help and climbed under the steering wheel. Debra hugged Delbert, kissed him on the cheek, and told him how much she appreciated everything he had done for them.

He smiled and said, "It was a great pleasure, ma'am."

She jumped in the backseat of the car. "If you ever get down in Albany, Georgia, look me up!" Delbert yelled. Debra waved good-bye as they drove out of the parking lot toward the interstate.

CHAPTER 14

After driving for a short time with very little conversation, Debra asked, "What's your name?"

"My name is Robert Mahoney," the cop replied.

"Are you married, Robert?"

"No," he quickly said.

"How old are you?"

"What difference does it make?" the young cop said. He turned and glared at her.

"I'm trying to be civil, Robert, but I can tell that you didn't do well in that how-to class, did you?"

"What how-to class?" he growled.

"The one where as a public servant, you learn *how to* treat people with dignity and respect." There was a long pause. Then, in a stern voice, Debra said, "In your profession, you need to be a little more cordial. You better learn that people are innocent until proven guilty. That's how our justice system is supposed to work."

"Okay, I'm supposed to believe you're innocent while you sit there pointing my gun at me?"

Debra's face flushed red with anger, and she said, "Jack Braco is my father, and he sent some thugs to kill David and me. They're the ones who killed that sheriff!" She hesitated for a moment. She leaned forward and said even louder, "All we have gotten from the cops so far is a dismissive attitude!" Robert leaned forward in the seat to get away from the high tones of her voice. "Don't you think it's kind of strange, Robert, that neither David nor I has a criminal record? If you would bother to check, you would know that in fact, David works for the FBI; you would think he could at least get a little consideration." Debra hesitated and drew a deep breath. "Do you think we were just sitting around one day and then all of a sudden we said, 'Hey let's go kill a cop'?" She smacked him on the back of the head.

He ducked his head down and said, "Take it easy, lady! Calm down."

"Why won't any of you listen when someone is trying to explain why things are the way they are? If all cops think like the ones we've been dealing with, it's a wonder there aren't more unsolved crimes and more innocent people in prison!" Debra leaned back in the seat, breathing hard. She shook her head in disgust and looked out the window.

"I'm an undercover FBI agent, Robert, and every word she just told you is the truth. Bill Rogers is head of the department where I work. He's conspiring with the men Jack Braco has hired to kill Debra."

"Are you talking about *Senator* Jack Braco, who's running for president?" Robert asked.

"Yes!"

"Now, why would he want her dead?"

"Because she is his illegitimate daughter, and he will do anything to keep the public from finding out about her. Bill Rogers set us up with the police. He knows the men chasing us are the ones who killed that sheriff from Utica. If you're with us when they catch up with us again, they'll kill you too," David said loudly. "They can't leave any witnesses." He kept looking over to see Robert's reaction.

"If all that you're telling me is true, then why haven't I heard about any of this?"

"You're hearing what Bill Rogers wants the cops to hear. He's a dirty cop. He would love for Debra and me to get killed in some kind of accidental police shooting, and then we would be out of the way. His secret would remain hidden, and so would Jack Braco's."

"What's your plan now? Where are you going?" Robert asked.

"I don't know yet. I need to contact someone at my department, someone I can trust, but we have to get back to the city first," David said.

The young cop looked at David for just a second, and then he turned around and stared at Debra. "What if I help you?"

David glanced over at Robert with a surprised look. Debra leaned forward and said, "Are you serious? You believe our story?"

"Yes, I guess I do, but I don't know how much help I can be."

"Well, the fact that you believe us is a start," David said.

"Since I believe what you're telling me, and I'm willing to help you get out of the mess you're in, how about taking these handcuffs off?" David looked at him for a brief moment.

"What do you think, Debra?" David asked, looking at her in the rearview mirror. There was a short pause as the two of them held a gaze. They each seemed to have an understanding of what the other was thinking. Finally Debra responded to his question.

"I guess we can chance it, David." David reached in his pocket and pulled out the handcuff keys and gave them to Robert. He unlocked the handcuffs, put them in the seat, and began rubbing his wrists. Debra had leaned forward, close to the back of the front seat. After a few seconds, Robert whirled around backward and grabbed the Glock out of Debra's hand and stuck the end of the barrel to David's head.

Debra stared at him in shock at how quickly he had moved. After a few seconds he began to laugh, drew the gun back, and put it in his holster on his right side. David drew a deep breath and then exhaled. "You made me a little nervous, Robert," David said, breathing normally again.

"I thought I would see if I could get your heart going a little faster."

"Well, it worked," David replied.

"How did you do that so quickly?" Debra asked.

"Just a little something I've been working on for several years."

They drove for a while and discussed their predicament at length with Robert.

"If I could get into the FBI headquarters and gain access to Bill's computer, maybe I could get something substantial to use against him," David said. "There might also be some evidence that would prove our innocence."

"If I can help, I will, but right now I need to use the restroom. I needed to go when this little trip started. So if you could take this exit coming up, I would greatly appreciate it," Robert said.

"Okay, I think we can do that. We need gas anyway," David replied as he flipped on his signal and turned onto the exit ramp. As they drove up to the nearest gas station, David asked, "Do you have any money left, Debra?"

"Let me check."

She reached in her pants pocket, but before she could finish, Robert said, "I'll get that. You pump the gas, and I'll pay." He then went into the store to use the restroom. Once Robert was inside the store, he stopped, turned, and looked out the window at David pumping the gas in the car. He quickly hurried to the back of the store and turned down the short hallway toward the restrooms. A young teenage girl was using the payphone. Robert walked over to her.

"Excuse me, miss. I need to use this phone." The young woman just looked at him and kept talking. He grabbed the phone out of her hand and pushed her to one side.

"Hey! What's your problem? You pig!" she shouted.

He put the phone to his ear. "She'll call you back." He looked at her and said, "You need to respect your elders, young lady." He turned his back to her, pushed the button down, and began to dial. The young woman stomped off, huffing and puffing.

After dialing the operator and giving her some numbers, someone answered.

"Hey, it's me, Robert. Yeah, they're with me now … yes, they did. Your plan worked perfectly. I stopped at a couple of truck stops, and they all knew who I was talking about. They told me that Georgia redneck always stops to see that old Chinese man and woman. They even told me what exit it was … yeah, that's right. The police uniform was just the right touch. I tried to not make it easy for them to take me with them … no, they don't suspect a thing. Where are you?" He turned around and looked down the hall. He turned back and continued his conversation. "Oh, you're not too far behind us. We're driving an old, green car. I think it's an old 1960s Chevrolet … okay, I'll hold them up as long as I can."

While Robert was on the phone, David finished pumping the gas and went inside the store. As he walked through the door, he bumped into the young woman who had been on the phone. Before he had time to apologize, she jumped back, looked at him, and said, "Why don't you just shove me around too, the way that jerk cop did back there when he took the phone away from me!" David just looked at her as she went out the door, mumbling as she walked. He turned and hurriedly walked back toward the restrooms. As he turned the corner to the hallway, Robert was hanging up the phone. David stood and looked at him for a moment. When Robert turned and saw David staring at him, he had a startled look on his face. He took a couple of steps forward and looked straight ahead.

"I–I was just letting the little woman know where I am and that everything is all right," Robert said, walking past David. David followed Robert to the cash register. Robert handed the clerk his credit card. After signing the receipt, Robert walked out of the store and sat in the car. David stood there momentarily, pondering what to make of Robert and the telephone. He knew Robert was too anxious to get back to the car. David had been a cop long enough to sense when something just didn't seem right.

David walked out of the store. Debra had gotten out of the car to stretch her legs, and she was standing beside the gas pumps.

David walked slowly past her and whispered, "When you get back in the car I want you to put your seat belt on. Don't ask any questions—just do as I say." They held a short gaze as David walked around to the driver's door and got in.

Debra quickly stepped over to the back door, opened it, and climbed in the backseat. David, trying to mask his increasing suspicion, thanked Robert for the use of his credit card. He pulled the seat belt across his lap, turning toward the back as it fastened to make sure that Debra did the same. When he saw that she had, David started the engine, and the old car rumbled out of the gas station.

They were coming upon the entrance ramp to the interstate when Robert said, "There's a souvenir shop down this road a short distance on the right. Do you mind if we stop for just a minute? I would like to get my niece a gift; it's her birthday."

"If it's all the same to you, I'd like to get back on the road. It's still a long drive until we get to New York City," David replied.

"Okay, you're the driver," Robert said. He looked at David and smiled. David turned down the entrance ramp leading onto Interstate 87 South.

After driving for a few minutes, David's skepticism of Robert continued to grow, and he decided to try a little interrogation to find out if he was really on their side.

"Where was your patrol car parked back at the restaurant? I don't recall seeing it."

"Oh…I parked back off the road. I didn't want you two to see it."

"You must have been awfully sure that we were there," David said, looking over at Robert. Robert looked at David with a smile. "Delbert told us that he had never seen any cops there before. How were you able to know to check at that particular restaurant?"

"Hey, what is this? Don't you trust me?" asked Robert.

"Well, being a cop myself, I'm just naturally suspicious," David said, looking at Robert from the corner of his eye.

"I totally understand your suspicions; I don't mind some questions," Robert said. He began to rub his hands together and fidget.

"I noticed you weren't wearing a personal radio. I thought all patrolmen wore a radio with a microphone attached to their shoulder."

"I don't wear mine most of the time," he replied.

"So. I suppose you called in before you left your patrol car to check out Delbert's truck, which means that the police are going to be looking for you, right?"

"No, I didn't call in," Robert said, growing even more nervous. David could sense Robert's uneasiness.

"Isn't that a requirement—anytime a police officer leaves his vehicle, he reports in to the station?"

"Well, I don't always follow the rules," Robert said, grinning nervously.

"Who did you say you called on the phone?" David asked, looking at Debra in the rearview mirror.

"I was just calling my wife to tell her where I was."

"I thought you said you weren't married," Debra quickly responded.

"Well…" Robert said with hesitation and a chuckle. "I guess I'm caught." With that he quickly drew his gun and put the barrel to David's head. "Now, we're going to take the next exit and wait for Bill Rogers to catch up with us. He's not very far behind." Robert quickly moved across the bench seat, closer to David, and put both hands on his gun. David had no time to react.

"Robert, if you really were a cop, then you should have noticed that your gun is much lighter with an empty magazine," Debra said.

"Okay, like I'm going to fall for that," Robert replied, still focused on David.

"Let me save you the trouble of checking," Debra said, holding up the fully loaded magazine with her left hand and shaking it back and forth. Robert looked at her from the left corner of his eye. "I replaced the loaded magazine with the empty one before you did all that fast, fancy handwork and took the gun from me." Robert slowly turned his head sideways far enough to see the loaded clip she was holding. "Oh, and I ejected the bullet from the barrel too," Debra said sarcastically. "I may be a girl, Robert, but I know how a gun works." Robert lowered his gun and pulled the slide back enough to see the empty chamber. His face quickly became the color of cotton, and he knew he had underestimated his adversaries.

Before Robert had time to think of an alternate plan, David pulled his gun from his waistband.

"This one is fully loaded," David said, pushing the barrel of his pistol into Robert's ribcage with his left hand. Robert gave a half-hearted laugh as he lowered the gun and moved back to the passenger side of the car.

"Now, Robert, I want you to stay facing forward and slowly hand that gun back here," Debra said. Robert just sat there for a moment without moving.

"Don't make me have to shoot you, Robert," David said. David kept his gun pointed at Robert's midsection. Looking straight ahead, Robert stuck his left arm backward over his left shoulder and handed the gun to Debra. She grabbed the gun and ejected the empty magazine. She shoved the loaded magazine into the handle, pulled back the slide, and chambered a round into the barrel.

"Did you think that we were stupid enough to let you have a loaded gun just because you said you would help us?" Debra asked.

"It doesn't matter," Robert said. "Bill is going to catch up with us anytime." Robert looked over at David and smiled. David stuffed his gun back in his belt and swung his right fist and punched Robert in the jaw, knocking his head sideways.

"Debra, if he moves, I want you to shoot him," David said.

"David, we have to get off this road," Debra said tensely.

"It's too late," David said, adjusting the rearview mirror. "There's a big sedan coming up fast." David pushed the gas pedal down on the old car. The car gave a loud roar and picked up speed quickly. All of a sudden, Robert jumped over on top of David and grabbed the steering wheel. The car went off the left side of the road and then back on. As David and Robert struggled for control of the vehicle, the car went from one side of the interstate to the other. David punched Robert, and he fell back in the seat while holding on to the steering wheel.

"Turn him loose!" Debra screamed as she leaned forward as far as her seatbelt would allow. She swung the pistol as hard as she could and hit Robert in the head with the barrel. The gun discharged, the bullet narrowly missing Robert's head. It blew a hole in the front windshield of the car. The bang was deafening inside the car. Robert lunged over on top of David when the gun went off. He pushed the steering wheel to the left and steered the car off the road, down an embankment, and through the fence that bordered the interstate.

When the car went off the road, Debra was thrown against her seatbelt, and the jolt caused her to lose her grip on the gun, and it fell to the floor. The heavy car didn't slow down as it went through the wire fence. It tore through the bushes and heavy brush as if they weren't even there. Debra tried to reach the gun, but the seatbelt was holding her back, and each time the car hit a bump, she was being thrown against it. She tried to unlatch the seat belt, but it was stuck.

David held the gas pedal down as he and Robert continued to fight for control of the vehicle. They both had a death grip on the wheel. Not wearing a seatbelt, Robert was being thrown around with each bump they encountered, but he held fast to the steering wheel.

The car kept going through the brush until David, trying to avoid a tree, jerked the wheel to the right. The car ran into a deep ravine and rolled over onto its top with a loud crash. Robert was almost thrown out the window as the car flipped. His head hit the post that supported the roof, and blood came from the gash. As the car rolled over, the engine stalled and the windshield shattered. Pieces of glass scattered inside the car. When the car came to a stop, Robert was lying facedown on the roof of the car, motionless and unconscious. The thick, heavy steel in the old car prevented the roof from crushing completely.

"Debra, are you okay?" David shouted as he loosened his seatbelt and dropped down onto the roof of the car.

"I'm okay, but I can't get this seat belt loose," Debra said as she struggled to free herself. David crawled across Robert to where Debra was hanging. He positioned himself underneath her and lifted her up. The car was creaking, cracking, and popping as it lay on the edge of the ravine. By lifting her, he took the weight off the belt, and she was able to unlatch it. She dropped down onto the roof of the car. David knew the car was going to slide down into the ravine.

"Let's get out of here before this car rolls over again!" David shouted. He was able to force the back door open just enough for the two of them to crawl out of the upper side of the car.

After they crawled out of the car, David asked, "Are you hurt? Do you have any injuries?"

"I don't think so."

"We have to get out of here. Bill was right behind us just before the car went off the road. He'll be here shortly," David said and grabbed Debra's hand. They ran through the brush as quickly as possible in the opposite direction of the interstate.

Bill was coming up fast when he saw the old Chevrolet begin to swerve from one side of the interstate to the other as David and Robert struggled for control of the car. All he could do was watch as the car took off down the embankment. He pulled his car off the road, jumped out, ran down the bank, and followed the path through the brush cut down by the big car. The car traveled several hundred yards into the brush before it flipped over.

When Bill reached the car, he found Robert barely moving inside. He was groaning and beginning to regain consciousness.

"Where are they?" Bill shouted as he looked inside the car, his gun in his hand.

"I ... don't know. Oh ... my head," Robert mumbled as he rubbed the bloody gash. The car began to move slowly, sliding farther down into the ditch.

"This car is going to roll over again!" Robert yelled. "Help me out of here," he demanded.

"If you weren't Carmine's nephew, I would leave you in there," Bill grumbled. Bill reached in through the door that David had forced open and grabbed Robert by the arms, dragging him out of the car. Robert staggered to his feet as the car rolled down into the deep ravine. He held onto Bill for balance.

"Sit down and wait here. I'm going to look for them!" Bill said as he pushed Robert to the ground and ran in the direction he thought they had gone.

After about ten minutes, Bill came back, cursing and yelling at Robert. "They could be anywhere! I'm surrounded by incapable morons! Come on; let's get out of here. I don't want to explain to every cop in the state why you're wearing a police uniform," he said. He grabbed Robert by the arm, lifted him up, and helped him back to his car.

By the time they reached Bill's car, a few people who had witnessed the accident had pulled over and were standing near where David's car had left the road.

"Go on about your business," Bill said, flashing his FBI badge. "Just chasing some fugitives." He helped Robert into the passenger side of the car. Blood from the cut on Robert's head had run down the back of his neck and soaked his shirt. Bill jumped in the driver's seat and drove away.

"You have to take me to a hospital," Robert mumbled and then passed out.

"I have to get you out of that cop uniform first," Bill said as he drove away. "One ace in the hole down and one to go."

After getting some clothes and helping Robert change, he took Robert to the nearest emergency room. He flashed his badge, thinking that would keep him from explaining about Robert's condition, but they told him to take a seat. Not wanting to attract any attention, he waited patiently. After speaking with the head nurse and answering several questions, he was allowed to leave. By the time Bill left the hospital, it was too late to pursue David and Debra. He decided to spend the night in a motel and resume his search the next day.

CHAPTER 15

David and Debra ran as fast as they could after leaving Robert in the car unconscious. They stopped only a few times to rest. When they determined that they weren't being followed, they sat down to talk strategy.

"I lost Robert's gun when the car flipped over," Debra said.

"I still have mine," David commented as he paused to breathe. "We've got to be close to the Hudson River. We're going east from the interstate toward the river. It can't be much farther."

"What are we going to do when we get there?" Debra asked.

"Good question." David hesitated for an instant, and then he said, "If we're as close to Newburgh as I think we are, maybe we can contact someone I used to know. He was a commercial fisherman, and he lived just north of Newburgh, on the river. If we could get to his house, I believe he could take us down the river to the city, or at least close to where we need to be."

"We've used almost all forms of transportation since this mess started—we might as well use a boat too," Debra said. They both chuckled.

They began traveling toward the river again. They crossed State Route 9W, so David knew the river wasn't too far away.

It was nearly dark when they finally reached the Hudson River. In the dim light, they were able to find an old shed near the water and decided to spend the night there. Piling up fishing nets into a big pile, they were able to make a bed.

The clouds began to roll in, and the wind rattled the door to the shack. Just as they lay down on the nets, the rain began to fall. For a short time, they were very still and listened to the rain. There was very little conversation as they waited with great anticipation for the cover of darkness. Just as Debra was thinking of how grateful she was to be out of the rain, water began to drip beside them. Debra turned her attention to a spider in one corner of the shed near the ceiling, working feverishly spinning its web. As she watched the small creature work, she felt slightly envious. It had nothing to worry about— no one to be accountable to. An evil world was going on around this creature, and it was oblivious. She wished life could be that simple for humans. She prayed for a better day tomorrow. After a short time, the rhythm of the patter of rain lulled them off to sleep.

The next morning, they awakened to the noise of a motorboat running. They jumped up and looked out the door of the shack. They saw a young boy sitting in a boat tied up to a small dock. He was revving the motor, which occasionally missed and sputtered. When they walked out of the shed, they could see a house a short distance from the water. They walked down to the dock, and David exchanged greetings with the young man.

"Henry Lipinski used to live close by here. He owned a commercial fishing boat. Do you know him?"

"Yes, I know who you're talking about," the young man replied.

"Where does he live?"

"About six or so miles down the river."

"Would you take us to his house?"

"Well, I need to test this motor that I tuned up—I suppose I could. Hop in," the young man said. They climbed into the small boat, and the three of them started down the river. The boat didn't move very fast. The motor gave a sporadic sputter, and then would run smooth. They knew from the sound of the engine that the young man's expertise wasn't engine tune-up.

After several restarts, they finally reached Henry's house. As the young man maneuvered the boat up to the dock, they noticed how well the modest little house was maintained. An old commercial fishing boat was tied up on the right side of the dock, and a boathouse stood on the left side. Attached to the dock was a walkway about four feet wide leading up to the bank. The walkway was elevated above the ground, matching the height of the dock. There was a small building off to the left of the walkway and wooden steps with a handrail leading up the riverbank to the house. David thanked the young man, who refused any pay for the trip.

They began to make their way toward the steps.

"I remember riding that old boat when I came to visit Henry during my summer vacations," David said, pointing toward it as they walked by. After they climbed the wooden steps leading to the back of the house, David knocked on the door. They heard some rustling around, and finally an older man came to the door.

"What can I do for you?" he asked.

"Henry! It's me—David Kimble. Do you remember me?" The man looked at David for a few seconds, and then a big smile came across his face.

"I remember you. You used to come visit me when you were in college." He walked out on the porch and hugged David. David introduced Debra, and Henry invited them in.

As Debra walked through the house, she noticed that the décor had the touch of a woman, with antique furniture and little figurines. Henry invited them into the kitchen.

"I was just about to have some breakfast. Would you like some?"

"That sounds great!" they both said. Henry took a carton of eggs from the refrigerator and cracked them in a skillet. When the food was finished cooking, they all sat down to eat. Henry took a bottle of pills out of his pocket and popped one in his mouth. David looked at him.

"Oh...I have a heart condition. I take nitroglycerin pills occasionally, but I do okay here by myself," Henry said.

"Where's your wife?" David asked. Henry's expression changed to a more solemn look.

"She passed away four years ago. She got cancer and couldn't beat it. She fought right up to the end, but she's in a better place now."

"I'm so sorry, Henry. I wish I had known, but after college I went to work in the forestry service for a while. Then I decided to go to law school and into police work. I'm sorry I didn't keep in touch."

"It's okay, David. I know everyone has their own life to live." He hesitated for a moment. "Sarah kept waiting for that pot of gold that I promised her when we married. Before her passing, she told me something we both knew and had known for a long time: Life is what you make it. Your pot of gold is your life and the way you live it. You're only as happy as you want to be, and God blessed us with happiness. I really miss her" he said. A tear came to the corner of his eye. "She was a wonderful woman, and I am the luckiest man on earth to have known her. If you look around, you can still see signs of her. I left the house just the way she liked it."

Debra looked away and wiped the tears from her eyes as she listened to Henry talk about the woman he loved so much.

"What about you and this pretty young lady? You sure make a nice-looking couple." He smiled as he looked at David and then Debra. David just smiled, and Debra blushed as she finished wiping her eyes, looking at the floor. "You better not wait too long to marry her, son. You can lose the good ones to someone else," he said. He stood up from the table, took the coffee pot off the stove, and poured each of them another cup.

"I know, Henry. You're right." David looked at Debra, and they both smiled as they held a brief gaze. Henry sat back down and began to reminisce.

"I remember when you came to visit while you were in college." He turned and looked at Debra. "He lived just down the road from my brother, in the Catskill Mountains. When my brother came to visit, David would come with him in the summer. He was practically a son to me." He looked at David and smiled as he patted him on the back. "Sarah and I couldn't have children, so we really looked forward to his visits." He looked at Debra and smiled. Then he looked back at David and said, "I'm sorry, son. I don't mean to blab so much. I–I just don't get a chance to talk to anyone these days."

"That's okay, Henry. Those were some special times that I will always cherish, but the only thing I can think about right now is the pickle Debra and I are in."

They told Henry their story, and he listened intently while sipping his coffee.

"We need some transportation. Do you have a car we could borrow?"

"I have an old truck, but they're going to be looking for you on the highway. Wouldn't it make more sense to travel on the water?" Henry said.

"I was hoping you would say that, but do you have a boat we could use; something other than that old fishing trolley we saw tied up at the dock?"

"As a matter of fact, I do," Henry said and gave a big, boyish grin. "I have an old 1941 Chris Craft that I bought at a good price." There was a sudden look of skepticism on David's face.

"Nineteen forty-one?" David quickly commented.

"Now, hold on—let me finish. It's twenty-two-feet long, and it was in terrible shape when I bought it four years ago. I retired from my commercial fishing business when Sarah got sick. After Sarah died, I needed something to keep me busy. It kept me from being lonesome. It took three years of hard work, but I finished it last year. I named it *Sarah's Wind*. I rebuilt the V-8 engine, so it has a lot more horsepower now than it did originally." Henry paused to get more coffee. His face seemed to glow with pride as he described the old boat.

"There's a lot of great history behind the old Chris Craft boats from the 1920s. The bigger ones were called rumrunners. Gangsters used them to transport whiskey across the Great Lakes from Canada to the United States during the Prohibition. They would run from the coast guard. They were some of the fastest boats around back then." Henry paused for a moment as he looked at David and Debra, who was staring at him intently. "I'm sorry. I'm clattering on again, aren't I?"

"No, don't stop; it's fascinating to hear you tell about the old days," Debra said.

"Well, I didn't live in the twenties. I was born in 1934, but my grandfather told me lots of stories," he said with an enamored look on his face.

"Henry, I would love to hear more about that, but Bill Rogers may find out where we are, and we could put you in danger. We need to be going now," David said.

"Nonsense, you can stay here with me, and I will take you down the Hudson first thing tomorrow morning."

"I don't think we can wait that long. Besides, what about your heart condition? Can you ride a fast boat?"

"I built the engine before my heart condition. I've taken it out a few times, but I'm okay as long as I have my medicine," Henry said.

Henry took them down to the river and showed them the boat. It was in the boathouse Henry had built over the water. The boat was mahogany wood with several coats of clear marine polyurethane on it. It was beautiful, and Henry had done a great job restoring it.

After looking at the boat, they all sat on the back porch overlooking the river for a while. After much persuasion, David finally agreed to stay until the next day.

Bill left the motel and went back to where the car had gone off the road the day before. When he arrived, the state police were there and a wrecker was pulling the old Chevrolet up onto the side of the road.

Bill flashed his badge and introduced himself.

The police officer in charge said, "We were checking out the torn-down fence and saw the path cut down by that old Chevrolet we found in the ravine. We're running a make on the plates now. Would you know who it belongs to?"

"I was chasing two fugitives yesterday. They were driving that car, and they escaped on foot toward the river. It's probably stolen."

Bill explained to them whom he was chasing. The state police had gotten the APB on David and Debra earlier when they had escaped from Bill at the motel. Bill asked them how far it was to the Hudson River. They told him that the duo had most likely made it to the river the night before. The police told him that they would have the water patrol assist him with their watercraft. He followed them back to Newburgh.

After meeting with the water patrol, Bill explained to them where the car had gone off the road. They pinpointed the approximate location on their map and rode up the river from Newburgh. It was beginning to get late in the evening, and they ran out of time. They told Bill to come back the next day and that they would get an early start. Bill reluctantly spent another night in a motel without knowing where Debra and David were.

The next day, the water patrol took Bill up the river in one of their two-man patrol boats.

He told the patrolman approximately where the car had gone off the road. They rode to where they had marked the location on the map.

When they rode up the river, it had only been daylight a short time. Bill scanned the banks thoroughly. They came upon the young boy who had taken David and Debra down the river the day before. He was sitting on the dock, separating fishing nets.

The policeman said, "That's Bobby Coulter; let's ask him if he saw anyone. He's always out on the water." They floated up to the dock, and the policeman said, "Hey, Bobby."

"Hey, Officer Jones," Bobby replied, giving them a glance.

"Hey, kid, did you see a man and a woman come out of the woods around here anywhere yesterday?" Bill asked. The young man looked up again, but only for an instant.

"Nope," he replied. He looked down and continued his work.

"Are you sure, kid?" Bill asked.

"Yep," he said without looking at them.

Bill looked at the kid for a moment. He turned around toward the cop. "Give me one of your radios, and I'll call you in a little while. You go on up the river and keep looking. I'm going to look around here for a little while." The cop handed him a radio. He stepped off onto the dock and watched the cop drive away in the boat. He turned to the young man and asked, "Do you know who I am?" The boy looked up at him.

"You were with a cop, so I guess that makes you a cop, right?" he replied.

"I'm going to ask you that question again, son."

"If you ask it the same way, I'll answer it the same way," he said with a big grin, still focusing on his work and maintaining the same pace.

"What do you mean, kid?"

"You asked me if I saw a man and woman come out of those woods, and I said 'nope.' I didn't see them come out of the woods."

"Where did you see them?"

"They came out of that old shack over there." He raised his hand and pointed toward the shed. "They caused me more work," he said with a frown. "That's why I have to separate these fishing nets. They piled them up to make a bed, and now they're all tangled."

"Where did they go?"

"What's it worth to you, mister?" the young man said with an intent stare. Bill reached in his pocket, took out his billfold, and handed him a ten-dollar bill. He quickly snatched the money and stuffed it into his pocket.

"I took them down the river."

"Where down the river?" Bill asked with great anticipation. The young man held out his hand. Bill clenched his teeth, pulled out his billfold again, and took out a twenty. The boy grabbed the money and stuffed it into his pocket.

"I took them to Henry Lipinski's house."

"How far down river?" The kid held his hand out again.

"I gave you a twenty the last time, son," Bill said with an irritated glare.

"Okay, Henry lives about six or so miles down the river, on the right side."

Bill took out his cell phone and called Carmine.

"Where are you?"

"I'm at a motel in Newburgh. I've been waiting for your call. It's boring here."

"Find out how to get to Henry Lipinski's house. He lives on the Hudson River, north of Newburgh."

"Tell him to take 9W out of Newburgh; it's only about twenty miles. His name is on the mailbox." He hesitated for an instant. "That one's for free," Bobby said with a big grin. Bill repeated to Carmine what the young man had said.

"I'll wait and let you get there first, but you call me before you try to capture them. Do you understand?"

"Yeah, yeah, yeah," Carmine replied sarcastically.

"Carmine, you better not screw this up!" Bill said sternly and then closed up his cell phone.

He keyed the radio and called the water patrol to come pick him up.

"Hey, you little shyster! How much did you charge to take them down river?" Bill asked.

"Nothing."

"Nothing? Why did you charge me?"

"You're a cop—you can afford it." Bill looked at him and lightly scrubbed his knuckles across the boy's head.

The water patrol came and picked up Bill. He didn't mention anything about Henry or his conversation with the boy. Hoping to give Carmine a chance to get to Henry's house first, he decided to stall for time by directing the cop up the river to continue their search for the fleeing suspects.

Carmine and his sidekick drove the twenty miles on 9W and finally saw Henry's mailbox. Carmine tried to contact Bill, but there was no service.

"I'll take care of them myself. I don't need Bill's help," he said as he slowly drove down the long driveway toward Henry's house. To keep from giving away the element of surprise, Carmine parked a great distance from the house. The two men crept up close to the house with the demeanor of carnivorous animals sneaking up on their prey. The house was situated slightly under the bank on the river. Henry's truck was parked with the front pointing toward the house.

When Carmine saw the truck, his evil mind began to devise a plan. He slowly stood up and looked through the window of the truck. The keys were hanging in the ignition. A big smile came across his face. He explained the plan to his sidekick. He then looked around and found a big rock. He pointed it out to his sidekick and had him carry it over to the truck. He opened the door, turned the key, and started the truck. The man quickly picked up the big rock and put it on the gas pedal. The engine revved up with a loud roar. The man reached in and jerked the gearshift down into drive and jumped backward from the truck.

The kitchen was in the front of the house that faced the riverbank. Henry, David, and Debra were dressed and had just had their breakfast. They were sitting at the kitchen table drinking a cup of coffee and talking about their trip down the river when Henry heard the roar from his truck engine.

"What the heck is that? It sounds like... my truck," he commented. He walked over and looked through the small window at the top of the door just in time to see the old truck rumbling down the bank, seconds away from impact with the house. The truck suddenly slammed into the house with tremendous force. The wood-frame, lap-sided house was no match for the size and speed of Henry's big truck. The truck tore through the wall of the house with ease. Henry dove backward onto the floor when the truck came barreling through the door and the front wall of the house. Part of the doorjamb and wall came crashing down on top of Henry's right leg as the cab of the truck tore through the house. The truck came to a stop as it rammed a partition wall just across from the door. Almost half of the truck came inside the house before coming to a stop against the inside wall.

When the truck crashed through the wall, David jumped up, grabbed the table, and shoved it to one side. He grabbed Debra and pushed her to the floor. Debra screamed Henry's name as she and David scrambled over to him. David struggled with all his might to lift the partial wall, while Debra dragged Henry out from underneath it.

"Yeehaw!" they heard Carmine yell.

After getting Henry out from under the wall, David ran over to the hole and looked out. He saw Carmine and his sidekick standing there, laughing and cheering. David drew his gun, but just as he pointed it toward them, Carmine saw him.

"Move!" he yelled as he shoved the other man toward several big trees.

"You bastards! I'm going to kill you!" David shouted as he pulled the trigger of his pistol. The two men dove behind a big tree. David fired four shots at them. Carmine fired a few shots back at David. David ducked down behind what was left of the kitchen wall, stuck his arm above the wall, and fired several more shots. The breach of David's pistol stayed open, revealing an empty gun.

Debra was tending to Henry, who was moaning and groaning on the floor.

"His leg is badly broken, David!" Debra yelled.

"Henry, do you have a gun?" David shouted.

"There's a shotgun...behind that...cabinet in the corner! There's...some buckshot on the shelf," Henry mumbled, breathing rapidly. David found the shotgun and the shells. Carmine fired several more shots through the hole made by the truck. David stuck the shotgun over the partial wall and fired. The blast took a chunk of bark off the tree just above Carmine.

"Hey, David, that was a pretty good shot!" Carmine shouted, "but I've got all day! Now if you don't want that old man to get killed, you and Debra just come on out and we'll let him go!"

"He's got a broken leg. He needs a doctor!" David yelled.

Carmine, sporting a grin, winked at the man next to him and shouted, "Give up, and I'll see that he gets one!"

"Maybe we should," David said, looking at Debra. "It's my fault Henry is hurt."

"You know we can't trust them, David. They'll kill us all," Debra replied in a low tone.

"No … you can't … give up," Henry mumbled as he grabbed his chest and gasped for breath. "My pills, they were … on the shelf by the sink." David looked, and the part of the wall where the shelf was had fallen in.

"They must be under the wall!" David shouted. He and Debra began to move pieces of debris, looking frantically for Henry's nitroglycerin.

The engine had stalled on the truck when it came through the wall, and the impact had pushed the hood back near the windshield. The top of the wall over the door had fallen through the windshield, and smoke began to pour out from underneath the crushed hood.

"David, we have to get him out of here! That truck is going to catch fire!" Debra screamed. She grabbed Henry by the arms and began to drag him across the kitchen floor toward the living room. The smoke quickly became flames as the ruptured fuel line ignited. Flaming gasoline began running out from underneath the truck and quickly ignited the wood floor. The smoke and fire spread through-out the front rooms of the house.

Coughing and choking on the smoke, David grabbed the shot-gun and ran into the living room with Debra and Henry. He knew the flames would reach the gas tank on the truck any second. David knelt down on the floor beside Henry.

"I couldn't find your pills, Henry!" David exclaimed. The house began to fill with smoke. "We have to get out of here!" David shouted. "The gas tank is going to blow on that truck." He handed Debra the shotgun, picked Henry up, put him over his shoulder, and they ran out the back door. They ran across the back porch and down the wooden steps to the dock. Henry moaned with every step as his badly broken leg dangled around.

David ran in the direction of the boathouse. "Where are the keys to the boat, Henry?" David shouted as he ran.

"Pocket … pocket," was the only word Henry could utter. Debra put her hand in Henry's pocket and pulled out the keys. Just before they reached the boathouse, the truck exploded with a loud boom. The windows blew out of the house. Flames rolled out and curled up over the roof. The house was completely engulfed as the flames and black smoke rose several feet in the air.

Bill and the patrolman were coming down the river when they heard the explosion and saw the black smoke. Bill knew that it was Carmine's handiwork, but he said nothing as the patrolman increased his speed.

Debra jerked the door open, and she and David loaded Henry in the boat. Henry was no longer complaining about his broken leg. He was breathing very shallowly. They heard the patrol boat slowing down as Bill and the patrolman coasted up to the dock. David looked out the window of the small boathouse and saw Bill and the patrolman getting out of the boat. David's blood practically boiled as his eyes caught sight of Bill. David grabbed the shotgun from Debra.

She grabbed David by the arm. "David, don't go! Please, don't go! They'll kill you!" Debra begged, her voice quivering.

"I've had it! Bill's going to pay for this," David said. She saw the determination in his face, and she knew nothing she said was going to change his mind. She let go of his arm, and he ran to the door of the boathouse.

David waited until they had walked by the small building located next to the steps leading up to the house. When David ran out the door of the boathouse, Bill and the patrolman were standing with the building between them and David. The patrolman was standing behind Bill, calling the fire department.

When David came out of the boathouse, he was on a full run. He ran up behind the patrolman and hit him across the back of the head with the barrel of the shotgun. The cop fell from the walkway to the ground, instantly unconscious. Hearing the sound, Bill whirled around, reaching for his gun just as David leveled the shotgun on him.

"I'm going to kill you, Bill!" David shouted. Bill stood frozen with his hand under his coat. Suddenly Bill jumped to his left behind the small building as he pulled his gun. He fired a wild shot in the air just above David's head. David fired his shotgun and blew a chunk of wood off the corner of the little building as Bill scampered out of sight.

"Come on out, you murdering pig!" David shouted. "Come on out, you gutless piece of slime, and do your own dirty work, you low-life coward!" Bill tried to move out from the building on the other side to get a shot. David pulled the trigger on the other barrel of the shotgun. The pellets took a big piece of wood off the left side of the building, knocking the gun from Bill's hand as he moved it out from the wall. Bill fell backward as he grabbed for the gun.

Carmine and the other man heard the gunshots and came running around the side of the burning house. David was reloading his shotgun as Bill reached for his pistol. Debra was standing in the door of the boathouse when she saw Carmine come around the house.

"David!" she screamed and pointed at Carmine. David ran toward the boathouse as he fired a shot in Carmine's direction. Carmine and the other man dropped to the ground.

Just as David reached the door of the boathouse, Bill found his pistol and began firing at him. At the same time, Carmine and the other man both began firing. The bullets blew pieces of wood off the door as it closed behind David.

Debra grabbed him and hugged him for half a second.

"Grab the towline!" he shouted. She grabbed the line and threw it in the boat. They jumped in the boat, and David started the engine. They created a great wake as they took off down the river. Neither Carmine, his sidekick, nor Bill could get a shot off. They were all reloading when David and Debra sped away in the boat.

Debra checked Henry's vital signs. He was lying very still, with his eyes open.

"David, Henry's not breathing!" she shouted. She began shaking him, slapping his face, and crying hysterically while screaming his name.

"Drive the boat!" David yelled. She jumped forward and grabbed the wheel. David began to perform CPR, but after several minutes, he still was getting no response. He stood up and walked up beside Debra, breathing hard, sweating profusely, and with tears streaming down his face. He took the wheel from her, and pulled over close to the bank. After getting the boat stopped, he turned and looked at Debra in total disbelief of what had happened. He stood there for a moment then held out his hands and looked at them and began to tremble. He raised his fist in the air and began to scream with everything in him. He leaned forward and pounded his fists on the side of the boat.

"This is all my fault!" he shouted. "He's dead because of me! I'm the one who brought us here!" Debra grabbed David. She put her arms around him, crying, and they stood holding on to each other.

CHAPTER 16

After David and Debra had driven away in the boat, Carmine came running down the hill to where Bill was just getting up from the ground.

"What happened, you idiot? You were supposed to call me!" Bill shouted. He climbed up on the walkway that was connected to the dock. "I was going to cover the back door so they couldn't get away."

"I don't like the way you talk to me, Bill. You should show a little more respect," Carmine said with a smug look.

"When you earn some respect, I'll show it. Now, you were supposed to call me," Bill said sternly. "Why didn't you?"

"Your cell phone didn't work, Bill. I wasn't going to wait all day," Carmine said.

All of a sudden, the house began to fall as it burned behind them, and debris rolled down the hill toward the dock.

"You better leave before the police and the fire department get here. I don't want to have to explain your presence to them," Bill said. He jumped down and took hold of the cop David had knocked out. "Help me lay him up on the dock."

Carmine motioned for the other man to help Bill. Carmine stood there and watched, with his arm in the sling.

Bill climbed into the patrol boat after placing the cop on the dock where he could be found. "I'm going after them. I'll be in touch. Now get out of here," Bill said. He took off down the river, picked up the microphone, contacted the police and told them that David and Debra had robbed an old man, kidnapped him, and burned his house. He told them David had knocked out the cop who was lying on the dock below the burning house and asked them to send the river rescue squad.

Carmine and company hurried past what was left of the burning house. They jumped in their car and drove away. Shortly afterward, the fire department and the police arrived.

After David and Debra regained their composure, they started down the river. They soon met the river rescue squad coming up the river. David flagged them down and gave them Henry's body. He explained to them that Henry had had a heart attack. They told David they needed him to answer some questions about Henry's death. David tried to explain to them that he was an FBI agent, but they wanted him to stay and talk to the police. David jumped in the boat, grabbed the wheel, and took off down the river.

"They're going to be looking for this boat," David said. "We're going to have to ditch it." At that moment, several shots rang out and pieces of wood splintered up as bullets tore holes in the back of the beautiful boat. They looked behind them and saw Bill rapidly approaching them in the patrol boat.

"David, it's Bill!" Debra shouted.

David pushed the throttle all the way open, but they could not pull away. The patrol boat was much faster, and it was quickly gaining on them.

"Hand me the shotgun, and get down behind the seats!" David shouted. Debra complied.

While steering the boat, David pointed the gun behind him and fired. Pellets peppered the front of the patrol boat. Bill ducked his head down as the windshield cracked from the blast.

Smoke began to roll from the engine compartment of Henry's old boat. One of Bill's bullets had ruptured the oil filter, and oil was spraying onto the exhaust manifold. David made a quick U-turn and headed straight for Bill.

As the two boats neared each other, both David and Bill jumped on the floor. The bow of each boat glanced off, and the two boats scrubbed down each other's sides. After they had passed and the back of the two boats were still close together, David stood up. He swung his shotgun around and fired at the back of the patrol boat as it went by. The blast hit one of the two big outboard engines. The fuel line ruptured, and the engine instantly erupted into a ball of fire. Bill dove out of the boat as it traveled on down the river. After coasting only a few more yards, the boat exploded with a tremendous blast. Burning debris scattered over a large area of the water. Several pieces rained down near Bill as he swam through the water.

David had lost track of the direction of his boat when he had looked back at the patrol boat. When he turned around, the boat was only a few feet from the shoreline, the throttle all the way open. He dropped the shotgun as he tried to turn the wheel, but the boat was too close to the bank. The bow caught the bank as David jerked the throttle lever backward, but there wasn't enough time to slow the boat down. The impact threw David into the windshield and Debra against the doors of the boat's lower compartment. The windshield cracked with the impact of David's head. David stepped backward, holding the knot that was forming on his head. Debra tried to stand up, holding her shoulder. The engine began missing and sputtering, and black smoke poured from the engine compartment.

David quickly turned the engine off. Most of the front of the boat was wedged up against the bank.

"Are you okay, Debra?" David asked as he reached out and took hold of her hand, helping her to her feet. A small trickle of blood came down his face from the bump on his forehead.

"I'm okay. I just landed on my shoulder." She reached for him. "David, you're bleeding."

"I'm okay—it's just a bump."

They looked back through the thick, black smoke and saw Bill in the river, swimming toward them, his gun in his hand. David looked around for the shotgun and realized that when he had tried to regain control of the boat, the gun had fallen overboard.

"We have to go. Here comes that maniac!" David yelled. He grabbed Debra by the hand, and the two of them crawled over the windshield, walked across the bow of the boat, and jumped to the bank.

They climbed up the steep hill from the riverbank. When they reached the top, they stopped to catch their breath. They looked down and saw Bill crawling out onto the bank, utterly exhausted. He lay there struggling to breathe. The engine compartment of the boat was now starting to burn, and the flames were getting bigger by the second. While lying on the shore, Bill looked over and saw the flames spreading on the boat and crawled away from the boat as quickly as he could.

David and Debra rested for a few minutes and then started walking. After they had walked for a couple of miles, they came across State Route 9W.

"We can't stay on this road. One of Bill's hired killers may come by," David said. They walked along the road, but they hid each time they heard a car coming. They stayed out of sight as much as they could. "If a truck comes by, maybe we can catch a ride," David commented.

"I hope we can get to Newburgh before dark. I don't fancy sleeping outside again," Debra said. She looked at David and smiled. He put his arm around her.

"I destroyed Henry's beautiful boat, Debra." He kept looking forward and didn't make eye contact with her.

"No, those no-good thugs destroyed Henry's boat," Debra said. She looked at David as they walked. She knew he was grieving over Henry, and she knew the reason he wasn't talking about it, he was still blaming himself for Henry's death. She put her arm around David's waist and leaned her head over against his shoulder. She didn't want to force him to talk about it. She knew that at the right time he would reveal his true feelings of guilt because of Henry's death, and she would be there to help him feel better.

After walking for about two hours and avoiding every car that came by, they heard a truck coming. They stepped out to flag it down and saw that it was a big diesel wrecker that towed big tractor-trailers. When the man saw them out in the road waving, dirty, and sweaty, he took pity on them and stopped. They climbed up into the big truck. "Are you two in some kind of trouble?" the man asked as they sat down in the seat.

"Yes, we need a ride to New York City."

"I'm only going to Newburgh," the driver said, "but you're welcome to ride there with me."

"That will have to do for now," said David.

"I'm Jason Osborne," he said as he put out his hand. David shook his hand. He didn't know what the driver had heard, so he quickly decided to give him fake names.

"I'm Danny Smith, and this is Brenda Stone. David only told him they were involved in an accident and needed to get somewhere to make a phone call. While driving along, they met several police cars with their lights flashing, speeding toward Henry's house.

"Wonder what that's all about," the driver commented. "There have been more cops on this road today than I have ever seen."

David, hoping to change the subject, asked, "How far is it to Newburgh?"

"It's only about twelve more miles."

"Great," David said.

Asking an occasional question and hoping to keep the driver's mind off the reason for all the cops, they sat back and listened as the driver talked about his job and his life.

When they were about four miles from Newburgh, the local news came on the radio. They began to talk about the fire at Henry's house. The reporter said, "The police are looking for a man and a woman believed to be responsible for the fire and the death of the owner of the house. Police are looking for David Kimble and Debra Benson. If you see these people, do not approach them. They are believed to be armed and extremely dangerous, according to Bill Rogers, Special Agent for the FBI." The reporter began to describe them and the clothes they were wearing. Jason looked over at them and realized that they were the persons being described on the radio. He said, "Oh God! Please don't kill me!" He held up one hand and moved away from them, pressing himself against his door as he swerved back and forth on the road.

"No! We're not killers! It's okay! It's okay!" they both shouted. Jason slammed on the brakes and slowed the truck to an almost-complete stop. He jumped out the door and ran down the road in the opposite direction. He left the engine running and the truck still rolling. David jumped under the steering wheel.

"David, can you drive this truck?"

"I used to drive a delivery truck years ago—it can't be that different," he commented. He put the truck into gear, and they drove on toward Newburgh.

"What now, David?"

"We need to find a motel where we can hide so I can think," David said.

Jason was running down the road when a cop drove up and stopped. He explained to the cop what had happened. The cop told Jason to get in the backseat, and they started out after David and Debra. The cop called over his radio, and several cars responded. Two of them came out of Newburgh, traveling north on Route 9W.

David was almost to Newburgh when he met the cops. One of them slid his car across the road in front of them.

"Hold on, Debra!" David shouted. He tried to steer away from the cop car, but there wasn't enough room left to pass. The big truck hit the front of the car, tearing the front section almost completely off. The car spun around in a circle several times and slid off the opposite side of the road. David struggled to maintain control of the truck. After regaining control, he looked in his side mirror and saw the cop jump out of the car and start shooting at them. The other cop had turned around and was now chasing them. They drove into town and met two more police cars. After the two police cars turned around, the three of them came up quickly behind the truck. Two of them pulled along the side of the truck and began ramming it. David tried desperately to avoid them, but they forced the truck into the side of some parked cars, pushing them onto the sidewalk.

"David, they're trying to kill us! How can we get away?" Debra shouted while she bounced around in the seat.

"I have to find a place to ditch this truck!" David yelled. He steered the truck into the side of one of the cop cars. He looked down the street and saw an alley running between two buildings to his left. He had to try anything to get away from them. Hoping it would be narrow enough to keep the cops behind the truck, he made a left turn and slammed the pedal down. His quick turn forced one of the cop cars into a parked car on the left side of the street. David turned in front of oncoming traffic. Several cars slid crosswise in the road. Two of them ran into the back of the others. David was able to turn the big truck down the alley. The truck glanced off one of the corners of the building with a loud *bang*. David had to stay over to the right side to miss rows of garbage Dumpsters. The fender, the running board, and the fuel tank hung onto the wall of the building on the right side as they squeezed down the narrow alley. Sparks were coming from the metal as the truck scraped the wall of the building. The truck hung on to a fire escape ladder on the side of one of the buildings, ripping the ladder loose and dragging it along with them for a short distance.

"I'm going to slide this truck sideways to keep the cops behind us. When we stop, we need to jump out on the driver's side," David said. He jerked the wheel to the right. The back end of the truck slid around and caught the building on the left. The front of the truck slammed into the building on the right.

With the truck wedged, David jerked the driver's door open and grabbed Debra by the hand. "Come on!" he shouted. He helped her out onto the running board, and they exited the truck.

Two police cars followed down the alley behind the truck. When David slid the truck sideways, the cops came up behind it. They jumped out of their cars with their guns drawn. They jumped up on the back of the wrecker and worked their way forward. They looked down the side of the truck and saw David and Debra running down the alley. One of the cops raised his gun and shouted, "Stop where you are!" They stopped and turned around. "Don't you move!" he shouted.

At that moment, the diesel fuel that was leaking out of the ruptured fuel tank ignited and flames came up the side of the truck.

One of the cops looked down and saw the flames, and shouted, "Get down! This thing is going to blow!" The two cops lowered their guns and scrambled down from the truck.

As they ran, the cop in the rear shouted, "Go, go, go!" They ran back to their cars and backed them out of the ally just as the truck erupted into a ball of fire and black smoke.

When they saw the cops disappear off the back of the truck, Debra and David ran to the end of the alley. They paused for an instant, looked back, and saw the truck burst into flames.

They turned right and ran across the parking lot of a gas station. They crossed the street and went down another alley, walking as fast as they could. A few minutes later they could hear sirens.

"We have to find a taxi, Debra, before the cops find us."

After walking for a few minutes, they came to a part of the town where there was heavier traffic. They hurried down the street, and David flagged down a taxi that was driving by. David told the driver to go south to any motel just south of Newburgh.

While they were stopped at a red light, the police went by with their lights and sirens on. David and Debra sank down in the backseat, trying to be as inconspicuous as possible.

The taxi driver drove south a couple of miles out of the city. When they came upon a small motel, David told the driver to pull in. They paid the driver and left the taxi. Not wanting to be seen together, Debra waited outside while David rented a room.

After they went in the motel room, Debra plopped down on the bed. "I'm exhausted," she said as she lay back on the bed and expelled a rush of air from her lungs.

"We can't be seen outside until the cops are through looking for us in this area," David said.

"What can we do now?"

"We've run out of options. The only thing I can think of is to call a friend of mine at the office. I think I can trust him to help us," David said. He sat down beside Debra. She sat up on the bed, and David put his arm around her. She laid her head on his shoulder.

"Who is he?" she asked.

"I've known him a long time. His name is John Parks, and he's an honest person. I'm going to call him and ask for help."

"While you make your phone call, I'm going to take a shower," Debra said.

David picked up the phone and asked the operator to connect him with the FBI headquarters in New York City. After the connection was made, David told the person that answered the phone that he wanted to talk to John Parks. After a brief moment, John picked up the phone.

"Hello, John Parks speaking."

"John, this is David."

"David," John whispered, looking around to see if anyone could hear him. "Everybody in law enforcement is looking for you and that woman who's with you. They said you killed a cop and now some old man."

"He wasn't just some old man—he was my friend. I know what they're saying, but it's not true, John. Bill Rogers has been paid off by Senator Jack Braco. Debra Benson is Senator Braco's illegitimate daughter, and he is trying to keep the public from finding out about her. He's paid Bill to kill her. I don't have time to explain it all now, but I need your help."

"What can I do to help you, David?"

"Are you alone?"

"What?"

"Is there anyone that could hear our conversation?" John looked around again.

"No, there's no one close enough to hear us."

"Okay, I'm at Dan's Motel, just south of Newburgh. Can you meet me here?"

"I'll be there as soon as I can. Give me the phone and room number where you're staying." David gave him the numbers.

"We'll be waiting. John, please come alone. I don't trust anyone else."

"Okay, David." They hung up the phone.

John sat there a little while, trying to decide whether or not to call Bill. Finally, he picked up the phone and dialed Bill's cell phone number.

The water patrol had rescued Bill from the riverbank. His cell phone was destroyed by the water when he went in the river. He had left the water patrol and gone to a cell phone store in Newburgh to get a new phone. He had heard about the chase that David and Debra had given the police and knew they were close by. He was driving south through Newburgh when his cell phone rang.

When Bill answered, John said, "Bill this is John Parks. I just got a phone call from David."

"Where is he?"

"He's at a motel."

"What motel? Where?"

"He said you've been bought off by Senator Braco and that you are trying to kill him and the girl."

"That's ridiculous, John. That woman has him completely under her control. You can't believe anything he says."

"He wants me to meet him there," John said.

"Is he in Newburgh?"

"He's close by," John replied.

"Give me the motel name, and I'll meet you there. We'll go meet him together."

"No, I'll call just before I get there and tell you the name of the motel. I'm not going to betray his trust."

"John, just tell me the name of the motel," Bill said. "I only want to help him."

"I'll call you just before I get there," John said and hung up.

"No! No, don't hang up!" Bill shouted as the phone went dead. He snapped the cell phone closed. He put the phone down and began yelling and banging the steering wheel with the heel of his hand.

After regaining his composure, he said to himself, "At least I'll be close by if that little jerk does call me."

He thought for a moment, and then he began to smile. He dialed a number on his cell phone. When someone answered he said, "Stan, this is Bill; is John Parks still at his desk?"

"He's just getting up and putting on his coat. Do you want me to get him for you?"

"No. No, I want you to follow him," Bill said.

"What!" Stan asked, surprised. "What's this about, Bill?"

"John's conspiring with David. He's going to meet him right now."

"What's going on with David? Is all that they're saying about him true?"

"Yes, it's all true, but right now I need you to follow John and call me on my cell phone when he gets to where he's going."

"Okay, Bill," Stan said and hung up.

Bill closed his cell phone and smiled. He drove around Newburgh, checking in the offices of several motels to see if anyone recognized Debra's or David's photos.

After David hung up the phone from his conversation with John Parks, he lay back on the bed and looked at the ceiling. Debra came out of the bathroom after she had taken a shower and gotten dressed.

"It sure feels better to get a shower, but I don't like putting the same clothes back on," she said as she scrubbed a towel through her wet hair. She looked at David lying there, staring at the ceiling. She lay down on the bed beside him, leaning on one elbow. "What are you thinking about, David? Debra asked.

"It's my fault Henry's dead. I should never have agreed to spend the night." David slammed his fist down on the table beside the bed. He sat up and swung his legs over the side of the bed to the floor. "If we had left, Henry would be alive right now." He sat on the edge of the bed, with his back to Debra and his fingers laced together. He leaned forward and put his elbows on his knees, his thumbs underneath his chin, and pressed his laced fingers against his lips as he stared at the floor.

"It's not your fault, David," Debra said. She leaned over and rubbed David's back. "Henry was so glad to see you; he begged you to stay. It breaks my heart to see you sad and blaming yourself. Besides, if anyone is to blame, it's me. This whole mess is my fault." She sat back in the middle of the bed. David turned and looked at her. She looked up at him as her eyes filled with tears. "Think of all the people who would still be alive today if not for me. You would've been better off to never have met me, David." She covered her face with her hands as she began to sob. She rolled over and buried her face in the pillows. She pounded the pillow with her right fist. Between muffled sobs she shouted, "Your friend is dead because of me!"

"I don't care about all these problems, Debra," David said. He turned around and lay down beside her. While leaning on his elbow, he put his hand on the back of her head and stroked her hair. He pushed her long brown hair to one side and began to rub her neck and back. "If not for this mess, I would never have met you. I certainly don't regret that."

Debra rolled over and looked up at him, still sobbing. Leaning over her, David rubbed some of the tears from her face. He slid his right hand underneath her neck, with his thumb caressing her left cheek. He put his face down inches from hers, and looked into her eyes.

"I don't care about the mess, Debra. I love you. Sure, I regret what happened to Henry, but that's not your fault." She could see the love in his eyes. He gently lifted her head as he put his lips on hers, and they kissed with great passion. He drew back from her as she held his face in her hands. "I could never blame you for Henry's death, Debra. It was just an unfortunate accident created by evil people who believe their only purpose in life is to make everyone else as miserable as they are, so please don't blame yourself."

"I love you too, David." She smiled, and they kissed again.

David went in and took a shower. After getting dressed, he lay down on the bed beside Debra as they waited for John.

"I don't know about John," David said. "He sounded kind of strange. I'm not sure he believed what I told him about Bill." David looked over at Debra. "He didn't even act surprised. I just wonder if Bill's gotten to him."

"You know him, David. Are sure you can trust him? He wouldn't bring Bill here, would he?"

"I'm not sure anymore. We'll just have to wait and see."

Debra leaned over and kissed him and then laid her head on his shoulder.

"David, try to rest. I know you're tired. Maybe you'll feel better when you wake up."

"Yes, I am tired," David said. After a few minutes, they both faded off to sleep with the hope that John would be able help them end this nightmare.

CHAPTER 17

Stan followed John Parks out to his car. John drove north toward Newburgh. Because of heavy traffic delays, it took almost two and a half hours. While driving, he noticed Stan's car following him. He dialed the number David had given him.

When David heard the phone ringing, he quickly sat up in bed and grabbed the receiver.

"Hello!" he said in a sleepy, raspy voice.

"David, it's me, John. I have a problem. Someone is following me."

"Do you know who it is?"

"No, I don't, but I can't meet you. I'll lead them right to you."

"Is it Bill?"

"It could be. He called me a few days ago and told me all this crazy stuff about you and asked me to call him if I heard from you."

"Well, did you call him, John?"

"Yes, but I didn't tell him where you were. He said he wanted to help you, David. He said you killed that sheriff and that this bad woman was controlling you."

"John, Bill is a liar! I think he's lost his mind. He's been bought by Jack Braco. He is responsible for several people's deaths!"

"But, he sa—"

"John, how long have you known me? You know that I would never purposely hurt anyone."

"Okay, you're right, David. I believe you, but what do we do about the car that's following me?"

"Where are you now?"

"I'm only a few miles from Newburgh."

"Drive on through Newburgh if you have to. Then pull over and wait for a while. Give me your cell number in case I need to call you." John gave him his phone number.

"I'll call you back when the coast is clear, David."

They hung up the phone, and John kept driving for a while.

After driving into Newburgh, he pulled in the lot at the I-84 Diner, a stainless-steel restaurant shaped like a train car. He pulled into a parking space and just sat in his car.

Stan drove down the street, then turned and came back. He maneuvered his car behind a building across the street from the restaurant where John had parked. He parked so he could clearly see John's car without John being able to see him. He called Bill and told him where he was. After twenty minutes or so, Bill pulled in next to Stan, walked around his car, and came over to talk to him.

"Stan, there's lots of money in this, if you help me," Bill said, leaning into Stan's car window. A smile came across his face. It was obvious that Bill had chosen the right man. Stan's greed for money was on the same scale as his.

"How much money are we talking about, Bill?"

"Lots and lots of money; just take my word for it," Bill said with an evil grin.

"What do I have to do?"

"I need your help to get information from John. He knows where David is." Stan's expression changed and a sour look came over his face.

"I never liked that little dweeb John anyway, and I certainly never liked David, either. Those two always have their heads together. Everything has to be right by the book—always acting all holier than thou! They both need to be brought down off their high horses."

"Well, here's your chance to put them in their place," Bill said. He gave a devious smile. "Come on; let's go get John."

They walked across the road, being careful to keep cars between them and John's view. They crept up to his car, Bill on the driver's side and Stan on the passenger side. Bill jerked open the driver's door and put his gun to John's head.

"Put your hands on the steering wheel!" Bill said in a stern voice. John had his hand on his gun in the shoulder holster. He slowly put his hands on the steering wheel. Bill reached down and pushed the unlock button on John's door handle. Stan opened the passenger door, slid across the seat, reached under John's coat and took out his gun.

"What are you doing here, Stan?"

"I'm here to make some money," Stan said with an evil grin.

John looked at Bill and said, "So David *was* telling the truth about you, wasn't he, Bill?"

"Just shut up and do as you're told. Now, I'm going to put my gun away, and you're going to walk with me back to my car without any incident, aren't you, John?"

John slowly stepped out of the car, and Bill directed him across the street. They forced John in the backseat of Bill's car. Stan sat down in the seat beside him, poking him in the ribs with his gun. After getting under the steering wheel, Bill just sat there. He didn't start the car.

John looked at Stan and said, "You're enjoying this aren't you, Stan?"

"You bet I am—every minute of it!" Stan said with glee in his voice and a grin on his face.

"I can't wait to see the look on David's face when I stick this gun up one of his nostrils!"

"Why do you hate him so, Stan?"

"You know why, John. He testified against me."

"You were wrong, Stan," John said.

"I don't care. Cops are supposed to stick together."

"Not if one of them is doing something against the law."

"Here we go," Stan said. "Go ahead, John. Get up on your soap-box and tell us how you always do the right thing and how we should all be the same way too. Just save your preaching for your kids!" Stan said.

"Both of you shut up!" Bill shouted. "Now, we have to talk strategy, Stan. I'm sure John must have spotted you following him, and that's why he stopped. Did you call David, John?"

"No, I stopped to get something to eat, but you two interrupted me."

"You're a liar, John! I saw you eating a burger at your desk not long before you left," Stan said in a condescending tone.

"What did you tell David?" Bill demanded, looking at John through the rearview mirror.

"I told you I didn't call anyone."

Stan hit John across the back of the head with his gun and said, "You heard the question. What did you tell him?"

John grabbed the back of his head as he flew forward from the impact and said, "Okay, okay. I just told him that someone was following me and that I would call him back." Stan reached inside John's coat and took his cell phone.

"You're not calling him back, so you won't need this," Stan said. He started to toss the phone out the window.

"No, hang on to that phone for a while," Bill said. "It may come in handy." He looked at John in the mirror again. "Now, John, I'm only going to ask you one time. Where's the motel?"

"What are you going to do to David if I tell you?"

"Nothing, nothing; I just want to talk. I just want to try to reason with him."

"You're a liar. I'm not telling you anything, Bill."

Stan grabbed John by the hair, shoved the gun barrel against his ear, jerked his head around, and shouted, "You're going to tell us everything we want to know!" John screamed as Stan began beating him. Bill put the car in gear and drove out of the parking lot in the direction that John had been traveling.

Stan tortured John while Bill drove around until John finally told them the name of the motel. They drove to the motel and parked down the street. Bill and Stan forced John out of the car and made him walk to the door. They stood behind John as he knocked on the door. There was no answer. Stan stepped back, kicked the door open, and shoved John inside. They drew their guns, ran inside, and looked the room over.

"They're not here. I should have known David would be too smart to just sit here and let us walk in on him," Bill said. At that moment, John's phone rang in Stan's pocket. Stan looked at Bill as he took John's phone out of his pocket. Bill grabbed the phone out of Stan's hand and opened it.

"Hello!"

"Bill, where's John?"

"The question is, David, where are you?"

"Enough people have been hurt. I want you to let John go."

"You and Debra turn yourselves in to me, and I'll let John go."

"I see you have that creep Stan with you."

Bill walked to the door and looked out. He looked across the parking lot and up and down the street.

"Where are you David? How do you know I have Stan with me?"

Stan shoved John over to the door. "I saw you as you drove by. Besides, I knew you would have someone with you. You're much too gutless and spineless to do this on your own. That's why you have those killers following us."

Bill grabbed John by the arm and pushed him in the doorway of the room, facing the parking lot. While Stan held on to John, Bill put his gun to John's head.

"I'll kill him right here if you don't give up right now!" Bill shouted into the phone.

"Look up the street at the department store. There's a warehouse behind the store. Meet me in the warehouse parking lot in a few minutes," David said and hung up the phone.

He and Debra left the phone booth they had called from and went through the store to the back. They walked out through the gardening department and went behind the building. They went in a side door of the warehouse section of the department store and walked down a dark aisle with stacks of boxes on either side.

"David, what are we going to do now? How are we going to get them to turn your friend loose?" Debra asked.

"I don't know, but I can't stand by and watch anyone else get hurt or killed," David said. "I want you to hide in here, and I'll come and get you if I can get away. If I don't come back, try to slip out and get away."

"David, please don't talk like that," Debra said as she stopped and hugged him. "Please, be careful." She put her hand on his face and kissed him.

"I'll be okay, but don't come out unless I call you."

Debra hid behind a shelf covered with stacks of products in paper boxes. David walked back to the door and waited.

Bill and Stan forced John in the car and drove down the street behind the department store where they parked their car. As they exited the car, John jerked loose from Stan and ran toward the warehouse door. John began shouting for David to get away.

"Go get him before someone hears that idiot and we have to explain this to them!" Bill shouted.

Stan chased after him, and just before John was able to reach the side door of the warehouse, Stan grabbed him and wrestled him to the ground. Stan jumped up, pulled John up from the ground, and pointed his gun at him.

At that moment, David threw the door open and came out of the warehouse, carrying a big piece wood. He hit Stan across the back and knocked him to the ground. Stan dropped his gun as he fell. John bent down and grabbed the Glock that Stan had taken from him. John and David ran back to the door of the warehouse. Just as they started in the door, Bill raised his gun to fire a shot, but they ran into the building before he could get a shot off. Bill ran over and helped Stan up. They jerked the door open, and hurried inside the warehouse. David and John rushed to where Debra was hiding. David grabbed Debra by the hand, and they hurried toward the rear of the building.

A man came up to them and asked them what they were doing in the warehouse. John showed the man his FBI badge and explained what was going on, but the man got frightened and tried to run away. John grabbed him by the arm.

"Go call the police," John said.

The man jerked loose from John and ran. The three of them raced out the back of the building onto the loading dock. A box-bed delivery truck was parked next to the loading dock, with the back doors open, and it was empty.

"Get in the back," John said. David and Debra jumped in the back of the truck, John closed the doors and latched the handle. John ran around to the door, climbed in the driver's seat, and started the truck. A man came running up to the door, yelling for John to stop, but John ignored him and drove away.

After they went inside the building, Bill and Stan made their way toward the back, near the loading area. They ran out onto the loading dock just as John was driving away in the truck.

"Let's get back to the car!" Bill shouted.

Several men had heard the commotion and came out onto the loading dock just as Bill and Stan were heading back to their car. Bill flashed his badge and explained to them that they were chasing three murder suspects. Bill and Stan ran back to the car and drove around the building. They sat in the car and watched the delivery truck leave the parking lot of the department store at the opposite end. They followed the truck as they headed south toward New York City.

The farther south out of the city they traveled, the more rural the area became. John noticed Bill's car following behind the truck and drove faster, but when he increased his speed, Bill drove faster also. When Bill saw that John increased his speed, he knew John had spotted him.

"Okay, John, let's see if you have any guts," Bill said. He then drove up behind the truck. "Stan, when you get a shot, I want you to shoot out the front tire on that truck!" Bill shouted. Stan pulled his pistol from his holster and leaned out the window as Bill steered the car to the left and drove up beside the truck.

John saw Bill's car drive up beside them. He tried to cut Bill off, but the big truck was not easy to maneuver.

When Stan had a clear shot of the front tire, he fired and the tire blew out. Bill slowed down and dropped back behind the truck as it began to swerve. John struggled to keep control, but with one flat tire on the front at the speed he was traveling, trying to steer the big truck and hold it straight in the road was virtually impossible. He lost control as the truck began to swerve, turned sideways and went into the left lane. John tried to steer the truck straight, but the truck ran off the road, crashed through the guardrail, and slid down a steep embankment.

The bank was about forty feet high, and a house with a short backyard was situated near the bottom of the hill. The truck traveled down the bank and across the yard toward the house. It began to tip over as it struck the right corner of the back of the house. On impact, the truck flipped over on its right side, knocking a chunk out of the house and ripping part of the cab off the truck. The impact threw John against the windshield, breaking it with his head.

While John was trying to evade Bill and Stan, David and Debra held on to each other in the dark confines of the box-bed truck. David had heard the gunshot just before the truck bounced down the hill and slammed against the house. They were being tossed around inside the box bed like rag dolls. When the truck flipped onto its side and stopped, David scrambled to his feet. He grabbed Debra by the hand and helped her up. He knew that Bill and Stan would be there shortly.

John crawled out through the broken windshield, his face covered with blood. He staggered to the back of the truck, wiping the blood from his eyes. He pulled the latch on the door and jumped back out of the way as the right door swung down to the ground. David and Debra climbed out the back of the truck and were horrified when they saw John's face covered with blood. One sleeve of his suit coat had been torn off when he crawled through the windshield. His white shirt was covered with blood from the cuts on his face and head.

At that moment, a young man came running out of the back door of the house. He stopped for a moment and looked at the truck lying on its side in his backyard. Then he ran to the back of the truck and saw John, with his bloody face and shirt. David and Debra had just staggered out of the truck when the young man came up to them.

"Hey, are you okay?" the young man asked, taking hold of John's shoulder.

"Can you get him to a doctor?" David asked.

"Yes, I have a jeep over there." He pointed toward the front yard. "But shouldn't we wait for the life squad?" the young man replied.

"We can't," David said. "There's some peo—"

"Hold it right there! This is the FBI!" Bill shouted, climbing down the steep hill with Stan following.

"Help us! They're trying to kill us!" David shouted. He and Debra grabbed John by the arms and they ran toward the jeep. The young man followed after them.

"But they said they were from the FBI!" the young man shouted. "Maybe they can help."

Suddenly, John jerked loose from David and Debra. He ran back toward the truck, pulling his coat off as he ran.

"I'll keep them busy while you two get away!" John shouted, as he ran around the back of the truck. He pulled the gun that he had picked up back at the warehouse. He began firing at Bill and Stan as they came down the hill into the backyard. He fired several shots at them, but the blood in his eyes impaired his vision. The shots John fired at them were wild and missed them by several feet.

Bill and Stan dropped to the ground when they heard the shots and saw John firing at them. Stan raised his gun and fired back, and John fell backward onto the ground at the back of the truck.

David, Debra, and the young man ran back toward John just as he fell back onto the ground. David knelt down and took hold of John and tried to lift him up, but he was limp, lifeless, and blood was coming from the center of his chest. David grabbed the gun lying next to John and pointed it at Stan. The slide on the Glock nine-millimeter was locked back and the breach was empty. David was so angry he tried to pull the trigger anyway. The rage in him instantly peaked at the breaking point. He sprang to his feet just as Stan came up to him. Stan shoved his gun in David's face. "Hold it right there, David!" Stan yelled. David looked at Stan with a death glare. With one quick move, he knocked the gun from Stan's hand. He grabbed Stan by the throat and began choking him. He slung Stan to the ground and pounced on top of him. David began beating him in the face as fast as he could throw the punches. He was screaming with everything in him. He was relieving the rage and the frustration that had been building up in him from seeing his friends get hurt and killed. He could not control his emotions as he continued to pummel Stan.

Debra dove for Stan's gun, but at that moment, Bill ran up and grabbed the gun off the ground and pointed it at Debra. He motioned her back, and quickly moved behind David, and hit him on the head, knocking him to the ground. David rolled over, semiconscious.

"Don't hurt him!" Debra screamed as she knelt down beside David and cradled his head in her lap. "You're a big man with a gun in your hand, Bill. Someday you're not going to be so lucky!" Debra yelled.

"Just shut up and put your hands behind your back," Bill said, pointing the gun at her. She put her hands behind her back, and Bill put handcuffs on her.

Stan crawled around and finally stood up, his face bloody and his nose and mouth bleeding. He was staggering as he stumbled over to David and kicked him in the ribs.

Debra screamed, "Leave him alone!" She jumped up, stepped forward past Bill, and kicked Stan in the groin. Stan howled and doubled over in pain. Bill grabbed Debra by the hair, pulled her backward, and slung her around in a half circle up against the top of the truck.

"You stay right there and don't move, or your boyfriend is not going to make it out of this alive!" Bill shouted.

Stan jumped up after a few seconds and shouted, "I'm going to kill you!" He lunged forward, reaching for her, but Bill grabbed him and held him back.

"Stan, we have other things to think about. You have to help me fix this mess," Bill whispered next to Stan's ear. Stan was slightly bent over as he glared at Debra leaning against the top of the truck. He raised his arm and put his coat sleeve up to his bleeding mouth and nose.

Bill looked over at the young man who was standing watching everything, his eyes wide and his mouth open. Bill took out his badge and showed it to the young man as he walked toward him. "Do you live here by yourself, son?" Bill asked.

"No, my mom and dad aren't home," the young man replied.

"I'm from the FBI, and these people are fugitives," Bill said.

"You're a liar and a murderer!" Debra shouted.

Bill pointed his finger at Debra and said, "I told you to keep your mouth shut!"

Stan ran over next to Debra, grabbed her by the arm, and forced her around to the other side of the truck. Bill looked at the young man and said, "You go in the house and call the police and the life squad. I'm going to take these two fugitives with me." He assured the young man that everything was okay.

The young man went inside and called the police. Bill went around to where Stan was holding Debra. "Come on, Stan. You have to help me get these two in the car. I don't want to be here when the cops get here. You're going to have to stay behind and explain it to them. If I stay here with these two, the cops are going to ask lots of questions," Bill said.

"What about the kid, Bill?"

"He's not going to say anything. He's too scared. Besides, you tell them who we captured and that John was helping them. You had no choice but to defend yourself. The kid will corroborate your story. He'll tell them that John shot first," Bill said.

"There better be a lot of money in this for me, Bill. You really owe me," Stan said, wiping blood from his lip.

"Don't worry, Stan. You're going to be a rich man after this," Bill said with a grin.

"You have it all worked out, don't you, Bill?" Debra said, sarcastically.

"Just keep quiet and do as you're told. Take her to my car," Bill said.

Stan grabbed Debra by the arm and forced her up the hill to the road. Bill walked over to David as he was regaining consciousness, grabbed his arm, and helped him up. He forced David's hands behind his back and put handcuffs on him then pointed his gun at David and forced him to climb the hill to the road.

Several cars had stopped because of the hole in the guardrail. Bill pulled his badge and explained that he was chasing criminals. No one questioned him as he put David in the back of the car, beside Debra. Bill drove away, and Stan went back down the hill to the house to wait for the police.

As Bill drove south toward New York City, he dialed a number on his cell phone.

"Yes, I have them with me now ... no, I don't trust Carmine. He's botched things up every time." He hesitated for a moment. "No, I don't know where that is ... okay, where is he? Yes, I do. What's the number?" Bill repeated a phone number several times. "Okay, talk to you later." He closed his cell phone. "We have to make one stop before we get where we're going," Bill said.

"Don't even talk to me, you murdering scum," David said. He looked at Bill's face in the rearview mirror.

"I'm sorry about John, David, but I didn't shoot him; Stan did."

"You may as well have pulled the trigger yourself," David said.

"Just settle down; we have a long ride ahead of us."

"Where are you taking us?"

"The person I talked to on the phone has a special place picked out for you two," Bill said with a smile.

"Jack Braco, I presume?" David said, glaring at Bill.

"You'll see when we get there."

Bill drove to New York City. He called someone who directed him to an apartment building. He pulled into the parking lot, and a large man came out of one of the apartments. Bill got out of the car and told the man to drive. He went around the car and sat down on the passenger side. They drove away as Bill began to whistle, and then he looked back at David and Debra.

"This will be over soon," he said with a smile. David could not believe how nonchalant Bill was over John's death. He wondered how this man that he'd known for years could be so coldhearted.

After driving for some time, David complained about their hands being cuffed behind their backs and how uncomfortable it was. After a while, he finally convinced Bill to move the handcuffs around and cuff their hands in front. They were both surprised that Bill had enough compassion to do as David asked. They sat back in the seat, unsure of where they were headed or what was in store for them when they got there.

CHAPTER 18

The big man Bill referred to as Bob drove to New York City and crossed over into New Jersey. They drove down through New Jersey until they were near the Lincoln Tunnel. Bob pulled off the street onto a gravel parking lot near a building in a railroad yard in Hoboken, New Jersey. He drove around the building two hundred yards to another building located near the back of the lot and stopped the car. Bill stepped out with his gun in his hand and opened the back door. He motioned with his gun for Debra and David to get out of the car.

Bill forced them to walk over to the door of the big, metal building. Bob opened the door and stepped to one side, motioning for David to go through the door. David suddenly spun around, and kicked him in the groin. He dropped to his knees. David then whirled around and grabbed Bill by the coat lapel. Bill raised his gun hand and swung at David. David jerked Bill forward as he kneed him in the midsection. Bill fell backward on the gravel parking lot.

"Run, Debra!" David shouted. Debra ran past the car, toward the street. David ran around the side of the building in the opposite direction. Stunned, Bill jumped up and chased after David.

"Get the girl, you idiot!" Bill shouted, looking back at Bob as he ran around the building. The man stumbled to his feet, holding his crotch, moaning and groaning. He ran in the direction Debra had gone.

David jumped across a train track and rolled under a boxcar that was sitting there. He ran between the train cars, rolled underneath another car, and crawled to the other side. He crouched down quietly behind a set of train wheels.

Bill ran around the building, but he didn't see David. He stood momentarily with his hand on his midsection. He knew he had to catch Debra if he wanted to get David to give up. He decided to pursue her instead of David. Bill turned around and ran back in the direction Debra had gone. He caught up with the big man, who gingerly ran in Debra's direction.

"Where did she go, Bob?" questioned Bill as he came running up beside him. Bob stopped and bent over, breathing hard. All he could do was point toward an old, abandoned fuel truck sitting along the side of one of the buildings. "Is she in that old truck, Bob?" Bill asked.

"I think…she is," he said, gasping for breath, still holding his crotch.

Bill motioned with his gun and said disgustedly, "You let them get away. Now you go open the door to that truck."

Still trying to catch his breath, Bob stumbled over, jerked the door open, and quickly stepped forward. As he grabbed for Debra, she instantly swung her foot out, and the heel of her boot caught the big man in the mouth. The impact shoved him backward. He lost his balance and fell onto the gravel parking lot. The door closed back slowly. Bill grabbed the door handle, jerked it open, and pointed his gun at Debra.

"Put your hands up and get out or I'll shoot you where you are!" he shouted. Debra put her handcuffed hands in the air and crawled out of the truck. Bob slowly struggled to his feet, spitting blood from his split lip. He wiped his mouth as he grabbed her by the hair.

"You're hurting me, you jerk!" she yelled as he shoved her forward. Bill grabbed Debra by the arm and pulled her in the direction of the metal building.

"If David doesn't give up, he can watch me put a bullet in that pretty little head of yours," Bill said as they walked up to the left corner of the building, where the car was parked. He grabbed Debra by the hair with his left hand. Standing behind her, he put the gun to the right side of her head and yelled, "David, I have a gun to Debra's head, and I'll kill her right now if you don't come out!" There was no response. He jerked Debra's hair and said, "Make some noise." Debra howled in pain.

"Did you hear that, David? Come out, or I'll kill her."

"Don't come out, David—run!" Debra yelled. Bill jerked Debra's hair, and then he shoved her to the ground. She screamed as she fell.

"I'm coming out!" David yelled. "Don't hurt her!"

David rolled under the boxcar and came walking up beside the tracks, his cuffed hands in the air. As he walked toward them, Debra was getting up from the ground.

He looked at her and said, "I'm sorry, Debra. I couldn't watch this scumbag hurt you." With that, he swung his doubled-up fists and caught Bill on the left side of his jaw and knocked him to the ground.

"No, David!" Debra shouted.

"If you ever put your grubby paws on her again, I'll kill you! Do you understand?" David screamed as he stood over Bill with his fists clenched. Bob came up behind David, punched him in his lower back, and knocked him to the ground.

"No!" Debra screamed. She bent down and took hold of David's arm. Bill slowly staggered to his feet, walked over, and kicked David in the ribs. "Leave him alone!" Debra shouted.

Bill pushed Debra out of the way and grabbed David's arm. "You understand this? You do as you're told!" Bill shouted. "Get his arm, Bob."

Bill and Bob dragged David to the door, jerked it open, and threw him inside the building. Bob was still wiping the blood from his mouth as he grabbed Debra's arm and shoved her toward the door. He opened the door, threw her inside, and she fell on top of David.

As David and Debra stood up from the dirty concrete floor, they looked around inside the building. It looked like a repair shop for the railroad. There were plates of steel and steel rods stored on racks; long sections of steel railroad track were piled up on the floor. There were several different types of fabrication equipment around the shop, from drill presses to grinders and welding machines.

"How do you like our facility, David?" Bill asked as he walked up behind them. "We paid the security guard to let us use it for a short time. I bet Carmine's evil mind can figure out lots of ways to have fun with some of the items in this building. It won't be much fun for you two," Bill said, rubbing his jaw where David had slugged him.

"I'd like a chance to use some of those items on you, Bill," David said, giving Bill a menacing stare. Bill responded by motioning for them to walk over to a heavy-built steel table with four small chairs around it.

"Sit down there and keep your mouth shut!" Bill demanded.

He told David to sit at one end and Debra at the other. "What are you going to do with us?" David asked. Bill ignored him, took his cell phone out, and made a call.

"Yes, we're here. Sure … only a few minor problems. Okay, I'll see you in a few minutes." He closed the cell phone.

"I asked you what you're going to do with us."

"Carmine will be here in a little while, and we're going to leave that up to him. Like I said before, I'm sure he'll keep you entertained. I'm told he has a very vivid imagination," Bill said as he began to laugh. David looked at him, still not understanding how Bill could have turned out to be so evil. *How can this be the man that I worked with for all these years?* he thought. *How could he have pretended to like his job and to want to help people and then just suddenly throw all that away?*

"I suppose the person on the phone is the 'we' that you keep referring to, isn't it, Bill?"

"I told you to keep your mouth shut."

"No, I'm not going to keep my mouth shut. I want to know who's working with you, Bill."

"It doesn't matter. You're not going to live long enough to benefit from it!" Bill said.

"So humor me. I like to know who my enemies are."

"They're on their way here. You're going to meet them in just a few minutes. They wanted to talk to the two of you before we turn Carmine loose on you," Bill said with a snicker. David glanced at Debra, and they held a gaze for a moment.

Debra leaned forward in her chair and looked at the floor. She wondered what she was going to say to Jack Braco when he came through that door. Anger began to build as she thought about all the people whose deaths he had been responsible for. She waited for his arrival with mixed feelings of anxiety and anticipation.

After a few minutes had gone by, a car pulled up, the door to the building swung open, and someone stepped inside. Debra strained to see in the dimly lit building.

Expecting to see Jack Braco, Debra was caught completely by surprise when a slender, very pretty, and professional-looking woman walked into view. Debra thought she recognized her immediately. She looked much younger than her years. She was dressed in an expensive dress and was wearing expensive jewelry, and she walked with her head erect. As she walked, she held her purse that matched her shoes perfectly under her right arm. She wore thin, tightly fitting white gloves on her slender hands. She took steps as though she might step in something very unpleasant. With each step she took, she seemed to beam with confidence and determination. She pranced like a show horse, her heels clicking loudly on the concrete floor. Her bleached-blond hair was perfectly rolled and tucked on top of her head, and not one strand was out of place. It was obvious she had an important engagement, someplace where the cameras might be. As she came closer and the light was better, Debra knew for certain who she was.

"Remember, I told you once before that I wasn't doing this just for the money, David," Bill said.

"Yes, and I told you that only money or a woman can make a man do crazy things."

"Well, you were right, David, but this woman is worth it." Bill motioned for her to come over. "In case you haven't met her, this is Ellen Braco." Debra stared at Ellen with a puzzled look on her face. Bill reached out to take her by the arm as she walked up. She shoved her purse into Bill's hand, looked past him, and kept walking. She moved as if she was on a mission. She began pulling her gloves off as she walked.

"Well, well, well, Debra." She hesitated as she put both gloves in one hand. "I finally get to meet the little bastard that's made my life a living hell for such a long time," Ellen said with a smirk as she walked over and stood directly in front of Debra.

"Mrs. Braco, I—"

"Shut up!" Ellen interrupted. "Your very existence has practically destroyed my life!" She gritted her teeth, closed her right hand into a fist, and pounded the gloves in her left hand. "My husband slipped around behind my back and kept seeing that whore mother of yours for years. I didn't even suspect it. What a stupid, gullible fool I was!"

Debra looked down at the floor. Ellen moved over closer and stood in front of Debra. She reached out, grabbed her chin, jerked her face up, and said, "Don't look away from me. I've waited a long time for this." She hesitated for a moment, looking into Debra's face. She stared directly into her eyes and said, "You have his eyes." Her face flushed red, and her expression had even more fury and hatred in it. She shoved Debra's head to the side and turned her back, walked a couple of steps away, and stood there for a few seconds with her back toward Debra. She lifted the gloves with her right hand and began smacking them into her left hand.

"I wanted to meet you. I wanted to be the one to tell you what you are not going to get from Jack or from me. Jack set up a trust fund through your mother's lawyer. All the money goes to you six months after your mother's death—that's only a few days away." She spun around and stared intently at Debra. "So you see why you have to die, Debra?" She clenched her fists. "That fat lawyer of your mother's was going to tell you about the trust fund. I sent Carmine and some of his men to take care of him before he could tell you anything. They were supposed to take care of you too, but you left for the mountains the next day."

"So you're the one behind all this. You hired those men who followed me and Ashley in the black car the day I went to the airport," Debra said.

Before Ellen could respond, David said, "She has done nothing to deserve any of this. It's not her fault. She didn't choose to be born into this situation. Leave her alone!" Ellen walked the length of the table and stood in front of David.

"So this is the lover boy you told me about?" she said, looking at Bill. "I can see how it would be easy to fall for him, Debra." She gave a quick glance toward Debra. "He is awfully easy to look at." She put her hand on his face. David quickly jerked his head away. "It's too bad you won't get to spend much more time with him. You're both going to be dead shortly," she said. She walked back over and stood in front of Debra.

"Why did you kill Ashley and Ben?" Debra asked.

"When I learned about the blackmail, I didn't know who was behind it. I let Jack pay it for a while, to keep it quiet, but then I discovered there was a trust fund. I decided instantly. I wasn't going let Jack pay any more money out to anyone. I had to find out who was blackmailing him. I wasn't going to let you destroy our life, Debra. I decided immediately that you were not going to get one penny of that money. Can you believe that Jack was going to leave you almost half the money that he and I have worked for all these years? Just hand it over to you, Debra—his only child!" Ellen said, contorting her face and waving her hands. "Of course, that's entirely my fault too. You see, I can't have children. A few years ago, I found out about you, Debra, and I blamed myself. *It's my fault,* I thought. He went to another woman because of me. I couldn't give him children, so he had a child with someone else. But after finding out about the trust fund, I stopped blaming myself. I knew you had to die. I should've had you killed years ago. Why couldn't you have been in that apartment with your mother when she died?"

"You leave my mother out of this!" Debra shouted.

"Don't you dare bark at me!" Ellen screamed.

With Ellen's anger escalating by the second, David knew he would have to try to get her attention away from Debra.

"How did you get Bill involved in this?" David asked.

Ellen looked at David. "Bill is a friend of Jack's, and after I knew about the trust fund, I met with Bill and persuaded him to investigate the blackmail. Then Bill recruited you, David."

"You started an affair with Bill just to get rid of Debra?"

"Why shouldn't I have an affair? Jack did."

"So when Bill came to me with the story that Jack wanted to keep the blackmail secret, that was a lie, wasn't it?" David asked, looking at Ellen. "It was you who started all of this trouble? Jack didn't know about the FBI getting involved. He had nothing to do with it," David said as he looked at Bill and shook his head in disgust.

David looked at Ellen. "I reported to Bill who the blackmailers were, and he told you."

"That's right, David," Ellen said with a smile. "When Bill called me and told me that Ashley was the other person involved in the blackmail, it all kind of made sense. She was the closest to Jack, and she discovered his connection to you, Debra. Then I intercepted that picture the little twit sent to Jack. I knew if Jack saw his precious daughter all tied up and ransom money being demanded for her, he would give them everything he had. I sent Carmine and that bunch of incompetent morons he has working for him." She turned and looked at Bob standing by the door. He looked away then turned and walked out the door. "They were supposed to take care of those two and both of you at the same time at that cabin."

"So my telling Bill about Ashley and Ben got them killed. My friends Henry and John Parks are dead too," David said, staring at Bill. "You must really be proud of yourself, Bill. Do you realize how many people have lost their lives because you let this woman control you? You're sworn to uphold the law, and you've just thrown all that away over this woman."

"I love her, David—just like you love Debra—and I'll do anything for her." Ellen walked over to Bill, smiled, and put a hand on his face. She teasingly rubbed her body up against him as she walked by. It was obvious that she had lured him from reality into a world in which she had complete control over him. Bill reached out to hug her, but she snatched her purse from him, stuffed her gloves in it, quickly turned, and walked away.

"She's using you, Bill. Can't you see that?" David asked.

Ellen rushed over and slapped David. "Shut up!" she shouted.

Debra jumped up and ran toward Ellen. Bill moved forward, grabbed her by the shoulders, and shoved her back into the chair. "Leave him alone, or I'll—"

"You'll what?" Ellen interrupted as she quickly moved back over and stood in front of Debra.

"I'm the one you hate. Just leave him alone," Debra said.

Ellen drew her hand back and slapped Debra across the face and said, "How dare you glare at me with Jack's eyes!" Debra took a swing at her, but Bill grabbed her and held her down in the chair. She kicked at Ellen, but she moved away.

Debra hesitated for a second, and then she jerked loose from Bill. David stood up from his chair. Bill moved toward him. Debra looked at Ellen and began to smile. "My father really does love me, doesn't he?" Ellen's fury grew quickly as she glared at Debra.

"Your knowledge of that is going to be short lived, honey!" She turned and looked at Bill. "Bill, I want both of them handcuffed to that table."

"You're used to everything going your way, aren't you?" Debra said. "I bet you were one of those spoiled brats that got everything you wanted growing up, but this is one thing you can't control. My father loves me, and you can't do anything about that. Oh sure, you can kill me, but you'll never be able to remove me from his memory. Just like my mother—she's in his memory too, and there's nothing you can do about it, you hateful, despicable cow!" Debra shouted.

Ellen rushed toward Debra, screaming obscenities. "You sniveling little bastard! Who do you think you are spouting off at me?" Bill ran past Ellen and stepped between them. He tried to calm Ellen down. David jumped out of his chair and started toward them. Bill drew his gun and pointed it at David.

"Sit back down, or I'll use this!" he shouted.

"Shooting you would be too quick. If I had time, I would stay and watch Carmine cut you up in little pieces!" Ellen shouted as Bill held her away from Debra.

Ellen struggled to get loose from Bill. "I'm okay!" Ellen said. "Now handcuff them to the table right now!" She shoved Bill away and straightened up her clothes.

With Ellen watching, Bill took Debra's handcuffs loose from one hand and latched it around the table leg.

"That's a good little puppy, Bill!" David said.

"I told you to shut up!" Ellen said. She darted over and stood in front of David. Bill walked over, unlatched David's handcuffs, and cuffed one arm to the table leg. He stuffed his gun in his shoulder holster, and then he punched David in the mouth. The blow knocked David's head sideways.

"Leave him alone!" Debra screamed. Blood ran out of the corner of David's mouth as he straightened up in his chair. David swung at Bill with his free hand, but Bill moved out of the way. David spit blood on the floor as it pooled in the corner of his mouth. He wiped his mouth as he looked at Bill.

With fury in his eyes and contempt in his voice, he shouted, "That's twice you've hit me, Bill, while my hands have been cuffed! Like I said before, you want to try that without them cuffed?" Bill ignored him, walked over, and stood behind Ellen. He began to massage and caress her shoulders.

While massaging her, the smell of Ellen's cologne and the softness of her hair as he leaned forward and put his face to the back of her head were more than Bill could stand. He was captivated by the allure of her beauty and his love for her. He caught himself wishing they were far away.

"Let's get out of here and let Carmine finish these two. We can leave the country tonight." Ellen jerked away from Bill. She turned and looked straight at him with a surprised look on her face.

"Don't be stupid," she said with a hateful stare. "I told you from the start that we can't be together until after the election. I'm not going to throw all this away." She began staring off into space as if she were in a sudden trance. She raised one hand and motioned left to right. "I can see it all now—my name in lights! I'm going to be the first lady of the United States after Jack gets elected," she said with a devious smile on her face.

Then, as suddenly as she had left reality, she returned. Her expression and the tone of her voice changed. Speaking in a low tone, with a solemn look on her face, she said, "We'll spend some time together then, Bill. Right now I have to go to a campaign rally in Central Park and support my husband. Jack's going to be making a speech, and all the media is going to be there." She turned to walk away. Bill reached over and grabbed her by the arm.

"You said if I helped you with all this mess, we would go away together."

"Let go of my arm, Bill!" Bill tightened his grip even harder. She struggled to get free.

"You promised me!" Bill shouted.

"You're hurting me, Bill." She broke free from him and shoved him backward. As she moved away, she reached under his coat with her right hand, grabbed his gun, and pulled it from the shoulder holster.

"Ellen, I'm sorry. I wouldn't hurt you for anything." He reached out toward her.

Ellen took a couple of steps backward. She raised his gun and pointed it at him. Bill looked at her with a bewildered look on his face.

"What are you going to do, Ellen? Shoot me? I gave up everything for you! When this is over, you have no intention of ever having anything to do with me, do you? You've been using me, just like David said, haven't you?" Bill put his arms out and reached for her again as he took a step forward.

"I love—" A gunshot interrupted Bill. Debra screamed and turned her face away. Smoke came from the barrel of Bill's gun as Ellen kept it pointed at him. Bill staggered backward, groaning and holding the left side of his stomach. He looked at Ellen with complete shock on his face. "Ellen ... I ... love you!" Bill said as he fell to the floor. Ellen's hand was shaking as she held on to the gun. She slowly lowered it to her side.

"No one manhandles me like that, Bill. You should know that by now." The door to the building flew open, and Bob came running inside.

"What happened?" he yelled. Ellen stepped over Bill as if he were just an obstacle in the way. She tossed the gun on the floor as she walked away.

Debra and David sat there in total shock. They could not believe what they had just witnessed. They had seen firsthand just how heartless and coldblooded Ellen Braco really was, pretending she cared for Bill one minute and shooting him with his own gun the next.

She walked over to Bob and said, "When Carmine gets here, tell him to take care of those three and clean up this mess. There'll be a bonus for all of you. Now go get Bill's gun and guard this door until Carmine gets here."

Ellen walked out the door, jumped in her car, and sped away. Bob went over to Bill. He was moving around and groaning on the floor. Then he picked up Bill's gun and put it in his belt. Just as he turned to walk away, David said, "You have to help him. You can't just leave him lying there. He'll bleed to death!" Bob just looked at David.

"Hey, man, that's not my job. My job is to guard the door," he said. Then he turned and walked across the room.

"Wait! You can't just leave!" David shouted. Bob ignored them, kept walking, and went out the door.

Bill was lying on the floor bleeding to death, both of them were handcuffed to a steel table, and a killer was on his way there—how could their situation get any worse? With these thoughts in their heads, and not knowing what they were going to do next, Debra and David just stared at the door as Bob locked it behind him.

CHAPTER 19

With the turn of the lock in the door, David and Debra knew they only had a short time left before Carmine's arrival. They knew that their fate was sealed. If they could not get away before Carmine got there, both they and Bill would die. Debra looked at David, and as their eyes met, she exclaimed, "David, we have to find a way to get loose and get out of here! Carmine will be here anytime now. Without help, Bill is going to bleed to death!" "Yes, I know. I have to get the keys to take these cuffs off of us," David said, leaning forward, trying desperately to reach Bill, lying about fifteen feet away from David's end of the table. David stood up and tried with all his strength to lift the steel table. He couldn't budge it. He turned toward Bill. "Bill, you need to help us!" David yelled. "You have to give us the key to these handcuffs. This table is too heavy to lift and you heard what she said. You know Carmine will kill us all!" Bill moaned and rolled over on his back. Blood was oozing from the left side of his stomach.

"Come on, Bill. We can't help you if we can't get loose!" Debra said.

Bill struggled and moaned even more as he dragged himself across the floor toward David. He fumbled in his pocket, found the keys, and pushed himself up with all his strength onto one elbow. With blood-covered, trembling hands, he tossed them toward David. They fell short on the floor just in front of David, and Bill fell backward, exhaling a long breath.

David stretched out as far as he could, but even with his leg extended out, he still could not reach the keys.

"Debra, help me move this table!" David said as he began jerking on the heavy steel table. Debra started pushing on the other end, and after several times pulling and pushing with all their strength, they were able to move the table just enough for David to get his foot behind the key and drag it to him. When the key was close enough, he grabbed it and hurriedly unlocked his cuffs.

"David, please hurry. Bill's not moving anymore!" Debra said. David ran to Debra and unlocked her cuffs. Debra jerked the cuffs off, ran over, and knelt down beside Bill, checking his vital signs. She smacked Bill's face several times. "Come on, Bill. Stay with me now!" Bill moved his head from side to side and groaned. "David, please see if you can find a rag or some kind of cloth so I can put pressure on his wound." David ran all around the building, looking desperately for something they could use to stop the bleeding. After a short time, he came back with an old shop rag and a partial roll of duct tape in his hand.

"This is all I could find. You can put this tape over the wound, and it will help to stop the bleeding."

"It'll have to do," Debra said. She pulled the tail of her shirt out of her pants and tore a piece off of it. She rolled the clean piece of cloth around the old shop rag, put it inside Bill's shirt and pressed on the wound. Bill moaned in pain. "I'm sorry, Bill, but I have to stop the bleeding." Debra said.

"You should let me die with the way I have treated the two of you," Bill muttered.

"You're right, Bill. That's what you deserve. We should leave you right here with all the evil things you've done and all the people you've hurt, but the only way we have of proving our innocence is to keep you alive," David said. He looked intently at Bill. Debra stared at David for a moment, but she understood how he felt. "I have to find away out of here. I'll be right back," David said. Then he ran toward the front of the building.

Debra thought of all the pain and suffering that Bill had caused them and other people. With Bill lying helpless and bleeding, she had great empathy for him. She knew how it felt to be used and betrayed.

"Well, Bill, everyone makes mistakes. I know I've made plenty of them." She reached over and picked up a small paper box lying nearby on the floor, folded it, and put it under his head. She took the duct tape and tore several pieces off the roll. "Bill, this may be painful," she said putting her hand on his arm. "I am going to tape this rag over your wound. Do you understand?" He shook his head that he understood. She opened his shirt and began to tape the rolled-up cloth over his wound. He moaned and kept fading in and out of consciousness each time she touched him. She loosened his tie to make him more comfortable.

"Come on, Bill; stay with me."

In the meantime, David looked all around the building and tried to find a way out, but with no success. He came back to where Debra and Bill were.

"There's no way out of this building except through the locked steel door where Carmine's sidekick is standing; the back door is blocked from the outside."

"What about those two fans in the windows in the back of the building?" Debra asked.

"They have heavy, steel wire mesh welded over them, and there's nothing to cut it with. The garage door is locked from the outside, but I have an idea how we can get through that steel door," David said. He turned and pointed to the stack of train track rails lying on the floor. "I think we can use those steel rails, but I need your help."

"Bill, I'll be right back," Debra said. She sprang to her feet. "Okay, what do you want me to do?" She followed David as he hurried over to the stack of track rails.

"If we can pick up this stack of rails with that overhead crane,"—David hesitated and pointed up at the big crane hanging from the ceiling on rollers—"and if we can get it going fast enough, we might be able to break that steel side door completely down."

"What about the man outside with the guns?" Debra asked.

"That's where you come in. I need you to lure him over in front of the door just before I hit it with the rails."

"Oh, is that all?" she said with a pessimistic look on her face.

"I believe it will work if we raise the rails to just the right height, hit the door in just the right spot, and if you can lure him in front of the door," David said, looking at Debra with a big grin across his face.

"If all this comes together, it will be a miracle," she said with a half smile.

She walked over to David and hugged him. The two of them held on to each other for a moment. "Please be careful, David. Don't let that heavy steel fall on you," she said, pulling back from him. She put her hand on his face and looked into his eyes.

"Don't worry." He smiled. "I'll be okay. Now, we have to hurry."

As quietly as possible, David lowered the crane down to the floor. Then the two of them put the straps underneath each end of the stack of rails. They took a cable with a hook on each end and put the hooks in each loop of the straps. After attaching the cable onto the big boom of the crane, David raised the rails high enough in the air to be level with the middle of the small door. He pushed the left and right buttons of the crane switch and aligned the rails up even with the door. He rolled the crane as far back as he could, and just before he began moving it forward, Debra ran over to the door and yelled through the door at the man outside, "Hey, Romeo, why don't you let me out so we can get better acquainted?"

"Hey, how did you get loose?" he yelled through the door.

At that moment, David started moving the crane forward as fast as it would roll. Just as the rails reached the door, Debra could hear Bob rattling the lock to open it. She jumped backward as far away as possible. The rails hit the steel door with a loud *bang*. It ripped the hinges out of the doorjamb, and the door flew outward and fell flat on top of Bob. The heavy canvas strap in the front that impacted the door broke. That end of the rails came crashing down to the floor with an ear-splitting sound. Debra and David covered their ears as they ran away from the falling rails. David narrowly escaped when several of them slid out of the strap that hadn't broken and came crashing to the floor. Some of the ends of the rails landed on top of the door. David lowered the rest of the rails that hadn't fallen down to the floor.

"We have to hurry!" David yelled. They both ran back to where Bill was lying. "Carmine will be here anytime!" They positioned themselves on either side of Bill, put his arms around their necks, and stood him up on his feet. The pain was great, and Bill began screaming. They had to practically carry him over to the door. Bill screamed in pain as they desperately struggled to get him over all the train track rails lying in the doorway.

After they were able to get outside, they took Bill to the car they had arrived in and laid him down in the backseat. David opened the driver's door of the car and hesitated for a moment when he saw that there were no keys in the ignition.

"Check Bill's pocket for the car keys!" David said, looking across the top of the car. Debra quickly checked Bill's pockets.

"I can't find them," she replied.

"I was afraid of that; Bob was driving when we got here. They must be in his pocket," David said. He turned and ran toward the building. "I'll see if I can get the keys from our friend under the door."

"David, please hurry! We have to go!" Debra yelled. She jumped in the passenger seat.

"I'll only be a minute!" David yelled as he ran to where the door was lying. He knelt down and tried to reach Bob. He was making noises and slightly moving around underneath the door. David stretched out as far as he could and was just able to reach his coat pocket. He fumbled in his pocket and found the keys.

All of a sudden, he heard a car turn into the gravel lot off the street. David jumped to his feet and ran back to the car. He slid in the driver's seat, shoved the key in the ignition, started the car, and fastened his seatbelt.

"I couldn't reach any of the guns, but we have a bigger problem. I think Carmine just turned in off the street."

"Oh no! Now how do we get away from him?"

David jerked the car in gear, looked at Debra, and said, "You better fasten your seatbelt and pray that this car is faster than his." He shoved the pedal to the floor and spun the car around in a circle and headed toward the street.

They met Carmine coming around one of the buildings. There was another man in the car with him. David swerved toward Carmine's car and slammed into the driver's door with the big, heavy sedan. Bill rolled out of the seat and into the floor. He screamed in pain as he fell. David stepped on the gas and scraped down the side of Carmine's car with the sound of metal-to-metal. Carmine's eyes were wide with shock and disbelief to see them as the two cars scraped each other. Carmine's car slid sideways and spun around.

David held the gas pedal down. His tires were spinning and throwing gravel all over the side of Carmine's car. Debra leaned over the back of her seat and helped Bill get out of the floor and back into the seat. She put her hand on his wound.

"David, his wound is bleeding again. We have to get him to a hospital." David looked in his rearview mirror and saw Carmine turning his car around to follow them.

"I know, Debra, but Carmine is chasing us now, and the only chance we have is to get to your father at Central Park so he can help us."

"How do we find where the campaign rally is? Central Park is 843 acres," Debra said.

"We have to find out from Bill if he knows where in Central Park Jack is going to be speaking." Debra shook Bill a couple of times before he responded. She asked him where the rally was.

In a low and barely audible tone, he said. "I think Ellen said he's speaking at Central Park West. Go up Eighth Street to Columbus Circle." Debra repeated the directions.

"The police and the Secret Service will be at the campaign rally. Carmine won't be able to harm us there, and we can get some help for Bill there too." David glanced back at Bill. "Bill, hold on for a few more minutes."

"Just do what you have to do, and don't worry about me," Bill mumbled in a low, weak tone.

David turned onto the street, tires spinning. He took Willow Avenue over to 495 toward the Lincoln Tunnel.

"David, we're coming up on the toll booth for the Lincoln Tunnel."

"Maybe if we run it and don't pay they will send the police."

"No, David, that won't work. There's an E-Z pass on the window of this car." She pointed to the little box behind the rearview mirror. David looked back and could see Carmine's car coming up fast. There were two cars between them. Just then, the traffic started slowing up for the tollbooths. "It doesn't matter; the traffic is too heavy. We can't run it anyway," said Debra.

As they pulled up to the booth, David motioned to the attendant and said, "Get the license plate number of the black car two cars back and call the police! They're trying to kill us!" The man just looked at him with no expression on his face. David took off quickly.

Carmine had seen David gesturing with his hands to the attendant. When he pulled up to the booth, he was pointing his gun just over the top of the door at the man. The man ducked down, and Carmine took off quickly before the man could get a license plate number.

Carmine caught up with them while they were still in the tunnel and began ramming their car from behind. He maneuvered around and came up beside them. He steered his car into the side of their car. David swerved, and both cars were locked together. Debra screamed and held on to the dash of the car. Bill moaned and groaned in pain each time the cars collided. The two cars rammed into the back of another car, which spun around and slammed into two other cars. One of the cars flipped over, and they all three slid into the wall of the tunnel on the opposite side. The car that flipped over exploded into flames seconds after the driver crawled out of it. The drivers of the other two cars jumped out as well.

David jerked the steering wheel to the left with all his strength, trying to force Carmine into the wall. Carmine only had the use of his right arm; the left one was still in a cast and sling. He could not hold his car off the wall of the tunnel. Just as he hit the wall, another car rammed Carmine in the rear and pushed the car around backward. Carmine jerked his car into reverse, slid it around, and was hit again as David sped away.

Carmine was able to maneuver his car around and drove away quickly, following David.

When David and Debra reached the Manhattan side of the tunnel, David took West Thirty-ninth Street. He then turned left onto Eighth Avenue and drove toward Central Park West.

After driving several blocks, they slid up to a red light on West Fifty-first Street, just as a group of young men were crossing the street.

"Debra, give me all the money you have."

"I only have thirty-eight dollars."

"Check Bill's wallet."

"Why do you need money?" she asked, retrieving money from Bill's wallet.

"Just watch."

David motioned for the young men to come over to his car. They gathered around the driver's side of the car. "Hey, you guys want to earn some quick cash and have a little fun while you're at it?"

"What do you have in mind, man?" one of the men asked.

"There's a car coming up behind me in just a couple of minutes. It's black like this one, and it's bent up really bad like this one. There are two men in the car, and they're going to be driving crazy—you can't miss them. The one on the passenger side is a big guy and the driver is smaller." Debra handed David a handful of money. The man looked down the street, and he could hear Carmine blowing his horn. He saw a black car darting in and out of the traffic.

"I see him down the street, coming this way," the young man said.

"There's one hundred seventy-three dollars here, and that's all there is," Debra said. David stuck the money out the window toward one of the men.

"Please help us. The men in the black car are trying to kill us," David said, pushing the money in one of the man's hands.

"I don't know, man. It sounds dangerous to me," the young man said as he took the money. The light changed to green.

"Please, all you have to do is delay them for a few minutes!" David yelled out of the car window as he quickly drove away.

The men ran to the street corner as the traffic began to move and stood there for a few moments, trying to decide what to do. Carmine got trapped behind traffic at a light down the street; they could hear him blowing his horn.

One of them said, "There's one hundred and seventy-three dollars here. We can just keep this and not do anything."

Another one spoke up and said, "Hey, there was a dude lying in the backseat of that car, and he had blood all over him. I think we should help them." They all agreed as they put their heads together and quickly came up with a plan.

After a few moments, Carmine came sliding up to the red light where the men were. There was a car in front of him, and he was blowing his horn and yelling obscenities. He was trying desperately to force the car in front of him to run the red light. One of the young men walked out in the street. He walked up to Carmine's door with a rag and began wiping his windshield "Hey, man, want me to clean your windshield?"

Carmine looked at the young man, shook his fist, and screamed, "I want you to get away from me, you little punk!" The rest of the group ran over to the passenger door of the car and began yelling at the big man. They jerked on the door handle, banged on the car, and began rocking it back and forth. The man with Carmine shoved his arm out the window and swung his fist at them.

"You got any money, man? Come on, man; I'm just trying to make a little money here. Give a man a break!" the young man with the rag yelled.

"I told you to get away from the car, you street bum, before I have to do something that you're going to regret!"

"What's with the insults, man?"

"You and your street, hoodlum friends better get away from me!"

While the two were arguing, Carmine didn't see one of the other men squat down and sneak up to his door. Carmine stuck his gun out the window and pointed it at the man.

"Beat it, you little punk, or I'll put a bullet in you!"

The young man threw his hands up, jumped backward, and yelled, "Hey, chill out, man! Chill out! It's cool! It's cool, man!"

At that moment the other man stuck his hand up above the door and squirted pepper spray in Carmine's eyes. He let go of his gun, and it fell back inside the car. He grabbed his face with his one good hand and let out a scream as he inadvertently stomped on the gas and rammed into the car in front of him. The impact pushed the car through the intersection.

Just as Carmine's car flew out in the intersection, a big truck was coming down the cross street. It slammed into the passenger door of his car with a loud *bang*, and the sound of exploding glass and crunching metal echoed down the street. The man on the passenger side screamed as the truck plowed through the car. The car spun around, slid over sideways, and stopped up on the curb.

The young men took off running down the street, laughing and giving each other high-fives.

The driver of the truck jumped out and ran over to Carmine to see if he was hurt. The passenger was wedged in the floor of the car, and Carmine was on top of him. Carmine crawled up off of the big man, covered with glass.

He looked up at the truck driver with cuts on his face and red watery eyes from the pepper spray and shouted, "You stupid bastard! What are you, a moron? You almost killed me!" The driver's expression changed from serious concern to rage in an instant. His face flushed red.

"How about I wring your neck, you scrawny little runt," bellowed the truck driver. He lunged in through the car window and grabbed Carmine by the throat, choking him with his big hands. With the pepper spray in his eyes, Carmine could scarcely see to defend himself.

The police were there in a couple minutes. They pulled the truck driver away from Carmine. Carmine's eyes were swollen together from the pepper spray. He had cuts and bruises on his face and head. He was cursing and crying at the same time. The life squad pulled Carmine's sidekick out of the car. He was unconscious and bleeding from his head.

When the police looked in Carmine's car and saw his gun lying in the floor, they put handcuffs on him and read him the Miranda rights before they loaded him in the ambulance.

CHAPTER 20

David and Debra continued on Eighth Street toward Central Park West.

"Debra, do you see Carmine's car?" She turned around in the seat and looked out the back window.

"No, I think your plan worked, David. I don't see him. I think those guys held Carmine up." She leaned over the back of the seat. "You're still going to have to hurry, David." She checked Bill's vital signs. "Bill has lost a lot of blood. I think he's going into shock."

"We'll have to get him some help as soon as we get to your father."

After driving several more blocks, David slid the car to a stop in Columbus Circle in front of the Central Park West entrance. Barricades were preventing vehicles from entering. They jumped out of the car and ran inside the park. Just inside the entrance, they encountered the large crowd that had gathered for the rally. The podium was several yards from the entrance. They began pushing their way through the crowd.

While struggling to make their way toward the front, Debra could see Jack Braco standing at the podium as he spoke. The platform was three steps higher than the crowd at ground level. Two Secret Service agents were standing at the end of the platform, one on either side of Jack.

The mayor of New York City, the governor of New York, and several other political figures, along with Ellen Braco, were seated in a row directly behind Jack. People were cheering and waving campaign banners all around.

After a couple of minutes of pushing and shoving their way through the horde of people, they were getting close to the front near the platform. Ellen Braco looked down and saw them pushing their way through the crowd. She jumped up and went over to one of the Secret Service agents standing near the end of the platform, whispered something to him, and pointed at them. The agent she spoke to took a couple of steps forward and motioned for the other agent to come over beside him. The agent walked across the podium behind Jack, and the two of them walked the three steps down off the platform to the right. Ellen stood watching David and Debra.

While he was speaking, Jack looked over and saw Ellen standing to his right, staring down into the crowd. He looked in the direction of her stare and saw Debra and David coming toward the front.

They pushed their way into the open in front of the cheering crowd. Jack stopped speaking in mid-sentence.

Ellen looked in the direction of the two agents and shouted, "Shoot them!" She pointed at Debra and David. "They're trying to assassinate the senator!" The two agents drew their guns. A hush came over the crowd. "Shoot them!" Ellen screamed again.

"No! Stop! Don't shoot!" Jack shouted. The sound of his shout echoed through the speakers over the crowd.

Ellen ran down to where the two agents were standing with their guns drawn. She looked at one of them and shouted, "I told you to shoot those two!" She pointed at them again.

The people had moved back away from where David and Debra were standing. Debra was standing in front of David, with David slightly to her right side. They were about ten feet from the two agents. Debra looked up at Jack. Jack looked at Debra.

Jack thought about the years of his love for Debra and her mother and all the lies. At that moment he knew he could not keep this secret hidden any longer. After a brief moment, Jack said into the microphone, "It's time everyone found out the truth; I've harbored this secret long enough." Ellen looked at Jack. A tense silence fell over the crowd. "She's my daughter!" There was a collective gasp and murmuring sounds from the crowd.

"No!" Ellen screamed. She grabbed a gun from one of the agents and pointed it at Debra.

As she fired, Jack shouted, "Ellen! No!"

Debra screamed as she jumped out of the way. The bullet went just past Debra's right shoulder and hit David, and he fell to the ground. Debra turned around and saw David falling, and she dropped to the ground beside him, screaming.

"David! David!" she screamed. "Oh God, no!" She was on her knees, hovering over him. She had her hands on his chest, crying and screaming his name over and over.

The two agents grabbed the gun and wrestled it from Ellen before she could fire a second shot. While the two agents were holding on to Ellen's arms, Debra jumped up and lunged forward and grabbed Ellen by the throat. She began choking and shaking her while crying and screaming at the top of her lungs. Ellen's perfectly pinned hair fell down around her face.

"No, Debra, I'm okay!" David said, still lying on the ground. Debra let go of Ellen's throat and dropped quickly to the ground beside David. The crowd had moved in a half circle around them. Several more Secret Service agents joined the other two.

"Let … go of me!" Ellen demanded. The agents released her. She put her hands on her throat.

Jack ran down from the podium, stopped briefly, and looked at Ellen. She was standing with several agents around her, slightly bent over, coughing and holding her throat.

All of a sudden, screams came from the back of the crowd as they parted out of the way. Bill Rogers came stumbling through the crowd, covered with blood, holding the left side of his stomach.

As he staggered closer to the front, he weakly shouted, "Ellen … I love you. I would have followed you … to the end of the earth. Why … did you shoot me?" Then he collapsed to the ground. All eyes turned to Ellen.

"Ellen, what did you do?"

"Jack, I-I did it for you; someone had to keep this quiet"

"You don't care about me … you never did. It's all about the power, isn't it?" he shouted.

"Jack!" Ellen held out her hand toward him.

"Arrest her!" Jack shouted as he pointed his finger at Ellen.

"Jack, I'm your wife!" Ellen shouted as she looked at Jack with a puzzled expression. The agents grabbed her arms, forced them behind her, and put handcuffs on her. "What are you doing? Take your hands off of me! I'm going to be the first lady of the country!" she cried as they escorted her through the crowd, put her in a car, and drove away.

"Someone call the life squad!" Jack yelled.

A voice from the crowd called, "I've already called them, Senator."

David struggled to his feet, bloodstains down the front of his shirt. He held on to Debra as he stumbled over to Bill.

He knelt down beside him and said, "Bill, help is on the way." Then he collapsed beside him on the ground. Debra screamed his name and began to cry even louder.

Jack walked over to Debra and knelt down beside her and put his arm around her. She looked up at him with her tear-soaked face. Jack drew her to him as she wept. All of her emotions pent up for so long came flowing from her. She thought of her mother, Ashley, David, and all the things she had been through. She could not hold any of her feelings back as she clung to him and wept uncontrollably. Reporters gathered around them with their cameras and microphones, shouting questions at Jack as he held on to Debra.

The life squad came to take David and Bill to the hospital. After they were loaded in the ambulance, Debra climbed in to ride with David. Reporters surrounded Jack as he watched Debra get in the ambulance. Debra's and Jack's eyes were locked through the window of the ambulance door for an instant. Jack watched as the ambulance disappeared out of sight.

Three days latter, Debra stroked Annabelle's fur as she carried her through the living room in her Manhattan apartment. The TV was playing behind her. A news reporter came on the screen. Debra stopped and turned around when she heard what was said by the reporter.

"The whole country is abuzz after presidential nominee Senator Jack Braco revealed to the world that he has a daughter. The young woman's name is Debra Benson, a local writer here in New York City. This was the scene three days ago at Central Park at a campaign rally for Senator Braco." The news report replayed everything that had taken place at the rally. "Bill Rogers and David Kimble, both FBI agents, were taken to the hospital with gunshot wounds, both listed in serious condition. Ellen Braco was arrested at the scene and charged with the shootings.

"From what we know so far, Ellen Braco was having an affair with Bill Rogers of the FBI and using him to carry out her orders. It's reported that he conspired with her to try to murder Miss Benson. It seems Ellen Braco was trying to prevent the public from finding out about Debra Benson. Police are saying that Mr. Rogers is cooperating with investigators. Due to his confession, several arrests have already been made."

Then the camera cut to a shot of Carmine and one of his accomplices being dragged from an apartment, both in handcuffs.

"This man posted bail for a weapons violation a few days ago after being involved in a car accident. Police are now saying that he and his henchman are responsible for several deaths. The deposition that Bill Rogers gave police names several people who were murdered—from a New York lawyer to a Utica sheriff—by this gang, and they were controlled and funded by Ellen Braco. Investigators are probing deeper into the New York office of the FBI. Officials say that we can expect more arrests later. According to Bill Rogers, other agents were involved, and one agent was killed.

"We have learned that one of Senator Braco's aids, Ashley Bolton, and another man who was blackmailing Senator Braco were also murdered by Ellen Braco's hired killers. 'The limit of her endeavor to become the most powerful woman in America had no boundaries,' according to FBI agent Bill Rogers.

"Jack Braco has a press conference scheduled for later today. Early poll indications are that Senator Braco still has a slight lead over his opponent, although the lead has narrowed since this story broke. We'll have more on this breaking story later."

Debra went across the room and turned off the TV.

"I'm so glad this is over, Annabelle," Debra said. She put the cat down. "I have to meet my father now." She smiled. "I like the way that sounds, Annabelle, don't you? My father, my father," she kept repeating as she walked toward the bedroom.

After getting dressed, she called a taxi and walked down to the street. As soon as she walked out the door of her apartment building, she was mobbed by reporters. She covered her head and ran for the taxi. She could hardly close the door with all the reporters shoving their microphones in her face and bombarding her with questions. She told the driver to take her to Cypress Hills Cemetery in Brooklyn, New York. The taxi drove away, with the reporters chasing after the car.

After driving for a while, they arrived at the Cypress Hills Cemetery on Jamaica Avenue in Brooklyn. The taxi driver parked behind a long black limousine. After paying the driver, Debra turned and began walking across the grass toward her mother's grave. She saw Jack Braco standing by her mother's headstone. There were two Secret Service agents standing about five feet from him on either side. She walked over and stood beside him. He looked at her, put his hand out, and she put her hand in his. They stood there and looked down at the headstone that read, 'Elizabeth Benson, beloved mother.'

Jack turned and looked at Debra and said, "Debra, I've been dodging the press for the past three days. I wanted to try to explain why things were the way they were to you first. I don't care what the public or the press think about me. I care what you think about me. That's why I want you to know why I haven't been a part of your life." He looked at Elizabeth's headstone momentarily. "I loved your mother more than anything. We had a stupid fight. We were both young and dumb. I let my ego keep me from going back to her. I didn't find out until later that she was pregnant with you." He turned and looked at Debra and lifted her right hand and put both hands around hers. "We were just kids, and we made a mistake. We should have waited until we were married—the way God planned it to be—but we didn't, and by the time I found out she was pregnant, I was already married to Ellen. Ellen has always been a conniver. She tricked me into marrying her on the pretense that her father was a rich and powerful man. She said he could help me with my career, none of which was true. I never loved her, and I guess I just married her because I was mad at your mother.

"The choices you make when you're young affect your life forever. Make sure you make wise ones, Debra." He looked at her with concern. "I wanted to be with you, and I wanted you to be a part of my life, but Liz didn't want me to be with you. She knew what an evil, vindictive woman Ellen was, and she was afraid for me and for you. She said, 'If you can't be with us as a family, then I don't want you to be with Debra at all.' I didn't understand why she felt that way, unless it was her fear of what Ellen would do if she found out, but because of my respect for her, I honored her wishes.

"I was able to make my own way in my political career without anyone's help, but I never planned to pursue a career in politics this far; it just kind of slowly happened. I threw myself into the political arena, hoping it would take my mind off your mother, but that never worked. She was my first love, and I just couldn't forget her— or you.

"I couldn't keep my love for you and your mother hidden forever. Ellen found out a couple of years ago, but she stayed with me. Ellen was a power-hungry person; she was always bitter, hateful, and mean spirited, even before she found out about your mother. I should have divorced her, but I kept putting it off. I kept thinking that Ellen would change, but she never did. She didn't realize it, but the more power hungry and bitter she became, the more she pushed me away from her and toward Liz.

"Your mother was the most wonderful woman, Debra. She was kind and gentle to a fault. The three of us could've had a wonderful life together, but I blew it, Debra. I really blew it," Jack said as he looked into her eyes, still holding on to her hands. His eyes welled up with tears. "I want to spend the rest of my life making it up to you, Debra."

They hugged each other for a moment. Debra stepped back and looked at him with tears in her eyes and said, "What about this election?" She wiped her eyes with one hand. "I don't want to be the reason you didn't win the presidency." Jack hugged her again.

"Don't worry about that," he said. "If I don't win this time, I can always run the next time. You're more important to me than this election." He stepped back and looked at her as he held on to her shoulders. "I'm so glad this is finally out in the open. I want the whole world to know that I have a daughter." He smiled and hugged her close again.

As they stood talking for a while longer, a car pulled up and stopped behind the limousine. Debra looked around and saw David getting out. He came walking toward them, his right arm in a sling. Debra ran to meet him.

"What are *you* doing here? You're supposed to be in the hospital," she said with a smile as she approached him. She took hold of his left arm, tiptoed, and kissed him on the cheek. She laced her arm around his as they walked toward Jack.

"I was doing better than expected, so they released me early. I went to your apartment, and the manager told me you were here. He said there was a bunch of reporters there earlier."

"Yes, but I was able to get away from them, but enough about that. I want you to meet my father," she said with a great, big smile.

They walked up to Jack, and Debra introduced them.

"It's a pleasure to meet you, sir." David put his left hand out.

"Debra has told me about the ordeal the two of you went through. She said you saved her life. Thank you, David. I'm forever in your debt," Jack said, shaking David's hand.

"It was my pleasure. I'm in love with your daughter, sir." He looked at Debra and smiled.

"If you love her, don't let her get away. Don't make the same mistake I made, son."

"I don't intend to, sir." David put his arm around Debra.

"I must leave now. I have a press conference scheduled in a few minutes. I'm going to try to explain this to the public. Let's hope they understand." Jack took hold of Debra's hand, leaned forward, kissed her on the cheek, and smiled at her. "Call me later, and the three of us will go out to dinner." He walked toward his car, with the two agents following.

David and Debra watched Jack leave. David turned to Debra. He took hold of her left hand and knelt down on one knee.

He looked up at her and said, "I'm going to take the advice of two very wise men, Henry Lipinski and your father. I'm not going to let you get away, Debra. I love you. Will you marry me?" Debra gasped and put her right hand over her mouth.

"David!"

David reached inside his sling and pulled out a black box and handed it to Debra. She stood there shaking as she took the box, opened it, and looked at the diamond ring inside. He stood up and looked at her. She hugged him, tears streaming down her face.

Out of this nightmare, she had found her prince charming. Her dreams had come true. She wasn't alone anymore, and she had someone she could share her life with. She had the father she had always wanted too. *What a blessing from God,* she thought.

"Well? Will you marry me?"

"Yes, yes! You know I will!" They stood there looking into each other's eyes, and they kissed passionately. David took the ring and put it on her left hand. Debra took David's face and held it in her hands, smiled, and said, "I love you so much, David!"

After a short time, they turned and started walking toward David's car. Debra took hold of David's left arm, smiling as they walked.

"This is the most wonderful day!" she said excitedly. They walked a little farther, and she said, "I've been thinking. We have several people we need to thank for helping us, David."

"Yes, we certainly do."

"Maybe we could go visit Harry and Kevin, Tom and Kate, and maybe Delbert too," Debra said.

"That's a great idea."

"We can even visit Steve Tanner, but I'm not going to eat any more fried squirrel."

Joel Howard